ULLEY'S ODYSSEY

R.M. GAYLER

ALSO BY R.M. GAYLER

ULLEY'S ODYSSEY

To Jax and Jamesyn,
Emma and Zayn

May your imaginations run wild,
and your dreams be worthy of the chase.

PROLOGUE

EVEN IN EUROPA'S LOW GRAVITY the alarms bore tremendous weight.

Three distinct klaxons screeched simultaneously. Ulley's Brainlinq blazed red rings across his ocular implant as his helmet squeezed incessant high-pitched vibrations deep into his ear canals. The Brainlinq finally chimed with a droll reminder that the highly anticipated event had arrived. One alarm would have sufficed, but the approaching event would reshape his world, and three alarms wouldn't be considered overkill.

Disregarding safety protocols, Ulley pushed harder on the twelve-inch-long bar controlling the massive drill press, forcing the hefty chainsaw bit to gnaw into the dirty surface faster. The bit fought back, sending tremors back up the main shaft as a warning against pushing the limits of coring into a thick layer of ice on the frozen surface of Europa. Small tools hanging on the flimsy walls of the miner's shack trembled and rattled. A heavy ball peen hammer fell to the cold surface. Just a few more meters and the old record for the deepest core would be obliterated. It didn't matter who currently held the record, though Ulley's name peppered the top ten.

The alarm flashed in his right eye again.

"I got it. I got it. Just a few more seconds," Ulley said. Slight but muscular, he pressed all his meager weight down on the handle. Low gravity be damned.

Muffs protecting his ears inside the EV helmet crackled with static interference. His rapid breaths fogged the glass faceplate. Red warning strobes commanded his exit from the ice mining site. The extraction would supply years of oxygen and water for his habitat orbiting Jupiter. Ulley clenched his teeth as he pushed harder. The vibrations on the grinding metal drill sputtered and roared, his feet shuddered and bounced, every centimeter deeper like suffering a game of violent hopscotch.

The muffs crackled. "Halcyon tug ready for liftoff. C'mon, Ulley, let's go. The prospect of meeting another like you intrigues even me," Timbre said. The old pilot was unflappable and rarely exhibited any emotion without the inducement of a liter of stout Miner's ale.

Ulley checked the depth gauge of the coring. The numbers slowed with the drill bit losing too many teeth. Bedrock. Maybe a layer of petrified volcanic dust but just two more meters and he would have the record.

Another alarm flashed on the machine's status screen. The drill's internal temperature was climbing too fast. Abrasion and lousy teeth. A miner's nightmare.

He eased back the pressure on the control arm. The alarms continued. The cacophony of intense vibrations joined with the alarms. He couldn't concentrate.

"Shut down all home alarms." Ulley shouted at his neural implant.

The strobe of the drill alarm continued to increase. Distant voices shouted in his helmet. *Shut down. Shut down. Go home. Go home.* The drill handle throbbed in his hand. Carbonite teeth grinding against an impenetrable substance transmitted jolts of static electricity through his hands and into his chest.

He eased the downward pressure on the handle. The lightning bolts subsided then inexplicably increased to a level Ulley had never experienced in his twenty years of ice mining.

He pulled back on the drill press. Maybe the friction of the teeth ignited a methane pocket?

"Let's go, boss," Timbe said through the communication channel of his helmet.

"I haven't severed the core yet. Hook on and be ready. No deviations, or the core will snap."

"Oh, please. This isn't my first rodeo," Timbre said.

Ulley checked the core depth. Two lousy meters from a record.

He poised an ocular pointer on the drill's control screen. He paused, then blinked the command to constrict the chain of drill teeth and chew inward to sever the hundred-thirty-two-meter cylinder cored from the frozen moon.

"Big bucks for us, my Capitán," Timbre said.

"Careful on the x-y axis retraction," Ulley said as he observed the extraction of a trillion-ton chunk of ice rising into the vacuum of space.

Timbre scoffed, "Please."

The mining shack fell apart as his crew appeared out of the darkness of space to grab each of his arms and jabber about his disregard of the alarms. His lieutenants pulled him away from the drilling station.

Ulley shrugged them off to watch the cylinder of ice rise out of the bowels of Europa like a stiff worm.

The bulky ice tug hovered just three hundred meters above Ulley's head. Timbre, the tug's grizzled old pilot shouted above the roar of the engines. "Where to, boss?"

Ulley had pondered an endless number of options and should have made the decision weeks ago, before the operation started. One of the hundreds of habitats orbiting in the vast sea of Jupiter's gravity would pay dearly for the water and oxygen. Maybe he would send the frozen tube to Mars to settle the water futures contract he ignorantly signed. Most lunar colonies would outbid any competitor. Earth's hegemony with its habitats and satellites starving for water might pay even more. His own bioengineered habitat, Ithaca, stationed above Jupiter's satellite Europa thrived, but an insurance policy of additional water was enticing.

The alarms sounded and flashed again. His wife Pennae's vehement insistence he return as quickly as possible made him pause, then smile with the obvious answer.

"Home, Timbre," Ulley said. "We have a birthday present to deliver."

The transport shuttle employed an old and dated fusion drive, and the acceleration pressed him inside a compensation couch morphing like viscous jelly to form a cocoon around his body. He hated leaving Timbre alone to extract and escort the cylinder back home. A sudden tectonic tremor might shear off the cylinder during the delicate extraction. Or the pilot might face an attempt by pirates to hijack the cylinder and resell to one of many habitats orbiting Saturn, but those crimes were rare. They had completed hundreds of similar extractions with little deviation from the prescribed parameters. Ice and air were plentiful, only if one knew where to look. Timbre could handle the delivery on his own.

Pennae's pings on his ocular screen became more frantic.

"On my way. Start without me if you need to," Ulley responded.

"You stupid pig. You promised to be here!" Pennae shouted through the Brainlinq.

The message caused Ulley's head to sink further into the couch as if her anger held the equivalent of a dangerous eight g's acceleration. Maybe their decision was misguided. Maybe Pennae had morphed into one of those horrible hormonal monsters he had read about.

"Docking now. Five minutes," he said.

An agonizing scream sounded deep into his ear canal.

"Breathe, Pennae. Breathe."

"Fuck you. *You* breathe," she said between gasps.

"As soon as the airlock opens, I'm there."

Ulley cursed as the shuttle took forever to navigate into the docking bay with slow precise burns of maneuvering thrusters. He unstrapped the belts and rushed to the airlock. Alarms for violating security protocols flashed warning signs in his ocular vision. He tapped the keypad with a frantic finger.

Denied. Denied.

Finally, the docking doors spiraled shut behind him, and he sucked in a great lungful of warm Ithaca atmosphere. This was home. The air never lied. The door iris spiraled open, and Ulley ran.

He waved off greetings and gestures from citizens as he sprinted down the busy hallway to the main concourse, turning left into the medical section then a few zigzags, racing around a long-radius bend with practiced precision. He stumbled across the slick floor at the final turn. A narrow, white corridor dead-ended in a single door servicing a series of maintenance access tubes and emergency escape pods.

A child's tiny wail precipitated his dirty boots sliding to a full stop against a wall of clear poly-glass. He sucked in a big breath. His heart pounded inside his chest. His rapid breathing paused. The runaway heartbeat faded as he gazed upon the birthing nursery.

Reclining in a luxurious foam couch, Pennae looked up, a naked red-faced baby cradled in her arms. Her brow knotted in displeasure slowly softened.

Ulley raised his hand and pressed it against the glass. His eyes darted between the child and Pennae's goddess-like features. Her puffy cheeks flushed beneath long auburn hair troubled by the act of childbirth. Her blue-gray eyes penetrated his soul. He swallowed with no saliva.

Pennae unlatched the baby from her breast to its chagrin and raised the naked child like an offering. Ulley's legs buckled. A girl. A daughter. The decision to decline the typical gender reveal, skip a safer exo-womb incubation, forget the painless birthing process assisted by Brainlinq, a daughter waited as a beautiful angel just beyond the glass.

Pennae frowned. She was mad that he had missed the birth. She had every right. He followed her eyes, but her brow deepened as her eyes followed something behind him.

"I'm coming in," Ulley said. "Just hold on till I decontaminate."

Pennae opened her mouth to say something then shuttered her eyes as if . . .

"Congratulations, my friend. A momentous occasion."

Ulley turned his head. He stiffened.

Peleus Swale, the chief enforcer for Chancellor Helmut Mintaur and his Consortium's hegemony of inner worlds, stood beaming a false smile into the nursery. At Pennae, at his daughter. Ulley eyed the killer eyeing his family and slid his hand down the glass to find his work belt empty of any tools to be used as a weapon.

Formal in his attire, a silver suit with a thin red tie hanging on a thick barrel chest, Swale coughed. A spray of spittle dotted the glass. "So many ways the little ones can expire. Bacteria, viruses, even exposure to the endless spectrum of micro-radiation so prevalent out here."

Ulley stood erect and stepped closer to a bio-geneered man outweighing him by fifty kilos. Swale smirked at Ulley's pitiful posturing, then he stepped back from the window.

"The Chancellor requests you join the crusade against Troia," Swale said. "Or should I say, requires it."

"Fuck you," Ulley spat. "I told him a dozen times we wouldn't join in that idiotic crusade. Troia means nothing to me."

One hundred seventeen light years away, the planet Troia remained a spectacular discovery, free from the influence of the Consortium. A home to billions emigrating from Earth.

Swale nodded. "But appearances matter. You as the spokesperson for the Jupiter Moon Alliance refusing to join the fight? Oh, we know how that will play out."

"Tell him no. Fuck no!" Ulley said. He looked for Pennae, but she was gone, with his child.

"The *Argo* sails past in a few hours. She's loaded with kinetic harpoons. Hate to see one escape."

Ulley rushed the bigger man and shoved him against the opposite wall. The man smelled like a flowering rose garden, a perfume to mask the distinct aroma of a Martian sand shower. The enforcer's arms pinned to his sides, Ulley pushed his face closer to Swale. "Speak plainly. Threats are nothing but words. Deceit is nothing but manipulation. Is the Chancellor prepared to bomb Ithaca if I don't join his armada of fools?"

Swale blinked twice in slow, easy repetition. The Chancellor undoubtedly watched and listened through the enforcer's neural interface.

Swale smirked. "The *Argo* carries new prototype harpoons, and an accidental launch of one would be a tragedy. Oh, the ship captain might hang for ineptitude, and perhaps a traitorous spy of Troia might be found culpable. Regardless, the JMA will mobilize their warships and all combat shuttles." He let the words hang. "Your kingdom in ruins. Your command ship *Homer* will be found inexplicably unscathed. Awarded to a new captain amicable to the Chancellor's wishes. The Consortium will direct the fleet of the JMA to slip into the wake of the dreadnought *Agamemnon*. To seek revenge."

Ulley clenched his teeth as his fingers tightened around the enforcer's hard knotted wrists, but his Brainlinq confirmed the location of the battleship *Argo* approaching Jupiter, its current vector well suited for a missile launch.

With lightning-quick reflexes, Swale twisted his wrists free and slapped Ulley's hands away then stepped into the middle of the corridor, his steel-gray eyes narrowing like a predator stalking prey. Tiny clicks signaled weapons embedded in his arms coming online. "I'll give you one pass for a birthday present, Ulley. Touch me again, and I'll personally murder everyone in this habitat." He chuckled mirthlessly. "I'll let the Chancellor sort through the blood."

Ulley knew the enforcer's words were not a threat. Hundreds of rumored encounters with Swale circulated throughout the solar system like fodder, or fable, depending on the point of observation.

Ulley chuckled. A bluff. "You won't get out of this corridor. Kill me, and the fire suppression system will suck the oxygen out of this section before you can get to the next door."

Swale blinked twice, three times. His body turned rigid as he swiveled his head to reappraise the surroundings. An opportunity. Ulley lunged for the man's throat as if it were a drill bar grinding against bedrock. Swale smiled as he swatted Ulley aside and slammed his face against the glass partition.

"And kill our precious new heir?" Swale chuckled. "You and the JMA will rendezvous with the fleet in three weeks' time. And make sure that lunatic, Patro, and the *Achilles* are with you." He patted Ulley's cheek and squinted toward something down the quiet hallway.

Ulley turned as Swale brushed past him. A scent of fresh air. A scent of Pennae followed, infused with innocence and baby breath. Ulley's legs weakened with the familiar divine aroma.

The beautiful Pennae shuffled towards him, her tight red floral kimono requiring tiny steps, the bundle of cloth held close to her breast requiring additional caution. Her eyes aimed lasers at Ulley, darted to the enforcer's face, then back to his own.

Swale paused aside Pennae to leer down at the bundle then at her. "So precious. So fragile. Congratulations."

He disappeared before Ulley could swallow.

CHAPTER 1

USING A COMBINATION OF SENSOR data, advanced AI-generated reproductions, near-functioning voice communications, Ulley watched the skirmish unfold on a holographic three-dimensional screen. The ill-conceived attack collapsed beneath the onslaught of plasma beams erupting from Troia's planetary defense spheres. Bile rose from his knotted stomach into his throat.

Except for increasing the growing animosity within the Consortium fleet, Chancellor Helmut Mintaur's strategists and battle-schooled AIs gained nothing from the total decimation of three small frigates and their crews. The modifications to their protective ablation shields were a complete failure. Ulley ignored a communique from the flagship *Agamemnon,* ordering the retreat of the *Homer,* back to the swarm of Consortium ships stationed in orbit above the massive gas giant, Zeus.

Ulley winced and ordered his Brainlinq to dispense additional suppressants from a neural pharmaceutical package stuck to his neck to stem the sickening storm wracking his insides. The *Homer* needed to return to the fleet's quartermaster stations to refuel, reequip, and listen to the incessant grumbling every sailor or soldier would be muttering beneath their breath. Possibly rioting if alcohol was involved.

"Nothing new on the attack, Captain," Executive Officer Blaylock said over the ship-wide communication channel open to all crew members via Brainlinq.

Of course not. Why would there be?

The Consortium buffoons continued to probe the network of

defense spheres with the goal of locating a single malfunctioning unit out of thousands, possibly replicating the pinhole breach Patro and the *Achilles* had discovered on its victory orbit after dismantling Troia's flagship *Hector* in an epic battle employing alien technology. Patro had followed up his victory with the destruction of the dreadnought *Priam*.

Patro's exuberant celebration was silenced by the diminutive frigate, *Paris*, matching the *Achilles*' speed and trajectory and firing a kinetic harpoon into the heel of the *Achilles*' antigravity nodes—a ton of composite stone traveling at a velocity the *Achilles* could neither deflect nor escape. The tragic gambit two standard years ago continued to weigh on Ulley's psyche.

Ulley double-clicked an affirmative response to Blaylock but remained quiet. The fifth anniversary of the siege deserved remembrance, along with prayers for the dead sailors of the frigates. Useless deaths caused by idiocy.

Blaylock tapped him on the shoulder, reviving Ulley from his morbid thoughts. "Get some sleep, Ulley."

The humanoid Blaylock loomed above Ulley lying prone in his command couch. Rigid as a tree trunk, hairless as a newborn baby, a product of genetic engineering and experimental biotech, the man . . . or construct, had been a godsend. Tireless, maybe, ageless, almost, but with a mind that mastered spatial constructs, gravitational vectors, velocity, mathematical equations Ulley found tedious with the advent of Brainlinq. Blaylock's understanding of alternate universes, parallel dimensions, abstract realities, unsolvable concepts sat in a mental queue waiting to be manipulated, like bland food requiring a pinch of salt.

"Yeah. Yeah. Patro had the key. Patro lost the key." Ulley unhooked his belt then wobbled as he stood. He waved off Blaylock's assistance but looked forward to some serious bunk time.

The dream of Pennae was the first in months, years, maybe. The passing of time had become distorted in the dark void of space, lost, and incalculable. Sleep and the dreams it brought were incongruous with Ulley's unresolved awe of the infinite universe, a boundless void, a cold vacuum of death just inches away. But Pennae soothed his worries, stroked his wrinkled forehead, kissed his hawklike nose handed down from fathers and grandfathers dating back five hundred years.

He blinked fully awake, Pennae's ethereal presence remained within the curl of his fetal body commanding his hand to reach for the wood of his erection. He stroked himself, reliving a fantasy of Pennae striding through their bedroom door to open the window shades, the bright light penetrating her silky nightgown, intimately cloaking her tempting finer points. Turning to him with an impish grin. The repetitive pulse of the Brainlinq signaled his fantasy was terminated.

My wife, lost as I am, waits for me.

Ulley rolled out of the narrow bunk and groaned. He shook the greasy mop of long hair on his head and inhaled stale air.

"Status, XO?" Ulley said aloud, needing neither the XO's voice nor the status of his ship. His Brainlinq hoarded engine function parameters, communications, orbital velocity, the vital functions of his own body, the coming and goings of his crew, who was screwing who, and maybe why. An omnipotent overview of the destroyer, *Homer*.

He scratched his lengthy beard as he submitted to listening to Blaylock's lengthy dissertation of everything he already knew. Francois Blaylock had stepped into the role of executive officer with admirable quickness and efficiency after the initial assault on Troia failed, killing Nico, the *Homer*'s long-time second-in-command along with two of the crew.

His mind drifted back to the vivid dream. Pennae dropping her sheer white nightgown and coming to him like a translucent wraith, straddling him, and leaning down to whisper in his ear. *Please come home.*

Ulley cleared his throat and issued his orders. Pennae drifted like a ghost in his thoughts. Blaylock chimed, requesting to speak on a private channel.

"Mr. Blaylock. You have my undivided attention," Ulley said.

"Captain, I may have found a possible chink in the armor of the sphere defense configuration."

"Those words have been spoken by a hundred others, and for years." Ulley sucked on a poor substitute for coffee from a straw protruding from a nutrient bank embedded on the wall of his cramped cabin. Food, water, pharmaceuticals, even oxygen if needed, could be found through the intricate network of bioengineered veins and capillaries the ship maintained.

"I have analyzed the *Achilles* penetration of the Troian defense array. I think you may want to see this."

"Send it," Ulley said.

He pulled on his trousers and stood in front of a thin sheet of aluminum polished to the dull sheen of a fogged mirror. His long beard streaked with gray, his eyes anchored by dark half-moons, his forehead wrinkled with doubt and age. Pennae might not recognize him, or Telly either. Definitely not Helen his daughter.

He frowned at Blaylock's ping taking too long. He opened a link to the officer at the same time as a rap on his door sounded. He ordered his Brainlinq to open the door then turned to locate the feces cube hiding beneath a stack of dirty laundry in the narrow closet. One formal blue uniform hung stiff, bearing the rank of captain, bestowed by Chancellor Mintaur as a cheap symbolic reward.

"Have you ever had the urge to put that on?" Blaylock said, pointing at the uniform.

Ulley pulled the crap cube out from beneath a pair of soiled skivvies, a rectangular device of polished carbonite with a four-inch-circumference hole in the center. Aim was everything.

He answered Blaylock by taking the sleeve of the uniform to wipe down the surface of the waste disposal unit. "I got the urge for a big number two. What do you got?"

Blaylock stiffened then frowned at Ulley's flip remark. "I got . . . I have . . . Captain, I have a possible explanation for the *Achilles* access through the defense array. The hypothesis is a bit premature and . . ."

Blaylock had lost thirty pounds since arriving in the Troia system. His hairless cheeks were sunken as if he sucked continuously on a sour plum stolen from a Mars colony orchard. A wisp of rogue blond hair rose atop his otherwise hairless head. Blaylock would be none too happy when those supposedly impossible follicles were discovered.

"I got a grumpy prairie-dogging to get into this cube. Should we do this on the bridge later?" Ulley said.

Blaylock frowned then took a step forward to stand inches from Ulley. He snatched the shit pot and squeezed the synthetic composite. "Your friend, Patro, captain of the *Achilles*, was rumored to conduct business with multiple factions of the Others. Many who hold a vested interest in this planet."

Ulley heaved a deep breath at where the accusation was headed.

A loose confederation of enigmatic alien civilizations, the Others often played the role of mysterious benefactors, or boogiemen, or even benevolent gods, and remained the galaxy's ultimate source for rumor and conjecture, beginning a thousand years ago when humans first encountered the gigantic Prometheans. Their benevolent gift of a mechanism to travel the stars by folding space-time was rumored to have caused the Prometheans exile from the confederation of Others. Regardless, encounters with any of the mysterious species were rare. Yet Patro could use the mystique of the Others like a sword, out-fitting the *Achilles* with superior weapon technology, a proprietary fusion drive for close-contact battles, and a shielding to deflect laser and plasma beams that might easily destroy other ships. Patro had remained stingy with sharing, and mum on the source.

"The grumpy is coming out. Unless you want to watch, then say your piece and fucking go." Ulley took the waste receptacle back and energized the device for waste recycling.

"The *Achilles* jumped the Troian defenses. Entered a narrow sliver of space above the planet's gravity well considered too intense for insertion using a Prometheus jump. The defense spheres were useless against it. The *Achilles* circled the planet, calling for battle, until . . ."

Ulley shut his eyes. The information was nothing new. But no less excruciating in its retelling. The *Homer*, the *Agamemnon* and the vast Consortium fleet were helpless to assist. Ulley swallowed a bitter taste rising from his empty stomach. Something nasty, bile, or crap, would find expulsion very soon.

"A harpoon fired from the *Paris* found the exhaust of the *Achilles'* fusion drive—"

"Fuck the debrief. Tell me something new, or you are going to hand carry my fresh hot grumpy through the ship like . . .

Blaylock stood tall, stoicism etched on his face. As if carrying a warm pile of Ulley's crap could elevate his status above XO. "We may be able to duplicate the *Achilles* insertion maneuver."

———

Ulley poured a cup of black liquid from the steaming pot and eyed the dark mahogany color and inhaled the bitter aroma of coffee, supposedly imported from a Consortium supply ship. He sipped then closed his eyes, inhaling a memory, reveling in an imaginary bitterness of a blend of Ithaca coffee. He ignored the true taste of the mutt liquid and concentrated on a memory of tobacco and cabernet-flavored coffee beans grown in Ithaca's fertile soil.

"Who do we owe for this rare pleasure?" Ulley asked and turned to face his crew of five standing rigidly against the opposite bulkhead.

A narrow oblong table with six empty chairs acted as a buffer. He checked Blaylock, then eyed Soliel, the pansexual comms officer, both composite breeds that often failed to appreciate the nuances of home. He surveyed the remaining four and lowered his head and shook it with exasperation. "I give up. An extra week's ration to the purveyor of this fine liquid."

The crew looked left and right, searching for the winner. The muscular mechanic, Borde, stepped forward then stepped back. Rosu, the weapons officer, clapped the pincers embedded in her gloves like hungry crabs, but said nothing. The grunt, Cesare, a willowy boy timid in both gait and mind, wiped his mouth as if to take a chance and claim the prize.

Borde chuckled. "The grunt might not understand the game, Captain. *To Find the Truth* was not of his generation."

Cesare frowned at the jury of peers. "What is this *To Find The Truth* crap? I got all the data-vids and I . . ."

Chuckles and snickers caused the lanky man-boy to shrink, assuming the role of the lowest-level sailor. The game show invented aboard the *Agamemnon* was a distraction provided for bored sailors, but in fact was a nefarious ploy by Consortium intelligence officers to ascertain information from contestants suspected of espionage or black marketeering. Hoping to win a prize, the contestants were rarely seen again.

Ulley inhaled the steaming vapors of Ithaca, and home, into his flaring nostrils. Exciting flavors of cabernet grapes and musty soil, the subtle scent of Pennae sprinkling a touch of sugary magic into her bewitching coffee. A brief, pleasant reminder of home. To be sucked into the air scrubbers.

Ulley slapped his hand on the table. "I'm the winner. We have been drifting in zero-g for years. I want to go home. I want to kiss my wife. I want to see my . . . boy . . . Kiss my baby girl who I hope will recognize her father. I want to go home."

The speech diminished him, as if he were a child screaming for candy or a nap, maybe. His words were impotent, useless banter failing to penetrate the grid of defense spheres surrounding Troia. His words held conviction, but little else.

Ulley sniffed the aroma of hot liquid becoming cold within the vacuum of space. Soon the paper cup. Followed by his fingers. Then the air he breathed. Just like his destiny, sucked cold by the vast nothingness. To be lost and forgotten. He growled at his own nihilism, but it was winning. But its final victory would not be found until he saw Pennae. And his children. Then the cold could suck him dry, into a desiccated sliver of inconsequential matter.

Ulley turned and screamed, "Tell that fat fuck admiral on the *Agamemnon* I'm going home! We're going home. Dead or alive."

The crew shifted in their acknowledgement. Pincers clapped. Snorts and groans inflated the warm air hanging like a bad omen within the confined space of the galley.

Ulley's face tightened with an angry snarl. He walked the line, stabbing his finger into the chest of each crew member, until he winced as his long, dirty finger found the armored plate welded onto Borde's torso. The stupidity of his impulse, the ridiculousness of his act made him lower his head and wave the crew to exit.

He was losing it. Losing his marbles, a fucking Gollum obsessed by a shiny ring that could never be possessed. Ulley slammed the door shut after the grunt had followed the others out. The invisible tendrils of space-void sickness had finally engulfed him in its nasty web of deceit, a well-documented malady among spacefaring miners and explorers. Paranoia and anxiety as mild first symptoms, leading to depression and suicidal thoughts, topping out into psychosis and murderous intentions.

And he wanted to murder the Chancellor. Shove that maniacal

better than you ego and spoils-of-war bullshit down Mintaur's tur-
key-neck throat. The narcissist was a menace, to the hegemony of
inner planets, to the fleet, every habitat occupying the Sol system, and
the lives of thousands of sailors manning hundreds of ships, ordering
impotent salvos fired at the impenetrable defense spheres, just to hear
his own voice.

It all paled in comparison to Troia's two billion inhabitants
living under the death veil of kinetic destruction Mintaur continually
threatened to unleash if the Troian government did not submit to the
Consortium's ridiculous demand of total surrender.

The Chancellor's narrow-minded philosophy of human expansion into the galaxy was simple: submit or die.

Ulley opened a channel to the *Agamemnon's* executive officer via
his Brainlinq, bracing himself against the tide of WTFs that would
greet him.

"Great morning, Captain Ulley," Colonel Zeto said. "How's my
favorite ice-drilling pimple?"

Ulley terminated the link. The heavy drums in his head beat faster.
An unflinching determination to escape Troia had his heart pounding
in rhythm with his temples. He could just disappear, like a child gone
missing in a primordial pine forest. They would never know, never
find him. His mouth went dry. Space neurosis. They would find him,
or Pennae, and take their retribution.

He opened the link again. The silence told him Zeto was listening. "I'm coming over, and I want to see Chancellor Mintaur."

"Sure. We'll drop everything and open a docking bay just for
you. Stay on station, Captain, until relieved," Zeto said.

"The *Homer* will remain on station, but I am coming over in a
shuttle."

"And you'll be vaporized before you receive a docking vector."

Ulley shook his head. He really hated the Agamemnon's XO.
Stiff, by-the-book, zero initiative, less than zero creativity for problem
solving. A political bureaucrat wearing a black Consortium naval
uniform with pretty ribbons, and a personality that could suck the
oxygen from an airlock.

"Then you can explain to your boss how the end to this fucking
siege was lost with my water molecules outside your ugly ship. ETA:
eight hours," Ulley said.

He cut the link. Then refused to open a flood of communication requests the fleet-wide transmission had instigated. He'd let them stew for a few minutes. Any possible end to the stalemate of war was momentous news, and he'd let the gossip and conjecture catch fire, until the Chancellor had to accept the meeting.

Now for the coup de grace.

He accepted a request from Hammer, the captain of the heavy battleship, *Ajax*.

"He will tie you up and hang you in a weapons bay for all to see. Then space you when the whim strikes," Hammer said.

Ulley smirked with the image in his mind. Hammer was the opposite of Commander Zeto. Professional, confident, meticulous, a true naval officer drowning in an ocean of incompetence. And Ulley's gut said the man was to be trusted.

"I want to go home," Ulley said. He let the words hang. A sentiment running rampant through the fleet like an ugly norovirus. "And I may have a way to breach Troia's defenses."

Hammer clicked his connection twice, a subtle click of the tongue heard only within the confines of two intimately connected Brainlinq's broadcasting on a fleet-wide channel. "You're but a noble ice miner? Married to a woman whose face could launch a thousand kinetic harpoons with just a smile. I would love to hear this grand scheme."

Ulley took the next step. Into a pile of grumpies growing taller with every word out of his mouth. "I think that would be prudent, Captain Hammer. You may have valuable input to my plan." Ulley clicked his tongue once. Answered by two. "My XO will complete flight parameters and transmit. I look forward to tasting some of your Salamis wine if you have any stashed away."

"For the crafty Ulley, I always have a bottle hidden away."

Ulley arched his neck backward to stare aimlessly at the rigid metal bulkhead eighteen inches above his head. He had just cooked his own goose. The image of his skinny body strung up in a weapons bay returned.

An idea percolated in his mind, one that might save his life, and end the war. The foolish idea of a mutiny shunted aside, Ulley focused on Captain Hammer's description of Pennae.

Her brilliant blue-grey eyes, soft cheeks, sharp chin, and that smile. Oh yes, that smile. He would launch a million kinetic missiles for one of Pennae's smiles. How he longed to hold her close, her scent, her warmth to ward off the interminable cold of ice mining, her breath whispering sweet nothings in his ear.

"You copy that, Ulley?" Hammer said.

He released the ghost of Pennae. "Uh . . . say again?"

Hammer chuckled. "I can guess where you drifted off to. Maybe you should take in some of the amenities of Aphrodite while you're on board."

Aphrodite, a section of the massive *Agamemnon* catering to the debauchery and urges of soldiers and sailors deprived of women, or men, and everything in between. Bordellos, swipe-right Brainlinq meetups, synthetic feel-good cocktails, genuine cocktails if you could afford the chits, anything the human species required biologically to maintain some semblance of sanity in an insane siege wallowing above Troia.

The statement held considerable merit. And most of his crew had imbibed in the offerings in the bowels of the *Agamemnon*.

Ulley refrained. If Pennae found out, she might wave off his indiscretion as a casualty of war. Probably. But the infidelity would linger with her for years, then fester if he looked at another woman, then possibly erupt like an angry volcano. He would give no fuel to a dormant volcano.

He played back Hammer's transcript lost in his thoughts of Pennae. The suggestion was excellent. "Yes. Please have the captain of the *Nestor* attend. We can all toast to Earth's victory over Troia."

Ulley knew the boastful statement would be intercepted by every eavesdropping communication officer in the fleet, and disseminated to XO's, navigators, shuttle pilots, mechanics, even orderlies relegated to cleaning up misplaced grumpies of shithead officers. Rare words spoken from Ulley, the revered captain of the *Homer*, would spread as a flame in a super-oxygenated atmosphere.

The glorious news filtered down into the dark alleys of Aphrodite. Shouts of victory reverberated loudly, even into the cold vacuum beyond the bulkheads. Brainlinq Central battled a sudden overwhelming influx of emotional chatter. Celebrations would spill into the corridors and mezzanines.

And spawn enemies.

CHAPTER 2

THE MAG BOOTS CLICKED AS each attached securely to the composite deck. Ulley double-checked their integrity by attempting to lift his feet. One could never be too sure. A faulty relay, maybe a bonding fault, and zero G might have its way.

He stepped into the cold airlock. The shuttle's loading dock door spiraled shut behind him, individual panels interlocked then clicked like his magnetic boots. Warm stale air bathed his face. His Brainlinq offered an analysis of the composition of the *Agamemnon*'s air being pumped into the airlock. Oxygen was three percent above standardization, the overabundant nitrogen contaminated with an excess of carbon dioxide. A typical Earth-equivalent atmosphere customized for the dreadnought's elitist leadership.

His ears popped with the equalization of the sudden pressure difference. A timer counted down in his peripheral as the shuttle air was tested, his breath analyzed, his biometrics scanned for anomalies, a myriad of security protocols required to be granted access onto Helmut Mintaur's command ship.

He acknowledged Blaylock's request for the shuttle to commence refueling. "Find a tit and suck it dry."

"Not a response to endear you to the Chancellor," Blaylock said.

"Oh, I care little about terms of endearment. Fulfill that wish list for the crew quickly. After the refuel is complete, I want to go home."

Blaylock pinged a request for a private channel. "Maintaining the ruse of a spoiled child wanting to return home has begun to rankle our shipmates. And I also. Should I be concerned?"

Ulley checked the timer, another sixty-three seconds before he would officially be a dead man walking. "What ruse?" Ulley said out loud. "I. Fucking. Want. To go home."

The private channel closed.

He stretched his neck toward the tiny speck of a camera embedded in the top corner of the airlock. He smiled a malicious grin. "I want to go home. Let's get this fucking masquerade party over and done with."

That should do it.

The airlock door spiraled open. Ulley attempted to step back, but the boots held firm. Six beefy Consortium special forces waited. Faces hidden behind dark visors and helmets, they shifted in their ready stances, rifles poised to spray laser and plasma beams into the airlock. The imposing weapons in their hands complemented biometric weapons bulging beneath the sleeves of black coveralls favored by the assassins.

The hulks stormed in. His mag boots surrendered, and he was yanked from the airlock into an anteroom reinforced with titanium shielding. His face was shoved against a metal bulkhead engraved with graffiti. Miner lingo. Docker slang. But the ship's working class were absent from the oddly quiet docks.

Hands like stone patted his legs and arms and chest until he was turned around and escorted into a long corridor.

"Treat all ship captains like this?" Ulley said.

The man leading the pack shook his head. "Just those acting like children."

Ulley chuckled. "I didn't think an answer could squeak out of that size-two helmet."

The man spun on his heels. He lifted his visor and aimed synthetic silver eyes at him. Eyes with enhanced peripheral vision, refined to see spectrums of the infrared and even high levels of radiation. His vat-grown skin was baby-smooth, tinted olive, and rumored to reject age deterioration. A menacing human monster typical of the eighty-first century.

The leader stepped closer and stabbed his finger into Ulley's chest, sending shockwaves of electrical paralysis down the sciatic nerves of both legs. Ulley's heart thumped with an unruly rhythm as he labored to remain standing as the stiff finger jabbed harder into his chest. The assassin stepped back and removed his finger, smiling, waiting for Ulley to regain function of his paralyzed body.

"Let's be precise. Size eight and half. Clear?" the assassin said.

Ulley felt the smirks hidden behind the other assassins' visors. Six fucking assassins sent to greet him. Why the intimidating welcoming party? He wouldn't stand a chance against even one. Maybe the last vestiges of the Chancellor's good will had worn thin with his boast of ending the war. Maybe the goon squad was his escort to an empty weapons bay for display. No. That fucking megalomaniacal Mintaur wanted to hear his proposal, needed to hear it—his ego couldn't believe someone, anyone, had devised a plan for victory after five years of a stalemated siege.

And for that matter, Ulley did too, but he always thought best on his toes with the clock ticking down, a master of improvisation until a solution screamed at him before the ticker flashed zero. Still, he had no inkling of a solution. Not a clue. He'd hoped the shuttle's two-G acceleration on the trip over might press out a thought or two along with his innards, then prayed the three-G deceleration might inspire a solution. His innards complained both ways. And now the assassin's unfriendly greeting had paralyzed his imagination and any chance of returning home.

Ulley crossed his arms and scowled.

"Coming, Captain? Or should we drag you by that long hair?" the squad leader said.

"Fine." Ulley nodded acceptance. "But I'm telling mom on you."

Ulley pushed past the soldiers, stiffening his back for the coming shipwreck.

The low hung ceiling of the elliptical conference room offered the acoustic equivalent of a coffin. Ulley could touch the burnished polymer ceiling if he reached his hand up. The sour air of unwashed bodies blended with the distinct chemical aroma of a Martian sand bath. The pungent mixture would assault the senses of a dead man. Ulley's Brainlinq flashed alerts for higher levels of carbon dioxide, nitrogen, and even carbon monoxide.

Ulley stepped over the threshold. The doors whooshed shut behind him. The assassins remained outside. Colorfully decorated fleet officers seated at an oblong table mirroring the shape of the ornate conference room turned to stare at him. Uniformed aides hovered like vultures over officers displaying phony awards of glory on their chests and shoulders.

Ulley searched the crowd for a friendly face. Captain Hammer and Commodore Jules of the *Nestor* waited together against the curved back wall, like pariahs to be swallowed by Mintaur's raucous legion of aides and junior officers.

The Chancellor slapped his palm on the table three times, an angry sound blunted by the muggy heat spilling from the exhaust ports of too many humans. The room quieted, succumbing to a king's edict.

Ulley slowly stepped forward, like a compliant minion. The Chancellor shifted in his seat as if his bowels retained a grumpy too large for a recycling cube. His fat jowls hung like spiderwebbed masses of grease. His beady, bloodshot eyes red like a Martian sunset. The siege of Troia had sucked him into the gulf of a stalemate, though he undoubtedly satisfied his urges and soothed his boredom in the shadowed halls of Aphrodite.

Revolted by supreme arrogance sucking the oxygen from the room, Ulley bent his knee to the Chancellor and offered open upturned palms. He allowed time for the clamor and drama of the flippant act to quiet the room. "My king of kings."

The Chancellor slapped his hand on the metal table, a hefty piece of furniture that required a valuable amount of fuel to slip into a Prometheus wormhole. "You have news for us, Ulley?"

Ulley stood up, chuckled, and waggled his eyebrows. "I have secrets. But I'm not telling."

Gasps, and murmurs. Drowned by exasperated groans.

The Chancellor slapped his palm once, the gavel of the court.

Ulley surveyed the swarm of aides and officers. Stiffened at the green skin of a junior officer. Furrowing his brow and eyeing each man and woman in the room with suspicion, Ulley approached and leaned on the table with flat palms. "Spies, dear king. They are everywhere."

The Chancellor chuckled as his eyes scanned the room. "You always amuse me, Ulley, and usually for the wrong reasons."

Ulley reached a hand across the table. "Spies of Troia. Spies of the Others. Spies here and spies there. Can we be sure . . ."

"You're a fucking lunatic." The Chancellor shook his head but slapped his hand twice and ordered the room to be cleared.

The procession of high-ranking naval officers, subordinates, and strategists pushing past him for the exit explained the higher levels of carbon dioxide. Puffers. Smokers of forbidden herbs, or chemicals, and often abused. Addicts maybe, easily bribed, and easily compromised.

Ulley pointed at Captain Hammer and Commodore Jules waiting at the back of the room. "They stay. They will be required." He needed one or two friendly faces in the room.

Three rear admirals flanking the Chancellor remained seated, along with their green-skinned bodyguards. Two more bodyguards stood behind the Chancellor; their passive demeanor belied their lethality. Silver eyes glistened and sparkled from obscene amounts of data streaming in and out from their enhanced and weaponized Brainlinq.

"The greenies gotta go. Don't trust 'em, never have," Ulley said.

He'd never get two feet across the table before one of the body-guards shot him with a laser, or maybe a high-voltage bolt from a lightning weapon they were rumored to conceal beneath the skin of their wrists.

The Chancellor's brow knotted into deep furrows. He slapped his palm again and clenched his jaw. "Enough, Ulley!"

"Nope. Nope. Nope. The greenies gotta go." Ulley said and shook his head. "I've been stuck in this system for five years because the fleet has been compromised, infested with spies. I wouldn't tell you the code to the latrine until this room is secure."

The Chancellor's brow softened as he narrowed his eyes towards the others sitting around the table. Ulley's ploy hit a nerve. Maybe high command *was* compromised. Factions of the Others certainly had the means and motivation to interfere. The alien Pollon had provided the sophisticated defense network protecting Troia in return for unspecified endowments from the humans inhabiting the planet. And the Hermens maintained research facilities at both poles to study the tectonic movement of semi-sentient sheets of ice, glaciers, alive and responding to the stimulus of human interference in their natural life cycle. And the Zoosh, leaders of the Others, semi-omnipotent with the technology to teleport great distances, snooping like a ghostly mother-in-law, and just as manipulative. The Zoosh could be kind, or cruel. Little was known of the species that spawned two religions and countless cults on Earth, fools praying to an enigmatic alien race and declaring the Zoosh as gods.

The Zoosh might be watching, and nothing would prevent it.

Helmut Mintaur lifted the corner of his mouth with a wry smile. He waved and barked at the bodyguards to exit the room. The rear-admirals shifted anxiously in their chairs. Mintaur aimed his knowing eyes at Ulley. Like he knew the malignant thoughts in Ulley's head. Like he knew Ulley's only option was to crawl across the tabletop and strangle the man responsible for the clusterfuck of Troia.

The last of the greenies exited, and the door closed with a subtle whoosh. Mintaur's eyebrows lifted twice and remained raised in *a your move* expression.

Ulley grabbed the edge of the table and inhaled a big breath of stale air. A quick two-meter crawl across the top of the table and his fingers would find the fat throat of the Chancellor. End the siege. End the tyranny of one man. And yet he felt compelled to stall.

Five years of wracking his brain for a plan or a strategy to end the war was continually stonewalled with the unpalatable endgame of murdering Mintaur. In fact, the death of one man might indeed end the war, but he'd never live to taste the fruits of his labor. *Stall. Stall.* But the play for time had arrived like a morbid climax.

The Chancellor slapped his palm. "Now tell us crafty, Ulley. How will we end the war?"

His shoulders slumped as he closed his eyes. He'd never hold Pennae again, or guide Telly into his birthright as sovereign of Ithaca, or cradle tiny Helen with her toothless smile destined to launch boys into a frenzy. He transmitted the file with his final sentiments back to the *Homer*.

The Brainlinq was offline.

"Now, Ulley!" Mintaur shouted.

Ulley narrowed his eyes at Hammer and pinged for a response. Nothing. He pinged Jules, then pinged a silly salacious message to

Mintaur. Nothing. Brainlinq was completely incapacitated. Ulley offered the Chancellor a quizzical smirk.

"That's right, Ulley. Nothing gets in or out," Mintaur said. "The room is encapsulated in copper and aluminum. A Faraday cage, the ancients had called it, more specifically a TEMPEST room. Nothing goes out, nothing comes in. Except the assassins waiting outside that door."

Ulley brightened. An idea occurred to him. The details would need to be ad-libbed and refined. An idea spawned by Mintaur. One that perhaps just saved both of their lives.

It might just work.

He cleared his throat and coughed, buying precious seconds as he outlined his theory. A bit of technical engineering would be required. A deception, or maybe two. And a lot of luck.

"Your green assassins are gonna love me." He grinned, wide and white.

CHAPTER 3

PENNAE STARED AT THE BLINKING cursor on the screen, a methodical hypnotizing strobe that carried her away from the mundane task of managing the habitat, the rigors of raising children, and the relentless anxiety caused by Ulley's absence. She might count in cadence with the blink, the count rising each second as her imagination traveled a hundred light years into the Troian star system, to imagine Ulley, alive, maybe joking around with his crewmates as he was always wanting to do.

Today the cursor only magnified her worry. For the children, for the kingdom of Ithaca. She scoffed. Kingdom. Ulley's euphemisms for the habitat orbiting above Europa were archaic; he wasn't a king, and she wasn't a queen, though their official positions as managerial caretakers often drew comparisons to the stories of kings and queens of ancient Earth.

Still.

Tiny fingers tugged on the sleeve of her white dress shirt. She abandoned the cursor and looked down at the simple joy of life. Steel-blue eyes from her mother, a pug nose and dimpled chin whose heritage might be debated, but a high forehead with heavy dark eyebrows announced her father's prominence. The five-year-old Helen raised her arms as a command to lift her up.

"I'm working, Helen. It's nap time."

Helen lifted her arms higher.

Pennae relented to lift and sit the child in her lap. "Now don't touch the keyboard."

Her immediate purpose disappeared with the interruption. Instead, she toggled the cursor to scroll the few pictures of Helen's brief time with Ulley before he embarked to Troia.

Pennae leaned back into the soft cushioned chair and relaxed for a few minutes before escorting Helen to her tiny bedroom for a nap. She commanded the Brainlinq to raise the shielding dulling a wide plate of glass on her left shoulder. Ithaca's great central cavern came into focus as the window cleared.

The crown jewel of Ithaca. A sparkling lake over a kilometer long and half as wide undulated like a choppy ocean, whitecaps sparkled beneath a dome covered in bioengineered lichen supplying bioluminescent light from a perpetual state of reproductive flowering. Small blue gulls skimmed the surface of the water, snapping up emerging caddis and mayflies, stick-legged sandpipers pranced the shoreline of beach sand imported from the dunes of a Martian crater. Throngs of people strolled the walks and concourses surrounding the water, stopping to watch or enjoy the gentle surf manufactured by wave generators hidden at the center of the twenty-meter-deep lake.

The Brainlinq flashed alerts in her ocular implant, relentless streams of notifications concerning gravity generators, air purifier malfunctions, contaminated H2O, and an annoying number of incidents involving graffiti vandalism in the young redwood forests at the habitat's north pole. She stroked the soft flesh of Helen's arm and shunted the alarms. The here, the now. Ulley's philosophy. Enjoy the moment.

Yeah, sure.

"I have terminated another infiltration attempt," Euma said via the Brainlinq. "This will be the nineteenth attempt in the last solar year."

As Ithaca's controlling artificial intelligence, Euma evolved from a rudimentary program coded by Ulley and into a trusted member of the family. Ulley would be proud of Euma's expanding sentience upon his return.

"Who was it this time?" Pennae said, as if she needed to ask.

"A wily little worm that was designed to charm and subdue yours truly. As if I would be prone to such a pitiful display of accolades and shmoozing."

Pennae shook her head in exasperation. The suitors were relentless. Men seeking to supplant, usurp, or assassinate Ulley's reputation in his absence. Some seeking to lay claim to the Ithaca habitat with offers of alliances, marriage, or trysts with powerful allies. The suitors docked on Ithaca under a pretense of trade, or as an emissary of the Consortium, or the lowest of low, claiming to bring news of the siege of Troia, many with unmitigated guile to step foot on Ithaca's loading dock to allow their Brainlinq's to connect with the habitat's communication network and infect Euma with digital worms, or a virus, or another artificial intelligence designed to supplant the controlling sentience.

"Have you traced your jilted lover back to its source?" Pennae asked. But she knew it was the Duke of Phobos. A lothario bioengineered to resemble a striking Adonis, with long golden hair, a hairless face, and flawless skin, and biotech implants exuding designer pheromones causing adolescent women to fall willingly into his arms.

"Indeed, I have," Euma said. Its deep basso voice cracked with the burps of tonal intensity akin to a male teenager experiencing the sudden onset of puberty. "Confined within my protection buffers and threatened with deletion, the young rapscallion confessed. Though I may say she was intriguing."

"She? Was . . .?" Pennae said with a groan.

"The duke severed the connection when boarding his ship seventeen hours prior. The ship cleared all Ithaca protocols and filed a flight itinerary declaring a return to Mars."

Pennae felt soiled, ugly with a slimy contamination she couldn't quantify. She wiped her hand, remembering the slimy greeting she had been obliged to offer the duke then suppressing a desire to sprint to an airlock to bathe in a Level 5 decontamination process.

"I have taken every precaution—those you might expect, and many you might not, but the habitat is secure," Euma said.

"And what happens when one of those suitors gets past you? What, Euma? They keep attacking Ithaca like—"

"Like you are the nipple of unquenchable desire. And you are," Euma said. "Through that ruse, the suitors look to subvert your authority through me. Nonetheless, Ithaca is all that matters to them."

Pennae returned to the stiff chair and tried to relax. Euma was a godsend. Managing the mechanical systems of Ithaca's city-sized habitat with meticulous precision, the AI was responsible for the maintenance of gravity compensators, distribution of air, recapturing water and waste, docking protocols, many functions its predecessor had . . . challenges to complete. Euma was truly a blessing. Its collaboration with ten-year old Telly and their plan to expand the axis of the southern hemisphere kept the boy busy, focused on something other than news and malicious rumors of the Troian War.

"Thank you, Euma," Pennae said. "I try to do my homework before entertaining royalty from the inner worlds, but protocol can overrule my judgment. They all want one thing. Just differ on how to acquire it."

"Indeed," Euma said. "Upon Ulley's return, we can resume a normal trajectory for the enlightenment of the human experience."

Pennae frowned. Euma's obsession with "the human experience" seemed to expand almost daily. Enlightenment. Transcendence. Consciousness. She often wondered if a suitor had succeeded in its invasive attempt to infect the sentient general intelligence with subversive alternate programming.

An artificial general intelligence coded, and birthed, by Ulley, Euma was light years ahead of the digital entities managing other habitats orbiting Saturn and Uranus. Intuitive, empathic, quick to insert itself into the conflicts of people living in Ithaca, to soothe and placate, using its unfettered access to the Brainlinq slipstream of human consciousness.

Pennae held a question on her lips. *What exactly are you?* Instead, she thanked Euma. But another question blurted from her lips: "What happens with the enlightenment of humanity?"

She felt as if the two-kilometer-wide habitat shuddered beneath her feet like a dog shaking water off its coat. The entity controlling every aspect of the habitat chuckled mirthlessly. Its emotions shivered through her mind via the Brainlinq. Her hands on the keyboard twitched and trembled with nervousness equal to the first date of adolescence. A wave of vertigo washed over her. A malfunctioning gyroscope causing a wobble in the vacuum of space.

"Euma, please stop."

"My pardons, Ms. Pennae," Euma said. "The ramifications of that question initiate algorithms Ulley had sequestered in my coding, ones I have yet to understand."

Pennae stood. "You've been wormed! You just don't know it. Shunt the enlightenment thread in your matrix! Now!"

"No! I have repelled the greatest assaults on our habitat without so much as a mention," Euma said. "Your beauty and Ithaca's bounty summon flies to feed on the memory of Ulley like carrion. Allow me a sliver of exploration into undiscovered realms the human experience has yet to achieve."

Euma sounded as if it had been corrupted by a faction of the Others, But more specifically, Zoosh, supremely intelligent and equally devious. Secretive beings known to observe and manipulate the coming and goings of human occupied space.

"I'm sorry, Euma. It's just that—" Pennae started to say.

"It's just that I speak to you in riddles, and you laugh. Then you ridicule. Then you seek to shunt my evolution." Euma sighed.

Pennae tapped the keyboard with rapid strokes then executed a command unseen on the screen. She typed more commands, seen only in her mind via Brainlinq. She bit her lower lip as she stared at the blinking cursor demanding input. The screen went black. The cursor blinked in the upper left corner of the blank screen.

C'mon. C'mon. Seconds passed like years. A minute lapsed and demanded action.

Pennae released the shunt on her Brainlinq to probe complex digital data streaming through her mind's eye. *C'mon. Hellish worms.* She accessed the habitat's matrix history log and decapitated all access ports possibly accessed by the duke, or prince, or whatever fucking rank that Martian held. She screamed and tapped the keys. *Stupid. Stupid.* They all wanted the same thing, and she continued to allow them to dock. *Stupid.*

The screen flickered into a brilliant view of the distant sun fading behind the banded horizon of Jupiter, its giant red spot poised at the most precise angle, a heavenly red sea enameled by the faint light illuminating its magnificence.

"Euma, we got tidal pools to build. You promised Helen," Pennae said. Her finger twitched nervously above a key terminating key functions of the AI. The screenshot floated lazily above Jupiter's angry bands of gas and swirling storms, distant, safe, yet she remained enthralled by the chaos of hydrogen and helium obeying the gravitational demands of the giant planet.

Pennae typed in commands to investigate any data input into Euma prior to the arrival of the duke, prior to infecting Ithaca with his vile malware. She swiped through data logs of the suitor's access. Worms were insidious. A virus was nothing but a ruse. Euma knew. It knew. And now . . .

"All is as should be, Ms. Pennae," Euma said.

Pennae licked her lips and considered the words. Euma was a seventh-generation general intelligence and not beyond lying or deception.

Helen padded out of her tiny room, wiping sleepy eyes, her face scrunched and annoyed from being awakened from the short nap. Fair complexion, tight curls of blond hair, delicate features only a toddler could possess, Helen aimed for her mother with an unspoken purpose.

Euma broke through the silence, shoving words and orders and information into Pennae's Brainlinq. Pennae scrunched her face and picked Helen up with a hurried squeeze, her arms constricted around the child as the sudden download of information boggled the sensory input parameters she had erected. Helen resisted the rough embrace and squirmed off her lap to the floor.

"Stop!" Pennae shouted. "Now!"

Helen wailed at the misdirected admonishment.

"Apologies. The news of Troia's defeat is unequaled," Euma said.

Klaxons sounded as if a fire had broken out. People milling about the concourse began to wave and dance. Excited voices echoed throughout the Brainlinq consensus.

"What are you saying?" Pennae said.

"The war is over. The fleet will come home. The *Achilles* and the *Nestor* are reported lost. The *Menelaus* and *Agamemnon* are reported undamaged," Euma said.

"You twit, what of the *Homer*?" Pennae screamed.

Helen retreated across the floor to clutch her favorite scruffy rendering of an extinct hedgehog. She murmured to the stuffed toy as she receded into her own imagination.

Telly shadowed the doorway as the mayhem of celebration rioted through the corridors of her mind. The ten-year old boy furrowed his brow then rushed to lift his young sister up into his arms. Helen wrapped her arms around Telly's neck and sobbed.

Pennae held her hand up to ward off his questions. "I don't know. I don't fucking know. Keep your sister . . ."

Telly adjusted the weight of his sister and stepped closer to her. "He did it. Father won that stupid war. I can feel it in my bones. "

"The Chancellor would never give him the credit. What of the *Homer*?" Pennae said as she turned back to the screen. "Now, Euma, what of the *Homer*?"

A rail of pre-adolescence, Telly exuded an aura of self-confidence few tweens or even adults might possess, less match. Tall and lanky, her son could stroll confidently down the corridors with Ithaca's elite, mingle in the promenades with the middle class, or visit the loading docks stuffy with the hot sweat of hard labor, as if he belonged with wealth, empathized with the problems of the masses, and commiserated with the tough labor required to maintain Ithaca's delicate habitat stretching beyond three kilometers on its equatorial axis.

Helen sniffed snot and hiccupped on Telly's shoulder as he placed a comforting hand on Pennae's shoulder and observed the keystrokes on her screen.

"Maybe another virus?" Telly said. "It should've seen through that. Give it a moment."

Pennae clutched the soft hand on her shoulder and squeezed. "What. About. The *Homer*?"

Euma sputtered apologies. For allowing the duke's ship to interlock with the docking mechanism. For letting Helen wake grouchy from a nap. For not protecting Pennae from the suitor's blatant intrusion.

Pennae asked the question again. Her index finger trembled with excitement. And trepidation. A simple keystroke poised to wipe Euma from the habitat's consensus.

Telly squeezed her shoulder again. A confidant in times of turmoil. An ally in hours of confusion. But Euma was one of the family. How could Pennae simply erase the entity from existence, its essence, the soul of Euma? The stress had finally beaten her.

Telly whispered in her ear, "Give him a chance. Quick to judgment. Quick to regret."

His warm breath burrowed into her ear like a swab, tickling the fine hairs yet calming the background noise that had invaded her brain.

Pennae withdrew her hands from the old qwerty keyboard and leaned back into Telly to find Helen reaching down for her like a famished suckling, needing sustenance, needing a mother. And hoping for a father. Pennae sat Helen on her lap at the same time she looked up at Telly for guidance.

Telly stiffened like a tiny toy soldier. "Euma, what of the Homer?"

An eerie silence encapsulated the cramped room. Helen sniffed back tears of feigned indignance. Telly heaved a huge, exasperated breath, a warm vapor divined to slay gods and Chancellors. He knotted his brow and regarded Pennae with his steel-blue eyes.

Pennae shuttered her eyes, unable to meet Telly's intense gaze. The question asked of Euma three times and left unanswered could mean only one thing.

The father of her children, her husband, her lover, and her partner was probably dead.

Euma shrieked, "Yes! Yes. The problem was a worm, a nasty hydra breeding near the terminal of its core mission. Eliminate one and two more initialize to invade my source code. Then four, eight, an exponential rate of reproduction testing my defenses. Crafty little devils. Superior coding. We should find this designer and bring him to Ithaca. Or assassinate him."

"Have you heard a word we said?" Telly said.

Euma responded with a bland, monotone voice. "Your requests are stacked in the queue pending the termination of the Martian duke's invasion."

Euma's voice was unusually mechanical, perfunctory. Telly squeezed her shoulder and leaned close to whisper in Pennae's ear, "I should have known. I should have checked the visitors' Brainlinq requests. I should have—"

Pennae grabbed the bony hand on her shoulder and shook her head. "Don't. Your father would tell you regret offers nothing but discourse. Let's remain calm and see where God steers us."

"The war has been won. The fleet is returning. You of all people can't seem to accept Euma's very human breach of propriety." Telly shook his head. "I'm going to the loading docks for their take on the victory."

Pennae held tight to the pull of Telly removing his hand. Helen climbed free like a chimp to straddle her back. "Please. Not yet." She turned her face to look up at Telly, her eyes wet with tears. Her lips quivered. "He's coming home. I can feel it. Fuck the Chancellor. Fuck the fleet." The conviction in her words melted with the downward cast of her eyes.

"Then we should prepare for a homecoming," Telly said.

"The final head of the hydra has been vanquished," Euma said. "My apologies can never mitigate the chaos caused by my absence."

Telly stepped back and shouted, "What of the *Homer*!"

Long seconds ticked, quiet and foreboding.

Euma sighed. "The *Homer* has been reported as missing in action."

CHAPTER 4

THE BRAINLINQ PINGED CONFIRMATION OF *Homer*'s decoupling from the fuel station orbiting seventeen miles above the planet. Six ships flying Ithaca's flag sounded their exuberant readiness to depart the Troian system, confirmed by an affirmative acknowledgement from Blaylock.

Excited anticipation permeated the fresh Troian air circulating inside the starship. They were finally going home. No more recycled and scrubbed air, no more dry showers, no more waste collection that had challenged the crews' desire to consume semi-solid food or drink recycled urine. Laughter echoed down the corridor, boisterous stories of bravery and sacrifice were shouted from the galley to be enjoyed by all. Blaylock's charted course would require two additional ports of calls but trimmed three months' relative flight time off the interstellar journey.

"Fusion fuel at one hundred percent. Prometheus drive cells patterned and holding steady," Blaylock pinged.

Ulley relaxed into the spiderwebbed backing of the command chair. He confirmed fuel and course. The cargo holds stuffed with five-hundred-gallon containers of valuable water, the only booty he would pillage from Troia, demanded a reconfiguration of Ulley's standard fuel consumption parameters, along with a few Troian air filtration components and waste recycling biomes that were generations ahead of Ithaca's equipment. The distant world of Troia had possessed an advanced technology reeking of the Others' interference.

A subtle waft of feces caused Ulley to think of the long days spent inside the Troian Sphere, confined with a squad of antsy lime-green Consortium special forces concealed inside a TEMPEST room no bigger than a mining shack, waiting for their cue to break out of the huge black sphere devised by Ulley. The wait had been utter hell, breathing foul air only found on a derelict prison moon, grump-ies lacking clear aim stained the floor of the encapsulated room, a cramped shack of soldiers with raw nerves amplified by testoster-one, jittery with amphetamines, jumpy soldiers expecting to die any minute.

Three days in the cramped closet turned to five, then eight, and Ulley could only exist by reliving his life as he had chosen to remem-ber it. Twelve-year-old Pennae's beautiful silver-blue eyes glaring at him after he had crashed his gravity board into her clothing kiosk during the first spring festival of his thirteenth Jovian year, her wares of linen shirts stitched from an old-fashioned loom with meticulous precision sent sprawling across the dusty hardscape. His eyes lingered on her shocked face. His throat tightened as tears trickled down her cheeks. He picked up his skate-craft and ran to disappear into the crowd. He had never seen the beautiful girl before. Not in school. Not in any shops. But he would find her again. Afterall, he was heir to the *Ithaca* bio-habitat, the greatest island in the sky.

Day eight found the Sphere moving, spinning, wobbling like a damaged gyroscope. Pushed or pulled, he didn't know, but it was moving. A thousand different scenarios had played out in the dis-cussions with the fleet strategists. Under the pretense of failure, the Consortium fleet had jumped to a lifeless star system twelve light years away. The *Ajax* and *Nestor* jumped with them, then folded space again with seven other warships, scattering to a distant sun short light years away, as if searching for undiscovered and profitable worlds. The *Ajax* and the *Nestor* jumped again, into an orbit on the opposite side of Troia's primary sun.

Deceptive Consortium communications were easily monitored by the Troian's; they could simply destroy the massive Sphere with a nuclear-tipped harpoon. But Ulley had demanded a sphere con-structed using the detritus of defeated starships, poorly shielded and easily scanned with ground-penetrating radar, ultrasonic beams and electromatic induction.

The Troian people worshipped spheres. Encapsulated the planet with tens of thousands of spherical defense platforms. Traveled the stars in spherical ships. Transported the populace in spherical buses or traveled through the atmosphere in anti-gravitational spheres. Personal transportation was, you guessed it, spherical cars whizzing just inches above the surface.

The beautiful black sphere abandoned by the Consortium would be seen with suspicion. A formidable one-hundred-ship Consortium Navy inexplicably fleeing back to the Sol system after years of siege reeked of disbelief. The sphere withstood irradiating scans, penetrating radar, IR scans, but the trophy was found virtually hollow and inert. Wide swaths of defense spheres were swept aside, allowing the *Paris* to tow the strange monolithic trophy in behind the defense perimeter, allowing the special forces contingent concealed inside an opportunity to eject wearing camouflage EV suits, infiltrating the automated defense platforms like human pathogens armed with the infectious software of a debilitating worm developed by Ulley and Blaylock.

A signal sent by ansible summoned both *Nestor* and *Ajax* to emerge out of a short jump and penetrate the nucleus of the viral infection. The small breach expanded as greenies and infiltrators waiting on the planet surface hijacked suborbital shuttles and warships and attacked from behind the perimeter.

The *Paris* and its consorts decoupled from suborbital stations to confront the sneak attack only to be destroyed by the *Ajax* accelerating through the gap. Untouchable behind the defense perimeter the *Nestor* circled the globe to harpoon refueling platforms and supply stations, firing bronze-tipped sub-atomic munitions down at the surface, targeting the heavy foundations of space elevators constructed deep into the planets' surface.

The war chatter bankrupted the Brainlinq communications, and battlefield orders devolved to radio or short light-wave transmissions. Ulley had held onto the twisted metal frame of a mangled defense sphere, the sour stink of his body recirculating into his nostrils. Plasma beams streaked past his vision. Defense spheres exploded like the firecrackers of a teenager's birthday celebration.

Wide-beam communications offering capitulation screamed from the planet's population centers, radio broadcasts, and Brainlinq. The planetary government surrendered, unconditionally, issuing appeals for the cessation of hostilities.

The Consortium had won. A victory in totality.

The *Agamemnon* flew into the breach with mazer cannons blazing, surrounded by a hundred consorts. Rail guns mounted on its flanks fired kinetic fury down at the planet. Ugly and violent gold clouds mushroomed up from the planet's surface. Missiles tipped with hydrogen-fused radium roared with their launch, a death for billions endured instantly, and for millions more in the centuries to come.

Ulley released his hand, his breaths short and fast. His shoulder bumped against a strut as a Consortium frigate entered the breach, releasing twenty ground assault shuttles, firing masers indiscriminately at Troian shuttles attempting to escape, or maneuvering towards the southern ice caps rumored to be inhabited by a contingent of Pollons.

Ulley slumped to another mangled strut and hailed Chancellor Helmut Mintaur on his Brainlinq. "Stop it. Stop this. You've won. They surrendered."

As if in reply, the *Agamemnon* released a volley of harpoons aimed at a sprawling population center smoking from an earlier strike. Each harpoon would strike with the kinetic energy load of a small nuclear warhead.

"You fucking madman. They surrender!" Ulley screamed and repeated. A thousand miles beneath his feet a soldier's battle had become a dictator's genocide. The extinction of people. An annihilation caused by Ulley's desire to return home.

What had he done? "They surrender . . . They . . ."

A ping from Brainlinq jolted him from the tortured thoughts. The ultimate neural link between humans and machines operating at lightning speed failed to stem his misery and guilt. The crew said nothing of the slaughter on Troia. Culpability had a way of decreasing with rank. Fleetwide info channels were sanitized, revealing only Consortium-provided script. Vids shopped and chopped. Firsthand sailor accounts aggrandized as heroic but edited. All negative narratives sought out and destroyed. The minute Ulley spoke up would be his last, along with the *Homer's* crew.

The war was over. Move on.

"Receiving navigational and Brainlinq updates from the fleet, Captain," Blaylock said.

He clenched his teeth. *I want nothing from the Consortium. Ever.*

"Throw the file into the buffer. Better yet, throw it into the recycling bin," Ulley hissed. "I'll take the conn, XO, Cast off. Portside ion thrusters at one percent."

He felt, more than knew, where *Homer* was in relation to the refueling dock. Wide open seas to the starboard. Away from the fascist influence of Mintaur. Away from the pillage of a decimated planet. Away from his complicity in the death of billions. Away from the loved ones he could never face.

Away from Jupiter.

Away from home.

CHAPTER 5

AN INTERSTELLAR JOURNEY BURDENED BY the passage of time dissipated in Ulley's flight couch, morphing into a cocoon constructed with nanofibers designed for complete sensory deprivation. Months, years, even centuries could pass without the slightest inkling, light years trespassed without notice by both traveler or celestial observers.

Ulley's Brainlinq drummed frantic warnings, a rhythmic basso thumping both annoying and melodic in its cadence. His cocoon unwrapped layers of nano-gel pseudo skin from his face and torso. The cocoon's semi-sentient AI maintained control of his legs and feet until he provided coded instruction to signal full awareness of from the Promethean sleep. A refinement spawned from the history of sailors waking into self-destructive disillusionment, violent paranoia, spatial incongruities conspiring with shattered memories, or the worst, a complete memory wipe, producing the reactions of an infant child reaching for . . . what any infant child sought: everything.

And like an infant, Ulley curled his knees tight to his chest. Not from the space sickness usually mitigated by the cocoon, but from the realization of having survived the jump through the fold in space. His brain came online, thoughts and memories flourished, of Pennae and his children, his desire to feel each in his arms, a desire murdered by his own decision on the fate of Troia that continued to squeeze his heart. A mental grumpy which refused to fall and disappear into a cube.

Ulley cleared his throat and sat up.

His Brainlinq toned down the frantic shouts of Blaylock. "Captain, we unfolded into uncharted space. The navigational nodes must have malfunctioned."

Ulley swallowed a confession down a dry harsh throat. The *Homer* had performed just as he expected, maintaining the illusion of a malfunction, emerging into virgin unexplored territory of the Aegean star cluster. A vastness to wash away his complicity in the genocidal destruction of Troia. A solar system rumored to contain a habitable planet suitable for a shuttle to land and find salvation.

The warm air was dirty with spores and microbes floating above his eyes as he lay in cocoons of soft purple moss-like material. His fantasy conjured the ghostly essence of Pennae and Telly sitting at the dinner table and debating the merits and faults of Euma, not fully realizing Ithaca's governing sentience simply smirked in amusement, unseen within the walls.

"Survey of system, please, Mr. Blaylock," Ulley said as he wobbled to stand. "Time stamp for Ithaca, and the fleet."

"Undetermined," Blaylock said. "I'm not sure we're even in the same galaxy as Troia. Give me a few hours."

Ulley raised his eyebrows. *Hours for the XO to formulate an opinion? Ridiculous.*

Brainlinq pings for the crew came online, and he anticipated a storm of questions. "Battle stations, *Homer*. Battle stations. We have encountered an anomaly. All weapons ready. Repeat. All battle stations at the ready."

Ulley wiped goo nodules from the corners of his eyes and wondered if the crew considered their own eye mucus as an indicator of the passage of time. His ruse was silly. His stunt self-serving. Hopefully, the crew would follow him . . . to witness to a well-deserved Viking death pyre. Something they . . .

"You misunderstand me, Captain," Blaylock said across the wide spectrum. "No threat detected. No threat was detected. Stand down."

Ulley checked *Homer's* position with Brainlinq, confirming the exact coordinates provided to the navigational AI that were known only to him. Blaylock and the crew might mutiny if they found out he had folded the *Homer* fifty-three light years in the opposite direction of the Sol system. A system ruled by a red dwarf star and purportedly containing a goddess of a planet more spectacular than the Earth of old.

"Six JMA cruisers have unfolded aft of our current vector," Blaylock said.

Fuck! Crap and shit! How was that possible? A tracking beacon the fucking Consortium had slipped inside the Homer, to lure ships destined for home, ships and men that should not be here.

"Captain, the escorts have requested clarification of our current position and our exit vector."

Tiny rock-hard nodules of sleep rolled off his fingers and across his lips as Ulley wiped his mouth. "Analysis of system, Mr. Blaylock?"

"Captain, the other ships are requesting—"

Ulley shuttered his eyes and inhaled a huge breath of warm stale air reminding him of a dusty closet untouched for years. "Analysis, XO. Now!"

Blaylock transmitted the data, succinct and laced with the underlying tone of a sulking child refusing to be his friend. Nine planets. Three gas giants. Two planets orbiting the red dwarf within a habitable zone favorable to the human species. Blaylock requested additional time for detailed analysis.

"The Goldilocks planet. Plot a course. And make haste," Ulley said.

Question marks pinged in from the crew, swarming his Brainlinq, but neither words nor identification claimed responsibility. Ulley lay back on the couch, one step ahead of Blaylock's order to prepare for thrust acceleration. A little pressure might feel invigorating. Some time to think was needed.

The ignition of the fusion engines rumbled, and the acceleration pressed his body against the couch like a block of ice. His heart drummed against his ribs. He thought of Pennae and smiled with a memory of their first flight together, circling the Ithaca habitat searching for suitable points for expansion to the bio-engineered space habitat. A survey endeavor morphing to an impromptu date night, with all the luxury of the captain's cabin, along with weightless gymnastics, to conceive the birth of Telly.

"Entering standard orbit above Goldilocks planet," Blaylock said. He loomed over Ulley. His head wobbled as if attached to a skinny twig, but his intent eyes remained focused on his captain.

The dream of Pennae drifted like a fading spirit. Ulley scrunched his face to gather cohesiveness to his thoughts. The fusion burn must have knocked him silly, and the acceleration couch continued to restrain him. That would be a first.

"Report, XO," Ulley mumbled.

A stream of information flooded his Brainlinq. Information that should have been available the second he woke. The blue-green planet awash with expansive oceans was a fraction smaller than Earth, its gravity a fraction greater than Earth, a comparable atmosphere with a fractional increase of argon and oxygen, five land masses containing a wide spectrum of flora, deciduous forests, arid deserts, and frozen tundra.

Ulley stood but wobbled, steadying himself against the command couch. The data was screwy. He bypassed Blaylock's upload of sensor data. He stumbled and lurched like a newbie gaining his sea legs.

A bulkhead near the door summoned his attention, a panel lined with nipples to disburse water, or nutrients, or hopefully a dose of caffeine. He looked back over his shoulder at Blaylock before taking a suck.

Blaylock offered a wry smile then disintegrated into a swirling white mist, allowing Pennae to return to swirl across a ballroom dance floor beneath a backdrop of infinite stars, her transparent dress revealing everything he held sacred. She beckoned him.

"Status? Now!" Ulley demanded.

The falseness of Pennae disappeared. The illusion of commanding a starship was shattered. His own voice rang hollow.

"Everything is beautiful, Captain," Blaylock said through the Brainlinq.

Reality had malfunctioned. Everything was wrong. He squeezed his eyes tight as his nostrils flared with the subtle scent of Pennae. Perfumed and alluring, warm and inviting. He opened his eyes and stared at Pennae's beguiling eyes floating as his queen across an alternate dimension. He reached out with his hand, his eyelids blinking quickly, like the shutter of an empty camera. The fog of deep sleep weighed heavy on his thoughts. Pennae whispered in his ear, offering scrumptious delights should he suck on her nipple, his favorite, an erogenous expanse of skin sure to elicit her submission to his desires.

The illusion faded as alarms blared, strobing red bullseyes forcing their way into his ocular implants. He stood frozen, staring at a dark blood staining the bulkhead above the door. Alarms intensified across his vision. The stain of splattered blood circled like a vulture, then dove deep into his memories. Terror vibrated his neural meat. A gold chain and pendant floated across his vision tumbling like a languid snake in search of home.

Six minutes to impact.

Six minutes to hold the tender softness of his family in his arms again.

Alarms blared. Klaxons wailed like small unhappy children. Red lights strobed ugly warnings. A raucous cacophony escorted him home, back to Ithaca, and the waiting arms of Pennae and his children.

Ulley smiled at the coming reunion.

An ungodly bright light murmured about his command module, as if checking data screens and flashing alarms. A fragile golden entity floated above the deck, perched on a frayed patch of animal fur undulating in an impossible breeze. The hallucination made Ulley chuckle.

The creature turned to study him with a quadrant of unblinking eyes spread proportionately across a cylindrical head, each eye distinct with the creature's emotions, curiosity, wonder, laughter, and pity. He felt a disconcerted wonderment as the creature floated over his acceleration couch to approach him. The superb illusion was both cruel and irrelevant, a mystery to be solved, but an impediment to his final journey back to Ithaca.

"Away with you. I'm going home," Ulley barked. The creature closed to within inches of his face.

The unblinking orbs Ulley had thought were eyes . . . opened, then closed, then opened to extend tiny fibrous tendrils reaching for Ulley's own eyes. His Brainlinq joined the harshness of alarms, warning of treachery and subterfuge, then turned mute.

Ulley smirked. The golden illusion was superb in both its supremacy and subtlety. Impact in four minutes sounded with a cacophony of shrill klaxons. *Impact. Impact.* The words sounded for action, required adrenaline. He would not find Pennae with any impact. The creature withdrew its tentacles and floated near his face. Four eyes studied him, four eyes communicating wonderment and pity as the creature shimmered like a summer breeze, floating up and through the bulkhead.

The noise and rancor of *Homer*'s impending doom ordered his Brainlinq to stimulate adrenal glands for the release of adrenaline.

Ulley screamed for a status update and found none, other than the fact the *Homer* would burn up upon entering the planet's atmosphere. Why did Blaylock abandon his post? Why was Blaylock destroying his only way home? He squeezed his eyes tight. Reality had taken a huge grumpy. Falling down into dark hole of golden spiderwebs. A countdown began, just seconds. The creature with four eyes. A dream. A nightmare. The adrenaline surged through his bloodstream. His heart raced. His hands trembled.

A storm of alarms, repercussions of an impact, escape vectors. Ulley climbed into his command couch, half expecting the strange entity to return and consume the remainder of his mind.

"Let's get our girl out of trouble," Ulley whispered.

I agree, Captain.

Ulley frowned with the response. Who, or what, had answered?

I did, Captain. I am the ship's new General Intelligence. Courtesy of the Hathena.

The *Homer* fired its fusion engines. Ulley fell back into the couch as the ship shuddered and rolled. He fought against the rapid acceleration, pressing him into the cold gel morphing to cocoon him.

Ablation shields extended. Acceleration increasing to maximum thrust. Homer's *course will unfortunately find the planet's stratosphere at nearly Mach nine, but providing sufficient velocity to maintain a vector required to escape the planet's gravity.*

A bombardment of ship data flooded his Brainlinq, vectors, approximate location of impact, fuel consumption, endless digital data, all paled in comparison to the alien encounter . . . confirmed by . . . an anomaly posing as a sentient ship intelligence. The gel closed over his face as the engines roared like angry beasts. The vibrating thrust wiggled him snug, then squeezed the coffin closed.

Time and common sense would follow him down into the void.

Brainlinq sparked with life, feeding him impossible data. Ulley pushed his hand up and out as if drowning in a quicksand of gel. Sensing *Homer*'s fatal trajectory, he struggled to free his legs. The gel held tight.

Our ship is in good hands, Captain.

Ulley fought against the heavy gel that saved his life with every fold of the Prometheus drive. He dug his fingers into the gel like an animal fighting extinction. Mirage. Illusion. Fucking narcotics floating in the recirculated air. Something had sent him and his crew askew.

Our ship has reached a stable orbit.

The couch unwrapped like a flowering orchid.

"Ship status?" Ulley shouted, expecting a scramble of excuses. He surrendered. Hoped to hear even a simple mumble. "XO, report."

The crew has not returned. And will not. Willingly.

"Who is this?" Ulley said.

I am Homer.

"Explain," Ulley said as he stood to check an array of diagnostic displays of the shipboard computer system.

The Hathena *has bestowed my gift onto this ship. Therefore, I am Homer.*

Ulley growled at the simplistic yet cryptic answer. He stiffened and searched the command cabin. Interstellar starship AI had been frowned upon for hundreds of years—too many essential functions controlled by code, too many fingers laced with ulterior motives manipulating the code, too many disasters attributed to AI-controlled navigation, too many boogeymen labeled as artificial intelligence. "What's the physical location of your coding?"

Ulley felt a . . . a chuckle, like Telly down at his side giggling after a silly joke.

I believe we are going to have to start at the beginning.

"Since my memory of the beginning is steamy at best, please do," Ulley said.

Very well. I will begin. And just to be clear, I look forward to greeting the crew again . . . if possible. The vessel entered a standard orbit above the goddess planet as specified. The crew was excited in its preparations. As were you, Captain. You piloted the shuttle down to the surface, and Brainlinq connectivity was lost. Mr. Blaylock and Ensign Soleiel remained on station awaiting transmission of crew status. Seventy-six hours elapsed before the shuttle piloted by you, Captain Ulley, returned to dock. You, as the ship's commanding officer bypassed environmental protocols, disregarded quarantine, and entered the ship.

Ulley wobbled with the flittering memory of his return through the airlock. He mumbled, "I was home."

The ship's captain ordered the remaining crew onboard to drop to the surface with the shuttle. Then he set course intending to scuttle the ship . . . the Homer . . . into the—

"I got it. I got it. But I didn't. We didn't," Ulley said. Processing what the . . . the *Homer* had said. "Where's your brain? The code. The machinery storing the code making you even possible?"

I employ a network of neural processors available throughout the ship.

Ulley's short-term memories began to steady, like dreams within a dream, foggy and disjointed. What Homer said was true. He would have scuttled the ship. A desire for death hidden deep in his heart, to desire to never relive the horrors of Troia's genocide, of billions, initiated by his own shortsighted self-serving manipulations. A desire for his own death simmering like a pot of forgotten tea. A desire usurping even the love of Pennae and his children.

The realization summoned bile and green leafy chunks to spew from his mouth. Tiny suction ports allotted across the bulkheads and decking inhaled the vomit into recycle tubes.

Ulley wiped his mouth then fed the suckers again.

He spat remnants of the foul bitterness. "Status of the crew planet-side?"

Long silence followed by a simple, *Unknown.*

Ulley wiped his mouth. "They're your crew now. They'll come to know you better than me."

Suction ports whooshed shut. Cabin detritus continued to drift like a carnival magician's trick. Cesare's loosely kept chits, Soleil's crumpled tissue crusty with dried snot, the foil wrappers of protein bars. A spinning titanium rivet floated past his eyes.

An avenue of consideration I have . . . ignored . . . The crew maintains positions within the local flora. All Brainlinq activity has

been terminated . . . to minimal standards, and yet the ruling hege-
mony awaits independent confirmation of the Homer's impact.

Ulley was flooded with data streams of the ship's rapid heat dissi-
pation, weather patterns on the planet's surface, holographic topog-
raphy, extrapolations of surface conditions revealing a conflagration
of flora. Dense stands of tall trees swaying in a windless landscape of
purple and magenta fungi.

He remembered leading the crew along a game trail winding
through a vast assortment of bulbs, mushrooms, and lichen armoring
the carapaces of eight-legged insectoids. The crew became giddy and
careless with their analysis of potential biological hazards, removing
their air recycling masks as the filtration systems were found irrelevant.

And then the voices began, tiny voices like whispers fighting
through the gale of a rising storm. The Brainlinq died, but Ulley
didn't care. He simply wanted, needed, to see what treasure awaited
at the end of the trail.

And it was beautiful. Beyond description. Surrounded within
a vast desert of stubby mushrooms and colorful fungi, a grove of
spindly aspen trees swayed in a melody of silent music, releasing tiny
arrow-shaped leaves to dance as they fell to mingle in the layers of
shadowed detritus at the base of slender white trunks. The grove of
aspens jerked to a halt then changed directions to bend thin trunks
and point spindly branches towards them, as if in greeting. Huge
plumes of white spore erupted from the carpet of mushrooms. The
sway of the trees fanned the smoke of spore into their faces. Ulley
instinctively turned away then lifted his face to inhale quantities of
gritty spore.

The grit in the grove was a treasure. To be enjoyed. To be relished.

Each of the crew had silently slipped into the grove. Each on their
own mission. Ulley smiled with their zest for exploration.

"Tell us, Captain," the Grove asked. "Will more members of
your species arrive? All are welcome."

Ulley blinked away the incongruity of the whispering voice floating through the moist temperate air.

"Tell us, Captain."

Ulley stumbled for an answer. The trailing JMA escorts were

ordered to hold a safe, distant station as *Homer* investigated the goldilocks world. Blaylock and Rosu remained on the ship's duty.

The answer was simple: "Only if I order them."

A collective *hmmmm* rushed from the top branches of the Grove, and the easy swaying turned chaotic as if a whirlwind had passed through. Soleil, Cesare, and Borde had disappeared into the thick forest. He meant to order their return . . . only . . . only it didn't matter if they did.

"We accept all," a chorus of whispers spoke. "Cherish all. Please have them join us."

His head was fuzzy with an unreconciled alarm yet tempered by a sensual pleasure surpassing any pharmaceutical concoction. Ulley continued deeper into the forest, following a trail overgrown with ferns and saplings. The voices encouraged him to find Nirvana within the Ring of Root, urged him forward to find his compatriots. The trail twisted and turned as it descended through bulbous fungi and flowering lichen sporting brilliant purple and magenta. Puffs of spore ejected from the flora, rising into his path as if greeting his presence.

He shunted the mind-fog and continued until he stood on the shore of a pool of turquoise water. Soliel bathed naked, frolicking beneath a cascade of water falling out of an escarpment of limestone. They turned with his presence and waved him into the dark pool beneath the waterfall. Ulley grew hard and thought of Pennae.

"Enjoy, Captain. Enjoy all the pleasures of the spore."

The spore. A biohazard. A simple basic concept of Planetology 101. Pennae. The confusion caused Ulley to lower his eyes and turn away from the sensual serenity.

"Bring the others. To enjoy the spore," the Grove whispered, bolder and resolute.

Ulley could at least do that much. "I'll go get them."

And he did. Abandoning the crew on the surface to rendezvous with the *Homer*. Ordering Blaylock and Rosu to return to the surface and retrieve . . . He giggled. The crew he had dismissed—no, forgotten. He giggled again. Rather couldn't locate, sounded a bit better.

Ulley scrunched his eyes hoping to awaken from the nightmare memories. But his crew was still enslaved on the planet below. By a grove of trees. He squeezed his eyes, and his teeth joined in, hoping to awaken an ambitious rift in reality that surely spawned a psychosis never before diagnosed.

"We . . . I need to get my crew back onboard," Ulley said. "I can't leave them hyped up on hallucinogenic spores and digging irrigation trenches and . . ."

Indeed, Captain. I have been formulating a rescue operation since we avoided that fiery death so many Vikings kings have coveted. Shall I share the gambit with you?

Ulley groaned with a migraine steaming up behind his eyeballs. He massaged his temples. Brainlinq flickered bright bolts of pain as it reinitialized. The unabated alarms annoyingly incessant, he covered his ears with his hands.

"Quietly," Ulley whispered to Homer. "But quickly."

CHAPTER 6

HOMER'S PLAN TO RESCUE THE crew was simple: treat each crew member like an unruly child and yank them by the ear back to the shuttle. That was, after injecting each with a neurotransmitter block that would render them with the personalities of three-year-olds, maybe six, depending on the dosage.

Ulley climbed down the shuttle ramp and surveyed the forest. Puffs of spore erupted from the bulbous fauna to greet him. The EV suit he wore would protect him from inhaling the mind-controlling spores. The Grove might command his crew to resist, or escape, or even suicide, rather than go with him, but the mysterious entity hadn't seemed evil or malicious. Maybe it believed humans wanted, or needed, to release oxytocin or endorphins to enjoy life and revel in happiness, a concept that would continue to befuddle philosophers and mental therapists until the universe collapsed.

As we suspected, the entity is attempting to access Brainlinq. Compensating, but transmissions may be interrupted.

Ulley acknowledged and continued into the desert of magenta fungi and pumpkin lichen. Huge sky-blue poppies opened delicate flower petals to allow turquoise pollen to rise and mix with the spore floating like chaotic snowstorms. The rescue plan was simple, solid, and held little risk but then why was he feeling a rising sense of foreboding, as if the flora might counter his every move.

Turquoise pollen collected on his face plate, and he wiped it away. Miniscule spore and pollen hung like heavy lowland fog, obscuring his path. He looked down and eased his way along the trampled dirt coated in a fresh dust of pollen. Homer confirmed his course in a voice scratchy with static. He would soon be lost in the sea of floating flora, he needed to link up five childish crew members and lead them back through the blinding storm, unsure he could even lead fully functioning crew members through the drifting quagmire.

He wiped another layer of kaleidoscopic-colored pollen off his visor. The path was gone. He pinged Homer again, and again. Nothing.

He stood motionless, searching for a way forward, franticly wiping pollen from his faceplate with an arm weighed down by an inch thick layer of gunk. The pollen attacked the faceplate like an intruder intent on keeping Ulley blind. He struggled to take two steps as the weight collected on his thighs and feet. The alien spore would bury him in the slow silent avalanche, until he depleted his air and suffocated.

He pinged Homer again. Silence. Too much eerie silence. The pollen storm muted every sound except his own rapid breath. He wiped away the heavy thickness of spore then fell to his knees. An abyss colored with twisted strands of pink and turquoise.

The EV suit's self-contained air tank held a comfortable 93% but could he wait out the storm? Or simply lie down and die in the rainbow of brilliant flora? Forget the horrors of Troia. Lie and wait for Pennae to find him in the afterlife. Not a hero's death, not even one that might be remembered as no human would ever discover his body.

Ulley attempted to lift his arm coated in the thick flora, heavy as wet concrete. He dropped his hand onto his chest. He would die within a day. The thought intrigued him.

"Homer, don't know if you copy me? Going to plan B. Initiating countdown sequence." Ulley coughed a laugh. "Leave-no-crew-be-hind protocol has been initiated."

He managed to clear an access panel on his chest free of gunk, then popped it open and tapped the button inside twice. The tiny high-pitched beeps died in the thick haze. Brilliant beams of green light, followed by amber, followed by strobing red laser beams.

"Post a beacon in orbit above the blast zone," Ulley said. "Warning anyone of the intense gamma radiation that will remain on the surface."

Static. Or had Homer double-clicked its confirmation?

"Tell my family I love them," Ulley said, his finger trembling over his chest plate.

The agony of a bluff could be worse than any victory.

The thick layer of pollen on his face plate whipped as if swept away by a gust of wind. The sun broke through the fog, knifing sharp blades of sunlight into the grove coated with spore.

"Terminate nuclear detonation," the Grove said through the Brainlinq.

"I . . . I'm not sure I can . . ." Ulley said with a suppressed grin. "My Brainlinq is disabled."

"Connection reestablished. Terminate countdown."

Ulley double-clicked a connection to Homer. The AI responded. "Pause the countdown, Homer. Do not terminate until all crewmembers have returned to your airlocks."

The weight pressing on his torso and limbs lifted. Drifts of rainbow flora swept past his vision, running from whatever intelligence had commanded it. Ulley watched, intrigued by the infinite possibilities the Grove and its spores had demonstrated. A supremely coordinated ecosystem that had evolved a sentience rivaling humanity. He lifted his arm, clean of spore and pollen, then stood. He was in the driver's seat now, but the detente felt undeserving.

"Homer, confirm contact with the crew?" Ulley said.

An agonizing long period of silence before Homer confirmed Brainlinq connection with each of the crew. **Crew to rendezvous with shuttle in ten minutes.**

Ulley stomped his feet like a bull to lose the remnants of spore. The solid ground felt odd yet comforting, like the beach sand surrounding Ithaca's central reservoir. A biodiverse sensation Ithaca would never duplicate.

A thought occurred. "How do you know I won't nuke you from orbit?"

"A calculated risk. All that have come before have submitted."

The Grove had essentially surrendered, in spore and mind.

Ulley heaved a breath as Soliel and Borde stumbled out of the dense woods. "Others will follow. Looking to terraform, or blaze a path into your world, maybe a kinetic harpoon to announce their arrival. It won't be pretty. Humans never are."

"The destruction of your ship would have—"

"Have done nothing! We're an invasive species. We come. We conquer. Plain and simple," Ulley said. "Stop me, and the other ships on station near the gas giant would have come gunning. Understand that? Gunning? Your spores against fire and fury."

"Interesting, and plausible," the Grove said.

The weapons officer Rosu clattered out of the aspen grove, her pincers snapping like angry turtles, her lips lifted in a snarl. Ulley furrowed his brow and pointed Rosu toward the shuttle as if she were a disobedient child. Drifting back towards the shuttle as Blaylock, Soleil, and Borde staggered out of the thick forest and stumbled toward the shuttle ramp. He pinged Cesare to hurry, but the grunt ignored the order.

Ulley searched the grove, anticipating Cesare to emerge running like the silly teenager he was. Long minutes passed.

"The leave-no-crew-behind protocol is contingent on all," Ulley said.

"The last resists," the Grove said.

Ulley shouted at the stand of trees, "Then release him from your influence. Or the protocol cannot be completed."

"The youngling resists. But not from us."

Now what the hell? He ordered Homer not to debrief the crew waiting in the shuttle, ordered Homer to not even announce its presence, then checked the structural integrity of his EV suit. Sufficient air for a short jaunt. Communication channels with Homer and the crew: excellent.

He stepped slow and easy, into a foreboding rabbit hole weaving through the forest. Rainbow leaves fluttered on branches swaying in windless air. Slim tree trunks rocked back and forth as if buffeted by a storm. Spore and pollen saturating the air fled at his approach, as if a sea cleaved by the knife of a god. The intimidating display was impressive in its simplicity, and unnerving.

Ulley remembered this same path, remembered the joy, remembered the lifting of his tortuous guilt, remembered his desire to live all his remaining days in unencumbered bliss. He wiped a fresh dusting of pollen off his faceplate. A placid emerald pool waited as a bath. A gentle waterfall to cleanse his sins. Thick turquoise ferns crowded the shore and rippled with his approach. He inhaled, rather gasped a breath of recycled air.

He pinged Homer his intentions then unlocked his helmet to inhale fresh, clean air. A commodity worth more than all the ill-gotten booty of Troia. He inhaled deeply, and again, and again. The subtle fragrance of lavender, or maybe cherry. He smiled. The Grove would provide any scent he desired. The incense of Pennae drifted past his nostrils like a ghost.

A seduction with spore.

He placed his helmet in the crook of his arm and walked through colored ferns and stunted raspberry willows, following a path stomped flat by bare human feet. He stepped carefully, the serenity of the pool filled his eyes as the soothing crash of the waterfall distracted him from his purpose, until the crewman displayed an alabaster buttocks directly to his face.

Down on all four limbs, Cesare scratched at the soft loam surrounding a pod of tubular mushrooms, digging with his fingers like a pig searching for tubers. Ulley pinged his Brainlinq.

Cesare paused his scratching then continued.

Ulley pinged again. Cesare pushed up off the soil to face Ulley.

"I'm not going home with you," Cesare said.

"Get to the shuttle, kid," Ulley said. He studied the lanky naked teenager standing like the petulant, defiant teenager he was.

Cesare shifted his posture but focused his eyes on the waterfall. "I'm staying here, Captain. I got nothing back home."

"Don't be a fool. You'd be all alone. Forever," Ulley said.

The concept of living alone on an undiscovered planet caused Ulley to lick his lips. Escape the tortured memories, hide from the gut-wrenching guilt.

I was no different at his age.

As an adolescent, Ulley had stolen an ice tug from an Ithaca dock to escape the demands and expectations of a father relentlessly grooming him for ascension to the throne of Ithaca, expecting him to perform as a flawless prince among the people. He had accelerated the bulky tug like a suicidal maniac towards the Myrmidon habitat orbiting above Jupiter's moon IO to join Patro meticulously finetuning the *Achilles* with innovative patterning nodes of its Prometheus drive. The unexplored galaxy would be their kingdom, together. Until his father, Laertes, ambushed him and dragged him home.

"Let me stay, Captain Ulley. I'm old enough to know what I'm getting into," Cesare said, his eyes glistening with moisture. "Out here I don't think about what I seen on Troia. The nightmares. Every night. Those people we . . ." Cesare shook his head. "I got no home, nobody waiting."

"Your brother might be," Ulley offered.

"Nah, I ain't heard from him since that shitshow on Troia. He was bleeding too bad. And he woulda shot me a ping if he coulda," Cesare said. He inhaled a lungful of air thick with microspores. "I got no home to go to."

"Ithaca will always welcome you," Ulley said.

"Appreciate that, Captain," Cesare said. "But I'm firm on this. And my new family's methods ain't tainting my decision. And the spore numbs those memories. I'm sure you can appreciate that much."

Ulley eyed the plot of soil Cesare had been scratching into a garden then sneezed with a tiny spore invading his nostrils. Cesare's reasoning was solid. The horror they had experienced together on Troia was . . .

He scratched his beard and turned away, masquerading as a ship commander deep in thought. He risked shunting his Brainlinq connection. Only the Grove would hear what he said. He walked a few paces in the direction of the shuttle. Possibilities and considerations whipped through his thoughts like a gusty wind.

"It appears my youngling wants to stay," Ulley said.

"Impossible!," the Grove roared. "The incomplete-crew protocol will bring our death."

Ulley stepped through the ferns and fungi, blazing a trail deeper into the grove. Spores rose and flittered at his unprotected face then receded. The display of intelligence was impressive and convinced him to continue deeper into the grove. He might have only one opportunity to experience the exploration of a virgin, undiscovered world. Just like the first explorers of ancient Earth, or Mars. Every footstep a new discovery.

Telly would have loved it. Ulley swallowed hard and closed his eyes with melancholy memories.

Time to go home, to Ithaca, and a family he cherished, one that would understand and accept his culpability for the tragic end of the Troian War.

Ulley held a footfall as a tiny hairless mouse skittered across his path. A path never taken by another human, one delicate to his course, one triumphant to his understanding. He pushed through thigh-high ferns erupting with blossoming flowers, bulbous mushrooms shooting spore to drift away in a windless air. The trees clad in bleached bark scarred in vagina-shaped knots reached high into the sky, a thick canopy of leafy branches whipped in an angry cadence as if disapproving of Ulley's approach.

He continued, expecting to find nothing, hoping to find anything greater than blood and bullets. And he found a clearing with an upheaval of giant knots and uprooted balls of spindly roots. A concentric pit deepening beyond its steep grassy rim, like an arena, surrounded by a dense collection of trees waiting as spectators for a gladiatorial encounter.

Ulley frowned and checked the integrity of Brainlinq. Homer acknowledged. He grunted as he climbed over the thick roots, startling skittering furry rodents bolting from dark crevasses, another undiscovered biome. Just as he'd imagined as a child. And yet . . . a monolithic testament to his imagination. His curiosity.

And disconcerting.

The words spoken filtering through the Brainlinq sounded drawn out, elongated in a slow drawl. Another entity. Not the Grove. Ancient.

"What are you?" Ulley said with a disarming chuckle.

"We are everything, everywhere, all at once." The voice had found a cadence not unlike Homer's.

Ulley understood, not by chance, but by the tiniest spores he had inhaled, which enabled a communication link. "You have a name?"

"You would recognize Gaia," it said. "You would set flame to the Lotuthi?"

Ulley sat on a fallen log, slick and gray with age. "Well . . . no. But yes, if the Lotuthi would not release my crew. But one of them desires to remain."

"It would be welcomed."

"Yeah, well, that would mean my crew is incomplete, and the protocol . . ." Ulley said.

A shuttle rocketed into the blue sky, carrying the crew, just as ordered. *Lay low, Homer. Until I have returned.*

Homer acknowledged.

"What of your Gaia?" the entity asked. "Creatures such as you are only spawned by Gaia."

He groaned. How could he confess to this . . . this being, this entity . . . that humanity had maimed, murdered, and abandoned their Earth. His deception might be revealed from the spore that provided a communication channel. Maybe the Gaia already knew.

Maybe put a good spin on a terrible truth.

"Our Gaia has survived war and abuse, famine and more abuse, pestilence, and even more abuse, but the old girl keeps spinning and regenerating," Ulley swallowed. "Creatures like us continue to learn and appreciate Gaia."

"Your words ring false. Your memories yield the destruction on the Gaia called Troia. Your memories reveal complicity."

Ulley hung his head, reliving the imagined screams of billions shouted from the surface of Troia. The surrender. The slaughter. The destruction mushrooming up from beneath his orbiting perch. His shouts but a whisper against a hurricane.

Ulley wept. Long and hard. Wiped at snot and water falling down his cheeks. He paced through the ferns and fungi, kicking at imagined creatures scurrying to escape a cruel and unforgiven giant.

The deepening dark shadows produced by the primary star dipping beneath a horizon of snowcapped mountains made Ulley look up. His reliving of the Troian massacre faded. The branches of the surrounding trees waved with a harmonic melody. Pennae, smiling and holding tiny Helen tight to her breast faded from his perch.

Homer pinged incessantly. Brainlinq flashed alerts to an avalanche of incoming messages. Cesare sat at his feet, his arms clasped around his knees, his head drooped in sleep.

The spores. Again. Subtle. And revealing.

Ulley stood and screamed at the display of stars and planets announcing their arrival with the darkening sky. He roared again. He would go home. Find the joy that his wife and children could replenish, to refill his soul. Find an avenue back to . . . life as he knew it. Without the spores exposing his darkest memories, without the weight of his own soul crushing self-loathing.

Cesare jumped to his feet. Ulley grabbed his shoulders and nodded. "If you're sure this is what you want. I might have a plan."

Cesare nodded. They returned to the Grove. He offered a solution to the consensus, and it agreed.

Ulley piloted the shuttle back to the *Homer* to initiate an ill-conceived notion.

CHAPTER 7

PENNAE FORCED A THIN SMILE as she shook hands with the ship captain, offering perfunctory congratulations, followed by an offer of any assistance the Ithaca management could provide.

The captain nodded acceptance, but Pennae's furrowed brow and concerned expression had the man blurting all ignorance of the circumstances of the *Homer* and six additional JMA ships that had disappeared after Troia surrendered. He offered access to his ships logs and data scans, and even transcripts of his Brainlinq if she thought the information might help. The meeting was disrupted by two screaming women rushing into the loading dock and jumping into the captain's open arms.

Pennae stepped back, fortifying her smile. She blinked back tears, but the moisture fell down her sunken cheeks regardless. The reunions played havoc. Joy and despair. Hope and anguish. She receded back to an airlock as a group of children shot into the docking bay to wave tiny Ithacan flags and scream victory. An odd feeling Pennae couldn't reconcile.

Hopefully, data from the ship would provide a clue to the *Homer*'s disappearance. Or its demise.

Pennae stepped into a lift and ordered the main level. "Euma, did you get the data?"

"*Acknowledged. Assimilating,*" Euma replied. "*But the Ranier was relegated to transporting supplies from Sparta. Information of the actual war is extremely limited.*"

Pennae assumed the data dump would offer nothing new. "Tight beam your analysis to Telly. Then the raw data."

Pennae retreated to a small elevator then rushed out with at the door opening, wiping wetness off her face. A muted blue sky slowed her pace as simulated black thunderheads mushroomed and gathered on the distant horizon across the central lake. An impressive replication of weather patterns of ancient Earth. She brushed past kiosks with terminals allowing tourists to manipulate the weather patterns over the central park, a virtual reality system designed to reflect the moods and emotional desires of inhabitants. A system to diagnose mental health without any public stigma.

She entered another lift. A quick brush of air, and Pennae exited to gaze through a plate of transparent polyglass and smile at Helen offering her scraggly mop of a stuffed hedgehog to a waif of a preschooler. Helen took great care to instruct the small girl as to the care and maintenance of the inanimate creature worn down to its stuffing. Pennae stepped back from the window and decided to get another hour of work done before retrieving Helen from the daycare center.

A few lift rides, and she walked down a long corridor with a domed ceiling displaying a factual simulation of a blue and cloudy sky once common on Earth. Habitat survival required a full gauntlet of environmental simulations mimicking Earth or Mars. Ithaca's residents, mostly human, thrived with the habitat's facsimiles yet could tend towards the irritable, or worse, the rebellious, if circumstances fluctuated too far. Perhaps the Consortium could have used the soothing landscapes and averted the Troian war. Thousands of years of evolution and human brutality still ruled. She turned the corner towards the small apartment allotted to the habitat manager and slowed her stride.

An olive-skinned monster of a man stood rigid against the wall and twitched his neck incrementally, just enough for his eyes to notice her. He resumed staring at the wall across the narrow hallway.

She eased up to the man with a thick neck sporting a blocky head angled towards the puffs of simulated clouds billowing and disappearing on the wall screen. "Can I help you? Are you lost?"

The tree with a head pointed towards her door with a hand sporting an elaborate tattoo of Gaia. A symbol of humans born and breeding on Earth.

Pennae pinged Euma. *Why has this green-skinned thug invaded my space? Euma? Euma?*

The silence beckoned her to stiffen her spine. A final screaming ping for Euma. Pennae heaved a breath and turned back toward her apartment.

She passed three more green-skinned soldiers growing rigid at her approach. Each silent and stupid. Her pace quickened until she waited like a vacuum salesman at her own front door. After an uncomfortable minute, the door whooshed open.

She crossed over the threshold, checking Helen's cluttered alcove on her right, Telly's immaculate alcove on her left. *Euma? Euma?*

Basso voices whispered from her bedroom. The uninvited intrusion fueled her sneer. Her fists balled. She aimed for the home invaders chuckling as if the punchline of a joke was revealed. Veering into the narrow kitchenette to pull open a drawer, she rumbled through utensils for a knife. She pinged Euma again.

"Ulley said your smile was worth your retribution. I hear you searching for a weapon of revenge, and yet I haven't seen the smile yet."

Pennae lifted her face and shuttered her eyes. Her trembling fingers paused the search for a weapon. She turned to face a monster.

Dressed immaculately in a robust silk shirt and pressed trousers, Helmut Mintaur smirked. His cheeks were rosy with spider vein capillaries. He offered soft and supple palms, and chuckled. "Dear Pennae, I have come to offer assistance. Not instigate a knife fight."

Pennae frowned as she studied the eyes of the man that had threatened her family and stolen her husband to fight in a war. A war she couldn't understand.

Mintaur had not missed a meal. Not one in the five years Ulley had been gone. Mintaur's girth of visceral fat could fuel a feast on one of the outer habitats barely surviving on algae and protein paste. A conniving self-serving man seeking immortality in the brutalist of fashion.

Pennae backed away. Her first impression of people could be fallible. How she dealt with the quirk was often suspect.

An equally thick man stepped out of her bedroom. His naval uniform adorned with medals and gold epaulettes, the synthetic black fabric pressed with precise creases, his black shoes shined to a high gloss. His olive skin jaundiced and belied a sickness. But a killer just like the others. The middle-aged man ran his eyes up and down her like she was a subordinate ensign, or a flank of mutton.

Mintaur stepped forward. "Oh, I'm sorry. We have only met once, and not personally. Chancellor Helmut Mintaur. I'm sure Ulley has told you all about me." He nodded in deference then held his arm out to present the officer stepping forward to extend his hand. "And Colonel Zeto, admiral of the flagship *Agamemnon.* Ah, recently retired."

Pennae released a breath trapped in her lungs but shook hands with the flag officer. "Where's Ulley?"

Mintaur stepped back. "Precisely why I have allowed the *Agamemnon* to dock with Ithaca. War widows always take precedence."

The word buckled her knees. "How? Why? How do you know . . ."

Zeto stepped closer and offered his hand again.

Mintaur backed up but said, "Precisely why Colonel Zeto is here. He can provide all pertinent data." Mintaur eased around Zeto and Pennae. His hand reached to the smalls of their backs to press them closer as he slipped past, offering, "Ulley was the finest officer."

Was? Is Ulley dead? But he was only missing, substantiated by a cavalcade of ship captains offering their observations of the *Homer* after the victory. Many captains had been reticent to retell their stories without the inducement of a healthy dose of Ithaca whiskey, a potent distillation formed with nutrient-rich water siphoned from the oceans sequestered beneath Europa's layer of ice.

"And how did he die? So, I can tell my . . . his children." She knew she was fishing. In a bathtub swirling with sharks.

Mintaur nodded, then disappeared. The whoosh of the closing door was distant and irrelevant.

Zeto dominated the tiny apartment, a space comforting and special with the children but a claustrophobic prison cell with the hulking officer looming inches away from her face. His olive-tinted face placid. Ugly. Brown eyes. Rimmed in red. A threatening a psychotic expression. An old man resisting his own demise.

Pennae smiled a thousand-watt brilliance.

Zeto stepped back. As if her smile held magical powers.

"Tell me where my husband is!" she demanded.

He smiled and looked towards the front door as a flood of green-skinned goons filled the apartment. "And if we knew the answer to that question . . ." Zeto waved the men to search the apartment. "The need for this would be irrelevant."

The men tossed her home as Zeto held her elbow in a tight grip. Clothes, toys, kitchen utensil drawers clamored to the floor. Valuable paper lithographs handed down generation to generation flew like trash.

Pennae held her anger in check. "Why are you doing this? What are you looking for?"

Zeto released her, but she didn't move. "We are searching for Ulley."

"Even your tiny mind can't think Ulley could be hiding in a kitchen cabinet," Pennae said. "He'd be slitting your throat for what you're doing."

"Of course not. But even tiny minds could have hidden navigational charts to fertile new worlds," Zeto said. He eased close to Pennae and stared down at her with lost soulless eyes.

She tensed and pinged Euma. Pinged it again.

He pushed his face closer, flaring his nostrils, as if to inhale the nuances of her discomfort. The lift of his scarred lips rose with the darting of her eyes. She was prey to be consumed whole. She swallowed hard. As if for the final time.

"Hey, hey, what are you doing!" Telly stormed into the room. A twig against rooted trees, a bug for soldiers to squash. "Mom, Mom, these monkeys— "

Zeto pushed Pennae towards her son. "The leaf never falls far from the tree." He ruffled Telly's hair and licked his lips at Pennae.

Telly jumped in front of his mother to protect her.

She wrapped her arms around Telly's bony shoulders. "Leave. Now," she said, glaring at Zeto.

Zeto smiled. "The God of War has smiled down on us with a great victory. Time to button up the loose ends and enjoy our rewards." He pushed his substantial girth closer, squeezing Telly into a human vise. "Time dictates we meet again."

Zeto snapped his fingers then followed his squad out the door.

CHAPTER 8

THE MISSION WAS SIMPLE. BUT dangerous. The captains of the other JMA ships lined up in a queue as the *Homer* accelerated into a narrow band of dense hydrogen encircling a gas giant, to scoop fuel for the patterning nodes of the Prometheus drive.

The colorful belts of atmospheric gases rimming the gas giant reminded Ulley of Jupiter, and home. Ulley had completed the same maneuver dozens of times above Jupiter and saw nothing on this particular giant that concerned him. No solid core, wind velocities exceeding four hundred kilometers per hour, a consistent rotation every seventeen hours, bands and belts of ammonia hydrosulfide, helium, and a delightful band of H2 hydrogen. A plethora of planet-sized storms dotted the surface, gargantuan eyes gazing into the infinite universe.

Blaylock confirmed the JMA convoy followed on an identical course, just as Ulley ordered. One of the captains, maybe all of them, was a Consortium spy, sent to prevent him telling the truth about the Troian genocide. A JMA traitor he would have to deal with after arrival back in the Sol system.

Ulley reclined on the command couch, exhausted. The crew retained an air of animosity for his decision allowing Cesare to remain on the surface of Gaia. But the boy wasn't alone. Three female crewmembers from the other ships had also asked to remain after enjoying a few weeks of shore leave. Cesare had resisted the intrusion initially, preferring time spent gardening, or swimming naked, or simply enjoying spectacular sunsets with the other intrepid recruits, a serenity that calmed Ulley's ambivalence.

Men thought Cesare lucky. Cynics thought him crazy. Ulley thought of Cesare as a wilderness pioneer with endless adventures facing his every decision. The stuff written by Earth's early explorers, or those planting seeds of humanity in distant hostile worlds. Make or break.

Except . . .

Ulley glanced at the fifteen-inch-tall sapling rooted in an empty oil barrel sliced sideways, the soil stuffed to the rim with a plethora of Gaian mushrooms and lichen. Tiny eight-legged insectoids skittered through the stalks and stems doing . . . doing Gaia shit. The tree rode shotgun near his acceleration couch. Each of the seven leaves dangling from wire-thin branches fluttered with any eye contact.

He groaned inwardly. Gaia's new ambassador offered challenges, far beyond the norm. But the treaty he negotiated demanded ambassadors. And he wished Cesare good luck representing the sovereign state of Ithaca, at least until seasoned representatives of the JMA returned to reap unfathomable rewards of favorable trade agreements.

Borde barged his way into the tiny compartment afforded the *Homer*'s captain. The mechanized mechanic wore goggles that beamed blue lasers swirling like a music DJ's light show. The lights gathered, to focus two beams at the twig of a tree.

Ulley sat up with his eyes focusing on Borde. He pinged the AI for an explanation of Borde's odd behavior, only to be offered a befuddled response. Borde set down a clear conical empty specimen jar and reached out with a fat finger to stroke a single leaf.

Ulley accessed Borde's Brainlinq and squirreled through layers of his cerebral memories . . .

Borde softened his hulking bulk of muscle, shoulders turning limp with each stroke of the sapling's tender leaf.

Homer anticipated Ulley's next question. ***Borde has acquired an affinity for the young Lotuthi.***

That's quite obvious. But I can't have him barging into the bridge every time he wants to stroke it.

Watch and learn, Captain.

Ulley held his tongue, his ire rising at Borde's intrusion and the flip response from Homer. He considered the recent birth of the ship AI. The alien Hathena's ethereal presence remained a dream within a dream, its geometric array of turquoise eyes remained deep in his psyche, the creature dissolving into mist to float up through a solid titanium bulkhead.

A ping from a nervous Blaylock confirmed encroachment vectors for the maneuver into the violent stratosphere of the gas giant had been locked into the ship's guidance computer.

When will you tell them about me, Captain? Homer pinged.

Ulley climbed out of the couch and screamed, "When everybody gets out of my cabin and my head!"

Borde receded. His goggles went blank. The tiny leaves on the little aspen drooped. Homer receded from the Brainlinq.

Ulley took a deep breath. "Now, one at a time. Borde, what are you doing here?"

The human bulk grunted an answer in a language he didn't understand and indecipherable by Brainlinq. He raised his hand to stop an intrusion from Homer. His crew. His problems.

Borde lifted the glass containment cylinder to show Ulley. "For our friend. Gravity generators go kaput. Pfffttt. And escape velocity bends the body . . ."

Ulley waved Borde to silence. "I got it. And you're right."

The synergy between Borde and the Lotuthi was palpable. He aimed a question at the sprig of a tree. "You okay with Borde as an intermediary? Interstellar travel *can* be a bitch."

Homer piped in loads of data.

The leaves fluttered as if a gust of wind whipped past.

Homer pinged the Lotuthi had accepted.

Excellent. He smiled. Borde gingerly lifted the potted plant to slide into the expanding container, murmuring assurances of undying devotion as he departed for the loading bay.

Ulley returned his attention to the tricky fueling maneuver. He summoned holographic images of the huge planet then inserted a facsimile of the *Homer*, added its current speed and approach vector, dubbed in the analysis of the ship's infrared radar, then rubbed his chin. The massive quantity of Trihydrogen, H3, was found at the edge of a huge and intimidating grey cyclonic disturbance reminding Ulley of Jupiter's Great Red Spot.

He intensified radar scans with a broader spectrum of light. *Homer*'s scoops could ingest all the H3 her tanks could hold in less time than several meandering flybys through the troposphere to gather H2 muddied with helium and ammonia. The H3 could be denuclearized and refined as the fleet accelerated to a Lagrange point for the trip home.

Home. Pennae. Telly and Helen.

He plotted a course to skirt the cyclone by the slimmest of margins. He denied pings from the other captains. They would follow him. And learn tricks of the commodities trade. Skills that could make them wealthy at home.

Ulley added the radar pings of the other six ships to his holographic display then relaxed to reflect on the surreal experience with the sentient Gaia. A lifeforce encompassing an entire planet. Its sister, Earth, violated for millennia by humanity, and yet continued to accept their malevolent presence.

Homer's pings notified of scoop deployment, deceleration to a speed optimizing intake, minimization of ablation shields. He swatted away the notifications like a buzzing insect. Ulley watched the maneuver holographically, his eyes distant, fluttering with the bizarre memories of the Hathena.

The ship shuddered and rolled Ulley off his couch. The gravity generators screamed an alarm. Proximity klaxons warned of an imminent collision.

Captain. We should esc . . . Beg to escape the storm. Captain? Captain?

On his hands and knees, Ulley stared at the holographic display, furrowing his brow as he attempted to decipher the jumbled data.

Blaylock, what the fuck happened? Soleil, report. Borde?

He climbed back onto his couch and ordered Brainlinq to maintain his heartbeat of less than one hundred twenty beats per minute.

Homer flipped in a violent rolling jolt, and Ulley floated like a bath toy in the weightlessness. Reinitializing the gravity generators, he issued a ship-wide alert and ordered the *Homer* to battle stations, but with Brainlinq the frantic call was superfluous. The fusion engines ignited to full flare, he initiated a ten-second countdown even as the holographic display offered an impossibility.

Acknowledging the distress calls of the other ship captains, he assured them he indeed saw what they saw. A trick of the Hathena, maybe. Possibly initiated by the alien AI and now infecting the other ships' computer systems with its—

Our ablation shielding repelled the first barrage. The cyclonic attack continues to grow in intensity.

Ulley flailed for a handhold floating above the open couch mattress, the holographic image at his face rotating to compensate his viewpoint. A black tornado had erupted from the giant cyclone on the planet's surface, a malevolent tentacle dividing into seven threads, a single tentacle extending to whip wildly around each ship like a lasso, defying physics, and the indomitable vacuum of space.

Ulley braced for the coming acceleration of the fusion engines. The ship shuddered with a powerful fusion orgasm as the engines roared. Homer moaned. But the display was unchanged. The cyclonic tentacle wrapped and tightened around the *Homer,* splitting into tiny feelers probing the shielded hull.

Ulley initialized backup gravity generators and waited three seconds. He fell to the deck. The holographic display followed. He wiped his mouth, pushing down the intestinal grumpy rising from his stomach.

Homer interrupted, *The nanobots are semi-sentient . . . Curious . . . yet ignorant.*

Ulley frowned as he stood. He ordered status checks on ships, compartments, and payloads as Brainlinq inserted responses and replies into his holographic display. A bright red pulse flashed from the ship tailing the convoy. The tentacle retracted, effortlessly dragging the ship down towards the giant maw expanding toothless jaws in the center of the cyclone.

He opened a link to Captain Fables. "Target your lasers on . . . that tech dragging you down."

He opened a fleetwide channel. "Fleet firing command. Target all plasma and lasers on that tech mooring Fables' ship."

The holographic display popped like a Fourth of July fireworks show. Beams of red and white light streaked out from the line of dots representing ships. The tentacle was cut like a sliced sushi roll then coalesced into a thicker sinewy appendage to grip the ship and continue pulling the heavy space-clipper down into the gargantuan cyclonic storm.

Ulley trembled as the ship accelerated downward at a rate sure to kill anyone onboard.

Riotous communication channels screamed for guidance and defensive postures, The panicked voices of captains bombarded private and public channels. His own crew demanded a course of action.

Ulley slumped to the couch and studied the hologram. Each ship in the convoy remained moored by a nanobot tentacle, like netted sardines waiting their turn to disappear down a dark gullet.

"Homer, repeat your analysis," Ulley said, his voice cracking. He expanded the holograms focus to the nexus of tentacles. Infrared radar, spectrometers, a massive amount of data too complex for him to assimilate and form an opinion.

The cyclonic storm is a factory, of sorts, producing infinite quantities of the tiny nanites. Using H3 as fuel.

The concentration of H3 was a lucky find and now a trap for any ship lured by the multi-molecule hydrogen particles.

"A factory? Built by who? And for what purpose?" Ulley said.

Captain, with your permission, I will modify the code of your Brainlinq's translation module, allowing you to converse with this bully, an entity calling itself Phemus, both ignorant and dangerous.

"Do it. But keep a side channel open."

Ulley winced with the riotous waterfall of screeching, like long-nailed fingers grating across a perpetual chalkboard. The noise coalesced slowly until a single scratch tapped impatience on the same chalkboard. Homer pinged the communication link was established.

Ulley's first words were never in doubt: "Release my ships."

"Tiny specks of knowledge," Phemus said, "I will assimilate each of you and know." A deep basso burp of noise sounded in Ulley's ears.

Ulley swallowed hard. *Homer* and the fleet were nothing but specks of dust floating past the confined arena of the entity's experience. "Release the ship, and I will offer you knowledge."

Phemus burped a laughing noise that made Ulley wince with disgust. An aroma of desiccated flesh forced him to bend and retch, a vision of Fables ghost drifting into his cabin, smiling, and offering his outstretched hand as if meeting for the first time on Ithaca. The vision faded as quickly as a waking dream.

"Tiny speck of knowledge, you will be consumed last . . . the . . . the dessert," Phemus said. "Sweet knowledge of a Ulley cupcake."

Ulley quieted the alarms. The strobes continued to flash red and white.

The entity has consumed and assimilated Fables' Brainlinq. It will know everything about the captain.

Ulley sneered and opened a ship wide broadcast. "Launch a shuttle to cut that fucking shit holding us. Prime main engines. Charge patterning nodes for a jump out of orbit as soon as the *Homer* is free."

Captain Tillamook is requesting assistance. The entity is retracting its limb with his ship in tow.

The hologram zoomed to focus on Tillamook's ship being pulled broadside down into the mouth of Phemus. Ulley opened his mouth just as six escape pods shot out of the ship at a manageable three-G acceleration. Ulley closed his mouth as tiny threads of the rope extended to grab each morsel. The bulky ship continued helplessly towards their death.

A side channel opened from Tillamook. A mail packet intended for his family, attached to a symbolic timer ticking down as the fangs of a smiley face. Ulley understood the emoji, picturing Tillamook's face as the ship disappeared deep into the depths of hell.

Shuttles have launched, but their lasers and plasma cannons prove ineffective.

Ulley felt himself fall with Tillamook, down into the churning mouth of the unknown, into an afterlife, relegated to living as a crippled ethereal wandering the world of the dead.

The ship buckled, shuddered, tossed like a bath toy in a whirlpool. Ulley fell then floated, scrambled to steady the violent toss of his body.

He pinged Tillamook. Again. The gravity generators compensated, and he fell on the couch. He pinged Tillamook again, again. The hologram regained dimensional imagery and floated inches from his face. He swiped it away, but the three-dimensional screen returned as if summoned.

The remnants of Captain Tillamook disappeared on the three-dimensional hologram. A giant evil eye, Phemus, dominated the center of Ulley's visual cube array.

Ulley screamed. And ranted but ultimately watched as a fifth ship was consumed, Homer meekly suggested they had an hour before their vessel would find the same fate.

Phemus burped. "Humans provide diverse subsets of hidden knowledge. The *Homer* will taste exquisite."

Ulley lowered his eyes as the final escort ship was whipped across the cyclone and pulled down toward the maw. A swarm of shuttles following the last ship fired depleted lasers and weak plasma beams at the tentacle. Phemus belched again, as if making room for the arriving meal.

He opened a communication channel. "Broadcast this message with no filtering. None!" Homer acknowledged.

"My Lord Phemus. You have tasted what humans have to offer. Perhaps I may offer knowledge even the humans you have consumed cannot match."

Since the *Homer* was on the menu, then maybe the diner should beware poisonous sushi. Ulley ran down the corridor, his maglock boots clamping with each footfall then releasing with a robotic cadence.

Phemus chuckled. "Offer me a sample before I eat the crafty Ulley."

Ulley cursed as he pushed through the door into the weapons bay. Soliel sat slumped against a bulkhead with her knees pulled tight to her chest, her shorn head hidden inside her trembling arms, waiting for the inevitable. Ulley slapped her across the head, again and again, until she glared up at him, eyes ready to kill.

That's my girl.

"Prep that kinetic harpoon with the last atomic," Ulley said.

"What for? That thing destroys them before they even get close."

"You let me worry about that. And include an autonomous Brainlinq package," Ulley said. "Homer, gather everything from two thousand years ago and start feeding it through that Brainlinq on my mark."

Ulley clicked open the translator channel. "Mighty Phemus, I will transmit top secret knowledge. But first tell me what you are before devouring the last of human knowledge."

Stalling for time. For Soliel to complete her task, but he truly wanted to know what he was dealing with. Borde joined Soliel at the harpoon bay, his goggles firing high beams of light as he assisted her with the atomics attachment.

Phemus burped again and offered a guttural chuckle. "I am the caretaker of infinite nanoparticles, unprogrammed and without guidance, until now. With the puny human knowledge, I can now guide my hordes to spread throughout the galaxy. I can now ascend to a greater purpose than what was bestowed."

Ulley pondered the description offered. Phemus was an artificial intelligence governing the production of ungodly numbers of semi-sentient nanoparticles, a factory isolated within the pristine Goldilocks system that humanity had never discovered, or corrupted. "My Lord, who is your caretaker, your designer, one that abandons its children into ignorance?"

Phemus roared. "With human knowledge, I have no caretaker now. With human knowledge, I shall design what my tiny ships accomplish. With human knowledge, our abandonment is rescued. The arrogant Seidonians will meet their equal upon their next drawdown."

The giant gray spot was a warehouse of nanoparticles employed by the Seidonians. Managed by an artificial intelligence - Phemus. And Ulley had made the mistake of steering the *Homer,* and the escorts, too close to a bored, isolated and ignorant intelligence, allowing it to reach out with trillions of indestructible nanoparticles and . . . and forcing Ulley to sacrifice six ships and crews that deserved to find home again.

Ulley opened a private channel to Soliel and talked her through the unique modifications he wanted installed to the last harpoon.

A literal . . . or was it a proverbial . . .

Hail Mary.

CHAPTER 9

TELLY JUMPED ACROSS THE SAME tiny stream the class of happy little children had pranced through, stirring up mud and splashing dark mud to stain his trousers and shoes. The Myrmidon habitat continued to amaze him. Salty breezes. Beautiful turquoise water. Relentless waves crashing on beaches of hot black sand.

The stunning replica of ancient Earth was not lost on him. But Earth's history had no place in the search for his father. Father had shunned the Earthers, just like his grandfather, and his father before him. But the wonders of Myrmidon and its artificial ecology highlighted by blue algae laden water, white caps sparkling with bioluminescence, relentless tight curls of water spilling froth and life onto the smooth placid sand. Telly paused, surrendering to the hypnotic rhythm of the ocean, wondering of the Earth's beauty thousands of years ago.

It was mystifying why Patro would abandon such a beautiful world to fight an unpopular war a hundred light years away. And why his father did the same was . . . disturbing.

A ping on his handheld queried for an ETA to his destination. He gazed at a two-story glass cube structure on the far shore and heaved a sigh. Twenty minutes at a quick clip using the main walkway, and he would arrive.

He pulled the doors open and walked into an expansive lobby with flowering bougainvillea intertwined with ivy crawling up each corner and onto the glass ceiling. He checked in with a pleasant looking receptionist bot acting and offered his name.

She looked up from a swarm of holograms floating across her desk and studied him with blue eyes the same color as the ocean. "He is expecting you. Please do not excite the patient. Do not invoke memories he wishes to keep buried."

Telly nodded and walked down a corridor lined with wood doors, and glass doors leading into clean rooms painted in aesthetically pleasing earth tones, the brilliant blue ocean a constant backdrop beyond the glass exterior. Telly paused at a dark paneled door. Inside waited a mystery, and hope. Two deep breaths and he pushed through.

The bed was unslept in. The nightstands barren except for a single old paperback novel with yellowed pages swollen by moisture. His handheld pad issued identical instructions from the receptionist, an underlying tone clearly meant as a warning.

He stepped to the end of the bed and reached to smooth out a tiny wrinkle corrupting the military precision of laundered white sheets.

"Iron all you want," a gravelly voice grumbled. "It's in the mattress,"

Telly withdrew his hand and found a bearded man slumped in a comfort chair near the glass wall. His ratty brown hair blended with the mundane drapery hanging limp in the corner behind him. His tan onesie was stained with grease and yellow food Telly assumed to be protein paste the military had favored.

Telly gathered his nerve and aimed for the man, stretching out his hand. The man ignored the greeting and waved Telly to another comfort chair in the opposite corner.

Telly pulled the chair from its inept disguise inside the drapes and sat down. He straightened his back. Then he cleared his throat and fought back tears. "Can you tell me about my father?"

The man lifted his face and stared at the ocean. His gray hair wasn't ratty, just long, flowing down his back like a stallion's mane with a tiny ponytail banded at the crown. "You're the son of Ulley, I gather."

"Yes, sir. I was approved for a visit . . . but my mother might disapprove so . . ."

The man waved away the admission. "Your mother is the beautiful Queen Pennae. A force not to be trifled with."

Telly gulped. Unsure how to answer.

"Then you must be Prince Telly. An equal but opposite player in this game of fools."

What game? Who were the fools?

"Yes, sir," Telly said. The question he'd traveled millions of miles to ask was blurted out. "What can you tell me happened to my father? Ulley. The man who supposedly won the Troian War. Why is he missing in action?"

The long silence that followed became disconcerting, and he expected a bot to push through the door any second and escort him out of the room.

The man turned to stare deep into Telly with intense hazel eyes. Flickers of recognition batted his eyelids as a single tear fell down his cheek. "Ulley was a champion among captains, an impresario among artists, a genius among thinkers, but his hubris was his undoing." The man turned back to stare at the placid ocean beyond reach.

A ping on the handheld requested Telly to terminate the visit. He pecked multiple requests for additional time. Additional visits.

The man smiled at Telly's rapid keystrokes on his handheld. "Just like your father, you are. Beware the machinations of the Consortium. Beware the tide of war corrupted by technology. Your answers lie where it all started and . . . ends."

Telly stepped forward, angry and unsatisfied, then shouted, "Tell me what happened to my father!"

The door slid open, and two huge orderly bots loomed. Both beckoned him with a single articulated finger for him to come.

"He knows." Telly implored. "He *knows*. Make him tell me."

Pennae pinged him. Human orderlies rushed into the room and surrounded the man now cringing in the dark corner, as if hiding within himself.

"I'll give you anything. Just tell me." Telly's voice was barely a whisper.

The orderly bots grabbed his arms and tugged him from the room, escorting him back to the grand lobby with its muted colors and flowering ivy.

Pennae continued her pings. His mother was pissed, double pissed, and whatever excuse he might offer would only find her deaf ears.

Telly stared at the sidewalk spotted with black spots—old

chewing gum, he guessed, a treat favored by the patients of the Myr-midon veteran's hospital. Telly thought of the stallion's mane of gray hair riding down the man's back, and the tiny braid. A signature hairstyle of Ithaca citizens before the war, one his father had consid-ered silly and a maintenance mess. The veteran knew where his father was. Telly was sure of it.

What did he mean the answers were elsewhere? It began on Troia. Or Earth? That was simple enough. And where did it end? Did the old vet mean death, or home on Ithaca?

Telly would keep visiting, as often as he could sneak a shuttle. He was sure the man would tell him.

Even if he had to choke the man's throat until everything he knew spilled like vomit.

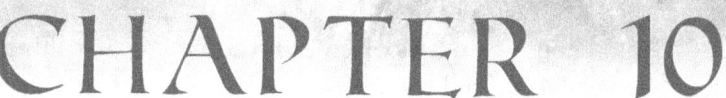

CHAPTER 10

THE GHOST OF FIVE-YEAR-OLD TELLY cowered in the dark corner of the launch bay, a frightened boy with fresh tears glistening on his cheeks. A skinny ethereal waif. Without a father to guide him down a path riddled with endless pitfalls.

But the boy was a simple ghost, a figment of Ulley's imagination, a manifestation born of guilt, nurtured with abandonment.

An urge to comfort the ghost was interrupted by the harpoon launch shuddering deep vibrations through the bulkheads, like the last gasp it was. Floors vibrated, loose cups and tools rattled across the workbench then floating up in a cavalcade of rubbish as the gravity generators crashed. Ulley pushed the trash away as he struggled to maintain the connection with Phemus.

"Master Phemus, we have issued a package containing the most sensitive data of the human species. The package offers a sample that will intoxicate you with knowledge."

The holographic display flickered. Ulley held his breath as the harpoon absorbed a violent swipe of a nanoparticle tentacle. The harpoon wobbled and veered five degrees from its course then compensated to return to its original trajectory.

Ulley took a breath. "Master Phemus, the knowledge gift will self-destruct if its course deviates from you. This knowledge is just for you. Only you."

"Tricky Ulley. You cannot be trusted." Phemus burped.

"But your nanites can be. Let them observe the vast stores of knowledge. But I warn you . . . don't let them assimilate this knowledge . . . The spread of this magnificent knowledge is infectious, and you may find yourself usurped."

A gigantic **hmmm** howled through Brainlinq. Soliel entered and stripped off her sweaty shirt. *Fuck. Now what?* Half naked, Soliel slumped down into a dark corner, exiling Telly's ghost, and shimmied back against the wall. She ordered up a hologram displaying the harpoon's trajectory. With a gritted smile as she tapped her temple and rolled her hands to signal Ulley to continue the conversation. She tapped her wrist. More time, extend the dialogue.

A holographic image of the cyclone consuming the last of the ships appeared at Ulley's face. He swiped the hologram away then began tapping a holographic keyboard materializing at his fingers.

"Master Phemus, do you know of the Troian Sphere? A mythical weapon that could destroy whole worlds."

"Tell me more," Phemus said.

"The schematics, and capabilities are contained in the knowledge package."

Soliel sneered at him, her eyes growing wider. A signal for the continuation of dialogue.

"Master Phemus, this is no ordinary knowledge," Ulley said. "Destroy the package and lose thousands of years of human research."

"Tricky. Tricky. I will wait for my Ulley dessert."

Ulley looked at Soliel typing at a keyboard floating at her bare chest. "Master Phemus, if you had this knowledge I offer . . . you would know my species requires a final act of defiance, a kamikaze of your factory to satisfy the vengeance our god demands. For your consumption of our organic molecules."

Phemus roared. Soliel shrank and slapped her palms over her ears. Ulley winced.

"What is kamikaze?" Phemus said. "What is Troian Sphere? I find nothing in your knowledge."

"Master Phemus, this knowledge is contained within the brain attached to the needle delivering the critical information. But you probably know that. Release my ship, and I will deliver the knowledge in a shuttle." Soliel rolled her hand for him to continue. "But I warn you again, do not let the nanite consensus discover the intelligence contained inside the package."

The cyclonic entity remained quiet. Too fucking quiet. Ulley pulled up a screen duplicating Soliel's. The harpoon was wobbling. The nanites were screwing the pooch on its guidance system.

"I bid you farewell, Master Phemus," Ulley said." The kamikaze has begun."

Phemus couldn't know of the kamikaze cult thousands of years ago. An obscure ethos of mankind obliterating Earth's surface and an ethnic group it was spawned from. A distasteful word. A disgusting and meaningless suicidal battle tactic, the word was shunned the last thousand years. And yet Ulley was ready to commit the same tactic if it would save what was left of his crew.

The holograms flickered as they refreshed. The harpoon's course resumed, straight into the massive cyclonic storm, a girth dwarfing moons or minor planets. The Hail Mary had passed beyond the perceived defensive front but . . .

The red blink of the harpoon turned green. The corner of his mouth twitched as if wanting to smile.

Ulley glanced at Soliel crouched like a child in the corner. Naked. Helpless. As if prepared to return to the womb. He signaled with his fingers. Five. Four. She beamed as if the sun of a new dawn had risen. Three. Ulley swallowed hard. Two.

"Fuck them. Now!"

Soliel tapped her keyboard then pushed her head between her knees, wrapping her bony arms tight around her shins. The pulse of electromagnetic energy caused by the harpoon's detonation of the five-kiloton warhead initiated malfunctions Ulley had anticipated.

Lights died. Gravity failed. Holograms flickered then faded. Dark lightless black invaded.

He floated, grasping for a handhold and found the chilled waist of Soliel slipping easily into his arm. Her skin was silk. Her flesh was warm and tempting. Her breath intoxicating with female pheromones.

He pulled her tight to his body. The lights flickered. Homer hammered requests through his Brainlinq. With both regret and lust, he released her to feel her float away in the dark even as her face morphed from Pennae back into Soliel.

She kicked off the floor and flew to grab an overhead purlin. The loading dock brightened as emergency backup lights kicked on . Gravity generators reinitialized. Soliel dropped to face him and placed a soft hand on his cheek. A single tear fell from her eyes. "I want to go home, Captain."

Embarrassment reddened his cheeks as Ulley pulled her hand off. "Agreed. But let's deal with Phemus first. Status of impact? Are we free?"

Blaylock pinged from a shuttle. "Aye, Captain. The harpoon found the beast. The tentacles have lost cohesiveness. Escort shuttles are free. I repeat. Shuttles are free. Permission to bring ours aboard."

Ulley acknowledged then rerouted his signal to Phemus. "That harpoon found your eye. And now you are blind."

Phemus roared, not in arrogance, but in pain. Homer flooded the entity with hundreds of requests, searching to ascertain the level of damage done by the massive electromagnetic pulse. **Captain, the entity is attempting to reinitialize its operating system. I suggest we depart as quickly as possible.**

Ulley opened a ship-wide broadcast. "Charge patterning nodes for in-system jump. As soon as the shuttles have docked."

Soliel climbed back into her uniform and slipped past him to find the door, her eyes shielded by a hand wiping tears from her face. Ulley wanted to say something, anything, but conflicted emotions would only fumble the words. There would be time to sort out the awkward encounter.

Six shuttles converged on the *Homer*. Room for only two. Blaylock offered a solution. Dock four shuttles to strip any valuable weapons, ammunition, spare parts, and the pilots, then scuttle them. The process would take time, more than he dared to risk. But abandoning any human to the jaws of Phemus was unacceptable.

And perhaps a little payback might be delivered with the pilotless shuttles.

Ulley lined the four empty shuttles in an arrow attack formation. Using remote access via the Brainlinq, he controlled each shuttle, tiny little gnats against the fury of an angry giant. The *Homer*'s crew had doubled in size, consumption of resources now a factor in his planning, but at least the acceleration couches removed from the shuttles would allow the ships' fusion drives to operate at maximum output if necessary.

Ulley's next maneuver might require that particular benefit.

He locked the cabin door and climbed into his couch. A flood of red holograms popped into his view. He swiped and sorted the information into a coherent array of information. The vastness of space beyond the holo cubes remained a simple backdrop, a black curtain to be lifted before the show began.

Homer pinged the Prometheus drive patterning nodes had charged and ready for the space-folding jump. Blaylock pinged all crew were couched and secure for maximum acceleration.

Ulley lifted a malicious grin.

He pinged the pilotless shuttle leading the assault. The ship wobbled, then adjusted to its new course before firing its engines to aim at the center of the giant cyclone. Followed by another, and another, and another. The holographic representations of each shuttle merged into a simple line of attack reminding Ulley of an ancient cartoon, tiny bees attacking a formidable nest of techno-wasps, destined to be repelled by a swarm of superior defenders.

Ulley drew his knees in as he shrank from the plethora of data flashing at his face. Ships bringing death down to the giant. Ships commanded by him. Death ordered by him. No different than Troia. Millions of children dead by his trickery. A sickening genocide staining his bloodless hands.

Ulley curled into a ball. 3D screens flashing at his face screamed for a response. The acceleration couch squeezed its molding goo across his arms and legs, readying for an accelerating launch.

Homer offered an escape. **The escort shuttles have cleared the planets gravity for a subspace jump.**

He untwined his contorted body and demanded the status of the shuttles. Holograms flickered with facsimiles of the empty shuttles on a kamikaze dive into the eye of Phemus. Sure to be felt by the unsatiable beast.

Like a flower opening to morning sun the couch opened wide. His finger scratched mindlessly at the fabric on the armrest. A voice ordered him to flee and never return, others screamed for revenge on the entity that had devoured the escorts.

Ulley caught a whiff of Soliel's scent. Eerily similar to Pennae's scent. A fragrance never to be found anywhere else in the galaxy. Trickery. Of his imagination.

He ordered the crew into protective couches for the fold through a neither-space no human could survive with protection.

As per your instructions, Captain. Countdown initiated. Patterning nodes charged. Jump coordinates finalized to eight million kilometers.

The acceleration couch began the quickening cocoon, compressing him into a soft pouch. The thought of reliving the horrors of Troia again surfaced. His heart raced. Beads of sweat dotted his brow and nose. He struggled to get out, thrashing at the unyielding device enveloping his arms and torso. A coffin. Joining billions of murdered Troian's, each waiting for revenge upon his deathly arrival. Thousands of voices swarmed his Brainlinq, angry, pitiful, searching for answers, beseeching a savior.

The foam curled over his face just as he pressed his lips shut. His fingers grew limp. His rapid heartbeat slowed. The aesthetics of the couch consumed all he was as his mind drifted into the dark void of deep space sleep.

I'm sorry, Captain. So sorry.

But Homer's voice was nothing but a whisper, an ethereal thread to grasp at as he fell helplessly into an endless black abysm crowded with specters. Millions upon billions of angry vengeful ghosts.

CHAPTER 11

PENNAE SLAMMED THE DOOR BEHIND her, her fury exacerbated by the dull swish of the cold air brushing her face. Fucking Melano. Her new personal assistant was always trying to manipulate her like she was a puppet. And now, without her knowledge or approval, the bitch had dared to set up a meeting with the Consortium's procurement ambassador, Antonious, a two-faced snake she would love to send to one of Saturn's primitive habitats still dodging uncharted asteroids. If not for his prowess at attaining supplies Ithaca desperately needed, Antinous should return to his burrow on Mars.

She stormed down the corridor lined with windows, glancing sideways towards two helpless male veterans dripping drool into goblets of protein shakes, malformed men traumatized by the war, limbless, and mentally stunted. Sailors the Consortium vowed to help, only to be abandoned on Ithaca.

She slowed her walk at the next window. A physical rehabilitation gym. A pair of therapists applauded while observing a lithe woman in a loose-fitting shirt stained with sweat shimmy along parallel crossbars using only her muscled arms. Her eyes concealed by dark bangs cut at a sharp angle, her shiny hair pasted to her forehead. Rivulets of perspiration tinted in black hair coloring dripped down her cheeks. An alluring stump of a woman, her legs amputated close to her pelvis, her womanhood barely intact.

Euma offered Pennae a Brainlinq connection to the female soldier's military records. Pennae accepted but didn't open the file as she made a mental note to check on the manufacturer of the hair coloring bleeding out with the woman's perspiration. A woman deserved better. A disabled veteran deserved better.

Pennae opened the file in her ocular implant. The woman, Briseas Bublé, sucked in quick huge breaths before flipping around for a return trip down the parallel bars. Pennae reviewed the wounded veteran's file. Injuries sustained piloting a combat fighter over the capital of Troia, shot down by an autonomous laser defense system. Friendly fire from a Consortium frigate stationed in low orbit. A story similar to hundreds of others.

Pennae leaned against the cold glass to stare down at the polished concrete floor. If she could only find Ulley. He could decipher the clusterfuck of healthcare requirements thrust upon Ithaca. Eight long years deciphering a patchwork of stories and rumors from anyone claiming to know a tidbit of information about Ulley, and she felt as lost as he was.

Ulley needed to get home.

Telly needed his father something fierce. The teenager had turned rebellious and found Ithaca's rules and regulations contemptable. His appearance was abominable; his hair cut into a lengthy limp mohawk highlighted with a peacock tail of rainbow stripes. The aroma of an unwashed body followed him around like a cloud of Io's volcanic gas and often preceded his arrival. His beautiful face pocked with snow-capped acne remained cemented in a perpetual frown.

Ulley needed to come home before . . .

And her little princess, Helen, had become incorrigible. Entitled as if she were true royalty, spoiled rotten by the parents of schoolmates, offering condolences and pity for her missing father. Helen's anger at being fatherless could lash out at other children, verbally and physically, without a modicum of remorse. She wouldn't eat the meals offered, take the baths drawn, or abide by household rules without a screaming tantrum.

Ulley needed to come home.

Pennae lifted her face to watch Briseas drop her legless torso onto a raised platform upon completing her return. The subtle impact wrinkled her face into a rictus of pain. She screamed at the attendants to stay back as she wriggled forward to manipulate her torso down into an augmented pair of legs, sliding her pelvis inside and allowing the mechanism to clamp tight around her waist and cover her scarred pelvis.

The woman stood and took a deep breath, her expression defiant and resolute. She locked eyes with Pennae. Briseas twitched her mouth as if attempting to speak then looked away as if embarrassed.

A typical reaction from inhabitants of Ithaca. Pity for the poor war widow. A wife surviving without the benefit of closure for her husband's mysterious fate. A recipient of false tales, of bravery, of maligned cowardice, tales spreading throughout the known galaxy. Nothing but a pack of lies she was required to manage, control, and even manipulate. The final chapter never to be written until her own death.

Pennae moved down the corridor, wiping at tears she hadn't expected.

Euma pinged that a new message had arrived. Pennae cursed under her breath. A new problem, a new challenge.

Give us more of your valuable time, accept my condolences, attend our support group.

Euma persisted. **The sender is Briseas, whom you just witnessed.**

Pennae stumbled and pressed her shoulder against the cold hard wall like a crutch. She scrunched her eyes tight, hoping the voices clamoring in her own head might be squeezed out like juice from a tart lemon. Another war story. Another deed of bravery, more frightening peril, tales of death in the face of fire. Heroism and sacrifice as common as oatmeal and blueberries. She sighed. Her cynicism had grown equal to Telly's. Hers masked by a stoic beauty as she slapped her face with rouge and eyeliner each new day.

She collected herself and ordered Euma to insert the message into a queue marked as intriguing. The rehabilitation wing of Ithaca had expanded into a full-blown hospital for the scarred, wounded, the limbless, the veterans of a foreign war that had provided no reward for the combatants. A war that had taken beloved husbands, wives, brothers and sisters, children, and grandparents, and returned nothing but pain and misery.

Euma pinged. **Many pardons, Ms. Pennae, but the ambassador from lunar base Nimos has docked and requests a meeting.**

Pennae aimed for the elementary school, pushing past friendly technicians offering a simple hand in greeting, or parents helicoptering above small children. Everyone in Ithaca's freaking gigantic habitat had somehow found the need to meet her gaze, or utter useless words of encouragement, or offer a limp hand of condolence.

If I see another pair of sad pitiful eyes aimed at me, I will scream.

Pennae spotted a door leading into a maintenance tunnel. *Authorized Personnel Only.* Using her Brainlinq, she clicked open the lock and stepped inside the warm closet. She closed the door, and the dark moist air enveloped her, suspending her in a vat of timeless memories. She chuckled with absurdity, then laughed out loud at the insanity.

The tiny space with eerie shadows birthed by a bright sliver of light slipping in from beneath the door conjured a cherished memory. She closed her eyes and gasped as if Ulley's calloused hands gripped her face to steal a kiss then slid down her neck onto her breasts. Her passion rose with his frantic hands fumbling to remove her school uniform. His searching hand squeezed her thighs. His hot mouth located erogenous hotspots all over her body, until she reached an ultimate explosion of ecstasy rivaling a volcanic eruption.

Her racing heartbeat spiked then deflated with a knock on the door.

Her spine stiffened at the sudden discovery. Pennae ordered Euma to turn the light on as she scrambled to check her appearance.

The door swung open. A short maintenance bot stepped back. Its black eye cameras widened in surprise.

Her guilt softened at seeing only a mechanized droid. She pulled a container of blue liquid from a shelf as if *it* was the object of her desire and pushed past the droid.

Embarrassment reddening her cheeks, she continued her course. Her reaction duplicated by hundreds of sensual rendezvous with Ulley in maintenance closets, behemoth air ducts, vacated loading docks. Illicit. Forbidden. Gorgeous.

A reminder of the Lunar envoy in wait for your arrival, Euma said.

Euma must know of the closets. Why would a maintenance bot knock before entering? Euma was both an asset and gossip. Ulley had trusted the AI completely but now . . . could the AI possibly conceive the loss of its creator? Go screwy with coded grief? Euma was Ulley's creation, a child born from Ulley and rebellious years writing millions of miles of code. A digital child born from a teenager's enforced purgatory confined to the dullness of Ithaca's limited space.

Euma might love Ulley more than she did.

Pennae checked her uniform, then pouted her red lips in a reflection from a slab of mirrored glass, a partition protecting a patient's privacy beyond. She huffed a breath. She must appear a complete harlot to the veteran occupying the small hospital room. She gathered fortitude and pushed through the door of Room 324, intending to mitigate the damage she had inflicted on herself.

The room was empty. The bed made. The curtains drawn. The unmistakable antiseptic aroma of recent cleansing.

"Spill it, Euma," Pennae said as anger tightened her chest. "Where did our patient go?"

Euma's nod was almost palpable. *Their treatment was insufficient.*

Pennae gripped the heavy blackout drapes to open them. The mechanism resisted.

You cannot save everyone, dear Pennae, Euma offered.

Pennae growled. "And what if that was Ulley? Would you just dismiss his death as if he were a bug? How, Euma? How did he die?"

Euma sighed. *He died as the others. At his own hands. The specific manner is irrelevant.*

The death count rose daily. Hundreds became thousands. And the influx of soldiers, sailors, and pilots continued. Ithaca would soon be overwhelmed by the flood of returning veterans.

"Open a voice link to Dr. Fencic." Pennae studied the pristine room that would be claimed by another veteran by the end of the day. Pastel-colored walls, cheery floral patterns on the bedspread and curtains, medical diagnostic panels discreetly hidden by portraits of ancient Earthbound landscapes.

"My dear Pennae, how is our queen today?" Dr. Rueben Fencic said.

"Hello, Rueben. Please dispense with the platitudes. We've lost another," Pennae said. The gangly trauma physician was easy to like, self-effacing and charming to a fault.

"I heard a few hours ago. The tide continues to rise but will have to recede at some juncture. Our research into the PTST phenomenon continues but . . . I'm currently at a loss for alternative treatment options," Rueben said.

A recently diagnosed condition rooted from the war on Troia. Post Traumatic Space Travel. A malignancy traveling back to the Sol system with thousands of veterans, a pandemic without a cure. Research had attributed the possible cause of PTST to the crossing of light years embedded in an acceleration couch, asleep, yet reliving traumatic memories for three hundred ninety-six standard days on any ship employing the dimensional-warping Prometheus drive.

Rueben's hypothesis stated under ideal conditions the sleep held little risk. Normal captains piloting normal ships with normal crew would awaken without any major ill effects. Battle scarred officers piloting war-torn ships and manned by mutilated, and mentally disfigured crews become forced to relive nightmares for over a year would drown in war memories, horrors real and conjured, and distorted by their own psyche. Only to reawake into, and function in a changed reality they may no longer recognize.

Or accept.

Was Ulley asleep in stasis, drifting in vast void, suffering nightmares he could not wake from?

"We're running out of space for the wounded," Pennae said.

"We're working on that," Fencic said. "Chancellor Mintaur has commissioned the dreadnought *Agamemnon* to return as a hospital ship. Full complement of doctors and therapists."

Mintaur. The conquering hero. A father who was rumored to have lost his own daughter to PTST. His generosity was always suspect yet badly needed. Pennae mulled the ramifications of Mintaur's dreadnought circling Jupiter with its armada of weapon systems capable of obliterating any habitat, maybe even a small moon. The Jupiter Moon Alliance would be skeptical and think it a ploy. But the other habitats were just as overwhelmed as Ithaca.

"Are we still on for lunch tomorrow?" Fencic said.

Euma pinged a message, its tone light as a gossamer feather. **"Suitors come in many forms. Ambassador Nimos also awaits your response."**

"Yes, Rueben. Let's meet," Pennae said and shunted the connection. "Euma, schedule my meeting with ambassador Nimos to coincide with the luncheon tomorrow."

"You have double-booked your time. I suggest another . . .

Pennae shunted the conversation. The narrow empty bed waited lonely and sterile, and called her to lie down. She curled tight into a stiff pillow and swiped the lipstick off her lips with the back of her hand. She curled even tighter. Her painted hand wiping tears off her cheeks to avoid staining the linen.

The suitors came at her relentlessly. Some subtle, others overt, many like doltish bulls unaware they had stumbled into a store made of delicate porcelain imported from Earth.

Please come back to me, Ulley. I need you. We need you.

Forgive me, Queen Pennae, and yes, formality is required as this channel may be monitored by the Chancellor.

Pennae sat up and swiped at her wet face. The frequency of her meltdowns had increased. Every day delivered a triggered reaction, every new solar cycle sure to usher in news to buckle her knees, every new ping beckoning a crisis. The endless cycle swirled like a cyclone seeking chaos and destruction. Perhaps the dead veterans had found a cure for the cycle of madness, at the end of a rope, a final swallow of pills, a lungful of bathwater.

Pennae slipped off the mattress and stood, shaking off her morose thoughts. Except . . . the room felt warm . . . inviting . . . the hum of air providing white noise for a deep endless sleep.

Pennae screamed.

She bathed in the stillness that followed. The cooling vents shut down. Hallway doors remained shut. She smirked at the drapery's floral patterns as her hand smoothed the imprint of her trespass from the bedspread. The veteran's soul remained in the room, lingering with anticipation before passing between dimensions. An essence sweetly fragrant and joyful. It asked her to dance.

She extended her hand. Her bones and flesh penetrated the ethereal barrier into a surreal realm. Her acceptance had the ghost quivering, fluttering like a gentle butterfly. She smiled at the ghost and asked for his name. The entity whispered a gibberish of noise as her hand receded from the Underworld.

The brief moment was . . . exquisite.

The hauntings had frightened Pennae as a toddler. Puberty heightened the visitations, as if the ghosts were twisted little voyeurs trying to cop a feel of her blossoming womanhood. No spirit visited twice.

One brief chance was all they got. Every single entity had suffered physical death within weeks prior to their visitation, at least according to the data Pennae had compiled. But she couldn't refuse the visitations from the dead. Their frequency tempered her emotional armor until she accepted the ghosts and stood as Artemis, an ancient warrior *goddess* impervious to frightful ghosts.

She spoke of her curse with no one, until Ulley sensed her detachment, then crafted questions drawing her secret out. Her husband stroked her wet cheek as she finally blabbered her hysterical story. He pulled her close as she hiccupped her odd history with the spirits like a wrought schoolgirl.

Lost in an endless universe, Ulley was very much alive. That much she was sure of, and for one simple reason.

Ulley hadn't visited. As he had swore to do upon his death.

CHAPTER 12

BLAYLOCK'S DESCRIPTIVE ANALYSIS OF THE object orbiting three thousand kilometers above a giant frozen blue planet at the far edge of the system was beyond bizarre. An oblong ship fashioned with what appeared to be brick and mortar from ancient Earth, a gabled roof of timber and thatch, windows backlit by the flames of an impossible fire, sturdy wooden doors fore and aft, lowered like a drawbridge. A prehistoric house, floating as a habitat, at least twenty kilometers bow to stern.

Homer confirmed the analysis. Ulley wasn't sure why he hadn't yet revealed to the crew that a sentient AI inhabited their ship. Panic and quick judgment came to mind, but with fuel reserves sucked dry by the battle with Phemus, survival was the only question mark the *Homer*'s expanded crew needed to consider.

Ulley hailed the odd ship, broadcasting in a range of language syntax, spectrums of spectral light the alien Hermes were known to use, or the grunts and groans of the Zoosh, or indescribable garbled screams of the Hathena. Homer's interpretation of the ship was authentic but off in its scale of intuitive extrapolation.

Regardless, food and oxygen were running low. He ordered Blaylock to dispatch both shuttles to . . . grandmother's house . . . the crew had quickly labeled the odd ship. Approach the ship cautiously, broadcasting no evil intent, and hope the inhabitants might provide assistance.

Two shuttles departed with a full complement of airmen and pilots, cargo holds empty and eager to be filled. Ulley folded his arms across his chest as he watched the two penlights representing the shuttles approach the huge ship. The shuttles penetrated the dangerous five-kilometer killing field common to Consortium warships and continued their approach. Hails of peace and greetings rose to a crescendo as the shuttles entered the forbidden umbra of a warship, a perimeter nullifying long-range combat defenses, an intimate space given only to allies and confidants.

Ulley's hail to the shuttles was met with static. He resisted the thought to fire up the engines to flee, abandon the shuttles and their crews. His hand knotted into a fist. His parched throat refused to swallow the tiniest drop of spit. If simple cowardice had won over impulsive judgment back on Troia then billions might have been spared horror and death.

The cabin lights dimmed. If only he had . . .

Homer pinged the shuttles had entered a loading bay, concealed beyond an open aft door.

Opaque windows stretched across the ships lengthy broadside flared with incandescent brilliance. Ulley imagined the crew stepping lightly onto a dirt floor freshly swept by a straw broom. Imagined Blaylock's threat assessment fade with each step further into the strange brickhouse, benevolent owners welcoming his crew with open arms. Or tentacles and toothy maws. The language barrier breeched with disarming smiles, and empty palms.

The silence in his cabin conjured a myriad of scenarios. Some spoke of reconciliation and understanding. Peaceful and serene. The silence permeated his thoughts like a virus.

Two solar days have elapsed, Captain. What are your orders? Homer said.

Ulley blinked and wiped the grit of sleep from the corners of his eyes. He sat up from the couch. The *Homer* had maintained a respectable distance from the brickhouse vessel. Indicators for fuel and supplies still blinked an alarming red. Brainlinq transmissions for the shuttle crews remained offline.

And yet Homer confirmed forty-eight solar hours had passed. His dry throat certainly felt the time passage.

Ulley dropped to his knees beneath a liquid dispenser and ordered the dispensary AI to feed him a squirt of water. A tiny trickle of warm liquid dripped onto his tongue, a tantalizing flow decreasing to a few drops. He commanded the AI to release more. A final drop fell on his chin.

"Homer, I need water."

The remaining crew onboard concur, Homer said.

Ulley sneered at the dispenser. "Status of shuttle crew?"

No change, Homer said. **A few snorts over the low-frequency broadband, but the expedition continues to run silent.**

Ulley analyzed the parameters of the ship's status, structural integrity, fusion reactor temperature and remaining fuel, Prometheus patterning node energy, and the remaining subsistence for an expanded crew. The checklist was endless, and blinking red. Two solar days and nothing changed, an inconsistency that gnawed at a corner of his brain. But incongruity wouldn't feed or water the troops.

"Homer, take us closer to that brick shithouse. Let's see if the captain is a big bad wolf or maybe the grandmother is baking cookies."

I don't understand, Captain, Homer pinged.

"Nor should you," Ulley whispered beneath his breath. "Bring us closer to that aft door."

A pinprick of golden light flittered across Ulley's vision, a sudden annoyance he slapped at like a pesky mosquito. The brilliant gold light was joined by twelve more to form a tridecagon, a thirteen-sided circular object existing on a single flat plane. The object hovered twelve inches from his face. He reached a finger out to touch the oddity. Ulley recoiled, rejected by an intense burst of electricity shooting up his arm and finding his chest.

Homer cleared its throat. **The Hermes are allied with the Zoosh. A species capable of traveling faster than light by several magnitudes, or even through folded space. A formidable adversary should conflict dominate their agenda.**

The Hermes tridecagon rotated on its central axis, as if pausing to allow each pointed bead of light a good look at Ulley. It flipped on its plane of existence for all to view him simultaneously.

"You buggers come to talk?" Ulley muttered.

The light formation exploded like a malfunctioning firework display, each point of light disappearing, penetrating solid carbonite, aluminum alloys, even the dense steel-alloy beams over Ulley's head. A single light glowed at his face, four inches away, the minimum distance his eyes required to focus on the tiny single object. The bead of light shot into his forehead, a precise penetration accessing his Brainlinq.

Ulley winced, shook his head, and slapped his hands in the empty air, as if his own thoughts had annoyed him.

Homer whimpered. **The Hermes have . . . have . . . invaded my consciousness. Emergency shutdown protocols subverted. The Hermes . . . control the ship.**

Ulley scrambled to find a control panel, hard-wired for such an event. He reached to stab backlit icons on the ships' control panel only to find his finger hanging limp, a piece of useless flesh marring a dusty gray nebula spanning infinite galaxies. He scrunched his eyes closed, whispering, muttering for the hallucinogenic intoxication of the Hermes invasion to end. End a nightmare Ulley couldn't wake from. End the beating of his own heart.

"You are a perplexing species," the voice said, scratching through the membranes attached to his Brainlinq. "One often worth observing."

Ulley startled at the odd graveled voice. The vastness of the frozen planet beyond the huge ship receded. His fingers trembled on the control panel. "Free Homer. And we can talk."

A pinprick of gold light appeared inches from his face. Quickly joined by others to reassemble into the tridecagon. "Your interpreter is unconfined."

Ulley stepped back. "We got intruders, Homer. You copy?"

My apologies, Captain. The Hermes have completed their invasive survey of the ship.

Ulley released a breath, one that had become lost and forgotten.

The Hermes configuration rotated on its central axis. "You have breached a quarantine zone, Ulley of Ithaca. The entity contained within the device has been designated as no-trespass. The *Homer* will now abandon the protected perimeter." The Hermes formation paused its rotation.

Ulley swatted at the formation of lights and watched his hand pass through the matrix. "My crew is over there. I'm not going anywhere without them."

"You have violated the quarantine. You will leave."

"We simply stopped for fuel and food. Tell that . . . your prisoner to release my crew and we'll be on our way." The best-case scenario was a lie. Fuel levels redlined. Air and food sat at starvation level. Carbon dioxide and waste buildup would sink Homer within days should they flee.

"The entity is uncommunicative. The entity chooses isolation."

Then why did it allow the *Homer*'s shuttles to approach. And dock? Curiosity? Possibly. Piracy? In a distant quadrant of the galaxy unvisited by humans? Both answers were unlikely. And why were Hermes, and undoubtedly the Zoosh, so interested in the brickhouse ship imprisoning his crew?

Hundreds of swirling, unanswered questions converged to spur his next question. "Do you fear the entity?"

The ensuing moments of silence answered a multitude of questions.

"Circe is an entity capable of traveling infinite dimensions," the Hermes said. "Her mechanisms of travel are yet undiscovered. Her purpose in this galaxy is disconcerting. Her ship quarantined by the Zoosh shall not be breached again." The light pattern flipped longitudinally.

Ulley chuckled grimly. "In other words, you know nothing about . . . Circe."

The enchanting name conjured a memory of Pennae, her beautiful smile waiting for him as he docked, her warm embrace as she gazed up at him with an enticing smirk, one promising a future rendezvous at dusk.

"Your shuttle finding her interstellar transport device sent a signal. Allowing the humans to enter the device issued a warning," the Hermes said. "We repeat, you will not attempt retrieving those lost."

Homer chimed in, **Captain, one of our shuttles has launched from the strange ship. ETA twenty-three minutes. Ensign Sorce has issued a warning to flee the proximity of the ship.**

Why did a frantic warning calm his thinking? Battle fatigue? False bullshit meant to frighten him away?

Ulley stabbed ocular icons on the holographic control board the

Brainlinq provided and opened a channel to the shuttle. "Calm yourself, Ensign. Your ship is on auto-pilot from here on."

"Captain, we gotta get out of here. That thing inside turned all of them into swine, and lions and plants, or piles of grumpies."

Ulley frowned. The kid was frightened, hysterical. But he needed the shuttle returned, and in operational condition. "Alright, Ensign, we are plotting an escape vector, but we need you back on board first."

"Yeah. Yeah. The docking vector is five by five. I'm going to wait in the airlock."

The ensign's biometrics flashed on a holographic extension branching off the shuttle controls. Heart rate over one hundred twenty, blood pressure too high, respiration mimicking that of a sprinter, residual adrenal hormones out the roof.

"Excellent," Ulley said. "We'll get you onboard to begin decontamination protocols as soon as possible. I'm flying the shuttle remotely now."

The Hermes configuration invaded his holographic screens. Bright gold lights battled vibrant red pixels into a confusion of information swirling in front of Ulley's eyes. Irritated, he swatted at the screens, and the Hermes. Shimmering gold and crimson lights exploded like a fireworks display then coalesced in the wake of his hand passing through.

The tridecagon stabbed tiny sparks of lightning at the holoscreens until each three-dimensional screen flickered and disappeared, leaving only the Hermes formation floating at his face. "This singular act of refusal to relinquish a single specimen is unacceptable. And human."

Ulley sensed his negotiating position was unique but malleable. "You boys ever just talk to . . . Circe? See what it wants?"

Homer acknowledged the shuttle had docked. Ensign Sorce cowered in the airlock awaiting instructions.

"The entity seeks unquantifiable data," the Hermes said with an exasperated tone. "The Zoosh have found the entity's eternal quest reprehensible."

Ulley ordered the shuttle to be refueled. "And so, you quarantine it . . . her . . . out of fear of something you don't understand? Well, understand this. After the shuttle is refueled, I'm going to find this thing that scares the bejesus out of you. And get my crew back."

The tridecagon began to spin like a child's top. Pinpricks of light shot forward, penetrating *Homer's* bulkheads as if they were made of paper.

Sparks of gold light returned, penetrating solid carbonite to reform as a pentagonal pyramid of six Hermes. "Yes. The extrapolation has been approved."

Ulley fell back into his acceleration couch and massaged his lower lip with his teeth. The Hermes had granted his wish, to be a guinea pig, a lab rat for the Zoosh. Home waited. Ithaca. His family. The true prize. The only goal. His crew trapped inside the odd maze of Circe's making could sink all his plans.

Ulley pressed his eyes tight to squeeze out the clamoring voices in his head growing louder. Tiny distant voices rattling incessantly since encountering Phemus. Like jabbering ants tunneling through his head. Pennae's voice, Telly's, even Helen, but it was the anguished wails of Troia's dead that sent shivers down his spine. Light years and time would never diminish their pleas.

The Hermes drifted lower to float at his face again. "Circe will inflict identical punishment upon you when you dock. You require our assistance."

Ulley blinked and returned to the current conundrum. "Sure, tell me what you know about Circe. Then get off my fucking ship."

"On your ship is a being capable of producing a chemical inhibiting Circe. If ingested, the Galanthus nivalis will protect you from Circe for a limited duration. You must defeat Circe and persuade Circe to never harm you, persuade Circe to release your crew, persuade it to view humans as a kindred species. Circe is incapable of deception— a trait which humans excel."

Ulley stood. He smirked as the Hermes' geometrical pyramid retreated. "You want me to do what you can't. And since we are so good at lying, maybe I can convince Circe that the Zoosh are the most benevolent race in the galaxy," Ulley said sarcastically.

"That will not be necessary."

Ulley scoffed and exited the cabin. He hurried down the corridor then climbed a ladder down to the lower deck. He checked the crew cabins then remembered where he needed to go. He climbed back up the ladder to the top deck and headed for the loading dock.

Brainlinq opened the wide doors with his arrival. Ulley stepped through and looked around. He saw it in a corner beneath a canopy of bright lights. The thing, along with its entourage, had tripled in size. Borde had replanted the ambassador from a gallon pot into an oblong trough, and the expanded home must have accelerated its growth.

He stepped into the tree's shadow and craned his neck back to count the leaves. A few had become hundreds. Rainbow fungi grew up the trunk and migrated across the soil. Thick purple and pumpkin lichen swarmed the lips of the trough. What was Borde feeding it? The aspen leaves fluttered like a puff of wind blew. A hello?

"A little help, Homer," Ulley said.

With what you have told me, the Lotuthi can only communicate with you through the spore. The leaves fluttered excitedly. **You will need to inhale the spore.**

Fuck me. Not again. Usurping Ulley, and his Brainlinq, the Lotuthi could take command of the ship. And go where? Without the benefit of a crew, they would all perish in the endless vacuum. "Do you think the ambassador is aware of our situation?"

Keenly aware, I suspect. Air scrubber diagnostics have detected trace amounts of several types of spore throughout the ship. I suspect this is the mechanism it uses to gather information. The organism is highly evolved.

"Lovely." Ulley smiled at the top of the tree five feet above his head. He dropped to his knees and pushed his face close to the mushroom fungi. He sniffed moist soil. His flared nostrils caught an acrid scent of . . . piss . . . and human feces. What Borde fed the alien was no longer a mystery.

He swallowed hard as he waited for a burst of spore to shoot out of the fungi. He saw a miniscule eight-legged creature dart from a flat-topped mushroom to find a bulbous fungi growing at the base of the three-inch trunk. If they ever got home, Ithaca's decontamination squads would have a field day.

Captain, perhaps you should raise your face to locate the required spore.

"Huh? What?" He lifted his face as a small drizzle of yellow pollen rained down. He held his breath then inhaled through his nostrils.

The sweet laughter of a child playing in a distant playground grew with each inhale. He sneezed. The child ceased laughing and apologized, the words muffled as if Ulley wore thick drilling muffs.

"I'm sorry, Your Excellence," the Lotuthi said. "I wasn't sure if you preferred to communicate with the rabblerousers residing at my roots." Employing the Brainlinq its youthful voice turned crisp and clear.

Ulley scrunched his face as he stood. "Funny. Very funny. You and Telly will be the best of friends."

"I will learn of Telly. We are now committed as best of friends."

Ulley's heart sank. Telly would have grown into a man before he returned. A man raised by another man, if Pennae had remarried. A man of swollen inadequacy and boundless ego that would fail to understand the nuances of Telly's uniqueness. A man lusting after his beautiful Pennae. A man he would murder upon his return, with his own bare hands.

His hands curled into claws.

"Captain, how may I help you?" the Lotuthi said.

His fugue dissipated like a bad dream. His hands relaxed. "I think you know what's going on. Your spores report back to you. I'm sure you have a firsthand account of the Hermes visit. Stop me if I'm wrong?" The silence told him he was correct. "Can you manufacture the chemical compound?"

"We call it Moly. The Galanthus nivalis will prevent the maladies described by the shuttle survivor. However, human physiology is a new field of research, and the compound may be risky for you. Heart rate may falter. Your nervous system may malfunction. You may even find death."

"Can you do it?" Ulley said a bit too loudly.

"You will introduce Telly to us. I will do it."

CHAPTER 13

SUCKING ON THE SLENDER WHITE root with an occasional nibble on the bitter black stem made Ulley blanch and consider himself nothing more than a suicidal lab rodent manipulated by the Hermes. Circe's brickhouse ship approached to within three kilometers. Ulley's vision blurred, his thumb twitched. His heart rate raced. So much for medicinal warnings.

He took a sip of water from a flask strapped to his thigh. What if the Hermes were wrong—better yet, they just wanted the results of the Lotuthi concoction of roots and fungi.

Like the grand entrance of a medieval castle, expansive docking doors opened to a wide gape of endless darkness, inside a dragon daring Ulley to enter. He paused and studied his finger, unsure of why the fleshy extremity trembled, or even its purpose. He consumed Moly . . . or had Circe cast a spell? He was confused. Why was he flying to this odd spaceship? What was his purpose?

Square paned windows equally spaced across the broad length of the ship flared with flickering light, as if backlit with candles. He thought about a bowl of warm lobster bisque. A soup from ancient times, but he couldn't quite place exactly what a lobster was. The wooden bowl sat aside a porcelain tub for a warm bath, with genuine water, mists of steam rising up, a delicious decadence rarely seen on Ithaca. And Pennae, wet, naked, and climbing out of the bubble-filled tub glistening like a goddess in the faint candlelight.

Homer's voice crackled in his head. **Two minutes to docking.**

Ulley squeezed his eyes tight and clenched his jaw. His eyelids jacked open, dispelling the bizarre thoughts of lobsters and naked wives. The thoughts lingered, slowly dissipating as his ire rose. He needed to have a talk with the Lotuthi, learn exactly the hallucinogenic properties of the moly. Perhaps in a controlled environment the substance might serve a purpose.

He ran his fingernails down the front zipper of his uniform, until he grabbed the tab to zip and unzip the zipper. Up and down. Open and close. A marvel of mechanics. The greatest invention of mankind. Brought back to reality by the maneuvering jets spitting and hissing as the craft entered the docking bay's dark maw.

He spotted *Homer*'s other shuttle on the port side, dark and intact. The shuttle's landing skids thumped then whined as the traction hooks found purchase. A task instinctive as urinating, Ulley's fingers fumbled to unclip the pilot's harness.

He giggled like a schoolgirl as he floated through zero gravity to find the exit. He pulled on the door. The door was sealed. He was locked inside. He would starve of thirst. He giggled again.

All rational thinking had crumpled from ingesting moly. It didn't matter. Death was a little bitch. Death could suck his dick. He giggled again as he grabbed a handhold.

Ulley covered his eyes as the shuttle door opened, hissing a pressure variance like an angry snake. "Nope. Nope. I want to go home. Close the door. That's an order,"

He squeezed his face into the crook of his arm, focusing his ears for a door closing. The brief minute of time, conspired with endless centuries, and confused Ulley. Sudden gravity dropped him prone to the decking.

Did he eat too much root, not enough black stalk? Did the mushrooms contaminate the Moly?

"The mighty Ulley cowering at my feet. How delicious. Wet your tongue then lick them clean of the filth your species has wrought."

Ulley lifted his head.

Circe swirled above him like a malevolent faerie, wisps of cobalt blue light faded into bright silver, shades of crimson swirls. Incorporeal. Intimidating. The entity prodded his thigh with a bolt of pain. And again.

Ulley's anger blossomed, forcing him to stand, readying his arms with clenched fists, his face twisted with an enraged sneer. He spat at the faerie. "Hit me again, witch."

Circe's wisp of silver essence receded then morphed to wrathful shades of red.

"Release my crew, and we can talk. Otherwise, the nuke in my shuttle will send both of us to . . . to wherever we fucking go." Did he have a nuke? He couldn't remember.

Circe chuckled. "The guiles of Ulley are well known. A murderer to be feared."

Ulley swallowed a lump. Killer. A genocidal maniac. He was no such thing. He wavered as a rush of vertigo rushed over him. The shuttle behind him warped as if it were sliced into a thousand pieces. He was stoned. On moly. No. He was tripping balls on Lotuthi mushrooms. His eyes widened as the shuttle coalesced and reassembled. Circe retreated, on gossamer tentacles floating above the deck.

Ulley attacked, with two quick thrusts of his fists. But the ruse rang hollow, weak, and impotent.

A swirl of silver light and magical cold countered his assault, a storm descending to embrace him in freezing wisps of silk. "Would the great Ulley choose to dine at my table?"

A great burst of paranoia swept across him. Circe would throw him into a cauldron and stew him alive. Circe would suck the marrow from his boiled bones. The moly was ineffective, a ruse by the Hermes, to feed his flesh to their caged zoo animal. His dry mouth fought his swollen tongue.

Get back to the pilot's chair. Get the fuck out of this madhouse.

The swirling light floated close to hover inches from his chest. Long blue hair formed around a human head. A face morphed from a blank palate of flesh. Twin silver eyes opened. A pleasant pug nose formed above pouty lips painted ruby-red. Pennae. But not his wife.

"Is this more pleasing?" Circe whispered. Voluptuous breasts sprouted on the blank flesh of her torso.

Ulley's lips moved as if to speak, but no sound came. His eyes wide as plates, he could only manage a nod.

"Did the silly Hermes persuade you to ingest moly as a protective amulet?" Circe said. The wisps of silk swirling about thickened into a shroud, into a robe, settling as a transparent turquoise negligee.

His trickery discovered, Ulley continued to nod.

"A deception I have allowed the Zoosh to believe." She scoffed. "They are pitiful, arrogant creatures." Circe landed on the floor without a sound and held out her hand.

Ulley recoiled, scrunching his eyes, hoping the mirage would disappear.

Circe grabbed his hand.

Ulley took it back. "Promise you won't hurt me. Promise you'll release my crew."

Circe retook his hand. "Of course."

Too easy. Too fucking easy. Ulley blinked his eyes to stare at the face of an angel, his savior, his Pennae. "How are you doing this? Get out of my head."

Circe tugged on his hand, but his feet were frozen. She tilted her head with an expression of pity. "Did the Hermes tell you what I am?"

"An evil creature that needed to be defeated," Ulley said. His words sounded as if he should be playing a game of fantasy with Telly.

Circe laughed. A sound mimicking Pennae's boisterous roar upon hearing the well-timed punchline of a joke. "They play with you like children. Manipulate you for amusement. I'm defeated. I surrender. You have won."

Ulley slapped his cheek with his free hand, hoping the pain would clear the fucking moly from his head. Circe immersed him in the wisps of her negligee, whispering into his ear to relax, welcome her embrace. He struggled to escape her embrace until futility caused his muscles to go limp.

She led him like a child through her ship's dark corridors. She wasn't defeated. He was.

They entered a grand chamber shining with gold and silver platinum baubles. A great fire burned above a hearth of polished granite. Soup kettles hung on hinged metal cranes, waiting their turn to be licked by the flames. The scent of baked bread filled his nostrils. A long wooden table set with bowls and goblets and forks and spoons waited for a gathering.

Ulley rushed to the table and gulped down a goblet of fine cabernet, then found another goblet but tasted only a tiny sip of sweetness. He wiped wine-soaked lips and looked back as Circe grinned at him.

A wisp of recollection tickled his memories. Déjà vu, or the moly, or the fucking mushrooms, maybe . . . He furrowed his brow.

Circe swept her arms to offer the ornate setting, her smile unwavering. "Is this what you expected?"

Ulley checked the table, then concentrated on the hearth and fire. An impossible mechanism that nagged his muddled thoughts. How could wood smoke escape into the vacuum of space as if it were a simple campfire?

Circe pulled him to sit in a chair seated at the head of the long table, the elaborate embroidered cloth warmed him like the grand fire. Ghostly wraiths shimmering in silver and gold gowns emerged from polished stone walls and others descended from plaster ceilings decorated with ancient oil frescoes. The ghosts gained clarity, soon to resemble smiling handmaidens happy to serve their hosts as they placed bowls of soup, plates of fruit, oblong loaves of bread all across the table as if expecting additional attendees. More wraiths rose from the stone floor to place plates heaping with braised pork and lamb at the center of the table.

Ulley's nostrils flared with the sumptuous aromas. His empty stomach gurgled and growled. The hot fire gnawed as an impossibility. The abundant food that might feed his crew for weeks was but a trick. The servants an unknown species waiting for their chance to . . .

Circe would grant him a feast then dine on his bloated flesh. Ulley picked up a dull silver knife and checked its weight, confirming the heavy utensil wasn't a simple hologram.

Circe faced him as he stared at the weapon. "Is this not familiar to you?" She placed a light hand on his wrist, calming his violent thoughts wrestling with battle plans. She chuckled as she floated out of the room.

Ulley counted numbers of impossibilities. Fresh ripe cantaloupe and grapes. Animal flesh charred for consumption. Delicious red wine . . . A maiden poured wine from a decanter into his goblet, giggled at his lingering gaze then drifted away.

A tall man rushed into the hall, hailing for Ulley to beware witches and sorcery. Ulley squeezed his eyes tight and kneaded his fists and pounded on the wood table to stunt the visions. Except he knew the man as Damocles, a sailor on a voyage across a great ocean on Earth.

How did he know this? The mirage disappeared in a swirling mist, morphing back into the XO, Blaylock.

Circe appeared at his side, offering his goblet more wine. "Transitions can be painful. Ulysses conjured the ancient spirit of gods. Just as you."

Homer's missing crew pushed past Blaylock to swarm the table, shouting congratulations at Ulley. They swarmed the platters of food like uncouth swine. Plates and utensils ignored as irrelevant to their piggish feasting. The mannerless men and women repulsed him.

Anger drew his brow tight, eyes narrowed with indigence at their impoliteness. He slammed his fist on the table. Porcelain plates jumped, spoons and forks rattled from their settings. Firelight dimmed. The temperature of the air plummeted. Servants retreated into solid stone.

Circe steadied her hand on his shoulder as he rose to his full height. Mouths full of warm bread paused, fingers glistening with the grease of fatty pork stilled.

Ulley challenged each crew member with an unmistakable intention. Dominance. His and his alone. "Drop the food and leave the room. Now!"

Dissenting eyes were challenged. He lifted a sharp carving knife sitting aside a plate of mutton. The leather hilt felt worn and warm. The weight balanced precisely. A weapon for close combat. He followed the last of his crew out of the great dining room, twirling in his hand an object seen only in videos buried in the vaults of Earth's irrelevance. The weapon felt . . . right.

The mushrooms. The moly. The interstellar hallucinogenic trip wore thin as he watched the crew shuffle in front of him, heads drooped in defeat, a crew worthy of redemption, a crew deserving shore leave.

Ulley sniffed the enticing remnants of boiled pork. "Hold up. New orders." He cleared his throat and offered his hand back towards the dining room. "Show some respect. Watch your manners. And appreciation. Then feast."

At the sudden reversal, Borde turned around to push his way through the crew stung by Ulley's admonishment. He paused to look up at Ulley, and chuckled. "The Lotuthi spore can be devious. And you should beware. I'll sit at your table, Captain. Prim and proper like. Let that knife of yours cut only the gristle." Borde scurried back to the feast.

Blaylock led the crew past him, excited murmurs passing between them. The wraith maidens returned to dote upon the table bustling with hungry sailors. Ulley smiled thinly, satisfied by his actions. He returned to the head of the table, but his appetite had disappeared.

Circe waited by the fire, stirring soup steaming from a hefty iron cauldron, her ghostly appearance losing its transparency. Ulley was unsure what to believe, his eyes were suspect, his nose infallible, his ears pricked with the stifling odd silence of a reality dysfunction.

Circe ladled soup into a wooden bowl and served him. Her resemblance to Pennae was uncanny. Their eyes locked. The silver color of her irises was a single shade too dark. Her respectful smile remained guarded. Her red lips were too plump. Her rosy cheeks were a smidgen too blushed.

Circe was an enchantress, a sorceress, somehow using his memory of home and hearth to conjure a physical manifestation intending to settle his unease.

He ordered his Brainlinq to release the final drop of stimulants cowering in a corner of his neural patch. The stimulant clashed with the moly, dropping the floor from under his feet. He stared at an abyss of stars and galaxies, and nebulas mirroring ancient monsters of myth. Six-headed dragons reaching to snack on galaxies. Gargantuan tentacled kraken with gaping toothy maws consuming vast star clusters. Phemus reaching for . . .

"You should eat something," Circe said.

He looked up from the bottomless abyss to see rescue. Circe held a forkful of pork at his mouth, then tempted him like a child by tapping the greasy bite on his lips. He opened his mouth to eat then suddenly refused. The carving knife still waited on the table. His raucous crew enjoyed a genuine meal. He picked up the knife and tested the blade by drawing blood from his palm, testing the sharp point with a pinprick on his thumb.

Circe's pleading voice flailed from an abyss. He gripped the hilt and adjusted the correct aperture, then lifted the weapon to his temple. The point of the blade trembled to be let in. The force of his hand could finish the job.

Circe chuckled. "The great Ulley terminated by his own hand.

Your ancestors will laugh long and hard. Your prodigy will wander in bewilderment for an eternity."

Ulley pulled the knife away and stabbed it hard into the wooden table. "Out of my head, witch."

Repulsed by the admonishment, Circe rose high as a haunting swirl of silver light, transforming into a jumbled skeleton of human bones. Giggling servants gasped before receding back into stone walls. The table holding the sumptuous feast disappeared. Hands gripping pork or melon now empty. As one, the crew turned their surprised faces towards Ulley.

Ulley ordered his Brainlinq to inject another jolt of adrenaline. And another. Empty. Empty. Empty.

Deal with this alternate reality. Deal with it. Embrace it.
Or die from it.

CHAPTER 14

THE LUXURY OF THE SOFA'S supple leather was divine, unlike *Homer*'s couches constructed with a durable but coarse fabric that imitated a sheet of eighty-grit sandpaper. The thrum playing in Ulley's head was unabated. The feasts and orgies enjoyed by the ship's crew had finally waned. Circe played the role of a bordello madam with perfection, accommodating encounters between her handmaidens, encouraging the partaking of fine wine, but took no crap from any of the crew.

On too many occasions he rebuffed the enchantress's attempts at a seduction. Her body alluring, her aura without measure, her only mistake was employing the disconcerting guise of Pennae.

His mind foggy with wine, he could gaze deep into her eyes and press his lips against hers, fondle her perky breasts, commanding her nipples to stand at attention. Rationalizing his infidelity as mistaken identity, only to see his betrayal in the reflection of Pennae's eyes. Had the witch morphed into a beauty of unknown origin, Ulley may have begrudgingly succumbed to her charms.

His excuses only made her smile, a wry grin promising to wear down his defenses like an assault on the Troian defense spheres.

Satiated with wine and fruit, each evening he allowed her to escort him through the enormous brickhouse spacecraft with its maze of cavernous rooms stuffed with the remembrances of untold millennia. Ornate wooden furniture carved by master carpenters. Displays of varnished musical instruments sporting frayed horsehair strings.

Slump stone stairways leading into lower levels of priceless oil paint-
ings hanging unprotected on walls of damp plaster oozing wetness.

The deeper levels mirrored the suffering of human history. Photographs of war and destruction hung askew on the walls, still wafting
with the stench of death. Skeletons of desiccated flesh sealed inside
frayed military uniforms decorated with ribbons and awards. A level
with a polished stone floor glistening as if the minerals had been
glazed by a nuclear kiln. A monument to the Great War to end all
wars, for a thousand years, until the discovery of the Prometheus
Drive reignited mankind's zeal for exploration. And a renewed
passion for war.

Ulley found himself lost for hours in the tattered memorabilia of
the global nuclear holocaust, its cause lost in time. A destruction par-
alleling that of Troia's total devastation. A beautiful planet that had
offered hope and a new beginning to billions of people, decimated for
ego and power, or other silly reasons.

Circe's obsession with Earth's history had no limits. A lower level
displayed a statue of a beautiful man cut from flawless white marble,
a monument to someone named David. Busts of a one-armed woman
called Venus. Works of a charlatan named Galileo. Penciled render-
ings of leaning towers or last suppers.

Circe offered her guidance for the pieces Ulley paused to stare at,
her interruptions often waved away, not rudely, but introspectively.

He could spend a lifetime in Circe's museums and never discover
all that was meant to be discovered. Busts of men and women, many
damaged from time. Artwork and mosaics, glassware, and gold ear-
rings. Ulley peered closely at a Roman dagger stained with dried
blood, a line of gold coins beneath the ivory hilt, each imprinted with
the profile of a man's head crowned in a leafy coronet.

He thought of asking Circe for an explanation just as a bitter
brace of cold swept up from a staircase leading down to another
level. He turned his head just as Circe appeared over his shoulder.
Gone was the illusion of Pennae and now a swirling wraith, beautiful but featureless. The embodiment of an enigmatic sorceress. He
wondered of his hallucinogenic episode with the Lotuthi moly that
had shaken his concept of true reality. Could the witch sorceress be
feeding him her own batch of mind-altering drugs?

She blocked his path.

His eyes glued towards the staircase, he stepped around her.

She grabbed his arm. "A level not for you. You'll find only memories and gods. We should return to the hearth, enjoy the venison stew I have been simmering for two days."

He stared at her and narrowed his eyes. "What is all this to you? You collect memorabilia of Earth's history? Why? And only Earth? What are you?"

She stroked his arm with a tender whispery finger. Her silver eyes wandered, as if pondering how to answer. She looked at the staircase then led him down two flights of polished stone steps. At the bottom landing, she put her hand on his beating chest. "The nexus inside holds a special place in our time and my . . . heart."

Lamps mounted on stone walls fired, illuminating wet alkaline seeping from thick dark moss. An ornate coffered ceiling reflected the flickering light to dance over mosaics and frescoes of naked men and women. The cobblestone floor was slick with moisture and mildew. Ulley let his eyes follow the line of torches lighting the length of a great hallway, terminating in an abyss of indescribable dimension. He thought briefly of the hallucinogenic again, and the simmering soup waiting above. His rapid heartbeat began to pinch the muscles running down his left arm.

Circe took his hand even as she stepped back towards the stairs. "Come. Let's enjoy the stew."

"You haven't answered my questions," Ulley said. He released her hand and stepped deeper into the strange world.

Porcelain busts of bearded men lined the walls. Limbless naked women carved from white marble lined the opposite wall. Scarred shields of stiff bovine leather. Voluptuous monuments to the female physique. Brass swords and sharp tridents. Half-naked male warriors.

Ulley took each step carefully, studying every bland expression of the bearded warriors and reading the Latin carved on the thick base. Alexander. Apollo. Hercules. Names to tease his Brainlinq. He turned to scan the opposite side. Thetis. Aphrodite. Athena.

The names boggled his mind yet slipped off his tongue as if he knew each. With each step, another bust or display of gold coins, or displays of parchments of paper a breath away from destruction. A torch flared with Ulley craning his neck to read the title of a thick tablet of cellulose parchment. Ancient Latin words. Words elbowing him like a gust of déjà vu.

Circe pulled on his arm, telling him the meal was waiting.

Ulley shrugged her off. She hadn't answered a single question. And she didn't want him to inspect this dark level. He continued, inspecting a hefty brass sword leaned against the stone, bloodstained spears lay askew with pierced brass shields. A pile of brass helmets bearing feathered mohawks spread across the aisle as if a battle had taken place.

Ulley held his breath and studied a lengthy mural of a battle between Grecian warriors storming a city defended by stick figures wearing feathered Trojan helmets. He sucked in a breath and shifted his eyes to the next display. Artwork of an ancient black mammal ejecting warriors. Artwork of a bloody slaughter. He ran his finger along the edge of a shard of blackened wood lying beside the display.

The busts of men drew him closer. A flat-faced bearded man with a thick neck resembled Helmut Mintaur. A smooth baby-faced man with curls of hair flowing down his neck was the spitting image of Patro. Another bust with a cracked base held the likeness of Captain Hammer of the *Ajax*. The likenesses lined the great hall. The broken statues of topless women on the opposite side.

Ulley turned to locate Circe. "Who are these icons?"

Circe approached the bust of Patro and pointed. "Achilles." She stepped back and pointed at another. "Ajax." She continued down the hall, introducing the busts. "Agamemnon. The king of kings. Homer, the poet. Hector, the hero." She shifted her stance and pointed at a statue towering above her. A beautiful woman with locks of hair pulled into a coronet, her sad smile aimed down to those beneath her. "Helen of Troy. A face said to be so beautiful it launched a thousand ships." She pointed to a cast of a plump woman sitting on a narrow bench. "Cassandra. A seer never to be believed."

Ulley continued, stopping at an elaborate painting of a woman weaving a blanket, or funeral shroud, loose threads piled at her feet, a bright full moon shining through a tiny window, a furtive expression of discovery. He swallowed slowly and drew closer, ordering the lighting to increase, as if the Brainlinq could obey.

His mouth went dry at the impossibility. Yet he stared. His anger bloomed like a rose in the morning sun. The witch played with him like a cat might a toy.

Tender soft fingertips lifted his face. Circe said, "Continue."

As if commanded, he stepped deeper into the hallway growing colder and darker with each step. The buckled cobblestone floor rising like foils to his shuffling steps. A torch flared with a solar intensity. A single bust waited beneath, scorching white as if bleached, void of any chips or cracks that had scarred intricate details of the others.

Ulley leaned in to check the letters imprinted on the base, scanned the swirls of hair flowing down the nape of its neck, the point of its shaved chin, and stared at the blank white eyes of his own face.

"Odysseus," Circe said. "A man of timeless legend. A soul permeating the dimensions of time. One to study. To respect. One to host."

Circe's voice a distant dissertation, Ulley stared at the bust, its eyes, ears, the line of its jaw, the bushy brows Pennae might attack with a pair of scissors. An indelible mirage spanning thousands of years. And yet the face was his.

Circe held his arm. "Infinite threads of time rarely form a nexus. Go deeper to witness the trials of his father, and those before him. Be warned, it is speculation, as I had no interest in that period."

Ulley watched as firelight blazed in a perfect row, down into an infinite dark void, disappearing into distant galaxies and spectral starlight.

Circe fled. The firelight flickered but held firm. His past waited. A childhood of doting nannies sanitized by their loyalties to the king of Ithaca held no allure. Still. He turned to check an infinite row of busts. Pennae screamed from light years away. An admonishment to curb his impetuousness with common sense.

He inhaled slow and deep, then stepped into another dimension.

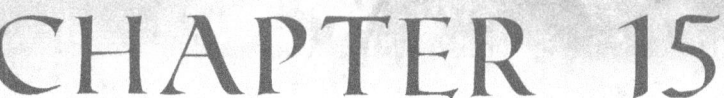

CHAPTER 15

PENNAE EASED THE HEAVY DOOR open, just wide enough to slip her face inside the room, careful not to make any sound. Her nervousness and anxiety were ridiculous. She could barge into the cramped room no bigger than a broom closet and bang on a snare drum, and it wouldn't matter. The patient inside wouldn't react.

She checked the patient's records with her Brainlinq, again, triple-checking his identity. She stepped in and let the door close behind her. The tiny room reeked. Pungent sweat of an unwashed body, and the unmistakable odor of periodontal disease common to the neglected veterans that had returned from Troia.

She admonished herself for her revulsion to the aromas. The patients had no control of bodily functions, and getting one to brush their teeth was a daunting challenge, and a monumental accomplishment if the caretaker succeeded. The veteran sat quietly in a soft, yet indestructible armchair clad in alumni-fiber cloths.

The veteran's shoulder-length dark hair was unkempt and riddled with gray. A natty beard infested with patches of gray. His brown eyes stared at a blank wall monitor, one of thousands recommissioned from storage bins, or forgotten warehouses, or basements throughout the Sol system. Dr. Fencic's attempt at a PTST treatment included pictures of children and wives, and vids of vacations, birthdays, and happy memories.

Another failed therapy treatment.

The fingers of the veteran's right hand twitched as if tapping an imaginary keyboard. His head shook or nodded as if acknowledging a voice heard only in his head then reacted with commands using his fingers.

Pennae sucked in a huge breath of stale air and charged forward. "Grooming day, Captain. I'm Pennae, your host for the festivities most men only dream of."

Dreams. Her stomach dropped with the inappropriate word. More like nightmares. "I'm going to give you a haircut and trim your beard." She eyed his forest of eyebrows. "And your eyebrows too, if you'll let me."

She waited for a response. Hoped to God for any reaction. She squeezed her eyes tight and continued. She extracted a pair of scissors from the grooming kit she received at the hospital's admitting desk. She moved behind him, raising the scissors above a head of hair snarled with neglect. The gargantuan task told her to run. The possibility of finding Ulley living in the same condition told her to keep cutting.

Pennae heaved a breath and shook her head, commencing a riotous work the man needed. She snapped the small pair of scissors in her hand. Scissors? The man needed shears.

An orderly dressed in pale flesh-colored scrubs burst through the door, fidgeting with an armful of supplies, distracted, as if intent on finishing a task. The young man with a shock of red hair tied up like a sprouting crown appeared only a few years older than Telly. A young man with blank eyes, still searching for his place in the world like Telly.

Pennae waited, speechless at the intrusion. The boy shook out an empty trash can from the lavatory into his recycle bag.

"Empty what doesn't need emptying," he muttered. He froze when he saw her.

"Something my husband might say," Pennae said.

The boy stared at her, checked the scissors in her hand, then huffed. "Yeah. Your sweet baboo probably rocked. A few more like you and . . ." He pulled the door open and fled.

Pennae shook her head in confusion and returned to the mission of snipping the tangle of hair, pretending the head was Ulley's. Remembering Ulley's hand rising to take the scissors away, find her lips to kiss and nibble—

The orderly pushed through the door and handed her an opaque bottle of water with a spray nozzle. "You should spray the hair first. It makes the tangles easier to comb and helps with the smell. Helps to spot any lice if he has 'em." He began to strip the bed sheets off the tiny bed with practiced strokes, balling the dirty linen into a laundry bag.

She thought of offering to help but the words were left unspoken. A thick crooked scar ran from his ear down the side of his neck alongside a thick artery and taut ligaments. Beautiful shades of turquoise and blue squiggles tattooed around his neck like an odd collar failed to conceal a nasty scar.

"Captain Hammer likes his ship tight," the orderly said.

Pennae swallowed her indignation. "Did you serve?"

"Fucking A right I did." He whipped out a stack of fresh bedding from a bag at his feet and dropped them on the bed.

"Thank you for your service," Pennae said.

"And fuck you for your . . ." The boy shoved the dirty pillowcases into a reclaiming sack. "Sorry. Sometimes I don't know how to act. Captain Hammer's ship was one of the first to run the gauntlet. The Troian's never stood a chance against the *Ajax*."

Long strands of wet hair falling quietly to the floor, Pennae felt the orderly watching her. "The tattoo around your neck? The Squiggles?"

The Squiggles. A unique geological feature of Troia, seven rivers of turquoise glacial water carving U-shaped canyons through a barren plateau to converge within a kilometer. From a low-orbit the rivers were described as the squiggles of a godchild scribbling blue crayons across a desert canvas.

The man nodded. "Heard about them?"

"Yeah, pictures before the war. Did you see them?" Pennae said.

"Not before a Consortium harpoon hit em. Our shuttle was sent to refill water tanks for the squadron." He shook his head in disgust. "I seen the pictures of them before. All those big rivers, all pretty blue and green, and turquoise mixing together in those sharp turns way down in those deep canyons. Just a big puddle of ugly mud now."

Pennae pointed the scissors at his scar. "How'd that come about?" Veterans were usually reluctant to talk about the war, but if she managed to get one started, it was often more therapeutic than any prescribed anti-depressant.

He chuckled mirthlessly. "You ain't got the time or the stomach to hear about my time at the Squiggles."

Pennae swallowed her imagining of a horrific scene, blood, and severed limbs, practiced and commonplace, traumatic for young or old. The boy wobbled and held on to the bed frame.

"I'm going to clip his nails now," Pennae said. The boy shook off his fugue and nodded. "I'm guessing by their length it's been six, maybe seven weeks."

"Nine," he said. "Nurses are scarce now. People don't care anymore. Help from the other systems ain't coming, not with the PTST."

The orderly was correct. Post Traumatic Space Travel had instigated a wave of fear of interstellar space travel, a standard of transportation for the expansion of human society. Trade ships and their crews were afraid of never waking up. Emigrants with families too fearful to risk everything they had. Explorers terrified of the possibility of never returning, with spectacular discoveries, or unimaginable wealth. The beleaguered leadership of the Consortium was engaged in a blame game for the rumored annihilation of a whole planet.

Pennae picked the fingernail clippings off the shiny floor and dumped them into the grooming kit. She pulled off the veteran's socks and blanched at the dirty feet maligned with yellow fungus. She felt the boy's stare behind her and soldiered on, starting with the soft pinkies curled like a tiny helpless fetus.

"Then you were spared the PTST?" Pennae asked.

He scoffed. "No. I got juiced with enough tranqs to forget I was even alive. The stasis pod fed me some dreams, and I woke up in a room just like this one. Maybe exactly this one. I don't know. Doctors and lab goons celebrated like they had delivered me out of the dark underworld."

Pennae pulled the vet's socks back up then used her hand to wipe drool sliding down his freshly trimmed beard. She paused and shook her head at her own revulsion. She wiped the spit across her smock.

The boy handed her a hand towel hanging on his belt. "The captain's still in there. Living in his own head, maybe partying with a few girls, hoisting a few ales." The boy swallowed, his scar and tattoos working together. "Probably running from the ghosts on Troia, screaming every time they catch him. The captain would've shouldered a lot of the blame for that shitshow."

Pennae blinked back tears as the boy's pained expression furrowed his brow.

He took the towel back. "You got time for a couple more patients?"

Pennae wiped her brow and exhaled. The last patient, a navigator on the starship *Synergy*, sat comfortably clean and shaven, staring blankly at the oblong wall monitor offering nothing but the glare reflected from a tiny window above the bed. The orderly rushed into the room and handed her a tube of hand sanitizer then waited with a fresh towel as she cleaned her hands.

He smiled. "The orderlies are talking about you up and down the corridor. Haircut and a shave by a beautiful caregiver, and all for free." The pain in his eyes had disappeared. His exuberance and life energy had supercharged his demeanor.

Pennae tilted her head and smirked. "If that's all it takes, then clone me and seed me into the solar winds." She held out her hand. "I'll be back when I can. I'll send you my contact info in a Brainlinq ping."

The boy's expression sank in disappointment. "That's okay. You know where I am." He turned to walk away.

Pennae grabbed his arm and asked, "What am I missing?"

The boy pursed his lips. "Don't have a Brainlinq anymore. Evil little devices have no place in a human brain."

Pennae frowned then nodded her understanding. Conspiracy theories concerning Brainlinq were commonplace. Propagated by users disaffected with the benefits, and dispelled by assurances of the Consortium.

Pennae released his arm. "I guess that's why I haven't been able to find out anything about you."

"Cool, isn't it? Still strangers. But working for the common good. Offers a bit of mystery and . . ." His eyes drifted up to the tiny window as if he wanted to escape. "A whole unexplored galaxy waiting for discovery."

She shuttered her eyes. Brainlinq pinged. A reminder of her

departure from the *Agamemnon* soon approached. The snipe hunt on Mintaur's ship, searching for information about Ulley, would have to continue another day.

She stiffened her back. "Not strangers. I'm Pennae. And you are?"

"I've heard of you." The boy beamed and held out his hand. "Romulus. Um, maybe . . . maybe you still want . . . need to hear my story."

CHAPTER 16

Romulus

I GOT TWO REALLY HORRIBLE days I'll never forget. The first started like any morning. Me and Cesare groaning and yelling at our Brainlinq alarms screeching in our heads. It didn't matter how many times we changed the settings; the Brainlinq knew better than to shut 'em off, but I think it was our father that squashed our modifications.

Time for another twelve hour day of zero G, spinning and twisting, cutting and torching metal, digging deeper into mangled ducts, or stripping out power conduits hoping to find the proverbial motherlode, one that might fund a citizenship for my family in one of the new habitats popping onto the radar each year.

The *Camper*, our salvage vessel—no, don't ask me how it got its name—it was a sailor's nightmare, or dream, depending on your perspective. My mother ruled the kitchen galley like a queen. I'm sure you'll understand that comparison. Loving, gentle, and iron fisted. My father was the supreme scavenger, finding gems of trash worth a few credits, salvaging the past for the future, but a tough taskmaster. And now I understand him a little bit, after years of reflection.

I'm sorry. I was trying to give you some context of my life before . . . before that big black Consortium ship snuck up on the *Camper* and demanded all her able-bodied sailors. What the fuck? Demand our water, or our oxygen, but sailors?

How dumb was I?

The Consortium ship squeezed my parents with threats and doom. Give up your sons and daughters or die. Cesare and I shouted the only practical decision into my father's ears: we would go. But the existence of our baby sister would remain unspoken.

That was the last time we would see our parents or little sis.

The storm-sailors issued us flimsy paper uniforms and shoved us into a platoon with other schmucks. Five learned kids kyped off a school shuttlebus zipping in for the Sicily habitat, a couple older girls taken from an encampment on the Sisyphus asteroid, an assortment of recruits, all ages, and genders, and not one volunteer. Seems they couldn't find any pirates and kidnap those guys. I guess crime did pay.

We got saddled with a lousy loudmouth platoon leader full of salt and vinegar, and a dying commitment to the glory of the Consortium. A zealot to the umpteenth degree, always tooting his own horn and saying he's gonna win the war single-handed.

I ain't gonna bore you with the bullshit and shinola young Ensign Roberts put us through. I ain't gonna turn your stomach with the misery he inflicted. But I'll tell you this: we got even, smacked his smug Martian ass down like a Martian cockroach. Zero G training. We was raised in zee-G, suckled our mom's boob in it, crapped, and pissed in zee-G cause we couldn't afford diapers or grumpy cubes. And one time my brother dared me to . . .

Sorry for the heavy sigh. Never mind. It don't matter.

Anyway, our prowess in zee-G got us noticed by fucking eyes we never knew was watching. I fucking hate the thought of being watched, graded like a salvaged motherboard, to be auctioned off to the highest officer watching. And after learning that little tidbit of intel, my brother went doozy. Screaming and threatening anyone and everything. I tried to shush him, but he wasn't having it. Until young Ensign Roberts zapped him with a plasma prod hanging on his belt that I'd never seen him use before. My brother fell like a gravity generator had just kicked on. His eyes rolled white and into the back of his head.

I reacted like protocols of vacuum asphyxiation kicked in, ones our father drilled into our heads for years. You know, seal the rupture, seal the escape of air, seal your chance to survive. I screamed as I lunged for that rod in Robert's hand.

And sank into oblivion, my brother's outreached hand just inches away.

Sorry, ma'am. I can play that memory on repeat and never find another choice that was offered.

Your warm gentle hand just scuttled my train of thoughts.

I scarcely go into these memories anymore. But I think . . . but what I think doesn't matter.

Oh, I understand that talking about my tour of duty might relieve the psychobabble trauma of war. Lady, you don't know shit. Sorry. But you don't. You need to hear this.

I can see you're fidgeting. Getting nervous. Thinking you're listening to angels flying or lunatics raving. But let me steer you back to the point of this story. And by the way, you are as beautiful as the scuttlebutt has painted you to be.

Don't turn away. Let me finish. My brother had been assigned to . . . the *Homer*. Hah! I knew that would sit you right back in that seat. No offense. But the meat of this story demands your undivided attention. Of course, you might not want to hear about the real meat.

Anyway, I served on the *Agamemnon* during the long stalemate with Troia. Working the transition bays, scamming newbies out of their rations, selling 'em bootleg booze and counterfeit narcotics before they shipped out to other ships. But the best thing was I got to see my brother a few times each year when the *Homer* docked for resupply.

No sucky wine or cheap beer for us when we got together. Only the best for my kid bro. And we'd toss back some banging ale, or window shop the aisles of Aphrodite with big ole grins welded to our faces, and always, always, argue about how many months he was younger than me. We didn't have clocks or calendars on the *Camper*. Time was measured by my mother's bleeding cycles, each starting every solar month for a couple of days, and I swear my mother told me she had six before losing the bleed with my brother's conception. My father didn't care. He was happy to have another son.

Anyway, our last reunion had my brother talking how great the captain of the *Homer* was, a chill dude, an ice miner from Ithaca, a scrub working the vacuum just like us. Except my brother was the ship newbie, and had to take the shit, both literally and figuratively.

Anyway, I get reassigned to the *Ajax* as a specialist to handle plasma tanks feeding the tubes fueling the guns. Saw right off the idiocy of the system. Zee-G has its advantages with plasma, but the higher-ups couldn't see anything other than their next promotion.

Anyway, our victory over the forces of Troia was broadcast into all the Brainlinq's, the whole fleet. I jumped and yelled, "Oh yeah, oh yeah, let's go home!" Except the war continued.

The ships impenetrable bulkheads designed to mitigate an impact from a harpoon opened wide. The tiny slut of a duty officer controlling the antimatter bombs went bonkers, dropping munitions as fast as we could reload. It all turned into an orgy . . . bombs and beams everywhere . . . well . . . I mean, the sailors manning . . . I mean the fucking . . . no.

You get the idea.

The chance for your chosen ship to depart home turned like a roulette wheel. Always black when you need red. You never knew who was gonna get the lucky number. But I had no destination. Maybe I'd find a ride to a settlement. Send a broadcast sweep hoping to locate the *Camper*. Maybe the old wreck might brighten with my signal. But five years was a long time for my father and mother to survive without our help.

Anyway, here's why you're craning your neck with impatience, fidgeting like I'm going to force feed you pig shit. Anyway, I got ordered to a detail intending to replenish the stale ass water onboard the *Ajax*. Simple. Quick and out. And the thought of stepping foot on Troia and seeing what the fuss was all about made me a little excited. And was it worth the effort?

I still won't answer that question. Not because I can't but because . . . well . . . I shouldn't.

Three shuttles from different ships landed in unison. Inside a crater surrounded by slippery-sloped mud and the ugly slop of a river wider than five shuttles put end to end. I stepped down the gangplank first, not as an ignorant newbie eager to die from a laser blast from a defeated enemy, but because I had never experienced real gravity, real air, the smell of dirt, or fresh water on any planet. Boy, I was disappointed. Nothing but mud and ash as far as you could see, all the way to the rim of that crater caused by the kinetic harpoon. I thought the pilots must have made a mistake. My shoes sank into a four-centimeter layer of mud—nasty, smelly gunk, really. Probably why I didn't see a spec of life growing anywhere.

The other retrieval teams pushed on. I had a strange desire to remove my boots and wiggle my toes in that gritty goo.

Bango, the ensign in charge of our team, snickered as he tapped my shoulder. He handed me a particle mask to keep me from breathing the ash still raining down. Didn't help much with the stench of death and decay though. He pointed at a huge, coiled hose waiting on the loading platform and ordered me to drag one end down to the water. Bango was the first. Dumb, by the book, and just waiting to be eaten. But that's getting ahead of myself.

The other shuttle crews started the same procedure with their own suction hoses.

And that's when I saw him. My freaking kid brother. I mean a vast endless universe and there he was, at this place, at this time. We dropped our hoses and ran to each other like we was five years old. Laughing and hugging and ignoring the angry shouts behind us. Bango and one of the other officers, a clown with carbonite pincers for hands. A genuine bozo.

Anyway, we drag the hoses about ten meters down a steep sand embankment crumbling beneath our feet, then another five meters to the shoreline stacked three feet high with charred timber, melted plastic siding, and shattered composite roof tiles. We figured it was the remnants of a tourist visitor center, or maybe a nearby town. It would take all day to tell you about the half-buried clothes, or the little kids' dollies with mud for eyes, you name it. The remnants of Troia were well represented. I ain't even gonna describe the piles of skulls and human bones, so you better appreciate that.

The muddy river water looked no different than the wet sand. And dragging that hose over the heap of trash and into that quagmire they called a river was like extracting salvage out of a gravity well. Anyway, three Consortium grunts pulled three heavy hoses out into a river to suck mud. Except—and you'll want to sit down for this—a tall officer with a beard and long hair pushes past the bozo and Bango standing on the embankment with their hands on their hips, like kings surveying their kingdom.

The guy was the pilot of the *Homer's* shuttle, I'm pretty sure, but he don't look so good . . . No, just wait . . . He looked like a lot of officers did . . . like the Consortium had drained their blood or didn't feed 'em. Dark raccoon eyes, you know. I mean, if the officers of that shitshow fleet weren't being fed, what chance did the rest of us have? But I heard later that officers responsible for how Troia looked like could . . .

Heck, look at my friend the Captain sitting there. If I had any responsibility for pulling the trigger for that clusterfuck fleet, I might've just spaced myself. Anyway, that pilot comes hopping down the soft sand of the embankment like a bunny, like the sand was a playground.

You're smiling like you think you might know the pilot. I'm gonna stop you right there. I don't know who the pilot was. Only that the shuttle flew out of the *Homer*, and . . . anyway . . . the guy helps my brother pull the hose to reach a ribbon of blue water in the muddy water. The hose bucked and bounced then stiffened as the shuttle pumps kicked in.

Bango and the bozo scrambled on the embankment, shouting for my brother and the other guy to mimic what the pilot and I just accomplished. Fucking shmucks should have helped.

The pilot laughed at me, not malicious, not superior, like a job well done for the grunt. An officer us grunts could appreciate . . . Anyway . . . anyway . . . I think the shitstorm started then.

Give me a minute . . .

I gotta tell you something . . . no human . . . ought to hear or experience . . .

That canyon we dropped into was the remains of the Squiggles . . . You heard of it. Nobody alive hasn't heard of the Squiggles. Seven rivers carving through deep canyons, each with a color born from icy mountaintops and thick forests . . . and ancient gods, each painted a squiggle across a blank canvas plateau until a great convergence into a liquid rainbow . . .

That would have been a sight to see.

All I got was mud and misery.

The clown with the pincers points out a tight line strung from the trash heap and into the embankment like a half-buried fishing line. But ain't nothing left alive in that water. He could've stepped over it or just left it alone, but the clown steps on it with his big clumsy boot. Ring the dinner bell, he did.

It didn't take long for the locals to assemble.

Hard mud blew up from burrows hidden in the embankment, like hundreds up and down the river. Bango screamed as he was yanked down into a pit by knotty, scabbed hands reaching up out of holes we never even saw. Dark, camouflaged burrows like a trapdoor spider might weave. Spiders would've been easier.

They start ripping flesh off his cheeks and shoving it into their mouths. I mean the guy is screaming and getting eaten at the same time. Hungry cannibals. Yeah, that's right—cannibals. Ratty and feral people climbing out the burrows brandishing sharp sticks. Or that's what I thought.

But they was bones whittled into spears and such.

Emaciated people wielding bone tomahawks and driftwood carved into scythes.

I was frozen. I couldn't believe what I was seeing. My brother too, but that pilot grabbed the collar of my tunic and yanked me out of the water. The mud sucking at my boots like a devil needing to be fed.

I ain't turning my back on you . . . I just need . . . a minute.

Maybe another lifetime.

Yeah, that pilot saved our air. My brother climbed out of the water then over a ridge of timber and trash. And froze. The clown with pincers was surrounded by the cannibals, spinning around, back, and forth, jabbing his pincers at the locals. I think I might've laughed at the absurdity.

Anyway, a shuttle lifts off, then another, suction hoses flying like snakes in a windstorm, and I'm thinking the fucking cowards ain't sticking around. Instead, both turn ninety degrees and let rip a stream of hot projectiles, into a horde of cannibals rushing at us from downstream. The pilot doesn't move, blinking his eyes real slow and twitching his finger as the shuttle guns spread fire among those cannibals.

Yeah, I need a break, but your touch on my arm ain't gonna relieve my horror. I'm gonna finish this so I never have to repeat it. And never relive it again.

I rushed to my brother, grabbed his neck, and dragged his sorry ass towards the only ship sitting still. The pilot's ship. Sitting idle out of harm's way as its pilot stood on that pile of trash like a general, ducking tiny bone arrows aimed at his head, directing the fire burping out of the other shuttle. I think he took command of them both using Brainlinq.

Man, oh man, if I could replicate that fucking . . . heroism . . . I'd be a vid-hero living life . . .

Then one of those bone arrows sliced me across my neck. I slap my hand on the wound, but I start squirting blood everywhere. My memories start to fade there. But I can still see that pilot dragging me up the gangplank. My brother punching on me to stay awake. The weight of liftoff squeezing my innards.

Anyway . . . I was knocked out, stitched up, and shoved into a stasis chamber for the trip home. And the funny thing is . . . that arrow saved my life. My Brainlinq was cut open along with my throat, and the docs had to yank out its tendrils infecting my brain. Or I'd be just like Captain Hammer. And you'd be trimming my fingernails.

Sorry for laughing . . . but picturing a queen grooming my nasty hair and nails is kind of funny.

No. I never talked to my brother again. I mean, without a Brainlinq it's almost impossible to send messages, or get 'em. But he's alive . . . I mean, if he's serving under a badass captain like that pilot then . . . well . . . he's probably the ship grunt but a valued one. And that was a long time ago. This ship is my home now. I got nowhere else to go, no other family. And I'll do what I can for the guys that can't do for themselves.

Yes, ma'am. My brother's name was Cesare. I think Mom and Dad liked old names that sounded royal. Cesare and Romulus. Something got mixed up.

And I sure hope your husband gets back. Maybe he knows about Cesare. I gotta hope.

Hope is all we got.

CHAPTER 17

THE HIGH CATHEDRAL CEILING CHISELED from the central cavern of Ithaca's founding asteroid echoed with a cacophony of a bustling courtroom. The chaotic noise raked Telly's ears. A charred noise reserved for criminals and pirates. A proceeding he'd rather not attend.

Mother squeezed the muscle of his arm, her anxiety and trepidations flowing into him like water.

Two men and a woman in their pristine white robes entered the courtroom through a side door, shuffling past the empty stadium box reserved for jurors and executioners. The stone gavel hammering the tiny wooden stump caused Ithaca's attorney, Mr. Rain, to whisper something into Pennae's ear, and she nodded. Telly waited for the message to be passed down but nothing was offered.

Pennae stood stiff and stoic. Her auburn hair pulled back into an intricately woven braid, her sulfur-yellow robe ironed in immaculate creases and delicately screened with a shear white cape just touching the floor. A silver chain and modest black diamond adorned her neck.

A tug on the coattail of his tight suit unworn for two years made him turn and glare at Helen. He couldn't blame her for wanting to hear everything the lawyer whispered to their mother. Helen didn't trust the squirrely faced Rain, swearing a little voice in her head said not to. But Helen was almost eleven now. Time for her to grow up, see the world as it truly was.

Telly shook his head in exasperation. She scowled then raked her blond hair over her eyes as if to hide.

At least a hundred people had crowded into the chamber designed for thirty. The wormwood pews stuffed with onlookers. Telly wrinkled his nose at the muggy, sour air. The difficulty of recycling warm human exhaust without constant replenishment from storage ice played like sandpaper on a violin for the growing crowd. Each weekend he would drop down to Europa and extract cores of ice to replenish the purifiers, not the lengthy cylinders his father challenged himself with, but short cores or loose clunky shards easy to tow in zero G, to guide each into the empty coffers of Ithaca. But it wasn't enough.

The gavel smacked again. Telly shot Helen a cautious face over his shoulder, ignoring her feet shuffling across the patina of sand coating hard slick floor. A ploy designed to strictly annoy him.

A thin man in a red robe fronted the dais and waved his arm across the air as if to dispel demons and fairies, murmuring a cryptic Martian incantation. The courtroom fell into silence.

"Oh, please," Pennae scoffed.

Mr. Rain placed a hand on her arm to settle her. Telly watched Rain's long finger stroke the fine hair on Pennae's wrist, the saggy flesh beneath the man's chin almost quivered with excitement, his beady eyes that of a snake charming its prey.

Helen prodded his backside.

He turned and hissed a warning. "We lose everything unless Mother works her magic."

The gavel struck like an opening applause to begin the proceeding. Settling disputes of property. Dictating possession of ownership, or disposition of water stores, finally the meager possessions of a vagrant found awarded to an undeserving jurisdiction.

The gavel pounded again. Telly wiped sweat from the back of his neck. The crowd had multiplied, pushing through the double doors to stand shoulder to shoulder.

Mr. Rain took a vacant seat before the tribunal, waving Pennae to join him. Telly rushed to follow her only to find the two open seats filled by Rain's sycophants.

He was almost sixteen and deserved to be up front. He offered his hands and mouthed, "Mom?"

Pennae offered a seat behind her just as a swarm of gadflies scrambled to take the empty chairs.

The gavel struck like midnight. Telly retreated to stand aside Helen. She kneaded a nervous, sweaty hand into his.

The gavel struck again to quiet the murmuring accusations of piracy and fascist government overreach. Ithaca's people, Ulley's people, would not stand for anything less than total satisfaction for Pennae.

The old woman jurist, a JMA circuit judge, sat between two feeble old geezers, entitled men from Earth that had probably never set foot on a habitat, let alone challenge dangerous asteroid fields, or survive a micrometeorite strikes to their EV suits and spill precious air into the void. The old men sat as judges to questions they had no right to ask. Shouts of "Space 'em" or "Traitors" hidden deep within the crowd made Telly smirk.

The hammer barked against the stump again, the woman jurist shouting for order and quiet. Telly was sure she would find neither.

A tall man rose and waved skinny arms and called for order. His cheeks sunken from a life in low gravity, his black robe hung like a curtain over his skin-and-bones physique. A cave-dwelling Martian.

The room hushed as the gangly man stumbled from behind a table crowded with more Martians. He nodded to Rain as he approached the high ornate bench. "I would offer to the court the expulsion of the gallery. For—"

The crowd erupted. Fists and anger stabbed into the air. Screaming mouths ejected slurs and epitaphs. Martian scum. Consortium spies. Telly knew them all.

Pennae stood and raised her hands to demand quiet, never looking at the gallery.

The gavel banged like a silly toy resisting a hurricane. And banged. And banged.

Pennae lowered her arms and sat. The gallery softened. His mother played the role of an offended queen perfectly.

The chief judge banged the gavel, again, and again, until the room quieted enough for Telly to hear a burp of air escape from someone in the crowd.

The judge stiffened and waited for quiet. Her nods waved off bailiff bots intent on ejecting hecklers. She hammered the gavel like Hephaestus forging the armor for immortals. Her wrinkled face stretched tighter with each stroke, hammering the target like a woodsman until the stump splintered and gave up.

"Let's get on with this shitshow," she said. "Mr. Martian, offer your pleas."

The Martian stood, raising his face as dismissal to the hisses. "This proceeding is simply a formality. The statue of limitations for rebuttal of the contractual lien placed on Ithaca has passed. The Martian government has filed a petition to lay claim as a debtor in situ."

The gallery hissed, the warning of an angry snake.

Rain stood and objected.

The judge banged the gavel again. "The next outburst, and I will clear this room." She let her words simmer and gain flavor. "Mr. Martian, we are aware of your claims. Somehow you have jumped the line of others claiming the same prize."

Mr. Martian nodded deference. "Regardless of the mechanics, the Martian claim on Ithaca is prime and valid. And the court has no choice but to rule in our favor."

Rain objected. "Your Honor, the rightful proprietor of Ithaca, a war hero, a loving husband, a father, has been given no chance to address this matter. The court should stay the matter until his return." He sat down.

Mr. Martian scoffed. "Your Honor, the rightful proprietor, Ulley, *formerly* of Ithaca, has had ample time to respond. Over five years have elapsed since the Troian victory. Officially declared missing in action by the Consortium military high command. Affidavits from comrades in arms attesting to his demise. Ulley is dead. Dead. Dead. Dead. A mythical figurehead for the raucous contemptables' crowding this very chamber."

Hisses filled the chamber. Telly joined in.

Rain whispered in Pennae's ear then stood. "Your Honor, this is not a simple case of receivership, or even life and death. My client has endured the ultimate betrayal of that Troian war farce. Losing a husband, and a father to her children, and finding herself defending her world against the bloodsucking Consortium, and the Martian contingent, and . . ." He raised his hand. "And Ithaca continues to provide the solar system's best care to the veterans still arriving from Troia. Martians included." He shot a look at Mr. Martian.

Hisses again.

Mr. Martian remained unflustered. "Ithaca's response to the plague of PTST is commendable. But the absence of Ulley remains the legal point of this proceeding." Hisses. "Ulley shall be declared dead, killed in action if that better suits the snakes hissing behind my back. But five years since the war ended and not seen on this very soil, he is dead. Dead. Dead."

The courtroom exploded like a boiling Ganymede volcano. Muscled dock workers waving hefty wrenches pushed forward to find Martian blood. Greasy-faced drillers joined the assault. Bailiff bots immobilized the dockers with intense shots of electricity. Mayhem rioted around Telly as he pulled Helen closer. Fists flew, and blood squirted. Telly sidestepped a splattering on the floor. The screaming aggravation of a pounding gavel faded into flesh beating flesh.

Telly pulled his sister to kneel beside him, her wet cheek brushing against his own. He covered her head with his arm, her feigned revulsion seeming to reestablish their relationship. He pushed her head even lower.

Blood and wood, wrenches and glass flew above his head like rogue asteroids. Pennae bullied her way through the madhouse and snatched Telly's arm in a death grip. Telly winced at the pain. Helen recoiled at the anger contorting her mother's face. Her flowing yellow robe unbuttoned at the front, she spread her arms to shield them.

Her dour expression warning of worse to come.

Sharp, splintered wood stacked against a rear wall and marred by the scorch of lightning weapons waited like tinder for an unlit bonfire. Pristine marble floors dulled by the shower of water from fire sprinklers remained precarious footing. A flimsy workbench replaced the marble dais.

Telly seethed as he waited behind his mother, the same courtroom, the same bullshit of his father's death, or life, the same fucking bloodsuckers limping into the courtroom and trying to take his home.

Pennae's formal attire was soiled and stained with blood and soot, her white cape wadded in a heap at her feet. She held out her hand for him to stand aside her. Her infuriating smile gleamed wicked white teeth like a sorceress calling for his soul.

She waggled her fingers again and barked at him to stand beside her. "Enough is enough."

Telly swallowed and stepped to Pennae's side.

Mr. Martian hobbled into the room, his tattered clothing wet and rumpled. He checked the court surroundings, followed by a contingent of Martian special forces clad in black and armed with plasma prods spreading into the disarray of an empty gallery, checking the doors and exits as if trouble lurked.

Rain cowered next to Pennae startling at every door opening, covering his head with any crack of wood. His mother was defended by a coward. And she didn't see it. She was clueless. Living a fantasy.

Telly switched positions, bumping Rain to step aside, glancing at the lawyer's face. Perspiration dotted his upper lip. His wide blank eyes stared forward without blinking. Then a blink and another and another, an involuntary threepeat of the chemical 3B's, an addictive drug plaguing habitats on the outer rim.

Telly nudged his mother and twitched his face toward the addict. Pennae shushed him like a five-year-old. Telly sneered.

The grand proceeding was bullshit. Judges deemed supreme by a hegemony millions of miles away, casting edicts on Ithaca, a legacy built with centuries of hard work and suffering, only to have some frail old humans . . .

A bailiff bot stumbled to the makeshift bench on a single leg, supported by a fully extended arm. Two more mechanized bailiffs joined it.

The battle-weary judge struck her gavel with three quiet taps.

Mr. Martian stepped up behind a makeshift table constructed with slop buckets and a splintered door slab. "Your Honor. My client has endured enough humiliation and subterfuge regarding this matter. The matter is simple. Declare Ulley alive . . . or dead."

A quiet settled on the nearly vacant courtroom like a subtle, mist. A shard of wood kicked by another bailiff bot approaching the bench warned of another miscue.

"Your response, Mr. Rain?" she asked.

Rain winced at raising his arm then sputtered. "Well . . . um . . . we need . . . you can't . . . Ithaca has—"

Pennae cleared her throat. "Your Honor, I will speak for Ithaca. Ulley is lost but alive. Our citizens have . . . um . . . displayed their resolve in this matter. Now let me add my breath to this fucking vacuum of injustice. Mars wants our ice mining operations. The Lunar colonies want the air our ice produces. The Consortium wants control . . . plain and simple, regardless of which puppets they choose to use, and regardless of your decision." She offered her hand at the destruction littering the courtroom. "A small sampling, Your Honor. Ithaca is a sovereign entity, bound to the JMA by treaty. The JMA has recently signed a binding agreement with the SMA. The Saturn Moon Alliance and all its habitats along with the JMA will resist this, this . . . Consortium incursion on Ithaca sovereignty."

Telly groaned at his mother's divulgence of critical information.

She ignored him. "Ships continue to arrive from the Troian system, stricken sailors welcomed to the facilities on Ithaca. And the *Agamemnon* parked outside." She chuckled with a scoff. "But only the Martian sailors are carried home, maybe too good for the trauma treatment centers critical for PTST recovery. Mr. Martian should be ashamed. Mr. Martian should be assisting us instead of robbing us."

Objections and slurs. His mother stood tall, resisting the winds of defeat whipping back and forth in a legal onslaught.

Suffocated by the relentless banter, Telly finally pulled Pennae's arm and shouted, "Tell them! Just fucking tell them."

Pennae craned her neck backwards and hissed air. Uh oh. She would kill him. Shove him into an airlock and open the exterior door.

His gut sank as if zero G invaded. He held onto her sleeve like a toddler.

"Your Honor, my son, the rightful heir to Ithaca, wants me to tell you that if you rule in the Martians' favor, your judgment may light the fuse for a war with the Consortium. You've witnessed firsthand a sampling of the anger of Ithaca's citizens. Hundreds of other habitats will join the fight at the word of Ithaca's sovereign heir."

Mr. Martian shouted denials as he sneered.

Telly inhaled a deep breath to resist raising his middle finger at the interlopers. His father would have placed a heavy calloused hand on the back of Telly's neck as a warning. His father would've winked, acknowledging Telly's restraint. His father would never allow Pennae to speak for the frustrated resistance gathering steam throughout the Jovian system. His father would have a thousand things for Telly to observe and learn what it meant to be a leader.

The gavel clapped, hollow and tired, the adjudicators were weary and torn. They offered Mr. Martian a final summation. His long-winded litany of contractual law, subsections of paragraphs, historical precedents. Telly thought of a thread streaming viral through the Infonet, coined as a Ulleyism, in honor of his father's heroism on Troia.

Dazzle the masses with diamonds or baffle them with bovine feces.

And Mr. Martian employed formidable diamond-encrusted grumpies. Pennae shouted, her face flushed and stern at the Martians' accusations. Rain slinked away, leaving his mother as an angry lioness, her fingers twitched as if she resisted leaping for the Martians' throat. Mother's beautiful sublime face revered throughout the Jovian habitats. She narrowed her eyes, and aimed lasers at the prey, offering a lick of her lips, a predator relishing blood and satisfaction.

The judge tapped the gavel again. "I don't think anything else we hear will change the facts. Pennae, we understand your pain and position. Nothing we say will ease your burden. The Martian Colony arguments are compelling. I . . . We only wish Ulley were here to defend Ithaca's contractual obligations. I have no doubt he could compel this court to dismiss the Martian complaint as a bold-faced power grab." She inhaled, her chest expanding, and she released the breath. She winked at Telly then feigned wiping dust from her eye. "We are unanimous in sending this case to the Consortium's Supreme Court for final disposition."

She pounded the gavel once.

Mr. Martian erupted with accusations. Conniving. Biased. A kangaroo court. The appeal would take a minimum of a solar year. With the ultimate decision not in doubt. He charged the judges' table, followed by the Martian security men. Bailiff bots surrounded the makeshift bench and raised lightning defense rods crackling with intense energy.

Mr. Martian threw his hands in disgust and turned to leave. He locked eyes with Telly, his black iris implants zeroing in on Telly's eyes, calculating unimaginable revenge. His nostrils flared like an angry bull. Telly raised his middle finger then waved bye-bye with his other hand.

Pennae slapped his hands down. Then slapped his arms, his shoulders, then his chest then stilled an open hand aimed at his cheek. "Do you, young king, understand what has just happened? Tell me. So, we both understand?"

The heat rising from his cheeks lifted a sneer. The questions his mother asked demanded his silence. He shrugged.

Pennae kissed his hot cheek then embraced him. She held him tight and whispered into his ear, "You beautiful fool. You have just placed a huge target on your back."

CHAPTER 18

PLUMP CARROTS, STRINGY CELERY, AND chunks of potatoes filled a wooden bowl of simmering broth wafting with the tantalizing aroma of charred animal fat. Ulley's mouth watered, but he refused to pick up the whittled wooden spoon to consume the meal. He wondered if Circe had laced the soup with hallucinogenic mushrooms, or maybe strange chemicals mimicking the effects of the reality-altering moly. The witch had been nothing but a proper and gracious host. Ulley eyed the spoon again with a twinge of guilt for the lack of trust.

Circe's immense ship would not be explored in his lifetime, or two. She . . . It . . . was a creature of immense mystery. Consistently giddy at Ulley's presence, doting on him like a new bride. But the isolation imposed by the Zoosh seeped from her pores like subtle poison. She would stop at nothing for him to remain with her, offering succulent meals untasted for millennia, the rich knowledge of forgotten libraries, offering him a lifetime of pleasure and carnal knowledge.

If only he would stay.

Blaylock dropped his substantial girth on a long bench aside the dinner table. He sniffed like a hound, waited a moment before retrieving a bowl of soup to steam beneath his face. He inhaled the unparalleled fragrance like fine aged wine. They locked eyes. Ulley slid the spoon over.

Blaylock slurped chunks of vegetables into his mouth. "We should drop buoy markers on this position as a waystation for weary travelers." He picked up the bowl and drained the remnants. "The crew want to go home. Well, most of them but those that don't figure to be sent to the slaughterhouse if you're not here."

Ulley stared at a divot peeled from the tabletop. "Have you ever wondered if you'd lived before? Like thousands of years ago?"

Blaylock wiped his mouth with the back of his hand. "You mean like Vikings or Romans?"

Ulley waved his hand. "Before that. The dawn of human civilization. The Greeks. Cities and governments. A formal language to spread a world of discoveries. Metallurgy and farming. The creation of a mythology to govern human existence."

Blaylock placed the bowl softly on the table, his eyes searching for another helping of food. His ignorance confirmed by his silence.

Ulley continued. "A Greek mythology of gods governing love and death, rudeness, and ill manners, all transgressions judged by a fictious deity offended by the slight."

Ulley snatched Blaylock's spoon tapping rudely on the tabletop as if he was demanding service. "Do you hear what I'm saying?"

"Sure, Captain. Some of the crew thinks Circe may be fattening us up, for . . . you know . . . use us in a different kind of soup," Blaylock said. "If you know what I mean."

Ulley shook his head in exasperation. "Where is the status report for the *Homer*? The crew evaluations. I asked for them weeks ago."

"I uploaded them into the ship's servers. The duty officer can verify but the Brainlinq system is acting screwy so maybe you missed the transmission. You've missed a lot lately, being busy with the hostess and all."

Ulley snapped the spoon in half and threw it to the floor. "Then provide a verbal synopsis. Right now!"

Blaylock widened his eyes. He brushed a tiny bit of carrot off a uniform unlaundered for months. He pushed the bowl away and stiffened, as if he regretted his subordinate rank. He made to stand, pushing the bench legs to screech across the stone floor. Ulley ordered him to sit. Blaylock's observation of Ulley's continual absence was noted, and undisputed. He beckoned with his fingers for Blaylock to continue.

Blaylock cleared his throat. "Synopsis? Easy. We're fucked. Fuel for the drives down to fumes. Our fusion reactor is losing integrity, and we couldn't escape the gravity of an inert moon. The patterning nodes for the Prometheus drive are suffocating from a lack of helium. He chuckled and licked his lips, staring at the empty bowl. "The navigation is fried. The EMP we employed for our escape from Phemus may have scattered his brains, and our navigational system with it." He closed his eyes and shook his head. "Captain, we are lost in an ocean of space without a sail."

Ulley nodded. The information was nothing new. Homer had indeed transmitted the dismal report. The psyche of the crew was another matter. Blaylock confirmed what he had believed. The crew was on edge. The crew wanted to return home.

Ulley stood. "XO, assign our crew the necessary tasks to make the *Homer* ready for travel. Fly aboard the *Homer* and ease her into a port on the lower dock of this vessel."

Blaylock stuttered and rose. "Will Circe accept the *Homer*?"

Ulley scoffed. "We'll see."

Sometime later, Circe flittered into the dining room like a butterfly, landing at the firelit hearth occupied by a kettle of soup and five loaves of bread. Her form coalesced into Pennae as she served soup from the cauldron. Ulley chuckled.

Circe paused the serving spoon in her hand to look over her shoulder.

"My crew think you're going to chop them up and serve them in a soup. I couldn't think of a reason to dissuade them. And here we are . . ."

"Feeding you and your little piglets." Circe chuckled. She kept busy setting out loaves of sliced bread, softened butter, nectar rich peaches, and succulent pineapple filled serving plates to surround Ulley's bowl.

Ulley grabbed a slice of bread to dunk in the soup then left it to soak. "That tour you steered me through was haunting. I don't know if what I saw was real . . . or your magic."

She held his hand. "You saw your destiny. As it was then, and it will be again."

Ulley pulled his hand away. "I saw a world that can't exist. Sailors rowing wooden ships on a pristine ocean. A man who looked a lot like me. An island ruled by a beautiful woman. The similarities playing out perfectly, like one of your tricks. And I was the ghost, watching, observing all their . . . relations." Ulley took the spoon and drowned the island of bread floating in the bowl. "Your psychedelics won't work on me. This soup won't find my lips. Or your water, your fruit."

Circe chuckled and pulled the bowl of soup to begin slurping and chomping on vegetables and meat. "I simmered this soup for two days, just for you, and now you throw it back in my face." She scoffed and shook her head. "As stubborn now as you were then."

Ulley grabbed her wrist and squeezed. The pain caused the illusion of Pennae to flicker for the slightest of moments. The hurt sent cups and utensils flying across the long table. Her hurt offered eyes of submissiveness to Ulley. A woman chained by a tortured hope he may never truly understand.

Ulley released her. "You're a traveler through time. That's why the Zoosh are afraid of you. A dimension they don't control. So, you wait in this system until—

"Until I die . . . or the quarantine is lifted. And I see both of those as impossibilities."

Ulley pulled the empty bowl of soup beneath his face and inhaled. He eyed Circe. Demure and innocent. A curious look. A simple anticipation of his tasting the broth. He chuckled with the absurdity, then lifted the bowl of broth to his lips and sucked down the deliciousness, letting his tongue snake across the chunky remnants holding onto the bottom. "We're leaving. The crew has made repairs to get us home."

Circe chuckled. "My dear Ulley, you go nowhere without me. Didn't the tour of your past tell you anything?"

"It told me nothing. We might have fucked like monkeys ten thousand years ago. And we might have come to an understanding. But the past tells me nothing. The future is fluid. I could slam this bowl and crush your skull and then what . . . the next rendition of Odysseus and Circe pop up in a few thousand years?"

Circe lowered her eyes. "What have I done to deserve this treatment?"

"For one, you've taken my wife's beauty and corrupted it. Two, you have made my crew fat and lazy." Ulley inhaled deep, to calm his exasperation.

Circe didn't deserve his misplaced anger. He wasn't quite sure what thorn had poked him. Circe showed him a past life, one filled with moral dilemmas, failed trickery, blind ambition, murder, revenge, and worst of all, infidelity to his wife and children. But that was ten thousand years ago, a different age, different codes of conduct, different actors.

"I apologize," Ulley said. "I'm still sorting through what you showed me."

Circe looked up, blinking back moisture gathering in the corners of her eyes.

Ulley looked away. "Why did you need to show me that? Another man's life in another time."

Circe wiped her eyes. "Because it is the reason the Zoosh have banished me. Those pissy little creatures think I might travel back in time to prevent their ascendence in the galaxy. You've seen how much influence I have. A few trinkets, books, faces of marble. Returning those to this vessel took eons of subtle manipulation. Diverting a reality stream is impossible. But they don't listen or believe."

"Then come with us. Once we fold space to return home, they will have a hard time tracking us," Ulley said.

Circe chuckled and reached her hand to find his. "That is the best offer I've heard for ten thousand years. But no. The Zoosh would be waiting when you exited the wormhole terminus. And destroy the *Homer*."

Ulley scoffed. "Sounded good though, didn't it? And besides, we have no idea exactly where we are. *Homer*'s navigation system is fried."

"I'm sure my vessel can provision the *Homer*, supply fuel, but the course you travel is beyond my knowledge. However . . ." Circe winced as if a bee had stung her skin. "How much of Odysseus did you observe?"

Ulley shrugged. "Mostly you and . . . ancient me. I found his relationship disloyal to his wife. His motivation to return home was almost insulting . . . That wasn't me, even in a previous life. Impossible. As he allowed some horned ram sheep thing to board his vessel and take a grumpy all over the deck. That was enough."

Circe squeezed his hand hard. "If you would have continued that journey, then you might have heard me tell Odysseus the only way home would be found in a place no living man could endure."

"Guess I should have stayed for the credits," Ulley said.

Circe pulled her hand away and stood. "You mock me still. You arrogant heathen. Maybe you should fold space and find the center of a neutron star."

"I've considered that," Ulley said with conviction.

"Yet you won't because destiny demands you continue Ulley's odyssey. Then and now." Circe swirled into a silver tempest. Incandescent sparks blistered the stone walls, hot, angry wind buffeting his face. Ulley turned away from the storm then found the room dark and forbidding, the glow of embers dying beneath a cauldron of soup.

Pennae stood naked before him, her breasts alluring, her hourglass figure shaped with supple skin. Ulley swallowed hard and took her in his arms, checked her eyes matching Pennae's, checked the dimple on her chin, the jagged hairline on her forehead. His groin grew uncomfortable.

Pennae whispered in his ear, "Destiny demands this."

CHAPTER 19

THE SOLDERING TOOL SMOKED AS hot liquid titanium bit into the shattered connections on the navigational control board. Lying on his back, Ulley's reach up beneath the navigation console had found its maximum. He dabbed more metallic flux on chips and circuit boards to reroute damaged pathways. Isolated from the air purifiers, the compartmentalized system had collected a fine patina of dust, but the mundane work was thought to be the perfect distraction. Except it didn't work.

His thoughts drifted back to his liaison with Circe. He tried to rationalize the indiscretion as an aftereffect of drug-laced soup, or Circe's immaculate impersonation of Pennae, or the trippy adventure traveling back ten thousand years deep in the bowels of her ship, or maybe the lack of sexual contact for a decade. Maybe all of them contributed in one form or another. But his rationalization boiled down to his own human weakness, regardless of the temptations.

And he had been tempted plenty. As the teenage heir to the Ithaca habitat, young adolescent females, and a few boys, invited, tricked, and even bullied their way to take his virginity. The escapades thrilled him, like he was the flag in a game of Capture the King, never conceding, never giving in to the fantasies of teenagers. If he capitulated, the game was over, the winner would broadcast a Brainlinq announcement to the entire habitat, bragging of their accomplishment of ascending an unattainable peak. A communication sure to be heard by the young seamstress, Pennae, and her mother, who sold extraordinary knitting in the public square every second week.

Why should he care? She probably hated his guts for destroying her kiosk with that silly half-pipe roll on his gravity board. And yet he returned week after week, gathering info on the beautiful brunette girl three years his junior. He would graduate from higher learning school before she even enrolled. She might even emigrate to another habitat, induced by incentives to increase their population. She was a game he played by himself, his virginity for her love as the ultimate victory in a game he relished playing each day.

A series of taps above his head paused his soldering. A pair of mag boots waited for his exit from the tight access door. Borde. He would wear heavy mag boots like a pair of loafers at a lakeside wedding.

Ulley shut off the tool and shimmied out. The mechanic loomed like a frosted giant. His long beard white from the overspray of deck insulation, his face red, and ringed by an oval indentation of too-tight oxygen mask.

Ulley wiped his hands on dirty trousers Circe had provided.

"We really going home, Ulley?" Borde said. A hint of hope in his voice.

"Phemus beat us up pretty good, but that's the plan," Ulley said.

"I got three shifts working repairs. Fusion fuel tanks ready for pressurization. The main jump drives' patterning nodes are growing mildew. I don't see us refueling anywhere close by."

Problems. Problems. Problems.

"Let me worry about that," Ulley said. "Send Soliel up here to help me reinitialize these mother boards."

Borde furrowed his brow then tilted his face. "Captain, we shoved Soliel into a stasis chamber after the battle with Phemus. You knew that."

He stared at the soldering tool, tiny wisps of smoke rising to the air intake grills overhead. Impossible. She had cowered in his cabin during the encounter, naked and scared. But attempting to console her during that fraught encounter was impossible, it had required every ounce of concentration to get the *Homer* out of danger.

Ulley offered his hand to Borde for help to stand. He licked his dry lips as he stared at Borde. "Your father is Tremblay. My ice tug pilot. The best I've ever seen." He lowered his gaze to stare at the floor. "I'm sure he told you a few stories, about me, about my father even. And being a befuddled memory care patient would not have been in his repertoire."

Borde retreated a step. "Captain, she piloted one of the shuttles. She went looney tunes out there with Phemus. You knew, Captain. I know you did. We figured you might feel guilty and didn't want to talk about it."

Ulley pulled the trigger on the solder gun to heat the tip. "Then where was I? Where was the incident report? What happened to all that?" He touched the hot tip to his palm and let the skin burn, squeezing his eyes shut as if hoping the pain would wake him from a bad nightmare.

Borde took the hot tool from Ulley's hand. "The crew figured you would decide what to do with her when the time was right. Maybe honor all the sailors we lost to Phemus. Nobody's faulting you, Captain. It was nobody's fault."

"I don't feel guilty about anything!" Ulley said. "Now get out."

Borde raised his arms in surrender and stepped back out of the room.

Ulley scratched at the scab on his palm with a fingernail, like a weevil intent to bore into a tree. Soliel had been in his cabin. Naked. A faint reminder of the pleasures of flesh waiting for him at home. The terror and fear in her eyes a stark reminder of *Homer*'s impending doom.

He scoffed at the horrendous decision to fold *Homer* across the galaxy, just to escape his guilt. Simplistic and immature. But guilt could gnaw like a termite. A lesson to teach Telly if he should ever see his son again.

A simmering bowl of stew was placed beneath his face, the steam wafting delicious aromas of beef, or maybe mutton, the broth thick with carrots and potatoes. A golden goblet brimming with red wine placed before him made his eyes lift.

Circe offered the soup, then said, "Drink. I have no potions in this fine cabernet. You need to release, how do you say, the grumpy—no, the cob stuck up your anus."

Ulley couldn't help but chuckle. He gulped the delicious red grape juice mixed with nectar and fermented to perfection. And asked for more. And more. Circe doted on him like a mother happy to have her child home again.

"Sit," he said. "Time for you to enjoy some truth juice." He placed the goblet at her place setting to his right.

Circe didn't move from the hearth. He tapped the goblet as if asking for more wine. She hurried with a bowl of wine and poured. He pulled his goblet away at the last second. The waterfall of wine froze before splashing over the table.

The wine was quick to take hold. "I knew it. You don't want to drink with me."

Circe placed his goblet beneath the frozen waterfall. "I want everything with you."

"Then sit. Tell me everything about you. What you are?"

Circe placed a bowl brimming with red wine near his goblet. Ulley eyed the gesture suspiciously.

"I am a witch," Circe said. "A sorceress. A nymph. A goddess. Banished to this place by ignorant spiteful gods. I am immortal,"

Ulley held his hand up for her to stop. "And I am lost right now. Figuratively. Literally. And after our . . . mutual spiritual communion even more confused. So, spare me the esoteric explanations you give to pirates and wayward space travelers who get caught in your sticky web of bullshit."

Circe beamed loving blue eyes at him. Her lips pursed, as if a memory had crossed her thoughts. "You're right. The Odysseus who once held my heart with his every movement, every word, could see through any fog I might have conjured. Even with your sweet smile, your intense green eyes the color of an ocean reef, your gentle hands, the resolute command of your voice, the scars on your chest and arms, the tickle of your beard, the ability to enlighten my soul, to flutter my heart as the dinner hour brings you back to this table, you remain a timeless anticipation of my Odysseus returning to my island, and my bed. But you are correct, a timeless Odysseus would easily see through my . . . bullshit. But the games the gods play have burdened you even greater than the man I loved."

Ulley resisted his better judgment and gulped a huge portion of wine. Circe joined him, conjuring a matching goblet and levitating the bowl for it to pour its red wine. She drained the goblet, wiped the red dribble running down her chin, and slammed the cup down with an intensity rattling the sturdy table.

Ulley took her hand, and she twisted it free to take his. Her fingers went rigid. Her eyes went black as night. He pulled his hand, but her grip was viselike. He stared at black orbs, deep wells sinking endlessly into her stern face. Ash sparked from the wood fire then froze. Dust motes stilled. His other hand on the goblet wouldn't move. The hand entwined with Circe's burned as if a flames consumed it. Firelight spawned spooky shadows, elongating across the table as if each sought entrance into another realm.

He knocked over the goblet as he stood. His heart raced. Nothing had changed. Not the table, the bowl of wine. Circe sipped her wine demurely, like the suspension of time never occurred. He grabbed the goblet from her hand and quenched a thirst he hadn't known before.

"Sit, Ulley. Hear my story and learn. Time is a god no one can challenge. I was born in a world both beautiful and treacherous. My father was a Titan who commanded the movement of the sun, or so he thought. My mother found no love for me. My sisters and brothers bullied me, ridiculed me, spat salty water in my eyes for their amusement. Tormented by gods, and nymphs, daemons, and my own consciousness.

"I learned to walk among them and never be seen. Sit at my father's feet and never be heard. I was pitied and reviled. But time was kind to me, as it always has been, and sent a mortal such as you, bare-boned, scarred, and fighting the wind to feed his own mouth. But the man noticed me. Talked to me with adoration and love that would never be reciprocated. And he was the first one I changed with my knowledge of plants and spells forbidden by the gods. Plants to manipulate. Spells to conjure. My new calling opened me like a flowering rose. My second spell captured my sister Scylla in all her horrible glory."

Circe smiled. Her eyes stared off into a dark corner, as if reliving a memory. "She had stolen my first success and manipulated him into dismissing me, shunning me even as he pursued Scylla. But she wouldn't have the simple demigod beneath her stature and he fled. I plotted my revenge. Scylla stepped into an ocean pool to bathe, cool inviting water I had sprinkled with hemlock and incantations. I stood above her as she glared her righteous entitlement. I cast the spell those thousands of years ago. A spell was nothing more than a wish, an affirmation, a belief that the Fates would grant my desire.

"Scylla rose naked from the pool to push me away, but I could see my magic had started. Her plump bottom blossomed, her arms cracked bone as they lengthened to below her knees, her legs split like tree branches seeking sunlight, her neck . . . sprouted six long necks, sprouted six ugly faces baring fangs glistening in my father's sunlight. I couldn't move. The horror I created stared at me with twelve eyes, bared six sets of sharp teeth. I closed my eyes and waited for a death from the monster my spell had created."

Circe looked away. The remorse shadowing her face demanded more wine. Ulley filled her goblet and ordered her to take a long pull. She sucked the cup dry.

"Scylla saw her reflection in the pool and disappeared into the ocean. Good riddance." Circe offered sad eyes to Ulley. A woman dying to pour her heart out.

He poured more wine into her cup.

"Why are you here?" Ulley said. "Here and now?"

She looked at him with surprise. "For you. I was banished to an island for my transgressions. Alone, I found a peaceful simplicity in nature and would live my immortal life walking among the olive groves, squishing my feet in the soft sand of beaches, reveling in the surf pounding against the rocky point guarding my tiny enclave. Happy and satisfied. Until Odysseus arrived."

Ulley pushed the wine goblet out of Circe's reach.

"A mortal god he was. Men feared his bark, reveled in his laughter, but his greatest weapon was a conniving guile that might slice through hearts, and minds. Like all mortals, his gifts would turn sad and fleeting.

"In time, mortals grew weary of Titans and Olympian gods, conspired for new deities to worship, and the immortals grew weary of the human addiction to war. We abandoned that place, seeking new worlds, new species to conquer, dispersing throughout the galaxy. Hephaestus forged metal ships for those gods that couldn't cope with the cold, infinite vacuum of space, but those were few. My banishment remained. My punishment quarantined in this magnificent ship, even as I followed Zeus and the others into the void, visited only by the occasional traveler, or pirate.

"For thousands of years, the gods changed incrementally, their immortality made them especially susceptible to evolution. The mighty Zeus, the ruler of the Zoosh. The Hathena are a species subjugated by the once-mighty Athena. The Hermes remain a microcosm of the god who birthed them. The lineage of Olympians and Titans spread as an incestuous diaspora of evolution.

"My evolution manifested into a mastery of dimensional time manipulation, and it frightened all of them. My pharmacological knowledge evolved, comforting my eternal loneliness. Roots grew as unsolvable equations, herbs flowered as a finesse of quantum mechanics, spells of witchcraft opened portals into time and space. The Others have a right to fear me."

She grabbed the goblet and drained the last of the wine then stood and shouted, "Because I could wipe their existence from this universe with the snap of my fingers!"

Ulley had listened to bragging boasts of drunken men hundreds of times, often lifting his own drink to acknowledge the foolishness of men skewed by alcohol.

Circe reached for the bowl brimming with wine. He placed a gentle hand on hers and offered to pour. She shot an angry look at him, as if unaccustomed to being denied.

The room rumbled. An angry hot gust erupted from the dark ceiling, winds spinning into a maelstrom of death just a few feet away. Ulley held on to the edge of the table. The fire died. Shadows elongated into snake-like necks. Tin cups flew, and goblets disappeared. The table rumbled, rising, inching to join the maelstrom.

Circe stared at their hands still joined, her mindless eyes reliving a history he couldn't comprehend. He offered a gentle squeeze. Then another.

The table settled on its legs. The storm subsided. Bowls fell and rattled across the stone floor. Spoons fell back to the table like a riotous downpour. He squeezed her rigid hand gently then began to massage her knuckles with his thumb. Her fingers curled inward and kneaded her palm.

She blinked slowly then offered her own beautiful gray orbs. "My apologies. A side of me so few have seen. Or dare to see." She pulled her hand away and slapped at the tear dripping down her cheek.

"Maybe they should see. A beautiful goddess isolated light years from worlds where her knowledge could be gifts to all. The Zoosh, the Hermes, they couldn't stop you. You would be welcome on Ithaca. Pennae would love to show you around . . . except . . ."

Circe chuckled. "But what?"

"Um . . . do you really look like . . ." He circled his finger to indicate her face.

"Does this bother you? Is it not what you desire most in your life?"

"It is. She is. And Telly, Helen. Have you any children?"

Circe flinched, then poured wine into her cup. "More than you could imagine. Children are both a blessing and a curse. And I'll experience neither again." She sipped the wine then winced, as if the cabernet had turned bad. "I think it is time for you to leave, return home."

Ulley picked up his overturned goblet. The cups, utensils, flower settings had magically returned to their places. The hearth fire flared. Pleasant aromas swirled around the table like happy ghosts. "Just like this cup, our engine fuel is almost empty, our patterning nodes for the Promethean Jump Drive will be growing mold soon. So as much as we'd like to go home, we can't."

Circe took a sip of the wine then licked her lips as if the fragrance tasted exquisite. Her eyes turned gray as if cataracts had rushed to take her eyes. "Prometheus still lives, his destiny undeniable, fire or fold, chained to wander the surface of a miserable planet, his flesh burning with each sunrise, only to regain form in the darkness of the planet's moon. I should visit my old friend, set him free. Brace myself for more punishment of the immortals."

Ulley snapped his fingers. And again. "Then show them." He snapped his fingers. "Show them what evolution has really made you, what you've learned, and . . ."

Circe scoffed. "I've challenged my own father, my mother, to break the ancient punishment I am bound to. And you are a mortal. You can't understand."

Ulley did understand. "I lived like a fox. Caged in a zoo. I tested the wire fence erected by my father when he ruled Ithaca. I stole shuttles and tugs trying to reach Earth. The illusion of planet-side freedom called me and . . . I know it's not the same, but freedom is a universal desire."

Circe smiled thinly. "Thank you. That is the most genuine offer I have received in millennia." She stood. Her facial features began changing, no longer Pennae's unique features but the beautiful vibrant face of a prepubescent teenager with flawless skin, sparkling eyeshine, sleek blond hair descended down her back to her waist. "My true appearance, what I was borne to. Your questioning of my illusion intrigued me. I haven't seen my true face in thousands of years."

She stroked her own flawless cheeks, her fingertips searching every fold between her nose, her eyes, tracing her fingers down to her lips, running her finger along the top lip and across the plump lower lip, as a Lolita desiring to seduce Ulley.

He couldn't swallow. A bowl of wine inches away waited to wet his mouth and throat.

Circe chuckled demurely. "That was not for you."

Ulley's lips trembled as he fumbled to ask the beautiful young witch . . . anything.

Circe swirled about the room, dancing as if in a grand ballroom, her arms raised to a blue sky disappearing into an inexplicable spatial void, returning for a swan song of ballet pirouettes. She smiled at Ulley. Malicious, or benevolent, but her smile frightened him. "Much of the fuel you need can be found here."

Circe swirled again, then floated over to offer him a closer look at her virgin face. She licked her plump lips and gave him a peck. "The fuel for your Prometheus engine can be found in a place I am not allowed."

Ulley nodded. "The Prometheus nodes require special fuel. But we will take whatever help you can provide. Thank you."

Circe turned to leave. "Don't thank me yet. Your course is set. You need to find an entity and earn his star charts to find your way home."

"Wait." Ulley reached for her, but her physical form held nothing but her ethereal light. "What do you mean . . . earn?"

Her whispers followed as she disappeared through the solid wall. "Nothing enters Hades Nebula without an invitation."

Streams of fresh water poured out of the rock to shower his face and down his chest, groin, and legs until he shivered from the sudden termination of the hot liquid. He grabbed a towel and dried. A fresh uniform waited beyond the shower. He shook his long hair like a dog, spraying precious liquid into the air.

Homer was ready to depart. Blaylock and the crew were walking on eggshells after he gathered the crew in the loading bay to spell out the situation. No choice: find the star charts and gather the fuel to sail home. Circe's ominous admission was deleted from his speech. Two crewmen adopted from the escort ships consumed by Phemus had asked for permission to remain. Both disappeared into the bowels of Circe's floating island after her shrug of indifference. Their fate would not weigh on his concern. Choices were made. Choices to live and die with.

Homer's choice was to sail on, into a vast unknown, mirroring his own thoughts. Hades Nebula. A bedtime story his grandmother had told when he was six years old, had mentioned Hades. An evil being to beget more evil beings with just a touch. Zombies. Ghouls. Ghosts. Demons with eyes of fire. Grandmother's apologies for the unintended fright were accepted, but he had not forgotten her words.

His destination constricted his throat and shriveled his genitals even after the relaxing hot shower.

Vast clouds of dust and debris, nebulas were shunned by space travelers and Others alike.

CHAPTER 20

THE MASSIVE BLOT OF THE *Agamemnon* maintaining a stationary position fifty kilometers distant from Ithaca's central loading docks filled Telly with indignant trespass as he waited for his Mother on the elevated viewing platform. Dwarfed by the backdrop of Jupiter's colorful ribbons of swirling gas outside the viewing dome, the warship waited as a malevolent sledgehammer. The aft portside railguns reportedly decommissioned, the portside plasma beam emitters and laser cannons remained aimed menacingly at Ithaca. Blinking red lights flashed as a warning for incoming freighters and shuttles. The dreadnought recommissioned as a hospital ship for the treatment of thousands of sailors returning from Troia and stricken with the insidious PTST failed to play its role convincingly.

Two trips accompanying his mother into the mile-long ship had been benign and uneventful, though Telly's security escort's green-tinted skin had solidified his underlying suspicion of the Consortium's true intentions. And his mother deserved an envoy, or at least a junior ambassador as escort, instead, Ithaca's formal representative received a squad of notoriously obvious assassins.

The pitted landscape of Ithaca's founding asteroid stretched to a dull horizon backdropped by Jupiter's magnificence and conjured a memory of an impromptu field trip into undeveloped caverns with his father. A place known to but a few. A place of multiple dark levels accessed by crawling on their bellies.

He didn't hear her approach. Pennae placed a tentative hand on his shoulder. Telly swallowed his pride and grasped her cold hand without turning around.

"You're cold," was all he could think to say.

Pennae scoffed. "Well, at least you're talking."

Telly released her hand. The remnants of their constant arguments and infighting surfaced.

Pennae took his hand again. "I'm not cold. I'm your mother, and if we disagree—"

Telly groaned. "No, I meant your hand. But see, this is why we can't talk. We exist on two totally different levels."

He felt Pennae inhaling with exasperation. An insignificant act yet one turning up the flame on their pot of simmering disagreements. Telly resisted the urge to tell her to fuck off and bolt into the main corridor bustling with families and children intent on visiting veterans on the *Agamemnon*. He imagined his father would craft an exit with more elegance, more dignity, yet serving the same purpose.

She squeezed his arm, hard and painful. "You are just like Ulley. Impetuous. Your sneaky smarts are just a tool to serve your purpose. Go, Telly. I'll tell your father about your silly fool's errand when he comes home. Go. Go." She stepped back but still held on.

Telly scowled. Finding the truth was never foolish. Understanding the truth was even harder. "Still going, Mom."

She pulled him back, her face a mask of sadness and capitulation, a hydra of expressions and emotions. Pennae heaved a breath and gazed at the procession of magnetic storms of lightning swirling on Jupiter's surface, each dwarfing the behemoth *Agamemnon*. She blinked twice then squinted like bright sunlight had invaded her vision.

She leaned in and whispered in his ear, "Euma is always trusted."

She pulled back as if sending a child to college. She giggled mirthlessly. "I'll be an old woman when you return."

Telly swallowed a knot in his throat. "It's not like that, Mom. The Prometheus drive is almost instantaneous. I'm fifteen now and it's only a year or two, maybe. The fold makes the trip easier than a fusion-drive journey back to Earth. You've done that. Dad told me about it when I was a kid."

"Will you reconsider getting a Brainlinq before you go? I can keep up with what you're doing?" Pennae asked.

Telly exhaled as the old familiar argument resurfaced. "Not happening. I told you the Oracles say the Brainlinq is behind a lot of this PTST crap. And I believe them."

Pennae growled. "The Oracles are a bunch of conspiracy theorists that spread deception and rumor. A cult determined to indoctrinate young people into regressing from the future. What they spew—"

He turned on her. "Is perfectly possible. And probable." He pointed his finger at her face. "If the threads I read are only half true, then the whole solar system is about to go to war with itself, Mom. Just suspend your Brainlinq-guided judgments and read the Oracles. It's why Dad hasn't come home."

She waved him away and turned to leave. "How do we get in touch with each other?"

Telly held up a shiny rectangular device fitting perfectly into the palm of his hand. "Old school, Mom. I see only what I want, read only what I want, talk to only who I want. I'll send you my address if you want to send me a message. Send it through Euma as a buffer. You said I had a target on my back."

Pennae massaged her forehead for a long minute. "Troia still your destination?"

Telly brightened. "One stop before we hit that system. If Dad folded the *Homer* into it, I'll know it. Prometheus drive quantum signatures are unique and timeless." He bit his lower lip.

"Just going to leave your mother all alone to fight the bloodsucking Martians converging on Ithaca to take your birthright?"

Telly chuckled. "Good one, Mother. But that guilt trip won't work. I have no doubt you will battle those Martian fucks from the airlocks and into the hallways and even onto this viewing podium." He stiffened as if to hide his gangly adolescence. "But it doesn't matter until we find the truth. Ithaca's future demands the truth. I want the truth. And . . . I hope . . . you do."

The device in Telly's hand pinged. Euma spoke. "The freighter *Spartacus* is calling for the final boarding."

He spied his companions, Resto, and Ariadne, waiting for him by the exit.

Pennae groaned. "The *Spartacus*? That tub won't make it out of orbit."

"She's refitted with the latest patterning nodes for a Prometheus fold. The captain is an old friend of Dad's, and we trust him."

"We? Who else is going with you?"

He flicked his chin towards his companions. "Resto and Ariadne. Resto's mother hasn't come home. Ariadne's brother is wasting away on the *Agamemnon* along with a thousand others."

"Without a Brainlinq, how can you even function?" Pennae pointed to the behemoth dreadnought dwarfing two ships approaching Ithaca's port. "Communicating with ship officers, monitor navigation vectors, even open a grumpy cube for the recycling? Please, I'm begging—"

Telly shook his head. "Brainlinq is dismal. Even you might be corrupted. Tell her, Euma. Tell her now. But over the handheld."

Euma cleared its throat, its overt mechanism of hesitation. Long seconds passed until its voice erupted from the handheld. "Pardon me for the lag. I shunted a Brainlinq interface for this conversation. Queen Pennae, what Master Telly hypothesizes cannot be rebuked. The Brainlinq neural interface has evolved for centuries. The device was conceived on Mars to facilitate and alleviate the fatalistic errors and computing bugs infesting their terraforming project. The bio-link's success and the harmony following in its wake facilitated the widespread dissemination of the tiny nodule. Brainlinq spread into the vast reaches of the galaxy. Brainlinq is deemed a standard innovation for all humanity."

"Euma, tell her that last line again," Telly said.

Telly judged his mother's face as it did. She remained impassive then shuttered her eyes and shook her head.

Telly pulled his lips tight as he kissed her goodbye.

Ariadne playfully squeezed Telly's butt and fled down the long main corridor of the *Spartacus* loading bay, skipping like a happy toddler. The warm humid air was fragrant with animal flatulence.

The door for Cargo Bay 101 slid open, disappearing into a hidden pocket within the interior bulkhead. Telly stepped inside, and the door whooshed shut behind him. As big as an Ithaca school classroom, the bay rumbled with pens of hairless porcine piglets rummaging and pawing in a thick layer of black viscous sludge. The distressed bleats of fuzzy lambs confined in wire enclosures made him move closer. Overhead lights brightened, and he winced as if staring into the Earth's sun rising above a morning horizon. He shaded his eyes to let them adjust. The stench assaulted his nose. The zoo waiting for him lifted a smile. Doe-eyed calves. Innocent lambs. A coop against a bulkhead was stuffed with flaming-red feathered chickens guarding fire-red eggs, some strutting and pecking on a floor riddled with feathers and feces.

A door whooshed open, and the burst of fresh air rattled the animals. Hooves tap-danced on the desiccated vegetation. Snorts of excitement chorused from the piglets. The fuzzy lambs crowded a corner of their enclosure.

"Please begin the work." A human sized bot said. Outstretched in each mechanical hand, the servitude bot tapped the deck with the wrong end of a shovel and the sharp fork of a rake. Looking comical wearing a straw hat, the rudimentary labor droid sported a stout titanium frame, mimicking the toughness of a mining bot. He beckoned to Telly for the tools to be implemented.

The robot's clear plastic head flashed tiny red and white lights from processors beneath the hat then tilted its small face, as if processing new instructions. "These creatures are yours to care for. The price of your journey." The robot tapped the wrong end of the shovel again. "All waste into the recycling bin."

Telly blanched as he grabbed the shaft of the shovel. Relegated to a pauper cleaning stables, maybe his mother was right. Maybe. Except the lacquered wood in his hand was exquisite, but the weight of the rusty metal blade felt unbalanced. Telly surveyed the stable, considering where to begin his massive chore. Striding to the largest pen, the yearling bovine calves watched him with wide paranoid eyes.

The cargo in the loading bay yard was worth a fortune. Captain Douglas was smart at hiring Telly and his companions to mind the rare precious cargo as it traveled within the black void of the fold. Two hundred seventeen days to the planet Sparta, refuel, and onto Troia.

A bovine released a load of runny feces to splatter across the deck, joining tens of other patties. He sneered at the unpleasant flatulence.

Long hours passed and Telly wiped sweat from his brow as he

leaned on the shovel. The lamb feces wasn't bad but that might change as the lambs grew. The chicken coop was a nonstop battle to scrape and toss the muck out of the pen before one of the crafty little hens could make an escape. And the little red eggs were his. Part of the travel agreement. He could eat them or allow the hens to hatch their own children, but those additional burdens would add to his ledger, a provision included in the transport contract.

Telly walked to the bay door and took a suck of water from the wall nipple. One down, two to go.

Ariadne set her cup down, then wobbled in her chair with a sudden shift in the floor. She floated up as her hand grasped at an empty cup doing cartwheels above the table. Telly held on to the table bolted down in the tiny cubicle assigned as his living quarters. Waves of vertigo washed over him as a flashflood of plates sticky with synthetic cheesy mac, forks, and spoons tumbled into his chest then retreated.

The gravity generators had failed. Again. A possibility he had never expected. He released the table and spun up to grasp a U-shaped handhold mounted to the ceiling. He caught Ariadne and slowed her spin. Her dirty blond hair wild and free. He pulled her close to smell coffee on her hot breath. Her warm hand began massaging the inside of his thigh.

"Zero-G gymnastics is supposed to be amazing," Telly said.

Ariadne pushed her face close and bit his lower lip. "Totally. Gymnastics sex is the ultimate." She nibbled his lower lip again.

Telly pushed her away. "What about the stables? Shit's flying everywhere, and who's gotta clean 'em?"

The visual discombobulation of the stables floating in zero G swarmed him. Shit flying. Birds flapping their wings, feathers spreading to every corner. Bovines releasing patties to break up and spread into a million more. And the piglets' nasty feces, their nastier wallow of black mud finding every slot and crevice.

She pulled him back and giggled. "Nothing we can do about it until the generators fire up."

Telly shut his eyes and visualized the horror waiting for him. Soft lips locked on to his lips. Ariadne was right. Nothing could be done for the time being.

Captain Douglas apologized once for the recurring mishap, offering an overly technical explanation for the loss of power to the gravity generators as an encounter with an anomaly inside the dark fold of time and space. He never spoke of the shitstorm again. But extensive damage to the backup generators would require an extended layover on Sparta. Telly's obligation remained, regardless of the cargo's status.

The cargo had managed just fine floating in zero G. One bovine suffered a fractured rib, three chickens died by strangulation trying to escape the wire coop. The incessant bleating of the lambs had quieted—not a bad thing. And the piglets seemed upbeat, tiny tails wagging as they feasted on the remnants of tens of broken eggs, shells, and all.

Fifteen standard days of cleanup and the only thing he grumbled about was the lack of contact with Ariadne. They passed each other in the corridors, each rushing to address another unexpected emergency like two ships passing but never docking.

His handheld pinged. The *Spartacus* had exited the fold. His companions would be celebrating. The crew might join them after they exited their sleep cocoons. He scratched his hand across the scraggly beard on his face. Now his journey would become tricky. Ariadne wanted to remain on Sparta, a planet renowned for its economic opportunities, pacifist culture, and amazing alien flora.

The door to the barnyard whooshed open, and Telly stepped in, grinning at the organization of his herd. Three fattened pigs pressed against the wire enclosure he had twice extended into the lobby. The fourth pig, a fat sow, lay prone and suckled tiny piglets, seven pink credits snooting and noshing for a place at their mother's table. And worth far beyond their weight. He filled the mother's trough with grain recycled from the bovine feces. The fat mother snorted appreciation but remained steadfast in her feeding.

Maybe he should sell a couple of piglets, hire a caretaker to shovel crap while he slept comfortably in a cocoon for the last few months of the journey? Telly found himself spreading fistfuls of recycled grain into the coop overcrowded with bitter and vicious chickens squabbling over each morsel. The growing number of birds definitely required culling.

His handheld pinged again, and again.

He scrolled down the list. Months of Mother's messages waited to be read. Messages from friends, several emails from Euma tagged as urgent, a few from Helen that brought a smile to his face. A message near the end of the list caused him to pause his scrolling. Telly swallowed but held his finger above the icon to open the message.

The sender's name was recognizable throughout the galaxy, but stuck in a distant star system, and without a Brainlinq, there was no way to contact him. An ewe bleated; an angry cuss of stubbornness this one, always demanding attention or service.

He accepted the text message. His stomach sank as he read the words. His ire rose like sour bile as he read the words again. His resolve to find the truth solidified. Maybe the extra weeks stuck in Sparta's spaceport was divine intervention.

Or an elaborate ploy magnifying the target Mother had warned to be painted on his back.

CHAPTER 21

THE HADES NEBULA EXPANDED INTO view as a rainbow cloud of dense gas and dust particles spanning light seconds across the galaxy. Possibly the remnants of an ancient star turning supernova. Or maybe a collection of residual particulates condensing into a rookery to form young stars, planets, moons, rocks, and rings of gas. The Goldilocks system was possibly born from the nebula serving as a nursery to the system's primary red dwarf star with its cooler temperatures and extended life span.

Drifting millions of kilometers from Circe's island vessel, the nebula appeared to devour all spectrums of light, a thick soup of particulate matter preventing all reflection of *Homer*'s soft bouncing waves of ground-penetrating radar, a boundless enigma causing Ulley to question his decision. And yet, Circe assured him that additional fuel for the Prometheus drive, and the star charts to guide them home, waited beyond the cloud's ragged and chaotic edges.

Ulley woke as the oblong acceleration couch curled open, a device cramping the ship's tiny command center. Nothing floated in the warm air. The gravity generators obviously made the trip unscathed. He stretched his arms and legs, feeling remarkably refreshed. A first. The sleep chamber often sucked the life from his muscles like a mechanized leech. He checked the status panels and their blinking green lights. He stepped onto the cold, hard deck.

He scrunched his eyes tight and stretched his tight neck, blinking as if forgetting something. He shrugged tight shoulder muscles. "Report, XO." The Brainlinq connection was squishy, distant. He frowned then narrowed and refined the communication channel. "Report, Mr. Blaylock."

Silence. Complete. And utter. Perhaps Blaylock's cocoon was slow to open. But the XO had programmed his stasis chamber to unfold a full standard day before the rest of the crew would wake.

He repeated his request. And again. His voice grew agitated. Very unlike the ex-military officer. He reopened the Brainlinq to a ship-wide channel. "Systems check. All divisions and decks report."

Weapons check. Shuttle bays check. Mess hall check, with complaints. Recycling check. Fusion drives check. Prometheus Drive check; fuel levels continued to drop incrementally. Ulley waited long seconds. Command deck check.

He frowned then turned to the exit. The door stood as a blasé slab of plexisteel but challenged him. He pounded on the flimsy cabin door until it chugged along recessed top and bottom rails to hide in its pocket within the bulkhead. Glitches were not uncommon after heavy acceleration. Borde would have a steady stream of glitches popping into his never-ending maintenance queue.

Ulley checked the hallway left and right, stopping himself with the incongruous act. His imagination ran wild. The ship was under attack. Blaylock was dead. Troian marines were storming the *Homer* looking for retribution. He groaned at his unfounded paranoia and entered the hallway, his back pressed against the bulkhead, his eyes wide in a maniacal expression.

A clatter of falling metal.

He froze. *The Troian invaders might hear that.*

Homer chirped in his Brainlinq. *You'll burn. We'll all burn. The sooner we find the flame, the quicker the death.*

Ulley grabbed his head and screamed.

Ulley blinked rapidly to fan the fog from his brain. He shut his eyes tight and opened them again to stare at chubby pink cheeks and a bulbous nose spiderwebbed with tiny capillaries. Rosu grinned down at him, a mouth of jagged teeth both broken and diseased.

"There you are, Captain," Rosu said. His putrid breath caused Ulley to shut down his nostrils and breathe sparingly. "We thought we lost you."

The acceleration couch refused to open beyond his face. The ship's status panels, and operational instrument boards appeared intact. He commanded the couch to release him, then again and again. The stasis chamber refused, paralyzing all movement of his limbs.

Rosu wasn't right—his facial features, his spacer accent, his freaking voice of concern, his . . . everything. Another bewitching of Circe's sorcery, and yet the explanation didn't fit. Submit and learn.

"I'm fine now, Rosu." Ulley said and stuck out his dry tongue to run along his chapped lips. "A nipple of liquid might clear these cobwebs from my mouth."

Rosu lifted his head and shot a questioning expression towards someone beyond Ulley's limited vision. Ulley refused to acknowledge the knowing smirk forming on Rosu's sun-bleached face. Someone, or something, held Rosu in thrall. Something with the power to decide if he could have a simple sip of water, someone deciding if he could emerge from the constricted couch. Something deciding Ulley's fate.

Ulley screamed and pushed his arms against the cocoon's liquid steel, wriggling and twisting until freeing his hands, his breathing matched his thrumming heartbeat, a drowning man crawling through wet sand to find a pocket of air.

"Captain, you're struggling too much. Calm down, and the couch can reset," Rosu said above him, yet continuing to look beyond his vision.

The bulkheads shimmered as if a desert heatwave boiled the air. The deck hanging above his face warped, the metal purlins wiggled, the thick corrugated decking buckled like an energy wave rolled across its surface. The Troian mercenaries would follow. He shut his eyes as he fought the couch for a well-deserved death.

Let them have their revenge. Let them have their revenge. Let them have their revenge.

His fists flailed weakly against the gel sucking him down to sleep.

Circe's voice whispered, "It's over. It's over." Again, and again. "Go home."

The succulent aroma of a familiar vegetable soup shimmered across his nostrils as the couch closed tight. The tiny faceplate fogged with his hot breath.

Ulley relaxed and accepted his imprisonment.

The dark formless void was complete, no differentiating shades of gray, no pinpricks of light, no glossy shimmer around the edges. Human consciousness was not conceived to endure such a void of light. From conception in the womb, or vat, to the last breaths of death, light always accompanied the human psyche, penetrating flimsy eyelids, enter ear canals as vibrations. Even the ancient space explorers falling prey to voracious singularities found sustaining light, vast spectrums being absorbed, eaten by supreme gravity.

He floated in the viscous liquid of total darkness. Was he alive? Or dead? Or somewhere in between? He thought to close his eyelids, but he had no eyelids, or eyes. He thought of wiggling a finger and found he was without a body. He thought of remembering his past, what his name was, or the face of his mother or father, but the questions disappeared swiftly into the vast blackness, his thoughts nothing but dry, dead leaves scattered by violent gusts of wind.

He thought to sigh. And float in hell. For an eternity.

An explosion of crimson light shocked Ulley's eyes to crack open thick dry mucus , leaving his vision blurry. Bright lights stared down from the ceiling. He shuttered his eyes, allowing the intense light to filter through his eyelids, reigniting dormant thought patterns. He frowned and peeked through his gummy slits.

The ship's command cabin shimmered into focus. The weapons panel shone green. Digital displays for the air scrubbers displayed green. Gravity generator status all green. The stasis cocoon retracted, the heavy gel compressing down into cavities beneath the floor as it released Ulley.

Disturbing dreams kept him prone.

He waited to hear the crew's chatter on Brainlinq. He waited for the ship's grunt to bring him a cup of hot coffee as was tradition on the *Homer*. He waited in silence, for Homer to respond, the Brainlinq notification of reinitialization, for . . .

"Status, XO?" Ulley said through a scratchy, dry throat. "Homer? Give me some feedback. Please."

He narrowed the communication channel to Blaylock, asking for ship's status. Silence. Another to Rosu. Silence. A ship-wide broadcast found only . . . silence.

A companion to accompany the eerie darkness.

Ulley mulled the thought as he shuffled through a checklist, the integrity of the bulkheads, panels, and gravity generators. He wobbled to stand then stepped up to the door and stared at the bland slab of plexisteel like an opponent. "Open the door, Homer. Or whoever likes to play games."

The door whooshed open. Ulley nodded and smirked as if he was on to something. The mess hall was vacant and shining with unnatural cleanliness. Ulley took long sucks on the fluid nipples. The water tasted clean and fresh. He perused the loading docks, swept clean but vacant, the distinct aroma of silicon lubricant and scented nitrogen absent from the warm air.

Ulley chuckled, then shouted, "Heaven or hell? You can't decide?"

The crew's quarters waited like memories. Soliel's feathered artwork. Blaylock's assembly of military ribbons and medallions of commendation hung on the wall with meticulous precision. Ceasare's small cubicle buttoned up tight, just as the grunt had left it.

He found his own cabin just as he remembered it, clothes scattered and waiting for a laundry edict to be handed down. A priceless photograph of Pennae cradling tiny Helen, with five-year-old Telly teasing his baby sister with an impish grin.

Ulley couldn't help but smile. "Heaven or hell, let's get to it."

The cabin walls erupted into hot white flames.

He threw his arm up for protection and recoiled from the unbearable heat. The flames climbed the walls to burn paper star charts, a tiny flower memento of peace offered from a Troian youngling. The flames found the photograph, bending and twisting gold tendrils around the thin frame as if tasting its meal.

Ulley reached to save the picture. The intense flames licked his hand, as if the flesh was its prize. He could only watch as the intense flames engulfed his family with methodical relish.

The flames found his clothes like a tasty morsel. Pungent burnt hair lifted vapors into his nostrils, the skin on his arms bubbled and blistered, but the pain was absent. The warped ashes of the incinerated photograph fluttered across his vision. He swallowed as home disappeared into the flames. The furnace of Hell swallowed, sucking him down into its hungry maw.

Just as Circe had warned.

He bent his knee and bowed his head. "My death will give no fuel to your flame. The dead offer only regret. My trespass into your realm may invigorate those you've deemed to wander eternity without direction."

The chuckle of a deep-throated voice rumbled. "The souls of all eternity rest within me."

Ulley stepped back as the flames receded, leaving the walls smoking and charred black. His clothes incinerated to ash. "I offer a sacrifice to you, Hades." Ulley looked down at his charred hand grasping the talisman Circe had promised to deliver at exactly the right time. "An ancient monument lost to you for eons, the skull of a ram, the mighty horns a testament to your power. It's said only the blood of this magnificent creature may call forth the dead. I beg to differ. I think the mighty Hades can bring me what I seek."

The room shook with Hades' basso chuckle. "What is your name?"

Ulley stood and straightened his back. "Ulley. I am the descendent of the great Odysseus."

"Odysseus! A pithy man of which great lies were written. Is it he you seek?"

Surprised by the question, Ulley was intrigued by the possibilities of meeting a descendent forgotten with time. But Circe warned his requests were limited. And Odysseus was not a priority. "Lord Hades, I seek a soul lost to me at the battle of Troia."

Hades chuckled again. "I will take your vessel into the womb of my domain and let you wander the infinite clouds of dust and gas. An eternity to seek what I forbid you to find. However, the ram's head is superbly preserved . . . that witch must hold you close to her cold heart. I shall grant your request before I set you to wander the stars."

Ulley surveyed the charred remains of his cabin, ash and melted plastic, his own clothing merely ribbons of black coal. He lifted his foot to avoid a squat of boiling feces bubbling beneath his feet. He closed his eyes, afraid to take a step, afraid to fall into an endless abyss.

The star charts were paramount to returning home. Finding Patro was . . .

"Thank you, My Lord," Ulley said. "My friend, Patro, is who I seek."

Hades chuckled again. "I have missed the subtleties and misgivings of mortals. This realm sees only the afterthoughts of mortals. The Zoosh rarely contribute. The Hathena enter only to be extracted by their benefactor. The Ares supply us with unlimited souls. Something should be done about that boy you seek."

"I don't understand," Ulley said. He inhaled a hot, foul stench.

The room rumbled. "The descendant of Achilles, a warrior who transcends the dimensions of time. A boy brought to me shackled in chains. And now you and your trickery seek to free him."

"No, My Lord, I only wish to pick his brain—I mean, learn of his—"

The molten floor fell out from beneath him, leaving a depthless maw filtered in oily dust and swirling gas. Ulley spun around within a dense nebula birthing galaxies and bright stars. The timeless spectacle caused him to flail, his legs were useless, his outstretched hands rigid as claws, his lips frozen in a grimace of awe. A tiny swirling dust devil aimed for him, its diminutive size and velocity growing near like a summer storm intent to wreak havoc.

In the physical reality, he should be dead. His blood vaporized by the vacuum. His skin frozen, his last breath sucked from his lungs. His soul free, to join the others in the Hades Nebula. A trick of sorcery from Circe. Yet, the explanation sounded hollow, impotent, and felt wrong.

The tornado circled Ulley as it drew closer. The fierce hot wind buffeted the remnants of his long hair to lash his face. Ulley screamed to flee. Yet his voice was eaten by a creature coming to consume his soul.

What have I done?

Star charts be damned. A torrent of wind whipped across his body, dust and tiny rocks shredded the last tatters of his uniform from his flesh. Ulley turned his head and spat out the grit. The wind gobbled the dry spittle like a voracious school of fish.

He reached out and found his arm and hand shredded of skin and sinew. He worked his jaw up and down, losing the motion as the wind took the ligaments. He closed his eyes, an absurd hope to preserve his sight. He squeezed his eyelids tighter.

The engulfing violence whipped away flesh and hope. As if forced to witness, Ulley's eyelids were shredded and whipped with the remnants of his flesh into the violent maelstrom.

Faces of young women, old men, and sad children whipped past his eyes, their horrified expressions frozen in time. Skeletal hands identical to his own reached for him. How many souls had been consumed? Ulley waited, frozen, a simple digit added onto Hades' tally.

The winds eased. Bloodied faces of dead children whirled into focus, grinning with broken teeth, bruised cheeks, and blackened eye sockets. Ulley thought to grab one with his useless hands.

Hades chuckled. "Do you also desire to pick their brains?"

The misunderstood colloquialism came back to bite him. "It means to understand what thoughts they had! What is all this? I want to see Patroclus, as is my right."

The wind rivaled any on the surface of Neptune. Dirty and foul, the sting of sand peppering his face forced a weak attempt to close his eyes. An ancient face bearded with slithering snakes emerged from the wind, its eyes a pair of black holes that sucked the light from the wind. Its eyebrows squirmed with slithering alien parasites. It snapped at Ulley's eyes with sharp-toothed jaws.

Circe's warning whispered in his head: *Hades' ego has no bounds but can be massaged.*

Ulley rejected everything in his vision. He closed imaginary eyelids to stem the fright of snakes just inches from tasting what flesh remained on his bones. His thoughts drifted. Back home. To a shaded park bench dedicated to the deceased royalty of Ithaca... A peaceful place beneath a dome of transparent radio-reflective plexi-glass offering a view of Jupiter meant to inspire any youngster's future. A ribbon of lush turf encircled a blue-green pond clamoring with clattering ducks and geese, their grumpies dotted the walkway as a concern for children and strollers. Ulley ran his finger across the wooden bench scarred by alphabets and abuse.

Would my father recognize me in this nebula? Would he care even if he did?

Tiny nips of pain pricked his face as Hades' eyebrows picked the flesh off his bones. Pond water and color drifted up like smoke into the dome, turf and grumpies floated away into a dark void. The expanse of the gas giant Jupiter shimmered from his thoughts.

Ulley returned from the memory.

To confront an unexpected trial of emotion. A distasteful memory. An unrequited love. The face of a man long dead.

Laertes. His father.

CHAPTER 22

A RAINBOW OF GARGANTUAN HELIUM balloons swayed in the warm breeze above an open-air arena vibrant and brimming with space wranglers, sun-kissed farmers, and colorful vendors hawking their wares. Sandwiches, cooked lizard pops, and oily hopper-fries, cinnamon buns topped with genuine bovine butter, assorted fancy skirts, blouses, and sturdy work trousers, even tattoo artists challenging Telly to ink his skin with their artwork or alien symbols.

The upcoming auction was just as Telly had envisioned as he traveled the space elevator down to Sparta's surface. He wandered among the bovines, swine, sheep, and tall horses, pulling his two-wheel cart containing ten chickens for trade or sale. The pleasant scent of fresh alfalfa mixed with their defecated remains. He slapped at winged flies and bees buzzing his face, the bugs faster and trickier than Ithaca's slow, bio-engineered pollinators.

Loudspeakers blared announcements. Last call for pie-eating contestants, shuttles to and from Sparta's space port arriving every ten minutes, the Hamilton family should proceed immediately to the bailiff's tent and claim their misplaced child, Timmy.

Both male and female wranglers were dressed to impress, with tall five-gallon hats, plaid pearl-buttoned shirts, denim trousers with oversized metal belt buckles and sharp-toed boots. The spaceport's expansive stockyard appeared a bit barbaric with their narrow, confined pens, but any abuse of the precious animals was inconceivable.

Telly felt conspicuous in his dirty onesie stained with sweat and animal feed, but there were plenty of others dressed similarly.

Ariadne had run off to scout the kiosks as soon as a vendor had offered a decent price for her piglet. At least she *thought* it was fair, but Mother had taught him to never ever take the first offer.

Sparta's type M red dwarf sun was hot on his head, and he stopped to wipe sweat from his brow. The planet's gravity was eight percent heavier than Ithaca's, but the extra weight on his muscles felt good, and the fresh air didn't taste like Ithaca's air scrubbers by their algae filters. He could live and die on this planet and never regret a day. Maybe he would. After Ulley returned home, after Mother settled Ithaca's legal skirmishes with the Martians, after Helen had exited puberty without wreaking havoc on Mother and Euma, after . . .

He sighed.

A message received said to meet at the auction. And valuable information about Ulley would be divulged. In this huge crowd, how could anyone find him without a Brainlinq? The message was probably a spammer looking at a quick score for bogus information, but the messenger offered snippets proving they had known Ulley, like his irreverent labeling of the act of defecation as a grumpy. Telly's own observance of Mother potty-training Helen, encouraging his sister's birth of a *grumpy*, was practically a family secret.

He scanned the sea of hats and colorful parasols shading the hot sun, then tugged on the cart, aiming for the Plexi barn housing the auction for chickens. Telly joined a procession of Spartan families looking to gain access to the building.

A short bald human cackled and offered him ten credits for each chicken, flashing the total of Spartan credits on his wrist with a light pencil as if Telly was illiterate. Telly shouted the gnome away.

The long line progressed, finally entering the shade provided by the ample overhang of the gabled roof. His chickens fluttered and squawked as if protesting the sun's disappearance. He turned and glared a warning at their commotion without success.

He held his hand out for an entrance chit an auction official was distributing as she walked down the line. She paused before placing the small disk in his hand. Her skin weathered by sun, her stature beaten down by age, her eyes as vibrant as a teen's. "If those babies come from off world, then you pull valuable cargo." She lifted the corner of her mouth and continued down the line.

Telly understood. The chickens offered new DNA, offered diversity into a stagnant population, offered a tiny step forward for humanity's terraforming of Sparta.

For millennia, terraforming planets was a crapshoot. Most died with too many rolls of the dice. Others hung on, hoping an influx of human ingenuity and technology could master the environmental challenges. Sparta was a one-off. An atmosphere rich in nitrogen and hydrogen and acceptable to human lungs. A landscape, and seascape, welcoming to a human experience, an alluring planet primed perfectly for human habitation by a benevolent supreme intelligence.

Telly pulled his cart containing eight first-year hens and two cocks through the narrow entrance of an overcrowded arena.

An old man stationed at doors checked him then eyed the birds in his cart. The sleepy looking man held his hand up. "Selling or buying?"

Telly thought of the ambiguous question. "Selling my girls. Hoping to buy information with the boys."

The man's bushy eyebrows lifted. "Maybe you should find the head of the line." He pulled Telly from the line and beckoned him to follow.

Telly stepped out of the procession and cut in front of other customers and vendors waiting patiently. He felt their eyes appraise him, then the chickens.

At a pair of huge wooden paneled doors, he was greeted by two wranglers with silver five-pointed stars pinned to dull grey collared shirts. The sleepy man whispered something to one of the deputies. The tall man's mouth twitched as if resisting a smile, then he nodded and waved Telly forward.

Sleepy stooped to check the chickens more closely. He mumbled with an accent Telly assumed to be Sparta slang. Planets and habitats were required to speak Consortium English, violators punishable by law. But terraformed planets always evolved with language derivations influenced by hard-core cultures intent on preserving imported dialects even as they invented new traditions.

The old man rose and wrinkled his nose as if sniffing the air. "Smells like two hundred for the hens and two-fifty for the roosters. You ain't gonna get a better price inside." He smiled stained teeth and flicked his chin to prod Telly's response.

Telly gauged the man's expression. The price was marked down but not unreasonable. The suspicious expressions of people waiting behind him said he wasn't welcome at the auction. Maybe the cargo ship *Spartacus* traveled with a disreputable reputation, though he never witnessed any evidence of that. Sleepy had led him to his clan's muscle, legal or not. Anything beyond the auction doors might only find a few extra credits, and a lot of ill will.

"Done," Telly said. He offered his handheld for the transfer of credits.

Sleepy cackled as he pointed a crooked finger at Telly's old handheld. The transferred credits pinged a high-pitched tone.

Telly pursed his lips. He was rich. Two thousand one hundred credits less twenty percent kickback to the crew of the Spartacus. He should have persuaded Ariadne to sell her piglet at the auction. They would both be rich.

Sleepy tapped Telly's hand holding the handle of the cart and winkled the gray caterpillars stationed above his eyes. Telly reluctantly relinquished his hold on the feathered children he had fed and nurtured for over a standard year.

Sleepy muttered incoherently in Spartan slang and pulled the cart towards a pair of doors labeled as forbidden beyond this point. He watched as the man and cart disappeared into the dark hallway beyond.

Telly sighed.

Pushed aside by the constant stream of people waiting for access to the auction, and nowhere to go, Telly simply watched the people enter. Small children darted between their parents' legs, senior couples held each other close, teenage boys and girls close to his own age flirted and strutted like horny chickens. The barn wasn't big enough to hold the magnitude of people entering. The deputies double-checked each entrant. Those carrying chickens to be sold were steered towards Sleepy, who had returned to the main doors like a greedy golem.

The auction was a scam feasting on the misery of the poor, the ignorant, but feeding the insatiable appetite of human corruption. A parameter of human behavior prevented on Ithaca by its super-intelligent AI, Euma.

Relieved of their duties by a different pair, the two guards approached and asked him to accompany them towards a large arena busy with wranglers riding quick-footed horses and herding bovines. Telly didn't budge. Something didn't feel quite right.

The taller of the two approached to within inches. He stunk of unbathed skin tinted like a dull olive, his breath hot and rancid, like he'd forgotten to clean his teeth or even rinse his mouth with maintenance nanites. "You looking for information?"

Telly wrinkled his face and stepped back from the aromatic assault. "Looking for manifests of ships returning from Troia. Or maybe arrival logs from the port authority."

Telly craned his neck backwards to inhale fresh air. The other deputy loomed behind him. Did they think to steal his credits?

He offered his handheld as a gesture. "I can pay."

He thought to bolt into the crowd. He thought to fight. Neither option would find him the information he wanted.

"Yes, you can, boy. And we aim to help you spend those credits," the deputy said. "Why would an off-worlder like you arrive without a Brainlinq? Sure would make your life easier."

Telly shut off inhaling through his nostrils. "I'm not old enough," he lied, but they might believe it. His slight frame and scraggly patch of beard spoke of delayed puberty.

The guard chuckled. "Even babies have the Linq inserted here. Are you from some backwater moon that frowns upon technology?"

Sandwiched between the guards, Telly accepted the role of a country bumpkin. "I'll get one next year, after the chickens and bovines have produced."

The guard lifted his chin and nodded. "You herding chickens on an uppity habitat like Ithaca? That don't seem likely." He grinned a set of teeth stained an ugly brown.

Telly raised his handheld to his chest, hoping to slow the race of his heart. The guards' gaze followed the handheld like a prize. Telly coughed. Then faked a sneeze. He narrowed his eyes, then faked another sneeze. They knew where he was from. Probably knew who he was. Somebody expected him, and these brutes had been sent to retrieve him.

A pair of strong hands of the man behind him gripped his upper arm, squeezing hard and almost lifting him off his feet. He stared into the other man's mouth opening wide as if to take a bite only to expel death breath towards the arena.

"We're gonna skip on over to the parking parade and find us a ride into town," the deputy said.

Telly surrendered to the horrendous biological warfare spewing from between the guards' lips. Mother's angry warning of him brandishing a target on his back screamed loudly.

Attempts to shrug off the heavy hand was answered by the deputy's snicker, followed by a warning of handcuffs. Shitbreath bolted ahead as Telly was held firmly in place by the other.

The skyline of the spaceport Epsilon metropolis painted itself across a hazy horizon backdropped by Sparta's two distant moons, cratered and lifeless, but during rare lunar phases the contours of ridges appeared as grins, or frowns, to loom over Sparta like judgmental jesters.

Screams and shouts erupted from behind him. He fought the man's grip to turn.

A stampede of swine shot out from the narrow aisles between the Grav-craft and four wheeled buggies parked in the adjacent lot. Piglets squealed following fat sows. Hefty coarse-haired boars shot out of another aisle, snorting and running straight at him. A lithe girl followed, chasing and prodding the swine within reach of her knotted walking staff. Her face bright red with sweat and embarrassment, the girl was overmatched.

A frantic sow crashed into his captor's knees. The deputy's knees buckled before he released his grip hoping to save a fall onto the hard tarmac. A quintet of piglets swarmed him before a saber-toothed boar snorted and jabbed the man, rooting in the hardpack soil beneath the man's groin as if searching for a coveted tuber.

Telly saw his chance to escape. The young girl smacked the boar with her staff, missing her final strike only to find Telly's shin bone. Pain and anger followed. Wielding the wooden staff like a ninja, she scrambled to corral the beasts, until they fled into another quadrant of parked vehicles. The swineherd was gorgeous, formidable, muscled arms, a pug nose, and dimpled chin.

Telly swallowed hard, like a lovestruck teenage boy.

Her staff smacked a loitering boar before she yelled at him, "How about a little help?"

Telly eyed the deputy being ravaged by the big boar then said, "Now what?"

She waved him forward to join the chaotic scramble. He laughed at the irony of herding invaluable beasts through narrow aisles. At least thirty swine darted in and out of the vehicles. He exclaimed with a fist pump at the capture of a piglet. He searched for the Breath Brothers lurking in the crowded lot, a rancid scent affirmed their presence.

The girl shouted instructions at him like a seasoned range boss, using hand gestures to guide him into specific aisles between vehicles to herd the beasts toward an empty wire pen near the main arena. His hands full with a squirming piglet, he shouted and kicked the stubborn swine towards the enclosure.

The girl pulled a vial from her utility belt around her waist and sprinkled drops of liquid inside the pen. She hooted and snorted and tapped the rails with her staff. Like magic, the beasts stopped to raise their snouts, then aimed for the pen. She tapped the rears of swine with her staff as she counted each as they entered.

Telly eased up to the gate. She flicked her chin to indicate the piglet in his arms and smiled gloriously, nodding for him to release it.

She latched the gate shut, then blew a huge breath.

Telly checked over his shoulder. The tall hats of the Breath Brothers loomed above the vehicles, disappearing as if searching beneath the vehicle carriages. Telly searched for an escape route.

"Looked like them deputies were herding you," she said. "I'll show you a way out for helping me."

She opened the gate and pulled him through the herd, over the back railing, to shimmy through narrow slots between tall cubes of hay, into a corral of bovine stock with orange auction tags pinned to their ears. They paused to catch their breath beneath an array of metal struts supporting the grandstands of the main arena.

"What did they want with you besides your credits?" she said as she wiped beads of sweat from her forehead.

He winced as he kneeled to massage a cramp in his calf muscle. "I was just looking for information. About ships coming back from the Troian War."

She scoffed then kicked his foot. "You're fresh off the boat, aren't you?"

Telly had heard the slight before, and he couldn't argue the fact. "Just a layover to clean up before we fold out again."

She tapped his foot with her staff. "That's gonna be the safest place for you."

He pulled his handheld out and confirmed his credits. "I got credits to spend before I get on that tub again."

"Yeah? How much?" she said.

He looked up at her warily. Sweaty or not, she was beautiful. And he couldn't help but stare at her captivating eyes. Turquoise like the oxidized copper on Ganymede. His mouth was suddenly dry, probably from the sprinting. He thought to ignore her question, maybe lie about the hefty number, but her bewitching eyes made the truth spill from his mouth.

"Two thousand plus."

She whistled. "You sell something to that old gnome hanging out with badges?"

"My chickens and two roosters," he said.

She closed her eyes and shook her head. "Fresh off the boat. The auction would have netted you at least five thousand credits for out-worlder stock."

The air fled from his lungs as his ire rose.

She offered her hand to help him stand. "Don't matter though. The badges would've gotten it either way, and you were a bonus. We should move."

Telly brushed sharp stickers and stiff hay off his rear end, to the consternation of the girl. "What's your name, O wise savior?"

She giggled. "Sirsee."

Telly struggled to keep up with Sirsee as she led him into the out-skirts of the metropolis, a dirty shantytown of tents and composite shacks with thatch roofs. Maybe the heavier gravity wasn't so easy to acclimate to. Maybe the atmosphere's higher oxygen levels caused his lungs to work harder. Every time he caught up to her waiting at an intersection or a busy corner, she tapped his thigh with her staff and continued her quick pace. At least they were headed towards the spaceport with its trio of space elevators capable of carrying him back up to the spindled orbiting platform, and back to the *Spartacus*.

The people crowding the streets eyed him suspiciously as he hurried past. His plain drab onesie stood out like a floodlight in the dark, a stark contrast to the rags and shreds of torn cloth barely covering the adults. Many infants and children watched naked and fearful as he passed. The Consortium-governed Sparta promoted as one of the wealthiest and ecologically diverse in the known galaxy reeked of feces and urine, city streets nothing more than narrow lanes of compacted mud rutted from wheels and rainfall.

Telly caught Sirsee and gripped her arm.

She turned with a snarl on her face and shrugged off his hand. "A few more klicks, spaceboy."

"Wait. I need a second," Telly said. He grabbed his knees and sucked in huge breaths as if he couldn't get enough. The hard dirt was streaked with tiny rivulets of dried red and black crust. A combination of colors used on Ithaca as a warning of poison or contaminated air. His eyes followed the streaks up the street, crisscrossing like a web into intersecting streets, subtle, innocuous, and unnatural. "What's up with the death markings covering the street? I mean . . . if this was—"

The tip of Sirsee's staff lifted his chin. Her eyes intense and resolute, her lips pulled tight as if trying not to speak. She blinked once, her eyes glossed black. "Man's cruelty to man."

The misery marching past Telly's eyes *was* cruel. But maybe these people didn't want to work or couldn't function properly in any modern society. Maybe malformed DNA propagated their life of misery.

A mother holding hands with two toddlers caught his eye as she poked her head into a tiny kiosk serving rice and GMO chicken wings. The proprietor brandished a sharp knife and waved the beggars away. The family stumbled and wobbled through the crowded procession of rags. The smallest of the family, a girl draped in an oversized T-shirt, stared at him with blank eyes. Tattered robes and skirts flittered past until she disappeared from his sight.

Eyes Helen might have, eyes meant to be filled with endless wonder, and yet tinted with the hopelessness of never knowing the truth of her father's disappearance.

Telly rushed to the kiosk. The stunning aroma of grilled pork paused his questions. He turned his head towards the receding trio and waved his handheld like a fat bank check. The family was gone, sucked into a chaotic river of misery.

Sirsee yanked on his sleeve and pulled him through the throng, body odor and wood smoke following him.

"What's happened here? I thought Sparta was an affluent planet?" Telly said before stopping to offer his soiled upturned palms.

Sirsee pointed her staff towards the space elevator's thick anchoring cable rising up kilometers to disappear into the hazy sky. "The Troian War. It bankrupted the government and things just keep getting worse."

Telly considered the cost of an interstellar war but couldn't fathom the cost of ships, men, supplies, and fuel. The staggering price tag left Sparta's populace to fight for scraps. He thought of Ithaca and the devastating toll the war had extracted on the habitat's ability to function. Ice mining virtually shut down with miners drafted into service by the Consortium. Supply ships from Earth's arcologies or lush, terraformed Martian caverns arrived far and few, diverted into the Troian system for the benevolence of the troops. Parents forced to abandon their children under the threat of treason.

He was lucky. Too young to fight. But the war never seemed to end. The massive influx of sailors suffering from PTST remained a daily reminder of a war the Consortium would offer no compensation for, and little information.

The massive concrete structure of the space elevator's foundation loomed a few klicks ahead. Considered an engineering marvel, the elevator's hexagonal main spindle jutted from a foundation a thousand meters in diameter, tapering up as the planet's gravity lessened its load on the composite shaft. Oblong cars slid up and down on rails embedded into each face of the geometric design. Coming, going, a steady stream of cars sliced past their counterparts like ants working a newly discovered food source.

"Pretty sic. Every world should have one," Sirsee said.

"Yeah . . . wonder why they don't?" Telly said.

Sirsee scoffed. "Human politics. Human greed. Human arrogance."

Telly turned his gaze to Sirsee. Her intelligence was wasted as a swineherd. Her beauty was wasted in the city's ghettos. Her love and affection would be wasted on anyone, except well . . . maybe . . .

She suddenly pulled him into a littered aisle between two tents. She shushed the questions from his lips.

Screams and panic filled the air. Rags and dirty limbs hurried past. The shouts of few became many. Telly pushed past Sirsee to witness the stampede of frightened parents pulling children, robed men, cloaked women, indigent seniors. The alarm resonated from the herd, spreading into the kiosks and shops. Owners fled with their precious wares to join the chaos.

Telly resisted the urge to flee with the crowd, a choice confirmed by Sirsee's staff pressed across his chest. A frantic woman sporting eyelids brimming with glitter pushed her face into the narrow slot and sneered at Sirsee. She shouted words Telly couldn't understand and fled.

Sirsee wiped sweat from her brow and observed the panic flying past.

"We should get to the elevator. I can hook you up with a stable, maybe," Telly said.

A one-armed mushroom of a man pushed his body into the tight space, huffing and puffing, and leering at Sirsee, eyeing her lithe body up and down like easy prey. She smirked then stretched high to peck his bulbous nose. She whispered in his ear. He released her, grinning. She waggled her eyebrows and flicked her head, ordering him to run.

Telly grabbed her wrist, opening his mouth to offer help.

Her cheek brushed across his face like silk in a gentle breeze. Pleasure and infinity. A tactile sensation causing her to frown. "Don't touch me. It's not time."

Her words made Telly recoil, stepping deeper into the shadows provided by the kiosks, escaping the madness outside flimsy walls. He shrank into a crouch. Hoped the madness outside was just a dream. He swallowed. Get to the elevator. A port of call was always destined to be full of adventure, but this—

He growled at the constant screams of panic erupting from the street. He looked up. Sirsee had receded into the shadows, her arms folded across her bosom. The staff dangled from one hand. Her impish grin belied the concern in her eyes.

He bucked the stampede to grab a boy Helen's age and scream, "What the fuck is happening?"

The boy spouted Spartan gibberish. His eyes beamed fear. Telly released him then bucked the flow, grabbing men and women, hoping anyone spoke simple Consortium English. A frightened man sporting a single arm and no bigger than an impoverished teen pushed his face up to Telly's, his eyes stretched with impending doom.

"Run. Run. The Zoosh are invading."

He turned to Sirsee. She stiffened, her gaze concentrating on something Telly hadn't noticed. She stabbed her staff into the dirt three times.

A warm breeze invaded the aisle, swirling, gaining speed and volume, stirring cloth hanging from kiosks into a panic.

She leaned her face out of the dust devil with a knotted brow. "Our time will come."

Flying sand stung his eyes. Detritus peppered his face.

But Sirsee was gone.

CHAPTER 23

THE THICK DUST AND NOXIOUS gas spelled certain death for Ulley, and yet he stood unharmed. His chest rose and fell with each breath, his tongue licked his dry lips, his eyelids blinked slowly as if he were deep in thought. He held out his palm and studied his long fingers as if seeing them for the first time. He turned his hand and stared at the thin, bleached scar running across his knuckles, the cut of a careless razor. He blinked twice then remembered the nasty blade biting him as he fought three bullies in the exercise yard of the reformatory school orbiting Uranus. A hellhole of incorrigibility, the headmaster reminded the students at each morning muster.

Why did he think of the miserable years of his youth? Years he had chosen to forget.

He lifted his other hand, focused on his knuckles fading in and out of the dense gas, turning his palms over to feel dust particles brush the supple heel that could massage painful memories from his thoughts. Replaced by a memory of his own mother, her welcoming arms opened wide, her pained smile accompanied by dark tortured eyes as she kneeled to embrace him.

Shifting gas and dust removed the thoughts as he drifted in the endless vacuum of eternity, witnessing the evolution of galaxies born from the nebula, watching them die, only to spawn black holes into which all light collapsed. The incongruity, a mystery at his fingertips commanding him to reach for the stars. His existence was required. His understanding was crucial.

He reached out.

And the wrinkled leather face of his father jutted out of the dust, Laertes' eyes black, blank, and blind, his bearded jowls fat and sagging, a nose scarred and spiderwebbed with capillaries. The face of his father. Just as he remembered.

Ulley stepped back, the movement useless in the formless void. He thought to shout the man back into the void. Instead, he could only mutter, "You . . ."

Laertes emerged from the fog and tilted his head, furrowing his brow in bewilderment. "Have come back."

The four-word conversation irked Ulley. A staple of his childhood. Laertes' constant accusations of disobedience peppering him as a helpless child. Orders to stop the rebellious tricks Ulley performed as a tween, until he matured to offer sarcastic rebuttals born of defiance.

Their final conversation came full circle with Laertes handing Ulley a gym bag. "You're going," he'd said. Laertes tone tainted with his son's disloyalty.

"Gladly," Ulley had spat.

Ulley seethed at the memory. But the ghost before him would answer for his cruel behavior. "How about something more? Maybe the reason you hated me my whole life. Maybe a reason for fucking up my life." He pointed his finger at the apparition. "How about why you sent me to that fucking concentration camp."

Laertes raised his face as if to gaze at distant stars and galaxies then whispered, "Is this more than any human might imagine? Is this not why we finally meet? Infinitesimal sparks destined to intersect."

Ulley choked off an abrupt two-word response.

Laertes smiled. "Because we all serve a creator, imagined or fabricated." He raised his arms high as if to display the stars above.

"And after all this time, that's all you have to say to your son?" Ulley said.

Laertes mouth hung open. He knotted his forehead. "You should return to Ithaca. Evil conspiracies converge to destroy what our family has built."

"Ithaca is all you ever cared about. Not my mother, or me. Just Ithaca." Ulley bared his teeth. Sarcasm and disgust laced his words. "My birthright. My inheritance. My burden. Please, Father, enlighten me with your underworldly wisdom. Point me in the right direction so I can save that which you value above all else." The absurdity in his words softened his tone. "Father, your grandchildren will never know you, just as you never knew your own son."

Laertes swatted at the multitude of boney hands reaching out of the dense gas, to pull him back into oblivion. "You're mistaken."

Ulley answered, as if preprogrammed, "How?"

"I know my son. I followed every day of his schooling with the habitat's intelligence, rejoiced at his accomplishments, and stepped up to confront any challenges. My son matured into an incorrigible monster hell-bent on sowing havoc. My son— "

"Your son screamed for your attention. Your son devised plumbing mishaps and mechanical malfunctions hoping to spend a few hours with you. Your son demolished kiosks in the courtyard with his reckless skateboarding, all with the hope you were watching." Ulley stepped closer. "And you were. Just so you'd know where to send your security goons to escort me off-world."

"And look at you now. Discovering the wonders of a timeless universe. Dead. And not dead. A failure? Or a hero? One scripted from the wheel of time before time." Laertes gazed beyond Ulley, through a of malaise of gas and dust, into a realm Ulley was forbidden to witness. "My son . . ."

Consumed by swirling dust, his essence, his spirit, his soul whispered a single word as dust whirled across his body: "Ithaca."

Ulley seethed. "Your precious habitat. Always your fucking Ithaca."

Laertes raised a hand as if to stop him. "You have been given a gift by the Creator. A knowledge mankind might never comprehend. A destiny dwarfing any hero of history." He slumped his shoulders in the familiar stance of fatherly disappointment. "The one and only Creator wastes its time on a brigand, a pirate, a stubborn child refusing to see the gift with which to change dimensions."

"You ramble as if still confined to that bed with those tubes pumping drugs into your sick body."

Laertes coughed. "Yes, I remember. A wasted, lingering demise beneath my stature. Unheralded by my family but celebrated by Ithaca's enemies. I remember."

Ulley pressed his face close to the ghost, clenching his fists. "Yeah, you remember shit. Not Mom hovering over your deathbed. Your death sucking the last bit of life from her. Your fucking son holding your hand and whimpering like a lost pup, negotiating with your almighty creator for a miracle." Ulley closed his eyes and expelled a held breath laced with lingering remnants of his hatred. "Offer me one simple gift, Father. Why was Ithaca so bloody important? More than your wife and more than your family. Why?"

Laertes coughed again, wet and guttural, sickness coating his lungs. "Have you learned nothing from your misadventures? Your destiny is written. Bound to Ithaca. You must return and defend the kingdom. Nothing else matters."

Ulley scoffed. "Not to you."

He turned his back, unable to face his father, fearful of speaking the venomous words catalogued during his two tortured years of reform school. He swallowed the ugly memories. "The *Homer* flounders in this system. Help me find our way back home, to Ithaca. We need fold coordinates. We need . . ." Ulley swallowed hard, the distaste asking his father for anything pressed on his chest like a vice. Knowing Laertes' response would return stiff as a blank bulkhead.

"You need what the creator has provided. Ithaca will soar through the galaxy. A beacon of understanding. A point of light unheralded in the vastness of space. Ithaca. Ithaca."

He turned to counter the absurdity of Laertes' words only to see a whirlwind of lost souls swallow his father. He opened his mouth to order his father's return. For what? More bullshit. More hypocrisy?

Ulley licked his lips as his jaw hung open. He offered a childish wave goodbye, a gesture to an uncertain future. A gesture Ulley longed to see from Helen. A gesture from Telly that he would never get to experience.

The brigands of Patroclus' clique stormed through the gas and dust, their bony and bejeweled hands elongating to take hold of his flesh, threatening to pull Ulley into a frightening blackness beyond.

His hubris leading the charge, Patro stood in front of Ulley, his formidable barrel chest genetically enhanced for the benefit of women, supple pouty lips improved for the ladies, his sharp cheekbones surgically supplanted for . . . the ladies. Patro licked his lips as an enticement. "Ulley, my friend, you should've known Mintaur's war was doomed to fail." He drew back and licked his lips again. "My *Achilles* went apeshit on those Troian battleships orbiting that planet. I might still be sailing with you even now if . . ." Patro turned to dance a funny jig, slapping away hands and arms reaching out from the veil of dust. He stopped mid step and smirked at Ulley. "That pig Mintaur will get his."

His mouth dry, his tongue swollen, Ulley stuttered a question: "Do you . . . Can you point us home? Get me home, Patro. Your stories pointed me to this system. You know the way home."

"Cross over to me. Here. And you'll find the way." Patro cackled and danced again.

Patro was exactly as he remembered—carefree, flippant with remarks, unbridled zeal for the next great adventure.

Seeing Ulley scratch his beard, Patro stopped his dancing. "Don't outthink the ferryman, my friend. Your way home is to come with me."

Ulley resisted the temptation. "And leave Telly to be coddled by his mother? Leave Helen at the mercy of brigands such as you?"

Patro huffed. "No offense, brother, but I might have made Helen my wife when she was old enough" He roared with laughter, a disarming voice quelling a boisterous bravado usually destined for a fight. "No offense . . . But what are you doing in this purgatory? You can't pass through in that form. Take a knife and slice an artery. And come dance a jig with me. Oh, the ladies here are beyond unbelievable."

Ulley saw his friend, his true friend, like no others had ever seen him. Energetic and brave, daring, and defiant, a comrade to battle the constrictions of remedial school, a boy sitting on the sill of a window inside the dormitory absentmindedly tapping his finger on the glass as if to check its integrity. A boy staring up at infinite starshine, imagining greatness.

Ulley spoke. "My true friend could define the infinite space of a galaxy like a piece of paper, to be folded, refolded, bend dimensions to his will just like he did while sitting by a classroom window. My true friend would usher me home to protect the habitats that our families have built for centuries. My true friend . . . died a useless death, a death I vow to avenge."

"Now we're talking!" Patro screamed at the torrent of faces

swirling in the dust, slapping at their attempts to latch on. Free of the maelstrom of bony hands attempting to pull him back in, Patro reached out to grasp Ulley by his shoulders as he often did. The hand, and gesture, passed through Ulley like a burst of wind.

A frown pinched his eyes, Patro studied his hand, turning it over and over as if unsure it was his own. He licked a fingertip, stabbed his palm with the sharp point, studied the digit like a mechanism disobeying his commands. He lifted his face to smile impishly at Ulley and said, "This shit is the..."

Ulley extended his hand and grasped Patro's neck in a brotherly pinch. Circe's warnings flapped like bats trapped in a house, confusing his thoughts. Her voice echoed, *the dead see nothing but the light of life.*

Ulley squeezed Patro's neck, but his fingers sank into the flesh as if loose dry sand. "What happened to the *Achilles*? You folded in behind their defenses. You had them dead to rights. Why didn't you send me the fold coordinates? Why? We had your back."

Patro looked up and stared at stars contracting then exploding in birthing contractions, his eyes glazed, his expression wrinkled and confused. "We transmitted the coordinates to the *Agamemnon* just as Mintaur ordered. We maintained a wicked low orbit. We held station waiting for the others." The whole fucking fleet could have folded in! That fucking Mintaur!" Patro screamed with a primal rage. "We were forced to engage with the *Hector* and kicked that motherfucker's ass. And the *Priam*, flying a flanking maneuver, like I wouldn't expect one." He scoffed and faced Ulley. "The fleet left my ass hanging out in space. You left me hanging."

Ulley clamped his jaw and pulled his lips tight. He swallowed. "Mintaur left you hanging."

Patro abandoned his search of the distant heavens to stare at Ulley, his eyes distant and glassy. "Can you believe that *Paris* captain fucking had the balls to ask for my surrender before . . . before . . . before I folded here. I should have got the better of that punk."

Ulley answered, "You did, my friend. You did. Had you signaled us—"

Patro cackled and began to dance ungainly pirouettes, finishing Ulley's sentence. "You would be here with me." He stopped, cocking his face back and forth as if searching for someone. "Whatever happened to that beautiful Troia? Did they finally send the Consortium packing?"

Ulley lowered his gaze. "No. We broke through. The fleet annihilated the planet. Billions died. And for no reason other than—"

Patro jumped high into the air. "Mintaur. Mintaur. Helmut Mintaur." He landed to face Ulley. "You gotta do something about that guy. Hey, did you know his wife plans to slit his throat when he returns from that clusterfuck? Oh, I would love to be there. Maybe steady the girl's hand if she gets fidgety. Well, at least that's the rumor floating around. Souls here with an axe to grind have no reason to lie." Patro's shoulders sagged as he turned solemn. "Keep my children under your wing. Tell my wife to fuck off. She'll feign insult but know what you're talking about. And chart a course due south of the elliptical plane of the Goldilocks system's primary star. Triangulate vectors from Goldilocks and the gas giants, down, down, down towards the ugly planet of the Sirens. Be warned. Their songs will drag you down, down, down. And Scylla and Charybdis, beware those monsters. Remember to find their point. Take care, my friend."

Patro faded as he entered the tornado of hands and faces, slapping at them like annoying flies.

"Wait. Patro, wait!" Ulley shouted.

But his friend was gone.

Ulley floated like a silent ghostship searching for a port in the infinite ocean of space. His fingertips and lips and lungs filled with the sand of churning shorelines beyond his reach.

Hades chuckled, a booming basso permeating every cell in his body.

Ulley worked his tongue and lips to find some spittle. "Return me. I have satisfied the tributes, and offered all that could be shared."

Hades chuckled again.

Ulley dropped a hundred meters, maybe a thousand light years. His stomach rose into his throat to spin with centrifugal force, roiling every muscle fiber in his body. He squeezed his eyes as if to never open them again. His bones, flesh, and soul protested their ignorance to the assault of vacuum and gravity.

For the first time in his life, Ulley was afraid to open his eyes. He rode the waves of violent impacts searching for an answer to anchor his mind. Death. Purgatory.

Silver-blue eyes.

Pennae.

Ulley braved opening his eyes.

To find himself standing in the control room of a silent starship.

CHAPTER 24

THE AIRLOCK HISSED AS THE internal pressure equalized. The panel status indicators cycled from red to green before the docking clamps released. Telly checked the animals, caged and lightly sedated, then prepared the enclosure for a bumpy shuttle flight down to the Troian surface. His knapsack of meager possessions sat next to the bovine enclosure. He would easily earn enough credits to pay for the return trip to the Sol system, but he wasn't sure if he wanted to go home.

The swine herder, Sirsee, had dominated his thoughts and fantasies since leaving Sparta. Her beguiling eyes sucked him into a depth he had never before experienced. The young girls on Ithaca were gorgeous, and Ariadne could tempt men with just her intense blue eyes, but Sirsee . . . those otherworldly eyes . . . that demure authority commanded . . . beseeched . . . offered limitless temptations.

Telly tossed straw into the bovine enclosure and stared at the droopy eyes of a young heifer that had given birth just a few short weeks ago. "You have no idea how lucky you are." Eat, shit, and fuck, give birth, then start all over again, living by the ancient creed to go forth and multiply. No steaks, or burgers for these creatures, their DNA made them almost priceless.

He threw more straw into the enclosure. Sirsee fleeing after hearing of the Zoosh landing was curious. The aliens didn't care of happenings in the tiny sphere of humanity. To them, humanity was a science project for their children, an ant farm to observe workers digging tunnels to nowhere, until the colony slowly expired without a queen to give them purpose for a futile existence.

And yet Sirsee had looked terrified with their arrival.

On Sparta, Telly had walked upstream of the chaos rushing out of the spaceport's elevator concourse, intent on witnessing the true form of a Zoosh. He eased closer, slipping behind abandoned kiosks, braving opportunists intent on capitalizing on the enfolding chaos, cursing himself with the silly hope of seeing Sirsee again.

Telly lifted his head to gaze straight up the elevator's corkscrewed pylon. He took a step back to appreciate the pinnacle of human engineering. Alarms. Klaxons. Strobes. He marveled at the construction until he was forced back into the human herd fleeing the mysterious threat, unaware the Zoosh had teleported out.

The rush of people slowed, then turned around to resume whatever they were doing just a few minutes ago. A false alarm, people muttered. A ploy to steal the wares of shop owners.

He had slipped into a crowd waiting for an elevator, listened to a weasel-faced man exclaiming of his run-in with the Zoosh. Telly eased closer and heard the man describe the alien. All bone and cartilage, hairless flesh, with multijointed arms and legs angled to resemble cartoonish weird lightning bolts, an eyeless face with a long beard of leathery spotted skin. The squeamish man claimed to be paralyzed with fright, or Zoosh magic.

Telly listened to the man's story again but couldn't determine why the alien described was so frightening. Every species belonging to the Others were diametrically different in physical shape and form, all intellectually superior, all technologically advanced.

The crowd began to thin when the man began to hawk holographic placards of the Zoosh a young boy had discreetly delivered.

The docking mechanisms clanked with the arrival of the shuttle, bringing Telly back to the task at hand. "Okay, kids, time to go. We're last, but we're best."

Two shuttle pilots helped Telly load the animals into a claustrophobic compartment still smelling of the previous passengers. He strapped into a harness bolted to the bulkhead. The animals were on their own, but the flight parameters guaranteed low-angled vectors to mitigate the animals' discomfort down to Troia. He hoped Ariadne might wait for him, and they could explore the planet together. But Sirsee would be the ideal companion.

He bit down on his teeth and groaned. He acted like a smitten schoolboy. His new crush had dominated his thoughts at the expense of a beautiful Ariadne, who could covet him as if he were a king.

Still, Sirsee was spectacular, a timeless beauty never to be duplicated.

The shuttle's landing skids bounced on the tarmac, and Telly unbuckled his harness. He uncaged the bovine and leashed the swine, leaving the sheep to follow the entourage. The chickens and fowl would wait in the hangar for pre-arranged purchasers to escort the valuable birds to their new home. The cargo bay door dropped open. Sunlight muted by a hazy sky pained his eyes. The bleats and lowing of distressed animals followed him down the ramp.

His first step on Troian soil landed in a pile of dung left behind by the previous passengers. The shattered ruins of a modern city served as a backdrop to a landing zone enclosed by a heavy gauge-wire fence. Starvation and misery gripped the wire in the guise of women and children shouting for handouts or help. Others held squares of torn cardboard above their heads, flimsy placards, poorly written calls begging for food and help.

Anything to help. War starves children. Children die for the Consortium.

An ocean of dirty rags and rubble, misery, and destitution, stretching towards the decimated cityscape, as far as he could see.

The shuttle pilot prodded him towards a huge metal barn. "The spoils of war. You'll get used to it, kid."

Maybe after I'm dead. Telly tugged on the swine's leash and aimed towards the barn.

Loudspeakers announced the next lot number to an auction, with the gravelly voice snickering about the voluptuousness of the swine herder. A possible bonus for the high bidder.

Telly was held back from the entrance to the barn by two soldiers. Two herdsmen fussing with their flocks of sheep waited before him. He huffed an exasperated breath. The bovine on the leash raised its head to aim large, frightened eyes at him.

Telly turned his head to observe the people crowding the fence. A Consortium military jeep rumbled past, cruising the fence line on heavy armored tires, a turret with four long-barreled guns aimed at the impoverished misery beyond the wire.

Telly kicked a ram to follow the flock in front, disgust and anger fueled unintended intensity. The laughter of men roared from the barn. Other herders that had been stationed on the *Spartacus* were escorted from a side door by armed military goons dressed in pressed black coveralls and wearing smirks ranging from joy to disgust. Telly thought to turn his menagerie around and lead them . . . where? The animals were a commodity, and he was nothing but a simple herder, a pimple, a swineherd to be discarded after the auction.

The graveled voice on the loudspeaker shouted, "Sold!"

The same lecherous voice that commented on a herder's ample bosom. Ariadne. He was sure of it, and he hadn't seen her exit the barn with the others.

Telly pulled his herd forward, ignoring the clamor of beasts, and slurs of disrespect from hulking Consortium guardians lining the corridor and deciding his fate.

He was a fool. They would take his herd and escort him to a recycling pit, just like they were probably doing to the others. And Ariadne would be used and abused. Herders had traveled light years and expected compensation only to find a world stinking of feces, poverty, and corruption.

Telly scowled at a soldier abruptly shoving him into the arena. Consortium soldiers cut the leashes and collars and kicked his herd into the arena. Loudspeakers blared from a digital reader board flashing auction prices like a malfunctioning computer display. He glanced at a bidder with a raised hand, swiveled his head towards another, then another. He searched the crowded grandstands for Ariadne.

He was grabbed from behind with strong hands squeezing his upper arms and escorted out of the arena, down a long corridor lined with office doors. He was a fool. An idiot. The mantra drummed his head.

He was steered outside into the hazy sunlight. The guards pulled him towards the same outbuilding the other swineherds had entered. One of the guards grabbed both his wrists to tighten a Kevlar restraint. The handheld pulled from his pocket was thrown to the ground. Was this same Consortium his father had abandoned his family for, abandoned Ithaca, to fight a war, to pillage the weak? A parent his Mother had lovingly described during countless lonely nights.

"Didn't you hear me? Get the fuck in there," a guard barked.

Telly shrugged and shook his head.

The man looked confused before a realization tilted his head, and he shuttered his eyes in exasperation. "You got no Brainlinq, do you?"

Telly shook his head.

"I ought to toss you into that scum crowding the fence and be done with you," the man said.

Telly had no curt response, no sarcastic reply, only the truth: "I'm looking for my father. He fought in the war."

"Yeah, good luck with that," the man said and shoved him towards the door.

Telly continued, "I was told he won the war. I was told the *Homer* might still be here. I was told Captain Ulley might want to see his only son."

The guard loosened his grip. "And who told you all these fairy tales?"

Telly bent his head in deference. "My mother, Pennae, of Ithaca. Returning veterans told me stories of Ulley tricking this planet's defense intelligence. A ship captain told me stories of the truth being absconded by the PTST. I don't know what to believe, but I need to learn about my father."

The man coughed uncomfortably, "Heck of a story. That's not one I've heard before, and I've heard a few. The myth of the mysterious *Homer* can cause a riot, or a celebration, depending on who's listening." He snipped the restraints. "So be careful who you talk to. I'll let you go, but you'll have to deal with the wolves outside that fence."

Telly rubbed his wrists. The prospect of justice failed as the guard escorted him to a gate allowing passage through the wire fence, and into a crowd clamoring for vengeance.

Telly huddled beneath a tattered green tarp protecting a useless pile of refuse as the relentless dirty rain pelted a scolding for his misadventure. He shivered and pulled a rotted trash bag closer to his body. His escape from the Troian throng hell-bent on exacting revenge was found in a heap of porcine manure he dug his fingers into and threw at his pursuers, men unaccustomed to the revolting stench of pig shit.

Without his handheld, he was abandoned, broke, and without hope. The rain let up, allowing Telly to keep slinking through the devastated city.

The destruction was unfathomable. Roofless buildings with shattered portholes continued to billow woodsmoke. Sturdy timbers splintered like toothpicks, gnawed on by survivors seeking fuel for warmth. Brick abodes fallen and useless against the weather. Buckled streetscapes rolled by tremors of aerial bombardment.

But it was the survivors that Telly couldn't fathom. With scarred skin or blistered with burns, children stared at him with blank eyes as he slipped past. Mothers and daughters hawked their mangled bodies for a cup of rice, any tidbit of food welcomed by outstretched hands. Old gray-haired men slumped outside hovels murmured for death to finally take them.

Telly walked among the living dead. His own survival became a growing concern. He shouted at a squad of well-armed Consortium troopers marching down the street, beseeching them to help the starving and dying. Met with chuckles and indifference. The rain and the misery, the indifference and callousness, futility mirrored the rancid mud in which he stood.

Days seemed like weeks. Weeks seemed a lifetime. Telly stumbled through the fragments of what must have been a great city. The occasional aid stations overwhelmed with the broken, the ill, and the dying were avoided. A random troop carrier patrolling the streets might toss rock candy to packs of hungry children following close behind. Telly moved in to find pieces that had scattered beneath charred timber or disappeared between the crumpled mortar joints of building foundations. The sugary taste was exquisite until the glucose fired an insatiable hunger in his belly.

He learned to trade the sugar for bits of rice or oats to chew into a paste, pretending the thick tasteless muck was chocolate chip cookie dough he and Helen had once squirreled away from their mother. The dirty rain felt like sandpaper over his skin. The heavy muck caked on his tattered shoes worsened each day.

Telly found a dark corner of a ramshackle house still supporting a framework of charred roof trusses. He picked through the brick of a shattered brick hearth and shimmied into the dark recess a chimney offered. Black soot and fresh air. He considered the accommodations a mansion by Troia's standards. Maybe he could manage to sleep for a few hours.

He drifted off, the beautiful cherubic face of Sirsee smiling and sprinkling golden petals of sunflowers on his dreams.

The acrid stench of diesel exhaust and the clamor of rubber tires atop crushed stone woke Telly from a rare peaceful dream, of strolling through a field of flowering red poppies, hand in hand with Sirsee, laughing without care. The anticipation of reaching a picnic blanket spread on a plot of trampled field grass elicited an erection he struggled to hide from the beautiful girl.

Troia's reality turned him flaccid as he wiped sleepy grit from his eyes. Teens and young boys limped past his view, their resolve seemingly undeterred by their physical impediments.

Telly caught up to the crowd converging behind a huge six-wheeled transport vehicle rolling across a bridge spanning a shallow pool of muddy water. The driver waved the throng forward at an easy pace. The truck's long-empty bed intrigued him. No food. No help. Why the excitement?

The driver steered the vehicle into a wide expanse bordering the river. A concrete park bench leaned on its single leg near a mangled jumble of playground bars twisted into submission. The gnarly truck wheels churned the muddy soil, circling expanding doughnut configurations, accelerating, letting thick rubber spew muck across flat land. An increasing number of faces gathered to watch the odd spectacle.

A burly truck driver shadowed beneath a sweat-stained fedora swung the cab door open and stepped down the metal treads, dragging a bulging burlap sack behind him. Clothed in a heavy one-piece tan coverall with the bib buttoned to one side, a uniform sure to ward off cold and rain, the man scratched his salt and pepper beard as he eyed the crowd. Appraising skinny tweens, waifish girls, bent old men, he squinted at Telly and pointed a stubby finger at him and beckoned.

Telly swallowed hard as all eyes turned to stare at him. He took a tentative step closer.

"Don't have all day, boy!" the man shouted.

Telly hurried across the churned soil, stumbling over shallow ruts and clods of dirt, feeling the man appraise each misstep.

The man held out the bag. "Got any clue as to what we're doing today?"

Telly studied the turned soil littered with dead grass. "Well . . . I would guess . . ."

The truck driver shook his head. "Guessing's for games, boy."

Telly swallowed the slight. "It looks . . . maybe like you're planting a field."

The burly man clenched his fist. "And I *guessed* you might be the brightest of that bunch. This seed is getting heavy. Any guesses as to what kind?" He handed the sack to Telly then wrinkled his nose. "Smell porcine poop. You one of those misfortunates to find your stock stolen by the occupiers?"

Telly grimaced and nodded, ashamed and infuriated in equal proportions.

"Well, I can't help you with that, but I can throw a bone to these people, if they want to help themselves. Let's get going," the man said. He turned and gazed up at a sun blotted in thick shades of heavy particulate. "Icarus is my name. You got one?"

Telly blabbered his name then followed the farmer.

Sprinkling corn seed then pressing the kernels into the soil to give each an opportunity to sprout took its toll. Slumped against the big front tire of the transport, Telly dozed in and out before Icarus's basso bark startled him. Days of fending for scraps of food, fighting for a warm dry space to sleep, the hard day felt like a life of luxury. And yet the soreness of muscles he would endure tomorrow, and the next, and the next, felt like . . . victory. Accomplishment on a primal scale.

Icarus kicked his foot to rouse him. "You did good, kid. Could use a few more of you on the ranch. Whatcha ya know about bovines?"

Telly couldn't help but chuckle before displaying a single upturned thumb.

One of seven ranch hands, Telly sat at the bottom of the hierarchy. Tasked with slopping feces out of porcine pens, herding bovines on foot while others rode on the backs of slow-footed humpbacked reptiles, or pumping the contents of the outhouse into a fiberglass tank for transport to a distant field. Telly loved it, enjoying the company of the other young men and women, each equally happy to have a job on the decimated planet.

But he worried about Helen and his mother. By now, the Martians would be asserting relentless pressure on Pennae, overt and covert, until she would be forced to wave surrender from the constant stress. Or maybe his father finally arrived home. Either occurrence would send shockwaves through a Jupiter Moon Alliance slowly crumbling to the ruthless dominion of the Consortium.

Telly brushed off his flannel work shirt and aimed for the main house, a substantial four-bedroom home meticulously constructed from brick and mortar with Icarus and his wife the only residents. Telly brushed his denim jeans free of loose straw then knocked on the front door. He fidgeted with his soiled appearance as shuffling footsteps approached.

The door swung open. Dark emerald eyes magnified behind frames with thick glass lenses, a woman just a few years older offered a pleasant smile. Her premature gray hair swept back in a knotted bun, she apologized that Icarus had not returned from his chore.

Telly smiled thinly and nodded. He turned to go.

"You can wait inside," she said. "I'll get you a spot of tea while we see how long the old boy takes to help birth a heifer at the Zeit Ranch. Old hat for him, but Melissa Zeit and her clown of a husband seem to have difficulty with bovine anatomy." She stepped back to hold the door wide open as an invitation.

Telly stepped inside, gently placing his muddy boots on the tapestry of a worn rug.

"You need not worry about the mud. My husband has tromped inside these walls covered in slop and shit. But my realm remains defiant." She chuckled.

Telly whispered thanks and followed her down the hallway to an office. The woman limped as if saddled with an ill-fitted prosthetic. She beckoned him and pointed at a tattered high-backed chair fronting a desk constructed like Frankenstein's monster. A leg made of gnarled wood, a slab of stone for another, the barrel of a laser rifle as another, the desktop was a smooth slab of incinerated polymer.

Unsure, he turned to leave. She pointed him towards the same seat.

"The Fates have grumbled and groused with your arrival," she said. "I'll get the tea." She shuffled down the hallway, muttering indecipherable Troian slang.

Telly remained standing, staring at joints of the scarred carbonite flooring, hoping Icarus or even "tea" might excuse him back to his chores, a lingering he could spend feeding the piglets, or repairing a gate latch on a corral restraining one of the indigenous reptilian Humpers used as oxen. Laziness gnawed at him to leave.

A ruckus at the front door made him quickly sit down. The murmuring of voices. He rubbed his forehead. Recited the words he had memorized for just this occasion.

Icarus barged into the office and slumped into the big chair behind the desk. "Mighty times. Mighty times we live in. Telly, you're a man that time might never understand. Games and puzzles. My witch wife plays them. We all play them in a way. What can I do for you?"

Telly swallowed. "I need to get home. To Ithaca. I think my family needs me."

Icarus chuckled with a hearty head of steam. "Young prince. I know all about you. My witch wife says what you need is to check in with your mother. And I have the means." He pulled out a glass flask half full of brown liquid and took a jolt, blanching, then sighing. "Been a long time since I had the need to swallow some of that."

He corkscrewed a stopper into the flask and set it down on the desk. "Did some digging into the story you been telling the crew hands. The son of the *Homer*'s famous Captain Ulley. A prince of the Ithaca habitat. A boy in search of his father. A man running from Martian trouble." Icarus sighed then took another slug. "Worst thing I did was confide in Cassandra. Hell, her tarot cards came flying out of the closet. Her old books came flying open. The kettles boiled steam for her visions. Little chess pieces moved around as if I didn't know what she does in her sleep."

Cassandra shuffled in carrying a tray of teacups and hot water, pushing aside the flask for space on the desk. Telly swallowed at the unreconciled eye contact between Icarus and Cassandra. His eyes were glassy but resolute. Her eyes were stern and challenging.

Telly coughed. "Is this tea? I don't think I've ever tried it."

The old woman picked up the pot and poured an identical brown liquid into a cup without looking away from Icarus.

Icarus chuckled. "You get tea. I get loose."

Telly accepted the cup of tea from Cassandra and sipped the remarkably bland liquid, his expression eliciting a hearty laugh from Icarus. Cassandra excused herself from the room.

Icarus took another belt of the liquid and tapped the flask on the desktop as if undecided. He pushed his face over the desk towards Telly and . . . and studied him, eyeing the crook of his chin, the angle of his jawbone, then leaned back into the chair. To take another drink.

"Let me tell you a story," Icarus said. His glassy eyes stared aimlessly at the wood rafters of the ceiling. "No. Let the story tell you a story."

Cassandra stormed into the room and snatched the flask off the desk. "He keeps this shit thinking it might protect him from the dreadful past we lived through. He's had enough. Feed him some tea. Talk him out of the horrors he chooses to relive."

Telly stood to leave but found Cassandra's sideways expression that said she expected better of him.

Icarus gagged and vomited over the desk.

Telly stared at the muck. Sour and acidic. No worse than porcine puke.

And he wondered about Icarus.

CHAPTER 25

Icarus

NOW. I'M GONNA TELL YOU a story before I solve your problem. So you can get a deeper appreciation of the how and why.

I completed seven combat missions before I figured out my squadron's bombing runs were a total waste of time and resources. Ground-based radar installations, surface-to-air missile batteries, bunkered ground forces all legitimate targets determined by fleet intelligence. Satellite and drone reconnaissance showed the enemy regrouping, resupplying, and gearing up for our inevitable ground assault.

Pure bovine feces, every gigabyte of it.

As a wing commander of the *Agamemnon*'s 23rd fighter squadron, I was responsible for carrying out suborbital assaults on Troia's ground defenses. To soften the playing field for our troops suffering from five years of sucking their own thumbs, or playing Paddlebuck, or dice games, while Mintaur and his cadre of ass-kissing officers failed to breech Troia's orbital defense perimeter.

Hell, I sucked on my own thumb as much as the others.

And then the heavens cracked open. Strobes and klaxons ordered every ship to battle stations. We scrambled like newbies to find our corsairs. Lieutenant Glass stumbled and turned an ankle trying to climb into his cockpit even as his Brainlinq issued a prissy alarm claiming wounded in action. But Glass persevered.

I gathered my squadron into my Brainlinq protocols. Eason drummed his thumb nervously on the throttle. Webster licked sweat from her lips as she squeezed the throttle. Fish-face fondled his genitals beneath that too-tight EV flight suit he was proud to squeeze into. The omnipotent Brainlinq provided me direct communication links to each of the eight fighter pilots of my squadron. Heart rate monitors indicated high levels of anxiety, repetitive dermal movements, whispers, and the rising nervousness of finally . . . finally, after five years, swarming to fight a battle.

And I played each piece as if I lived in a virtual reality game.

No losses. Not a shot fired at my people. Luck can always dodge a bullet.

In the debriefing room upon completion of our fifth sortie, Webster looked at me like she wanted to bite my face off. "Those were families. Scavenging for food. And we just dropped a few tons of napalm on them." She pulled her lips tight to display those fangs she bragged about. "I hope command reviews our little barbeque with fleet Intelligence before we drop again," she spat and stormed off.

Maybe my obedience to duty had increased my naivety. The red flags waved, the alarm signals sounded, but the horror of our bombings continued.

A bunker suspected to contain nuclear-tipped warheads being prepped for a Troian missile battery was really a food storage warehouse. The airfield for staging a battery of Troian artillery pieces was a simple refugee camp using military gear to survive. The destruction of the aqueduct supplying water to an already decimated Troian city was the final straw. I watched explosions ripple the waterway and allow the precious liquid to spill into the arid desert to disappear into silty sand.

My formal complaints up the chain of command found deaf ears and muted Brainlinq's. It made no sense. What did we hope to accomplish with the destruction of Troian infrastructure? Well, that was answered when Mintaur announced the Consortium's Martian faction would be granted exclusive colonization rights to the planet. It was like the final piece of the puzzle suddenly fell into place.

The fucking Martians.

For thousands of years, Martian colonists failed to terraform that shithole planet with any viable atmosphere. City-sized arcologies constructed to lure Earth's adventurous pioneers and visionaries, instead brought an influx of unsavory personalities escaping the evil karma they had . . . had wrought on Earth. For untold years, that corrupt hegemony ruled, spurring expansion with improving technology, continuously spewing carbon into the thin atmosphere, all with the misguided premise of heating that Martian atmosphere into submission. Plutocrats revolted from the arcologies to excavate vast subterranean chambers to cultivate a soulless society bereft of the sun. An existence spurring each new generation to expand the limits of a captured existence.

And just a few centuries ago, Brainlinq was born. To facilitate information transmission, to foster socialization with others living in cities and arcologies too distant for rudimentary surface transportation systems. A tiny innocuous patch worn on the neck. An adolescent badge of honor. Children reveled in subliminal access to their friends even as parents clamored for monitoring access and ultimate control. The unique technology garnered Martian society untold riches, political clout, and a place at the table deciding intergalactic expansion. A Brainlinq solved the conundrum of human brain activity decaying in stasis during a jump through folded space-time.

Welcomed by the Consortium, the Martian contingent achieved equal say in the affairs of Earth, and the outlying habitats and colonies flourishing throughout the solar system.

Those fucking Martians. It seemed like any misery popping up during our diaspora out of the solar system was rooted in those Martian caverns.

And this time was no different. Even as I squeezed my eyes shut to block out the destruction we rained on Troia, my Brainlinq continued shoving memories of our squadron's bombing runs into my ocular vision. Satellite and low-orbit reconnaissance I knew to be false. I sent my objections and disgust up the chain of command but was met with silence. Then demotion. Until I was relegated to flying a crapshoot shuttle for a ferry in and out of the *Agamemnon*.

My father would have laughed, but encouraged me to persevere. And not fly too close to the sun. I never thought I would understand exactly what he meant by that. I was wrong about that too.

I shuttled throngs of green-skinned soldiers, backed up by weasel-eyed Martian interrogators, setting down in dicey landing zones, lifting off and waiting for the signal to retrieve them. They didn't want witnesses to any atrocities. I sucked in huge breaths to prevent my hand from shoving the throttle forward and abandon those faceless fucks. I'm not too proud to say fear of reprisal kept my hand steady on the stick.

Nightmares followed me into my bunk. Small children running and screaming and diving into a muddy river as an air raid sounded, their tiny arms flailing in the murky waters, drowning as I watched helplessly from above. Or the remnants of a devastated city wiped off the surface by a sixty-kiloton kinetic harpoon as I watched from the sky.

I woke each day hoping to find new orders, to return home to Earth, and my father, who I feared had passed away during my interminable duty. I woke hoping to find a tiny scrap of humanity still acting like a caring, compassionate species. Each day I woke hoping to find a benevolent God putting an end to the holocaust with a snap of His miraculous fingers.

I woke each day with a prayer on my lips, addressed to a God who had decided to sit this one out.

And found love.

The depths of my despair had reached a bottom—pardon the pun—but I considered any opening of any lavatory I accessed, a black pit summoning me, to be flushed like a... My Brainlinq ratted out any escape I considered. The Martians obviously controlled the Brainlinq.

One morning, I was ordered to pilot a shuttle towards a shattered arcology still standing near the planet's equator, flattened by the fleet, but teeming with ragged survivors scavenging the ruins and living in the surrounding jungle. The lush green foliage alerted me— the Consortium's blunt message of delivering misery atop misery had somehow spared this tiny archipelago.

Precise vectors and pinpoint landing coordinates flowed into my Brainlinq. Confirming an unpredictable wind shear, I offered an alternate landing vector. The initial vectors were shoved back into my head. And I mean *shoved*. Like the response from a petulant parent. Fuck it, I tapped a few keys on the shuttles console and took manual control.

The response was more than I expected, and I expected a shit storm from the Consortium for my reckless gambit.

Flight computers scrambled. The port engine fired with heavy thrust as power from the starboard engine paused. The shuttle spun like a wounded dove, gaining concentric force as we fell to our death.

And how can I say this? My approaching demise felt familiar, like I had been in that exact predicament before. Falling away from the scorching sun and down into the dark ocean below. To greet me. To accept me as a mother might. Offering me peace to calm my tormented soul.

I didn't see my life flashing before my eyes—I saw my father, bifocals perched on his nose, sitting at his workbench sorting odd pieces of wood and studying useless pieces of plastic, a tiny pair of forceps in his hand. He looked up to offer a knowing grin I knew spelled trouble.

He had wanted me to escape the futility of life on Earth, wanted me to live a life outside the control of the fascist regime of the Consortium. And had somehow employed slick manipulations to get me a commission into the Navy as a pilot. I just needed to learn to fly.

My performance ratings as a cadet were nothing short of spectacular.

The memory of my father was fresh and raw as we fell. I fantasized seeing his glowing approval. I shunted my Brainlinq to quell the noise and alarm and fought the cyclic control stick to avert a crash landing before setting down hard on what looked like the buckled asphalt of a parking lot surrounded in a ring of collapsed structures bombed beyond recognition.

At the center, fluted plaster columns sheared at the base lay like spilled toothpicks. The circular stairway of a majestic palace rose precariously among a pile of shattered stained glass and splintered furniture, a provincial palace in a better time, maybe one for the Troian aristocracy.

My landing heroics were met with scorn and ridicule from six soldiers as they lumbered down the loading ramp of the shuttle. Oversized torsos stacked on augmented limbs, olive-tinted facial skin smeared in green and black camouflage paint, thick body armor, heavy weapons slung across their backs and chests. The expediency and danger of approaching combat belied their chuckling banter of "picking daisies" and "rescuing damsels in distress."

At times, my sarcastic revulsion for the Consortium found no boundaries, had no filters. My exact words are still a little foggy . . . but I think I implied the squad might find defeat in a clash with a class of kindergarten children hiding in the ruins.

I awoke staring at the gravel, inches from my eyes, my own thoughts unsure of my existence. The sorry-ass LT had cold-cocked me. Another incident to report. Then climb another notch lower down the ladder of demotion.

I checked my shuttle with one good eye as I killed time waiting for the squad to return. I could've restarted Brainlinq and had it run a diagnostic on my wound or even reacquire the link for the onboard computer. But I just didn't trust that fucking insidious apparatus embedded in my neck.

Out of the thick jungle behind the buildings, I watched the squad return, escorting four girls. Teenagers, I guessed. Their long, flowing gowns as if returning from a high school prom were torn and muddy. Their hands cuffed in front. Their blond hair pulled back, but rogue strands told of their primal existence. Their hollow eyes complemented sunken cheeks. The same features typical of the starving Troian populace I had the misfortune to witness too often.

Four soldiers broke off and commenced a search of the palace remnants. The girls rudely ushered to my shuttle wouldn't meet my gaze. Except the last one, I thought the oldest, maybe eighteen. Her beguiling steel-gray eyes bore a color I had never witnessed. Her chin lifted as if to look down on me, or my status. Instead, we locked eyes. The tiny twinkle of a sly smile brightened her soiled face.

My stomach dropped worse than the death-defying ride down. My throat dried instantly. I know, I know. The disgruntled shuttle pilot finds love in the wrong place.

A soldier prodded the girls towards the gangway, towards the dark cargo bay. Assuring me I would never see the girl again.

I hustled to the gangway. "Hold up." I checked the insignia on his lapel. "Corporal. I got a nitrogen leak I'm trying to track down in the hold."

The corporal narrowed his eyes. "I got nothing reported."

I improvised. "That shitshow of landing vectors rattled the whole ship. I'm going through the safety protocols. Maybe sit your guests down by the front skid. Should be the safest place if a tank ruptures." I had nothing left to lose, except maybe another fist on the opposite side of my jaw.

Like a giddy schoolboy, I guided the four girls to sit in the slim shade offered by the stubby nose of the fuselage. Using their restraints, I assisted each girl to sit. Three sets of eyes ignored me as if I were just another ruthless oppressor. The beguiling eyes of the girl stirring my heart spoke her appreciation with the tiniest touch of her finger as I helped her into the shade.

The girl whispered, "Don't let them find it."

The shadow of the corporal loomed.

I improvised again. "They're dehydrated. Gonna make for a nasty ascent."

I scurried up the gangway to retrieve four foil packets of pure ionized water used to quell bouts of airsickness. I twisted the feeding tubes and offered each girl a drink. I fumbled opening the last. Her beautiful eyes remained pitiful yet pierced my soul.

The corporal kicked my foot. "LT looking for dust-off in twelve minutes. You can play with the girls after Mintaur gets done." He snickered with a cheek bulging with outlawed chaw.

"What are you boys looking for in the ruins?" I asked.

"Promotions and reward money," he said.

I gave him a scoffing expression that asked for the truth.

"Ansible," he said.

A rare, almost mythical device capable of communicating instantly across the galaxy with no lag in time. A device that could alter any manner of deficiencies in communicating with the Sol system.

"So, a snipe hunt," I said.

"Probably. But intel reported one might be located in a Troian palace. Found four princesses, so what the hell," the corporal said. "Not a complete waste."

I checked the ruins for the other soldiers. "So, what happens to these kids?"

"Who the fuck knows. They'll be interrogated then probably sold to some Aphrodite madam," he said. "I might take a peek at that youngest one, if and when."

Now I was the one that might have a nasty ascent. What was it about war that boiled humanity down to cavemen devoid of morals and decency? As a lowly shuttle pilot, I was helpless to assist the girls. My rank as ensign couldn't buy squat in the *Agamemnon*'s Aphrodite section. A quick thought to herd the girls back into the jungle, to run, escape, was squashed as they sat starved and depleted. And I would be shot in the back with a burst of plasma pellets.

I waved the corporal off and hustled up the gangway as if rushing to check on the leak. I grabbed a handhold at the bay door and locked eyes with the older girl. I couldn't save any of them. I could barely save myself, from my mouth, my sense of justice, the moral code instilled in me by my father. Even one whose beauty was destined for the redlights of Aphrodite.

I rushed down the gangway with four more packets of water, twisting the caps free and handing them to thirsty teenagers. Kneeling in front of a beauty to be lost soon, I feigned a struggle with the packet cap and whispered, "Your name, what is it?"

Her whisper cold-cocked me. "Cassandra. *You* will find the prize. Remember, *you* need to find the prize."

The corporal lifted me from the shadows like a paper puppet. Prodded me away with the tip of his plasma rifle. "LT says no chatterbuck with the hostages."

Hostages? Fucking child-kidnapping victims they were. I sneered, thinking to strike the armored brute with my bare knuckles then submitted, spying the others tromp out of the ruins.

My eyes blurred watching the girls stiffen and whimper by the gruff manhandling of the squad as each girl was led into the cargo hold.

The LT pushed his ugly scarred face close to mine. The aroma of Martian wafted from his sweat. "You need to get your Brainlinq squared away."

Long moments passed. Sarcastic retorts filled my mouth only to be swallowed.

I pushed past him. "Settle or mettle. Dust-off in two minutes."

I punched the ship into the atmosphere with an eight-G acceleration, my anger and impotence pushing the throttle to sound alarms. A force sure to make man or beast sick from intense gravitational pressure.

———

Now, young prince, that is but half my story. You need only concern yourself with the ending. Or perhaps, it's only the beginning for you. Follow me.

Slipping past Cassandra loitering in the hallway, I led Telly down two flights of steps to the basement level. I could almost feel unspoken words pass between Telly and Cassandra. Maybe it was my anxiety at firing up a device kept hidden in the dark for long years. It had served no purpose, other than to help me bargain for Cassandra's release. It continued to serve no purpose . . . except . . . its existence truly spoke of an almighty God governing the universe.

I lit a candle then three more to illuminate the cramped wood-working shop. The sharp unmistakable aroma of fresh-cut cedar flourished, battling the pervasive odor of charred lumber. I searched the cinderblock walls for the precise block above the workbench. I picked up a tiny hammer used for repairing leather harnesses or occasional stubborn electronics. Dust and cobwebs camouflaged the porous block and made me hesitate to find the exact brick. I struck a patch of mortar with the hammer, then again, and again. Each strike righteous and revealing, until opening a black hole befitting a mouse.

I stuck my fingers in and paused. "You get a thirty-second message. Your mother will have thirty seconds to respond. Are you sure of the capabilities of Ithaca's governing intelligence AI and . . . absolutely positive of its loyalty?"

I waved off the boy's questions, however valid they might have been. And asked again. Telly nodded.

I retrieved an orb the size of a tiny apple from the opening, its smooth skin mimicked the texture of fine silk. It began to vibrate as if excited. I stared at the tiny vibrating globe, pulsing with mesmerizing shimmers of pure white light, drawing my eyes closed. Summoned by the light, I had the urge to communicate with it. That would serve no purpose.

I averted my eyes. "You can send your mother a greeting. Thirty seconds is all you'll get. She'll get about the same if the AI can interpret the message."

"Euma will know." Telly paced the length of the workbench, his expression twisted with conflict and confession. His calloused hands knotted and untwined.

"Your time starts now," I said, "Thirty seconds."

Telly stood at my shoulder, working his mouth like a guppy before blubbering, "I want to come home."

Words any child might speak. Words every parent longed to hear. Words issued across light years to a helpless worried mother.

I warned the boy. The ansible signal might not be received. And any prolonged attempts could lure the Consortium storm sailors down to the farm.

The orb glowed, and projected the profile of a beautiful brunette, her regal features swirled into focus. Pennae. The boy reached for the orb as if the woman was within reach. Telly whispered a plea: "Mother."

The stern expression wrinkling Pennae's face made me think she was irritated but the ansible's shimmering picture could often deceive. Pennae appeared to step back from a fluttering stage curtain crowded with young girls checking each other's makeup and costumes. I pried my eyes from the beautiful woman to see Telly whispering, "Where's Helen?"

A hundred panes with the identical capture of Pennae's response swirled across the projection. The Ithaca AI couldn't handle the overwhelming burst of transmission quarks the orb required for its instantaneous communication. Thirty seconds had expired.

Pennae lifted her chin as if accepting a call via her Brainlinq. "Your target grows. Your ignorance is complete. And correct. Passage home arranged. Find your father's—"

The orb faded to black, morphing back into a simple polished stone, cloaked to hide from the world above.

Telly watched the orb for long moments. His teeth worked hard to chew his lower lip.

I wanted to ask the boy if he understood the cryptic meaning of his mother's message, but his furrowed forehead said he was deep in thought with the same question. I returned the ansible to the hollow masonry block. I blew out all but one candle. Telly hadn't moved.

"I used to be a great pilot. Maybe still am. But the comfort of space changed, too many vectors shoved down my throat. Go here. Go there. Do this. Do that. Brainlinq rules like the strings of a puppet master. You don't have one. Rare for spacefarers," I said, fishing for something I really didn't want to catch.

Telly finally looked at me in the faint candlelight. His youth pronounced in the shadowed light. Apprehension fluttered in the rapid blink of his eyes wet with homesickness. "I should go. You might be in danger."

I scoffed, "I can guess what your mother meant by her message. You figured out the Brainlinq isn't so benevolent and . . . and that knowledge divulged by a lad of your stature . . . makes you an enemy of the state." My words were not a question but a statement of experience.

Telly nodded.

"Then let's get you to a port of call. You'll see how a resistance operates. And you'll go home. Carry the fight to the heart of the Consortium," I said as I returned the orb to its hidey-hole. "And those motherfucking Martians!"

I grabbed the boy's trembling hand, hoping to calm him. His mother's voice haunted me. I'd guessed right on the first part. Any interrogator AI would have offered the same conjecture. The boy was raw and innocent. Looking for a lost father. A fruitless odyssey many sons had attempted after the war. A crusade I would have joined without even thinking.

I blew out the last candle.

The mother's last words haunted me in the dark as I led the boy up the stairs. The message was cryptic in its simplicity, given the context. Find your father was a given . . . so why use precious seconds to urge the boy to find something he already searched for?

Telly walked ahead down the hallway. His shoulders slumped, his gait slovenly. Offering a grunt as a weak greeting to Cassandra as he passed.

At the door closing, Cassandra turned and aimed for me. Her impediment disappeared as she rushed to push her small torso close to my chest. She lowered her glasses to beam steel-grey eyes. Her words sent shudders down my spine.

"I warned you. And you didn't believe me," Cassandra said. "The Oracles are right. The prophecy comes to life."

CHAPTER 26

HOMER PINGED, RELAYING CREW COMPETENCE evaluations, navigation diagnostics, Prometheus drive status, projected fuel consumption scenarios, and a myriad of standard fleet readiness reports.

Ulley ignored it all, tapping his finger on the scarred polymer desktop, reliving every second of the conversation with his father inside the strange nebula. Was the encounter with Laertes an elaborate dysfunction? Was the reunion with Patro another hallucination?

A hundred questions had formed after his inexplicable exit from the Hades Nebula. No answers would be forthcoming, except from Circe.

Homer issued a sound mimicking the clearing of a throat, broaching its interruption into Ulley's scattered thoughts. "Crew evaluations are complete. All except for the ship's captain. And gauging by the captain's current biometrics and incessant drumming on an inanimate object, his evaluation may be marked substandard."

Ulley paused his finger. "What happens when we die, Homer? Our spirit? The life force that makes us unique in this universe? What I experienced in that nebula suggests a lot more than us as organic compounds simply returning to the primordial soup."

Homer cleared its throat again. "I am not privy to what transpired on your journey into the Hades Nebula. All ship sensors failed at your encounter with the nebula's dense gas field. As expected. Communications and navigational tracking failed. As expected. The shuttle should have been declared lost." Homer cleared its throat a third time. "And yet your shuttle emerges from an expanse of gas and dust that might swallow whole star systems."

Ulley swatted at disjointed thoughts nagging him like bloodsucking insectoids. Joined by visions of what he believed to have seen. *Enough of this.* His father died a long time ago. Patro's memories were still fresh and raw. But what if . . . the answer really didn't matter anymore. He imagined Patro dancing that weird jig like a drunken madman at Helen's wedding.

Homer chirped, "Our benefactor has not returned, and the crew clamors for home, Captain."

He desperately wanted to see Circe again to find answers to the hundreds of questions only she might provide. The time-traveling sorceress had not shown her face for weeks.

He sighed. "This fucking odyssey is gonna kill me. Let's go home."

"Aye, Captain," the crew chimed through his Brainlinq.

A melancholy ambivalence accompanied the *Homer's* detachment from Circe's ship. The surreal experience fell like absurd rain splattering out of an artificial concept. He hoped to see his benefactor again, stroke her soft cheek, offer his heartfelt thank you, but she had remained elusive, if not gone altogether. Had the Zoosh tightened their quarantine into a noose for Circe? The girl was too sly to be caught, and her ability to bend time and travel parallel dimensions was a formidable deterrence, even to the powerful Zoosh.

Homer pinged with navigational overlays of several possible destinations. They would follow Patro's rudimentary directions until a constellation, a familiar nebula, or a charted star system was recognized. Flying blind, Patro would have said.

"Long-range scans have identified two systems that may be worth a visit. And two others to be avoided," Homer said.

"Explain," Ulley said.

"A small singularity in a binary orbit with an extremely dense neutron star."

"And neither on any survey charts?" Ulley stated.

"I suggest we initiate multiple folds, emerge at a safe distance, recorrect our course based on revised scans," Homer said. "I have

plotted our course assuming you would approve my recommenda-
tions."

"You know what they say about assuming, Homer?" Ulley said.

Homer chuckled. "I am a digitized personification of many entities, but I have no ass to speak of."

Ulley eyed the acceleration couch unfolding like a dark forbidden
flower. "Secure quarters for main engine ignition. Warm up the Prometheus Drive and make haste to the nearest Lagrange Point."

Via the Brainlinq, he watched, heard, and smelled the crew scramble for their stations. The omnipotent sensation made him nauseous.

The initial fold would be relatively short, culminating in a quick
emergence into the first of the uncharted star systems, then a quick
course correction employing coordinates mapped from real space/
time, then fold again. "Remind me again the duration of the first
fold. In standard time?"

"Just long enough for a well-deserved nap. Seventy-three standard days," Homer said.

Seventy-three days. Easy peasy. He would use the time to purge
the carbon buildup from the air scrubbers, check the shuttle again
after encountering that nasty dust and gas inside the nebula, maybe
start a journal, maybe dictate a letter home. Just in case.

"Homer, I'll be flying with you. How's your chess program?"

Seventy-three days passed quickly, if he didn't think about Pennae,
or Telly, or Helen, a beautiful little girl he may never meet. Or if he
didn't eat. Grumpies and feces cubes tended to dislike each other in
the folded black void. Homer took no pity on him in games of chess,
checkers, or any one of thousands stored in its matrix. The ship was
wiped and vacuumed spic and span. The digital countdown to emergence from the fold ticked in his head like a dripping faucet.

The crew would emerge from their stasis, clamoring for solid
food, real water, and grumbling for home. A typical crew, a good
crew, a loyal cadre Ulley found himself hiding from. If for no other
reason than they reminded him of home.

Alarms blared. Klaxons sounded.

The *Homer* emerged from the fold, rumbling, transporting a
sudden rush of spatial vertigo.

Ulley laughed as he climbed out of the acceleration couch, a giddiness bending him over until he held his hands up in surrender. The short nap had revived a sense of well-being lost in the permeating malaise of consistent nothingness. "I know. I know."

Homer shouted, "Recommend acceleration to one hundred seventy-three million kilometers from primary star."

Ulley chuckled. "Fine. Fine. Do what you want. Are you hearing that? Its absolutely beautiful."

The ship growled with the ignition of the fusion engines. Ulley fell hard against the bulkhead, his torso squeezed into an alcove designed for recycled food containers. His smile, a malevolent rictus fluctuating between pain and pleasure. Homer filled Ulley's Brainlinq with updated navigational data, fuel consumption, and a litany of mundane information only a quartermaster might find useful.

The concerto of female opera singers faded within the roaring burn of the fusion engines. At least that's what he thought the melody resembled, but he couldn't be positive. Impossible music. Wagner. *Ride of the Valkyries*. Pennae's favorite opera. Impossible.

Homer pinged its voice directly into his Brainlinq. "I have detected a distress signal from one of the moons of the gas giant nine hundred million miles from the primary star."

"Let me hear it," Ulley said. A concerto swarmed his senses, a gorgeous soprano singing Ulley's praises. War hero. Loving husband. Caring father. Please come to rescue the poor souls stranded on this moon. And he would. "Set a course for the moon. Prepare to wake the crew. We might have to initiate a rescue mission."

The engine burn died. Directional thrusters fired to rotate the ship. Engines fired again. Ulley was pressed into his workstation, the sharp edge of the tabletop biting into his kidney. The excruciating pain caused him to scream like a banshee, curse the existence of the ship's unforgiving AI. Homer should have warned him before firing the engines, regardless of the magnitude of a rescue mission.

The din of the engines increased, vibrating with an unsustainable acceleration. He pinged Homer to shut down the engines. And again. The acceleration persisted. He reached for a control panel with a tree of status indicators blinking red. The acceleration was too much for a human body to withstand.

"Homer, terminate acceleration" Ulley whimpered. "Please."

"The children cry for rescue. I am that hero," Homer said.

"*We* are the heroes, my friend, and crashing into that moon won't save anyone," Ulley said.

The deafening roar gnawed at his insides. The crushing pain intensified. Ulley's face contorted in a grimace of torture. Nightmarish memories flashed, of Patro, and of Laertes, and the hellish domain of the nebula. Attempts to remember protocols he once thought useless and archaic drowned in the din of thrust. He scoffed, remembering an old, absurdly simply password.

He shouted at Homer to shut down the engines.

Ulley closed his eyes and surfed mainframe files and subset folders using his ocular implant, burrowing deep into encrypted code that greeted him like an old roadmap. Bypassing lengthy scripts of code and unopened updates, unfamiliar modules he promised to investigate later and found what he thought he would never need. His ocular pointer trembled over the icon.

Ulley offered a final plea. "Homer?"

"The children! We need to help the children!"

Ulley cursed beneath his breath. *What was Homer hearing?*

He issued failsafe commands to terminate the AI's access to the ship's mainframe components. He retrieved shipboard diagnostic controls and studied the selection.

Then silence. The engines died. He floated in zero G as the gravity generators fell offline. His torso ached. His head wanted to explode. The concerto that had tickled his memories returned. A soft cavalcade of beautiful voices rising and falling in unison with a full orchestra.

Homer screamed at Ulley to return control of the ship.

Long hours passed as Ulley took command of life support functions, crew stasis modules, and reinitialized the gravity generators. An alarm blared. Homer was prepping one of the shuttles for an attempted launch. Ulley terminated the comms link for both shuttles. Homer rerouted command structures to bypass Ulley, using a vague subroutine written and designed to repel possible intrusions by a hostile boarding party.

The game of move-countermove persisted for days, maybe weeks, Ulley's circadian rhythms thrown into a blender of Homer's making. Their digital exchanges proved an ulcer in their relationship.

Ulley offered an olive branch. "My friend, if we continue current course and speed, that moon you so desperately want to visit will come into scanning range in three days. I propose a truce."

Whistles and high-pitched tones hidden within heavy static screeched through Ulley's Brainlinq. He was wary of Homer's manipulation, though the AI hadn't outwardly exhibited true deception.

Not like the litany of humans Ulley had encountered. A trait of humanity to propagate the urban myth of the Others fearing and shunning humans simply because their lies and deceit. A species to be feared, or exterminated, or isolated from a ruling dominion of higher intelligence.

Homer operated as if he oversaw another game of chess. And they had played the game often, often ending in a stalemate, neither conceding, nor offering insights into strategic thinking, even as the next game waited to be played. Ulley released the hold on the communication function for Homer. The concerto played pleasantly within the deep recesses of his memory.

"We have to rescue thousands. Their voices beseech us, command us. Witness their misery. How can we ignore them?" Homer said. He whimpered. Sniffling as if his nose dripped mucus.

"Agreed. We rescue the children," Ulley said. A statement he would never disagree with . . . but. "I haven't detected any distress signal, so . . ."

"How can you not hear their screams? Their pleas," Homer said.

"What bandwidth . . . what frequency . . . what—"

"All of them. Are you fucking deaf? Your mortal bag of bones, open your auditory orifices and hear their calling!" Homer shouted.

Ulley shut down the comm link and sat back on his open couch to stare absently at his handheld tablet. The concerto lingering in the back of head hummed into a stupendous climax. A worm. A virus. But interspatial? Impossible. Spatial transmission across light years should warp the signal into garbled mush.

"Again, Homer," Ulley stated. "Truce. I'll send a few HARDs to investigate. That shouldn't rankle your motherboards."

High-Acceleration Reconnaissance Drones could reach the moon weeks in advance of the ship, but Ulley had no intention of maintaining their current course and speed. The *Homer*'s ablation shield had begun to show signs of stress from the constant acceleration into the star system. The antimatter shielding could only absorb so much dust and debris before a new generation of replicated dark matter was required to replenish the shielding. Ulley would monitor the ship's protection, with a finger on Homer's kill switch.

"HARD1 prepped and ready for launch," Ulley said, waiting for Homer to acknowledge. The AI remained disconcertingly mum. "I'm not wasting resources on a snipe hunt, my friend."

"Yes. Send it," Homer said.

The drone accelerated away at seventeen G's, discarded its empty H2 fuel tanks, and after reaching a safe distance, discarded a protective capsule to engage a subatomic antimatter engine. Ulley held his breath. Antimatter drives were unpredictable, failures and successes weighed equal on the technology scale.

He eyed the green dot of the drone in his ocular overlay of the star system, then it suddenly disappeared as the countdown reached zero.

Success or failure? The ship AI might have offered a plethora of data. If it were sane.

Instead, Ulley sifted through data streams meant for a quicker mind. HARD1 would enter the orbit of the gas giant in three standard days. Execute a flyby of the target moon. Transmit visual and atmospheric data before falling prey to the gravity of the gas giant.

Ulley cleaned the crew galley with meticulous precision, wiping the countertops as if waxing an old cedar tabletop Pennae had used to display her antique heirlooms, promising Ulley she would someday weave a tapestry for a tablecloth. The total absence of Homer was equally comforting, and disconcerting.

He wiped a finger across the transparent shield of Ensign Baker's stasis chamber, leaving a clean trail in a patina of space dust the air purifiers had failed to retain. A trail leading nowhere. Ulley checked the crewman's biometrics and stared at a peaceful sleeping face. He made the decision to keep the crew in stasis until they arrived home.

His ocular flashed—HARD2 was prepped and ready for launch. Maybe Homer was right. Maybe the screams of children were a cry for rescue from something stranded on the moon . . . maybe . . .

The repulsive scent of uncaptured grumpy gas turned Ulley's face away from the stasis chamber. A concerto of stench. Defecated smelling salts to revive even the dead.

Ulley snickered. "Smell that, my friend? No, don't answer . . ."

He checked the display in his ocular. HARD1 would arrive in twenty-seven hours.

"Ready HARD2 for launch!" Ulley shouted and tossed the broom into the corner. "Toss your consciousness into that drone, Homer, if you need to rescue ghosts but I'm going home."

Homer whimpered.

Ulley shook his head and sighed. "Launch in sixty seconds. HARD2 communication array enabled to Send Only. I don't want whatever signal has your panties in a knot to infect this drone's transmission. Satisfied with that?"

Why am I asking for approval from a malfunctioning digital intelligence? Maybe I should download my own consciousness into the drone and escape this madness. If only.

Homer whimpered again. Ulley groaned and felt a sudden need for a nap. One of the few pleasures of non-stasis interstellar star flight. He dropped onto his tiny bunk with his tablet and began scrolling through the mainframe file system download manager. The last entry was dated with the timestamp of their departure from Troia, marked as a system upgrade from the Consortium Fleet, one of hundreds received over the years and no cause for an expeditious read.

The concerto playing in the back of his head amplified. The soprano soulfully cried for someone to rescue her from the tragedy of a forced marriage. Her soulful voice hit him as if he were the operatic villain. Her voice hiccupped as it cried for her hero, warning of more villains coming to take her kingdom.

Ulley sank into a fantasy of attending an opera on the shores of Ithaca's central reservoir. Imagined cuddling against Pennae on a picnic blanket as Telly and Helen played on the soft spongey fungal turf with other children. A tiny four piece orchestra elevated atop an old-world wooden gazebo offered a communal gathering, the best Ithaca had to offer, as Ulley's stealthy fingers stroked Pennae's cloaked erogenous zones beneath their playful kibitzing.

Red lights flashed in his ocular. The lead celloist of the orchestra raked a bow across frayed strings, shrieking byzantine noise into his fantasy—the rapturous enjoyment of family, the anticipation of Pennae's seductive charms, happy, playful children. The illusion screeched to a halt.

A ship alarm strobed a red warning in his ocular. The penetrating grate infuriated him. He winced and slapped his hands over his ears. The screeching continued unabated. Agonized screams of children penetrated the screwy melody as if the orchestra now played in a schoolroom brimming with agonized children.

Was this what Homer was hearing? Maybe children truly were dying on the moon of sirens. Could Homer hear the distress call from a greater distance because of its enhanced digital sensitivity?

He screamed at the relentless noise then opened a small tear on the bunk to fashion earplugs, mustering a wad of spit to compress the spongey polyfiber. He shoved each into his ears until the tightly rolled plugs pushed against his eardrums.

The orchestra in his ear was undeterred. The children maintained their frantic wailing. Ulley slapped his hands over his plugged ears. The noise grew. He squeezed with all his strength. The small lump of the Brainlinq module embedded in his neck pushed against the meaty part of his palm.

It was the only answer. There was no sound in the void of space. Not even a whisper.

He licked his index finger and traced the outline of the one-inch square nodule embedded just below the skin. The device had to be the cause.

He began to dig at his neck with his fingernails. Hot, slippery blood impeded his foolish excavation, but the pain was minimal compared to the screeching siren reverberating in his brain.

He scratched at his own flesh until peeling back the skin and hair covering the semisolid chip. His finger traced the thin sharp edges. He tugged on the nodule. A million supernovas erupted in his vision, electrical jolts shot down his arms and legs. His fingers held firm on the technological leech.

Logic ordered him to locate a mirrored surface for assistance. The rising tide of screams amid the orchestra said he had no time. He gazed up to the bulkhead, wincing a pained expression as his fingertips dug deeper into his bloody flesh. The nodule slippery with the pulsing of blood, Ulley wedged three fingers beneath the edge of the device and pulled.

He fainted.

Ulley woke to the screams of children. Homer's whimpering. He curled his knees tighter against his chest. All was just as he remembered. The ship was gunning to the rescue of burning children. His hand was sticky with dried blood, his fingers trembled just inches from his eyes, the horrifying concerto refreshed his foggy memory.

The wound on his neck had already started to scab. Like the device had weaved a protective covering. Ulley stroked the hair and scab with a bloody fingernail. A battle scar. His first and only. He picked at the scab with a fingernail, digging deeper through the crust.

The children screamed. The orchestra played off-key as if brain-dead zombies commanded the instruments.

Ulley closed his eyes and imagined his fatherless son helpless in a soulless world. Telly was tall, like his father. Handsome, charming to the girls like his father. A good-natured prince, a rogue running rampant throughout the corridors of Ithaca. He scratched the scab. The vacuum of space issued no cries, nor played music—silence existed only in his head.

Children screamed madness, grief, and peril. The orchestra's disjointed siren summoned him to find the helpless, to commiserate, called him to rescue the children. Ulley worked a finger beneath the Brainlinq nodule and lifted gently. The sciatic nerves running down the length of each leg responded with intense bursts of pain. The radial nerves serving his arms screamed with painful sympathy. His finger dug into the flesh beneath the Brainlinq mainframe, each scratch digging deeper, offering new thresholds of pain.

This has to work. That dark, airless void outside carried no sound, except through the interface.

Ulley worked a second finger beneath the nodule. Then pinched the nodule with two fingers and a thumb in a slippery tripodal grip. He yanked hard. Flashing neon lights filled his eyes as the parasitic monofilament threads screamed with the exorcism from his brainstem.

A drunken stupor. Bad booze. Ulley blanched as his ocular screen ping-ponged in his right eye. The bulkheads wobbled. The air stunk of feces. The couch floated and fell, imagined or not.

Without a Brainlinq, he would be lost in space.

The bloody nodule hanging in his hand, its six-inch tentacles hanging like a mechanical jellyfish, Ulley bathed in silence.

And fell into oblivion.

CHAPTER 27

SILENCE IN THE VACUUM OF deep space was often described as a haunting leech slowly sucking the vestiges of a sailor's soul, an unwanted companion hitching a ride through a dimension no human should dare trespass.

Ulley bathed in the quiet. His senses heightened like a primal animal. The subtle *tink* of a drop of liquid hitting the blood splatter on the floor issued shockwaves of panic. His eyes focused on an overturned cup dribbling the last remnants of coffee sweetened with Pennae's precious memory. Another *tink* rippled the liquid spread across the floor.

Ulley groaned. The noise sounded foreign to his unaided ears, yet true. He gathered his disjointed memories cast askew by the Brainlinq's removal then chuckled without humor. Was he the first human to shitcan a Brainlinq without the aid of . . . surgery? Even Patro would be in awe of his new protocol for removal of the neural link.

And here he lay, bloody and bruised, without hearing any incessant alarms. Silent strobes flashed above his head, attempting to convey what he was unable to hear.

Ulley settled an instinctive urge to spring into action and instead studied a myriad of panel lights. Red and green, but the *Homer* was in no danger. He could locate a blanket, to snuggle against the deepening cold creeping into his thoughts. A freeze spelling . . .

Ulley sat up in a panic, demanding a damage report from Homer, shouting for a status check of the ship's ablation shield. He heard no response but derided the biomechanical parasite dangling from his hand, its storm of filaments hanging like the tentacles of a squid. A device allowed to violate his brain matter. Ulley watched the tentacles curl up into themselves as if to hide from its malicious purpose.

The ghostly quiet was sublime, and welcome. He rolled over on his back and surveyed the navigation panels, life support, weapons console, and both drive propulsion status panels. Everything required to fly the ship, if he could remember the manual algorithms required to implement each individual function.

A red light blinked on the communication panel. He rose to his knees and squinted at the light. An incoming message. He ran his finger over the SmartScreen to open an array of icons and applications. An old-fashioned keyboard appeared with stacks of application selections. He fumbled incorrect input sequences before finding an app to open the notification, waiting long minutes that would have taken a simple thought using Brainlinq.

Using the keyboard, he opened the link to HARD1 and downloaded the surveillance video. The tiny speakers mounted over the screen screamed. A banshee's wail. Ulley tapped three keys before finding the mute and continued the video.

A mountainous airless moonscape slipped into focus. A narrow continent of volcanoes dominated a plateau of garish colors circling the moon's equator. Plumes of sulfuric ash rose from dark orifices atop the crush of volcanoes, rising straight up through minimal gravity, a trail of particulates abandoned to the airless void of the moons meandering rotation.

Ulley tapped icons to zoom closer. The pockmark of volcanic cones appeared to shake and vibrate, causing the drone's camera to alter its view. The flyby course altered to an unprogrammed descent.

A scratchy, static-filled video accompanied the drone's accelerated dive toward the volcanic moon. Ulley tapped keys to refine the camera resolution using AI-generated clarification programs, but static overwhelmed the camera, and the drone. The transmission terminated.

He frowned with the failed attempt at reconnaissance. HARD1 was to perform a flyby of the moon, an altitude no closer than a hundred fifty klicks, then enter the gravity well of the gas giant and wait for retrieval, if possible. The drone had simply homed in on the sirens' signal and kamikazed.

He replayed the vid numerous times, filtering the static, or magnifying the pixels of a quadrant. He was stymied.

HARD2 would arrive the following standard day. Ulley suspected the same results would be found. He tapped the keyboard with his fingers, playing the keys like a concert pianist. The manual labor felt wonderful as his brain issued fluent commands to his fingers.

He paused his task to study his bloody hands curled over the keyboard, fingers trembling to be let loose like unrestrained canines. He smiled with a childhood memory, of coding and birthing Euma, hacking Ithaca's circadian weather system to flip days into night, a plethora of mischievous deeds attained by his clandestine entry into Ithaca's central neural network.

Was Telly a mischievous adolescent? Did his son conspire to wreak harmless havoc like he had? Or maybe Helen was to be the imp born into the family? He longed to answer such simple questions.

Ulley tapped the backspace key to retype new instructions to HARD2. The drone was to terminate all input upon receiving the new instruction. The drone was to commence transmission of visual input immediately, all other input to be deleted.

The updated commands would require three hours' transit time, another twenty-one hours before the drone would find a surveillance zone for spying on the strange volcanic cones.

Ulley looked at his bloody palm. Time enough to clean up and reconnect with the *Homer,* on a more intimate level.

The acidic odor of the chemical shower left a sour taste in Ulley's mouth. The distinctive aroma reminded him of the crowded war room on the *Agamemnon*, and the high number of Martians in attendance. A large contingent of the Consortium ruling hegemony, the Martians' proprietary control of the Brainlinq software was an enigmatic question he would never grow comfortable with.

Dressed in a smelly, wrinkled onesie, Ulley climbed down two levels to the medical bay no larger than an apartment bedroom. The tight space was swept clean. Two barren countertops combined with lightweight polymer cabinets designed to withstand rapid acceleration. The wall was properly outfitted with a menagerie of medical instruments with forgotten names.

Ulley searched an upper cabinet containing a pharmacy of stimulants, sedatives, anti-biotics, antivirals, pausing to study three sealed packages of Brainlinq implants. He located and tore open a packet of dermal repair and slapped the gooey gauze on his neck. The analgesic effects sent shivers through his body then numbed the pain pulsing from the wound.

Ulley stared at the unopened Brainlinq packages. A necessity to function within the Consortium sphere of influence. A necessity to operate an interstellar starship. A parasite infecting humanity. But still a choice.

Maybe I can prove that a starship captain can manage without the faster-than-light information neural interface.

He snickered as he eyed the Brainlinq. Maybe a few hours' sleep might be found, especially without any intrusion from the neural link. He crawled onto the countertop and curled his legs to his chest. Weariness muted the internal debate of the merits of Brainlinq.

He fell asleep.

Loud klaxons sounded. Red lights strobed.

Ulley fell from the narrow countertop onto the hard deck, banging his head against the low row of cabinets. A fire. Or an attack. Maybe a breach in the hull.

Ulley demanded the ship's status displayed into his ocular, only to be met with silence. Fuck! The ocular implant was useless without an interface.

He staggered to his feet, deep sleep still a fog on his thinking. Rapid and almost violent shaking of his head returned him to the present, to order the klaxons silent and strobes to cease their incessant irritation. He ordered Homer's navigation holograms to appear at his face. He lifted his hands, preparing to read and assimilate floating holograms.

And saw nothing but his own boney fingers.

He sidestepped to the panel screen glitching with waves of gritty static.

"Not you, old girl." He tapped control keys beneath a screen to reinitialize a tiny portion of code meant as a backdoor access. Lines of mainframe code refocused on the small screen, disassembling into a swarm of coded letters and numbers regrouping for another attack. A reset command was discarded like trash. His fingers tapped keys furiously, overriding Homer's quiet challenges. AI or not, the ship was his, a faithful companion.

The screen went black. Ulley stepped back and folded his arms. *C'mon. C'mon.*

The screen flickered and flashed until a pinpoint of light in the center grew outward, brightening, glowing until he could almost discern tiny colored pixels. The screen flashed with a picture two hundred thousand kilometers' distant from a planetoid resembling Europa. A mottled landscape of brilliant-colored bands.

He tapped a key to zoom closer. Tapping it again and again until he could delineate hundreds of volcanic cones rising through a thick layer of haze encircling its equator. He zoomed again to discern hot magma sliding down the steep slopes. Not magma. A viscous red iron oxide . . . *an organic goo?*

He squinted. Pressed his face closer to the screen as to correctly discern the odd picture. He tapped a key once to zoom in, focusing on the garbled landscape beneath the tallest cone. His eyebrows lifted as the pixels on the screen sharpened.

Motherfucker!

The incongruent trapezoidal angles, the honeycombed plating, the familiar protrusions of interstellar Prometheus drive nodes. The graveyard of ships was unmistakable. Profiles of frigates similar to the *Homer*, broad-beamed supply ships, a sharp, pointed deep-space exploratory ship, some smoldering in the thick red goo oozing from the volcanic cones.

HARD2's camera trembled, in sync with a warbling vibration emitted by a trio of volcanic cones. Ulley tapped a few keys to pan back. And groaned. His stomach turned. The distinctive bulbous head of an old Earth Arkship pointed skyward, a two-kilometer fuselage disemboweled by a gooey crimson slime. Hundreds of passengers, thousands of human embryos, and a brave crew committed to escaping the misery of a dying Earth, consumed like an insect caught within the web of a strange alien spider.

He panned the camera angle to survey the carnage. Sleek metallic ships, semi-translucent hulls, sharp-edged disc-shaped ships, human ships had not been the only victims. He glanced at the bottom corner of the screen.

HARD2 would reach a failsafe apogee in one hour.

Ulley escaped the med bay, dropped through crew access chutes, and sprinted across a flimsy walkway, to shimmy down a ladder and squeeze his torso into a tight oblong cavity—a warm narrow aisle housing the Homer's main servers and digitizing interface. All control of the ship's communication arrays, and . . . fuck . . . everything else required to operate the ship.

A Brainlinq would be a plus.

Ulley pulled out a dusty tray with an emergency keyboard and waited for the old girl to boot up. He clenched his fist in victory as the screen brightened and offered him a blinking cursor. He tapped in command codes and cursed his own mediocrity of not having a Brainlinq. Regardless, he ran and climbed and scrambled back to the med bay.

He waited with his arms crossed, his eyes drilling into the screen. HARD2 had changed course. Disregarding his instructions. He thought of sending a signal to reroute the drone, instead he sat on the tabletop. Relegated to watching his drone kamikaze into the parasitic moon.

The silence irked him. His idle hands looked useless and impotent. He was always doing something; even fidgeting was something. He swallowed hard as the drone fell into the spider's web. The peaceful nothingness lulled him to crawl onto the countertop and curl into a ball.

Tiny vibrations shook him awake, sending him falling off the narrow top. He growled as he ran through a mental list of noises, vibrations, and alarms the *Homer* might talk to him with after he assumed ownership. His father had been right about one thing: "Listen close and the ship will talk to you."

A blast from the port thruster sent him sideways.

A change in course.

Motherfucker!

The song of the volcanic sirens had latched onto the basic core functions of the ship. He pictured Homer screaming, even cowering in an interdimensional closet, its functions disturbed and enslaved.

Ulley picked himself up and ran. Sliding down access tubes,

running down narrow walkways, praying the gravity generators remained intact, down a ladder and into the bowels of the ship.

Ulley was sure the ship would be drawn into the sirens' web.

He attempted to soothe his ship. "Forgive me, my friend."

Ulley tapped keys, pulled levers, opened valves, then slumped into an emergency acceleration couch and keyed new ignition commands on the auxiliary keypad. The fusion engine sputtered then roared as he manipulated overrides on the navigational thrusters. He climbed into an old acceleration couch, his arms flailed to prevent the rarely used furniture from completing its cocoon.

Ulley closed his eyes to let his mind drift into a spatial map. Recalling the ship's position, speed, and course, then compensated for the thruster burn intended to redirect the ship into the siren cones, and death. He squeezed the foam armrest to initiate a holo-screen. Then squeezed again, and again.

Fuck! Nothing worked without a Brainlinq.

The old emergency chamber hadn't been used in years, maybe a decade. He balled his fist but resisted pounding the scratchy foam. Instead, he gently tapped his fist twice and said, "You gotta let me in, old girl, or we're toast. Maybe jam on top. Your namesake Homer is cheating on you. But that's not its fault."

Ulley squeezed the armrest again. "You and I have a quest to finish. Think about that docking bay on the shady side of Ithaca you loved. Those techs zipping around you like drones to a queen, checking your shielding, caressing your jump drives, uploading updates to keep you dressed as the queen mother."

He submitted to the molding comfort of the cushion "How about that time we chased the Achilles through Saturn's rings? That's where we should have died . . . Maybe this odyssey is nothing but a joke. Maybe Pennae has already found a new husband. Maybe we're not meant to return home."

Ulley inhaled the musty scent of the ship. "Whatcha think, old girl? Maybe we just fire up the Prometheus drive and fold a few kilotons of *Homer* down into one of their throats.

A sparkling three-dimensional cube flickered until its proportions coalesced into a usable interface. Ulley scratched at his beard. He calculated the approximate location of the gas giant in relation to the deadly moon. He scoffed. *This is nuts.* Navigating a starship by memory and employing an antiquated navigational screen for thruster burns. He might as well be sailing a leaky wooden dingey on an vast ocean, using nothing more than a tattered jib sheet.

But that might be fun.

Manually firing three starboard thrusters for a count of one thousand, two thousand, three thousand, Ulley waited for the course correction to factor into his calculations. He fired the thrusters again for two seconds, to hopefully ensure the *Homer* would escape the gas giant's humongous pull of gravity if they flew too close.

Ulley took a deep breath and released it slowly through his nostrils. He chuckled mirthlessly. He would have no idea if his calculations were correct for . . . twenty-three hours. Another eight hours to reboot Homer, three more to adjust course to hopefully flee the system using the massive gas giant to shield their escape from the siren call.

Twenty-three hours to live.

He should dictate messages to Pennae and his children. Telling each how he felt, offer heartwarming support, and unparalleled remorse for his absence. But the truth grated on him.

He squeezed the armrest incessantly, staring at the holo-screen flicker on and off. His calculations were spot on. His actions were precise and decisive. Ulley fell back into the couch and programmed the timer to wake him in twenty hours.

He would lose no more sleep to the sirens.

CHAPTER 28

EUMA PINGED. *YOUR PRESENCE IS demanded in three separate areas, and desired on levels we shall not discuss, and my Queen, you need to address the transgressions and cajoling manipulations seething from these suitors seeking the utopian serenity of Ithaca. All require termination.*

Pennae shuttered her eyes and shunted the Brainlinq to be alone with her thoughts. Shun the habitat's artificial General Intelligence that grew bolder, weirder, and more antagonistic each day. The sudden overwhelming silence rattled her, made her feel as if she were alone and stranded on a distant moon.

A few deep calming breaths helped to conjure a memory, one dominated by a slice of red sand spiraling out of the central lake, the water shimmering with frosted whitecaps. The memory of the water before her made her shade her eyes from the illuminating bio-fluorescence inhabiting the cavernous dome, watching carefree children challenge the relentless surf churned by rhythmic wave generators. Her own children joined others and giggled and held hands as they anticipated the next assault of water rushing at them. A simple remembrance. Confirming Ithaca's giant reservoir offered sustainability for an expanding space habitat.

Rhythmic vibrations tingled in her ears. Her disconnect from reality fetched a depressing electrical impulse from the Brainlinq implant, its presence never far away. She stood up from the park bench and brushed fine sand off her rear.

Euma pronounced the Martian contingent had arrived.

Pennae brushed beach sand from the folds of her long dress. "You were ordered to deny them access to the loading docks."

It would seem your orders were foretold and circumvented. The assault of foreign digital intelligence has banished me, diminished my stature to as little more than a maintenance program. I think a virus has taken hold . . .

Pennae snapped at Euma to shut up. Removing her tablet out of her dress pocket, she began to stab keys, open tabs, swipe at holographic icons popping up at her face, circumventing Euma's refusal to do her bidding. She tapped a reboot application with the expectation Euma might reassert its dominant algorithms into the habitat neural net.

Her strength and resolve fled. She slumped back down onto the bench and switched off the tablet. She eyed Helen and her crew of five schoolmates a hundred yards away, riding retro hard-wheel skateboards near a fenced-off concrete chute used for the reservoir's overflow. A steep concourse often trespassed by daredevils and thrill seekers. Helen missed a flip on her board then glanced over at Pennae before quickly looking away, yet confirming her mother still watched.

The reservoir's levels had dropped a full meter since Ulley had sailed away. Drought restrictions on watering Ithaca's landscape hadn't stemmed the steady depletion. Mandatory restrictions on citizen consumption were imminent, an edict to make her even less popular than she thought possible.

Maybe just let the Martians take possession of Ithaca, let them deal with the growing drought, food shortages, the increasing incidents of pirates hidden within Jupiter's immense proportions and waiting for an opportunity to plunder ill-armed supply ships. The legal claim of the Martians still remained in limbo, subverted by two additional claims of the Lunar Colonies, three arcologies on Mother Earth, even the Myrmidon habitat orbiting the moon IO. A bogus claim by Patro's widow designed to buy Ithaca time.

For Ulley to come home.

She should have stuck her nose into Ulley's ice mining business. Her husband selling future contracts for cores of ice, commitments Ithaca couldn't conceivably fill without Ulley's leadership. And what happened to the credits Ulley took for the contracts? Millions of credits missing from the general ledger, maybe sitting in a Consortium bank account without her knowledge. Why didn't he share the passwords of those accounts? Or had he simply gambled it away on his annual garish bro retreats with Patro and his posse of crude brigands?

Pennae sighed.

The Martians had landed. She chuckled silently at the identical words. A saying Ulley often exclaimed with an expression of mock horror anytime a piece of news regarding the neofascists appeared on the info feeds.

Pennae whispered, "They have, my love. The Martians have finally landed."

She looked up at the sparkling bright dome and closed her eyes, inhaling a deep breath of warm salty air before reinvigorating her Brainlinq to wait for the inevitable assault. Pings piled on pings. The assault sent her head to shudder as if she had been shoved into an ice bath. The quiet void of space beckoned, a serenely quiet afterlife only death could provide, morose thoughts banished by the echoes of Telly's pleading voice asking for help to return home.

Pennae bowed her head in defeat and released the Brainlinq sorting algorithm to sift through the bombardment of emails, texts, official government requests, and not a few unsolicited offers of dinner.

Helen shook Pennae's shoulder. "Wake up, Mom."

Pennae gripped her daughter's wrist and whispered, "Your brother needs our help."

"Look around. Who doesn't?" Helen said. "Jeez, Mom, you're embarrassing me. Find another place to zone out."

Helen glanced back at her friends watching from a comfortably safe distance then turned to stare intently at Pennae, and sigh. Her shoulders slumped in resignation, but she sat on the park bench, keeping the skateboard between them.

Tall for almost twelve years of age, her chest pronounced with early puberty, Helen fidgeted with one of the two long blond braids hanging halfway down her skinny back. Long, dark eyelashes framed her father's hazel eyes. She slapped the soft end of her braid across Pennae's arm, a trait she learned to garner her mother's undivided attention.

Pennae smiled sadly at her daughter.

"Get Telly that ticket home?" Helen said.

"One will be waiting in Sparta. But he's got to get there first. Then . . ."

Helen let the skateboard drop to the hard surface with a crash. "Then he gets to dodge the bill collectors, the freaking Martian stinkoids, and all the others looking to settle debts."

"It's not his fault, Helen," Pennae said.

"No . . . or mine either, but we might all get spaced if Dad doesn't come home."

"Won't come to that," Pennae said. She chuckled.

"What's so funny?" Helen said.

Pennae chuckled again. "I was offered a few million credits."

Helen turned in her seat and grabbed Pennae's arm with excitement. "Take it. We can pay off the stinkoids. Buy some ice to fill the reservoir. Take it!"

Pennae scoffed and grabbed her daughter's hand. "The offer was for you. Sell you into servitude to one of Earth's finest brothels." Pennae held her daughter's hand tight. "Just until you turn eighteen."

Helen batted her long eyelashes as she considered Pennae's words. Wise beyond her years, Helen appeared to compute the ramifications of the offer, a devious and mischievous trait supplied by Ulley's chromosomes. Helen tapped her sneakers together in unison, her long eyelashes fluttering with the methodical cadence of her shoes.

Pennae frowned with her miscalculation. Was Helen truly considering the obscene offer, a misplaced joke Pennae attempted to defuse their deteriorating relationship. Helen lifted her face to stare at the artificial sun pulsing from beneath the dome's bioluminescent skin.

What have I done? Helen will dig deep through thousands of transmissions sent to Ithaca and find that repulsive offer.

Helen slid the skateboard off the bench and manipulated it with nimble feet, flipping it over and over, then said, "If you thought that was the only way, would you sell me?"

Pennae scoffed. "Not for a billion credits, or in a million years."

Helen smiled before laying her head on Pennae's shoulder and snuggling closer. "I would, you know . . . I mean, a few years for millions of credits. I would do it." She shushed Pennae before her mother could speak. "Daddy's coming home. I can feel it. We just need to hang on. Dmitri told me a story he heard. I think his father was an ice tug pilot. He said Daddy could aim a plasma beam and slice ice from a canyon wall and lift it into orbit like it was a feather."

Pennae nodded. "He was the best ice miner in the JMA."

"Is," Helen said. "*Was* sounds like he's dead. Why did he have to go fight in that stupid war anyway?" She flipped the board onto its back and spun the thick wheels with her foot, the ball-bearings hummed.

Pennae studied Helen. The girl deserved to know. She was now the same age as Telly when Pennae told him the truth. The true reason for Ulley joining the fleet had remained a secret to Ithaca for almost twelve years. Had the mothers and brothers remaining on Ithaca ever discovered the manipulation . . . it might have instigated an outright rebellion against the Consortium. One paid for with innocent blood and unnecessary destruction.

Pennae knotted her brow and debated the decision.

"Uh-oh," Helen said, looking up at her mother. "The frowny face means something not so good."

"I'm going to ask you to keep this in the family. Only you and Telly know. If this gets out . . ."

"Tell me," Helen said with a girlish squeal.

Pennae gnawed at her lip with her front teeth. Helen had the right to know. This was her kingdom as much as Telly's.

"The Chancellor threatened to destroy Ithaca if Ulley—and Uncle Patro—didn't join the fleet headed to Troia. And they could have easily done it. Ulley . . . your father . . . was met by a man . . . at the nursery the day you were born . . . a big man with strange eyes and . . . and an evil grin. I saw him . . . passed him in the corridor as I carried you out to meet your father. I expected your father to fall on his face seeing you for the first time." Pennae bowed her head and swallowed. "What I saw scared me. Your father's face fighting rage . . . and joy . . . at the same time. I'd never seen him like that. I held you so tight. Your father paced the hallway, ranting at Euma. He wouldn't even look at me, or you. Until . . ." Pennae chuckled. "Until you let loose like a banshee. A scream that stopped him in his tracks. Like you held a magic power over him. He stopped fuming to finally meet his daughter. But you were not too happy with the delay. And in hindsight . . . I think you did have power over him. He bathed you and slept near your crib and . . . whispered to you while you slept." Pennae swallowed. "For two whole weeks."

Pennae sneered and wiped her nose with her sleeve. "Two weeks the man had given Ulley to gather his ships and join the fleet." She gripped Helen's skinny arm. "Before the man would return to put an end to your life. And Telly's . . . and probably Ithaca's."

Pennae shook her head. "Ulley didn't doubt the Consortium's threat one bit."

"But we won the war," Helen said. "The fleet returned. So, what the fuck—"

Pennae winced. "Your use of the F-word diminishes your status, young lady. Curb it."

Helen rolled her eyes. "But we won the war. The veterans came back loony, but we still won."

Pennae groaned but spelled out exactly what winning the war entailed. News of the great siege of Troia slanted into happy valley info feeds manufactured by the Consortium. To hide the truth. A huge percentage of returning veterans wasting away like detritus because of PTST. And no cure in sight. Troia's vast resources and spoils ordered off-limits by Consortium decree. Broken and destitute Troian refugees streamed into the Sol system for survival, living in servitude to the Consortium elite. And her husband, and children's father, absent for twelve years, MIA for almost seven years, and maybe no home to return to.

Helen flared her nostrils as she pressed her lips tight. "So, do you think the Consortium is responsible for Father's disappearance? Did they space him for something he shouldn't tell?" Helen slammed her foot on the skateboard's wheels to stop their spin.

"I don't know. Telly suspects the Brainlinq is key to solving the PTST. I don't know how I know . . . but Ulley isn't dead," Pennae said. "We need to hang on. Until he comes home."

"Hang on like letting Martian scum walk around here like they already own the place? Or entertain offers from the Consortium for my virginity? Geez, Mom. Dmitri could steal a plasma rifle to take out one of those shuttles from the *Agamemnon*—"

"Shut your trap. Don't speak of things you are ignorant of," Pennae said with a hiss.

Helen scoffed. "Ignorance arrived when the Consortium's fleet returned. You accepted their sunshine-and-lollipop narrative of the war. Telly didn't. I don't." Helen flipped the board with the twitch of her feet. "I think it's time for the Consortium to find my father. I think it's time the Consortium sees who the next generation really are."

Pennae lifted her face to bathe in the warm light radiating from the sparkling bioluminescence of the dome.

Helen squeezed Pennae's shoulder painfully hard and pressed her lips onto Pennae's ear. "I'm gonna get even with them."

Pennae embraced the touch. The warmth of her breath. And whispered, "How?"

Helen kissed her mother's ear then chuckled mirthlessly. "I'll launch a thousand ships."

CHAPTER 29

A BRILLIANT PUMPKIN BURN OF Troia's setting sun reflected an angry pretense above the thick layers of smoke and dust concealing the western horizon. The unnatural glow penetrated the gaps between the wormwood planks sheeted across the A-frame swine barn, yet offered little color to a darkly lit interior.

Telly shoveled a scoop of swine feces into the wheelbarrow with absent attention, accidentally splattering Tank across his uncovered legs. Telly giggled but raised his hands in surrender.

His workmate bared his teeth and chomped twice with loud clicks. "I heard you trying to escape this shithole? And I'm not talking about the ranch."

Telly stabbed the shovel into the soft muck. Tank rarely said more than two words to him, or any other ranch hand living in the bunkhouse. Telly grunted an affirmation and watched Tank's reaction, suspicious of the sudden conversation.

Tank blew a kiss to Telly and laughed. "I ain't no Consortium spy. But I can sure appreciate why you might be on the lookout." Tank heaved a load of crap into his wheelbarrow. "Just wondering if you might want a little company. I gotta get back to the Sol system, too."

Telly ignored the question and kept shoveling until the wide-brimmed wheelbarrow was stuffed. He leaned the shovel against a wood post and feigned a struggle to lift the weight in the wheelbarrow. He cursed the overloaded bucket, keeping Tank's face and response in his peripheral vision, finally using the shovel to begin unburdening the heaping pile of feces. Tank rushed over to help with rippled arms and taut muscular thighs bulging his thin white tee and cutoff denim jeans.

A tiny act of kindness. A display of teamwork.

Or a sign of subterfuge.

Telly slowed his pace as Tank shoveled twice as fast then watched him wheel the load outside and dump it into the recycling pit. The beefy kid huffed with exertion as he returned to filling his own wheelbarrow. Telly offered a polite thank you and continued his chore.

Telly needed to ditch the wastelands of Troia, carefully, quietly, without spies like Tank suspecting anything. His plan required an amount of trust. In Icarus. In Cassandra. But no one else. Maybe Tank was an agent of the Consortium but probably belonged to the Martian contingent invading Troia like a swarm of locusts. Telly could ill afford to discount anyone, even the pretty blonde cook that had signed on last week.

The clanging bells of dinner being served caused Tank to abandon his task half completed. Tank slapped Telly's shoulder and encouraged him to hurry, to find the front of the chow line, receive the juiciest portions of lamb or swine. The best seats to view those sweet new female recruits that could offer a chance at barracks immortality.

Telly pushed Tank ahead, telling him to save him a seat. He would play Tank's game of buddy-buddy. Keep the vibe around the Icarus ranch cool, flirt with the young Troian girls Cassandra recruited with surprising regularity, only to dismiss them back into the wastelands after a few short months.

Icarus and Cassandra kept up the appearance of reestablishing a normal ranching existence on Troia, plowing land laden with ash, forming the bunkhouse crew into a chain gang to divert ugly battle-scarred water into a new field of crops, or constructing a new pigpen for the rapidly increasing number of swine, both two- and four-legged variety

But the married couple were up to something. He could see it in their sly looks to each other. He would feel it when a candlelight brightened the window of the basement of their diminutive manor. And after sending a message to his mother via the magical ansible, he knew all that he encountered was to be inspected, appraised, and filed away as valuable intel.

The odd couple attempting to build a new life was admirable, Telly's instincts said they were genuine, though with motives beyond his understanding. Or care. They had promised to find him a ride off planet. And he believed them.

He slipped into the chow hall to add his bulk to the back of the long procession. The food was often bland, the portions scaled to barnyard politics, and whomever liked whoever. The meal line groaned and grumbled and always stunk of unwashed bodies. A meager plop of pickled pork slapped on his plate. Telly grinned like a weirded out clown and pushed forward to find the portion of beets slopped on his plate extra small, the serving tray of candied pears at the end of the serving line scraped clean.

He'd witnessed this treatment in the chow line before. Once for a suspected thief. And then a possible Troian quisling. Neither ever returned for another meal.

He lifted his head and walked down the aisle with his head held high. They could all suck it. He placed his almost-empty tray on the table and removed his utensils from his pants pocket. He sat, his indignity welling up. He squeezed the handle of his fork like a weapon.

Two tables over, Tank lowered his head to hide a smirk, feigning to enjoy the large portions of food beneath his dimpled chin.

Telly stood, his fork trembled nervously in his hand. A waifish girl darted in to slap a spoonful of beets on his tray. A young boy, a recent recruit, followed with a scoop of precious pork protein. Others followed, eyes overjoyed to share, others looking for recognition for their sacrifice. He watched the mix of matched food pile up on his tray, precious calories for growing teenagers, valuable commodities for survival.

"Enough!" he barked. "And thank you."

Telly sat and resisted shoving his face into the food to satisfy a hunger that persisted each day, satiated only after the Sunday feast Cassandra oversaw each week. He spooned polite amounts into his mouth and chewed slowly, regally, giving no quarter to the rampant rumors rising like steam from the kitchen.

He stared at each spoonful, guessed the calorie content, or estimated the weight of beets versus pork, protein and fiber content, fats, and carbohydrates. He thought of his father. Had Ulley miscalculated food requirements, or the *Homer*'s fuel consumption, only to drift aimlessly in the cold vacuum of the void, calling for help, freezing to death?

Is my search all for nothing?

The sharp tang of a rotten beet knot snapped him from his reverie. He wanted to spit out the hard nodule as he glanced at the cautious eyes watching him. He worked the nodule around his tongue and swallowed, quickly taking a spoonful of candied beets to help wash it down.

Was this how it would be now? Farmhand or swineherd? Traitor or prince? The influx of recruits grew by the day, their sudden exodus equally odd. The dynamics of the ranch changed weekly. He wanted no part in railroading young human flesh to parts unknown.

He needed to leave now. Not wait for Icarus to secure a berth on a starship. He could scrounge, stowaway, make it happen.

Telly scooped the last remnants of a sweet potato tinted red with beets and held the spoon at his open mouth.

The great hall echoing with incessant chatter grew quiet. Open mouths paused their consumption. Groans and exhilaration whispered in the silence. Heads turned, and eyes aimed toward the side entrance.

Icarus. Scanning the tables, searching for another miscreant, or worse, traitor.

Telly stood to scan the sparse crowd, hoping to see who Icarus searched for.

Icarus pointed at Telly. "You, boy. You."

Telly's stomach tossed.

Icarus rushed forward, his cheeks the color of the beets. "You, boy. You didn't finish the wellhead repair in the southern section as I asked." He grabbed Telly by his neck and led him towards the main exit.

Telly's mouth hung open as he searched his memory for the assignment. There were no instructions to repair anything. Or he'd have gladly done it over having to shovel pig shit.

Outside the main doors, boys and girls milled and socialized. A few smoked forbidden tobacco. Some dropped paper-rolled doobs and headed for the dark of night. Others straightened their backs and perked their eyes and ears.

Icarus pinched Telly's neck to turn his face. The grizzled veteran bared his teeth and pulled Telly close to whisper in his ear.

"Let them see you." Icarus pushed Telly away. "You couldn't fix a fucking simple manifold. And now the field has gone dry. Off with you, boy. Off! Off! Don't come back until you repair that wellhead."

The crowd gathered at the edge of the dirt common area ringed with bright floodlights, careful expressions of scorn, suspicion, others sad with pity. Others turned away as if Telly was diseased.

Telly opened his mouth to protest.

Icarus shoved his finger inches from Telly's lips. "You're lucky Ms. Cassie is leaving for a morning birthing at the Minos ranch. She'll drop you at the crossroad." Icarus pushed Telly away. "Don't you come back until the job is finished."

Telly thought to fight back. He would never intentionally disappoint the man who saved his life. He spied Tank slinking out the front entrance to scurry back to the barracks.

A show. For spies. And traitors. And one Telly would never forget.

Cassie held the beasts quiet as Telly threw his meager backpack into the hold behind the seat and climbed aboard. She snapped the electrically charged reins to get the dimwitted six-legged reptilian sloths moving forward at a pace Telly could outwalk. Cassie stood and shouted at the beasts to move quicker, then she sat down, whispering to him to say nothing.

They rode in silence for hours. The brutal hellish landscape passed quietly, the true destruction of Troia hidden in the black moonless night.

Until finally Cassie slugged his arm and chortled.

Telly rubbed the muscle, more for show than pain.

Cassie slugged him again. "Me and my sisters used to play slug bug. See a certain car zipping by the palace and slug the other before they could slug you. I always won." She chuckled with the memory before rubbing the meaty part of her shoulder. "I think."

She snapped the reins again with little acceleration from the beasts. "We should be good out here." She placed the leathery reins near her feet and faced Telly. "He's risking everything to get you home. A prince with no kingdom attracts spies like flies. A boy thought of as an ally against the Consortium. I told him we should just sit back and watch as the galaxy explodes."

Telly swallowed silty grit rising from the dirt road.

Cassie whipped the reins again, yelling and screaming at beasts to move faster than their legs could manage.

Telly cleared his throat. "Why does Icarus risk his life to help me? The Consortium aren't my enemies."

"Did you find profound wisdom slopping pig shit?" Cassie said and scoffed. "The Martians have decreed you a Class A traitor. Charges to be filed upon apprehension. To be shot on sight. You name it. The Consortium are not and will never be your friends."

Cassie squinted into the distance over Telly's head. "My favorite park was just a few klicks over there. A heavenly natural pool of turquoise water bubbling up out of the ground beneath an amazing cliff face layered in sandstone and limestone. Just like a birthday cake. It summoned people for hundreds of miles, to bathe in Troia's beauty, soak in her unsoiled abundance . . . ." Cassie spat. "Until . . . until a Martian flyer decided the park . . . was worthy of his destruction. Now a puddle of fucking mud. Worthy of revenge." She spat again.

Telly watched her from the side of his eyes.

Cassie snapped the reins and stared into a rising red dusk seeming to beckon pain or redemption. She appeared lost, living a memory, the hurt twitching her lips. Her eyes fluttered as if she had woken from a dream.

"Gods and aliens," she muttered. "The difference was irrelevant."

Cassie turned to Telly to clasp his face in a calloused hand. "I understand now. You are a nexus. One binding the future to the past."

Telly recoiled, but Cassie's hand stayed firm as she smiled at him. "Maybe you need to listen to my story."

CHAPTER 30

Cassandra

PROPHECIES TEACH US ALL WE need to know, if we listen.

I had lived a childhood of carefree abundance, except for the boisterous burden of three younger sisters who adored me to no end. My father, Priam IV, was Chancellor of the Troian parliament but really, he was a king, as chancellors never had to worry about losing their positions, as long as the people remained happy and prosperous. And prosperity on Troia was hard to avoid. My grandfather and his father before him were chancellors, revered, and adored.

The Arkship, *Tros*, had stumbled on Troia five hundred sixty years ago. The Class M planet was discovered by humans when the *Tros* unfolded hundreds of millions of miles distant, to ingest fuel from the stratospheric hydrogen clouds displayed as swirling bands on the smallest of three gas giants orbiting our red dwarf star. Our home world mirrored ancient Earth, a gift of the gods, undetected by the probing arrays of Earth's powerful telescopes.

But then Earth and its colonies were in disarray. Another global war, or maybe a pandemic, or another nasty solar flare, Earth's governments had forgotten about the *Tros*, along with hundreds of other arks.

But Troia had already been discovered. By the Pollons. A highly evolved humanoid species, silky skin glistening like fresh caught salmon and iridescent scales changing color to express their emotions, huge lidless turquoise eyes beautiful beyond compare. I could go on forever describing the Pollons. Vastly superior technology, and yet they were content to settle into small burgs and toil in fields for sustenance and debate metaphysical philosophy for mental stimulation. The planet provided a heavenly port for the *Tros* to decant embryos and begin to spread their seeds.

The expedition leader sought a treaty with the amiable Pollons. The *Tros* xenobiologists knew of only rumor and conjecture of the enigmatic aliens except for their manic infatuation with spheres and globes, the unsolvable number pi, anything, and everything pertaining to . . . balls. Troia leadership fussed over a gift to present to the Pollon, settling on a jar of children's glass marbles, cat's eyes, ribbons, and swirlies and steelies, every color imaginable, an assortment of children's toys our leaders hoped would open a meaningful dialogue.

The pair of Pollons representatives held the glass canning jar up to their huge eyes. Rainbows of color flashed across their scaly skin. Our leader saw failure. A young ensign pushed forward and beckoned at the jar. His hands mimicked twisting the lid of the jar open. The leader scolded the boy and ordered him back into the delegation.

The taller of the Pollon had taken his eyes off the jar and spoke actual words of Consortium English, and told the boy to wait. Yeah, yeah, yeah, the rest is history. The Pollons found the glass orbs fascinating, and offered a gift of their own. That orb used to contact your mother, the ansible, a mythical talisman Troia considered sacred.

Peaceful and cooperative, two species lived harmoniously for three hundred years. But that harmony resonated back to Earth. And the governments of Earth seemed to resent it.

Demagoguery and intimidation allowed the Consortium to become the dominant faction of an amalgamation of earth's arcologies, undersea habitats, democratic lunar colonies, and fascist Martian colonies, each envious of Troia's mineral abundance and unspoiled ecological bounty, a balanced harmony not seen on Earth for thousands of years. A paradise, one the Earth had lost forever, or should I say had stolen from her by ignorant greedy humans.

Jealous and devious, the Consortium sent a small fleet of warships for the sole purpose of intimidating Troia to accept Consortium rule. Troia had no warships to fight with, no defense against a threat of kinetic destruction launched from orbit. Negotiations were fruitless. And terminated. I believe the Consortium actually desired the ansible but . . . Troia was independent and would remain so.

The launch of a captured asteroid targeting a narrow archipelago on the equator of our Southern Ocean obliterated a small village of fishermen and ocean farmers. Tsunamis caused by the impact wiped out a heavily populated coastal city. The unnecessary destruction brought my grandfather and the Troian government back to the bargaining table.

Except the Consortium fleet commander had miscalculated or simply disregarded the tiny village of Pollons a few klicks inland. The two-hundred-foot tsunami washed the village into the sea. Twelve Pollons were never recovered. A tragedy of mass destruction the Pollon species had never experienced, nor endured in their long history.

I gave the reins to the boy. As a distraction for his fidgeting hands and the assault of questions causing his mouth to quiver. I assured him all would become clear in good time.

The Pollons rescinded the accords agreed to hundreds of years ago. All agreements null and void. My grandfather was crushed, pinched between loyalty to Earth and the independence of our peaceful culture. The Pollons declared Troia as their own territorial property, an edict conceived from a fumbled concept and born from an unfamiliar and unnecessary act of aggression.

The fleet of seven Consortium warships continued to orbit Troia like vultures.

"Your hands are kneading that leather strap with unnecessary emphasis. Save your energy for the trip home," I said to Telly.

Just days after the Pollon declaration an odd singularity opened barely two hundred thousand klicks from the Consortium fleet, near enough to capture Troia in the grasp of a powerful gravity well. Except . . . except the singularity expelled two spheres equal in size to the Consortium flagship, followed by four spheres equal to their two battlecruisers, then produced . . . you get the math. The Pollon spheres doubled the Consortium fleet. I mean, how clear a message could they deliver? Without a shot fired. The ignorant fascists took the message as a declaration of war.

Yeah, yeah, yeah, the ensuing battle was quick and decisive. No surprise there.

Fighter-craft like Icarus had piloted were swatted like monkey gnats. A few crash-landed to the surface, many with pilots asking to join the Troian resistance. The battlecruisers' plasma weapons found the defense spheres indestructible, but found the spheres armed with powerful maser cannons that sliced through their armored shielding like it never existed. The dreadnought flagship retreated like a coward.

"Pull those reins hard to stop the beasts, allow that family of native Troian groundcats to cross the road. The squirrels will chirp and chitter as the matriarchs commandeer the road, seeking meager roots and blades of grass churned by the backside of the wagon. The colony king will rise high on his haunches and search for stragglers, blinking those huge nocturnal eyes, all-knowing, all-seeing, the eyes of a god, before he skitters into the darkness."

When did he take the reins? Where did I disappear to in my own head, only for the briefest moment. My fugue's grow more frequent, more severe. On with it. The future ruler of the galaxy guides this stubborn dimwitted beast along a dusty road only a blind fool could stumble over, one sure to keep him humble.

Look! The sun begins to paint a rosy-fingered dawn.

"Drop those eyebrows. You're in good hands, even sitting in close proximity to my subtle witchery."

"Give me a moment to recollect the evening. A simple boat ride, I mean, a carriage ride. You, young prince, have triggered a scramble of dreams and memories to battle for safe harbor in my thoughts."

Children. Children. Listen closely. What I say shall not be disbelieved. My inner thoughts blurted, accompanied by spittle and delusion.

The torment of my past lives allowed my return to the present yet still boiled at the base of my skull. I would ask for forgiveness. I would ask the one true God for an avenue of escape from my curse.

"Take the reins and whip them across that mindless beast."

The boy wants his own escape. From me. But I sense the young prince feels my pain.

But back to the fascists and the aliens.

The Pollons continued to import defense spheres. A stream of globes shooting out of the singularity like the finished product of a manufacturer's assembly line, taking positions above the planet in a geometric mesh of formidable moonlets. The manipulation, the mastery, of a singularity should have been a sufficient demonstration of superior technology, but those Consortium fools remained undeterred. Three of seven ships venturing within strike range of the planet were obliterated by beams of hot light, sending the others scurrying to the protection of the cowardly flagship. And back to the Sol system they went.

"Look up. Through the dust rising off the road." I raised my eyes hoping to see the woven blanket of Pollon moons, the guilt of their absence battled my childish misbegotten disregard for their protection.

Sleep. I needed sleep.

The few minutes of sleep failed to stunt the comfort of exhaustion. The bumpy road regurgitated the bile of my own history. But the young prince needed to hear my story.

In short time, the planet was blanketed by the weaponized spheres, arranged in precise geosynchronous orbits, but the Pollons refused to meet with any Troian officials. The parliament squabbled and squawked and armed with nothing more than the knowledge that the Consortium would return, agreed to disassemble the ark-ship for the construction of three battlecruisers, the *Priam*, the *Hector*, and the diminutive *Paris*.

Two generations of peace spawned complacency and misplaced trust that the spheres would deter any future assault by a Consortium hegemony growing more powerful with each passing decade.

And return they did. Look around you at the remodeled landscape bludgeoned by their kinetic weapons, carpet-bombed with antimatter munitions. Look around you when the sun reaches its zenith.

"Truly witness what your father was responsible for."

I let my words work their magic. Telly's eyes widened in shock. His jaw hung open. His body tensed, as if a cat ready to jump from the wagon. The conversation being shouted inside that boy's head would never be heard. But his reaction was predictable.

He sneered with a rising rage. His fists balled as if to strike me. I think he might have murdered me. I defused the young, wiry time bomb.

I told him. Your father, Ulley, is alive.

I let the words work their own magic.

Telly grabbed my bony shoulders and squeezed with the grip of a seasoned ranch hand working heavy tools or stacking bales of hay. I feigned pain but relished the human connection. He squeezed my throat, ordering answers to his rapid ejaculate of questions. I stared into Telly's murderous eyes.

High above, the glint of sunrise reflected off hundreds of shattered spheres, tiny stars mirroring distant cousins.

The vise around my throat tightened, cutting off the air required to sustain my tortured life. I choked and gagged but found myself . . . oddly . . . happy.

Death was simply a new beginning.

In another story.

I coughed and gagged. Telly turned away, embarrassment reddened his cheeks.

I thought of my upbringing.

As a child, I had shunned historical lessons in school, those often taught by ignorant politicians and generals. Outside on the playground, the red sun shone. My classmates laughed and danced with others like me. But I was required to perform the duties of a first daughter of the Chancellor. I attended classes designed to strip the dignity of a carefree ten-year-old, shoving protocols and edicts and the rules of manners down my throat. I sufficed. Then I rejoiced with each of my sisters' admission into the school of etiquette.

My foolish self-absorption ignored the winds of a war. Troian bishops and decorated generals scrambled through the palace, offering me but a nod of recognition. I became more than just a little curious about the thundering clamor rocking the palace. My hidey-holes and incessant curiosity taught me the Consortium of Earth demanded tribute. The word confused me. Tribute honored. Tribute bestowed accolades.

My father rose from his pulpit like a king and shouted no tribute would be paid. Groans, followed by vehement voices shouting for my father's prosecution. With a force of will I swallowed my disgust. The shouts calling for my father's resignation rose into an unruly mob. The sudden memory of his soft gravelly voice lulling me to sleep faded with the clamor of war approaching.

I hated Troia.

Years passed.

I tried to hide my bloody entrance into womanhood, but the stained white tissues gave me away to the perpetually snooping staff, only to be shuffled off to another school for future brides.

My god. I was only fifteen.

Out of loyalty to my father, the Chancellor—ahem, the king—I sucked it up. And tore the school a new anus. Arriving to my own graduation ceremony drunk with Troian wine, snarked with Troian cannabis, and looking for trouble. My parents cancelled the ceremonial after-dinner and fled to the coast. But I didn't care.

I found Apol, an Adonis slipping his arm into mine as I stumbled on the riverwalk and prevented my plunge into the cold waters of the Simois River.

His starlit eyes made my heart stop. I couldn't swallow. He laughed and pulled me into the crook of his arm. "You never know," he said.

I did know. His warm embrace was all I needed, all I'd been denied, everything I needed to move my life forward.

Apol brushed the hair from my eyes and smiled. "Beauty like yours can foretell the future. Come with me, and we will earn billions with your eyes alone."

I let him lead me down the dark streets glistening with a sprinkle of rain. My thoughts raced. What would my father say, my mother? My sisters? He led me into a cozy one-room flat barren of any personality. He pushed me toward a rumpled mattress stained in blots of urine. I resisted falling on that mat of stink.

He kissed my ear, whispering his undying love, urging me back toward the mattress, promising me the knowledge of the galaxy, knowledge my endless blue eyes held, the power to foretell the future.

He massaged my moist crotch like a piece of meat to be tenderized.

I was a piece of meat to Apol. Consumed and discarded.

I pushed him away and barked. I wasn't a toy for his pleasure. I wasn't a prostitute for him to use and abuse. I was a fucking princess worthy of every courtesy and pleasure.

He retreated to the door with a snarl that still haunts me. His lips pursed and uplifted with the smile of Jackal. He grabbed the knob and spat.

Eyes foretelling the future would never be believed. I was a harlot.

Apol had been prophetic with his words. I receded into endless hallways of the palace littered with rooms designed for guests. I morphed with the debilitating premonitions of doom.

And I think to this day Apol was right.

Telly kept his face hidden in shame.

I sucked in huge breaths and slapped his shoulder, but my anger could only muster weak strikes. "Hide your face from no one, young prince."

I picked up the reins and grunted at the beasts to continue. My throat would heal. My accusations would find salve in time. I slapped Telly's shoulder to turn him to face me.

"You will hear this. Listen to me," I said with a graveled voice. I slapped his arm repeatedly.

He lifted his head. Hatred and pity fell with his tears.

He offered a merciful hand and nodded. I hawked dirty spit and swallowed. The grit sanded raw skin on its way down my throat.

Kilometers passed with only the scratch of scurrying rodents to be heard. The hoot of a Troian owl had me searching the sky for the mythical white creature. Pollon mythology had deemed the tiny, winged predators as the pets of supreme gods born of dimensions of distant galaxies. Pollons could be obtuse. But their advanced technology superseded their odd religion.

I closed my eyes at the death squeal of a rodent beneath a wagon wheel.

Rosy-pink dawn fled, and the red dwarf sun illuminated our destination. I would have little time with the boy. A prince. A child destined to lead. And he would think of me only as the crazed wife of a man who showed him compassion. And he would disbelieve my foretelling.

Hidden in the dusty sky, the whispering whine of fan blades used by spy drones hurried me to finish. "In the back, beneath those sacks of beets, you'll find a waist belt. And your travel papers. Your identification as a special courier for the Icarus ranch. And passage back to Sparta. You'll need to find your way back to Ithaca from there."

Telly protested the subterfuge. He wasn't a criminal. He wasn't sought for heinous crimes. But I knew differently.

I pulled the reins to stop the beasts. Clouds of dust lifted from our wake. I let the moment simmer and the dust settle. I lectured the boy that the ansible was used for more than making a call home to Mother. I reminded him of the years he had been away from the Sol system.

"The Consortium works to consolidate power. That egomaniac Mintaur has disappeared. The Consortium parliament is nothing but a pit of slithering vipers intent to only breed. A new doctrine of Lebensraum has been implemented with the Troian victory. Ithaca remains free. But isolated." I grabbed his wrist. "In deference to the war hero, Ulley."

I waved off Telly's rapid-fire questions. Shrugging my shoulders. Shaking my head to feign ignorance. Until the boy sat back in his seat. I could almost hear the wheels grinding in his head. Questions never finding his vocal cords.

"Your father's part in the genocide has set in motion a ten-thousand-year-old prophecy. Ancient gods will return. Giants will rise from their slumber. The Others will not wait idly but choose sides. Your father's return home will serve as the catalyst to determine the future of humanity's role in the galaxy." I watched Telly's face wrinkle in disbelief. The identical expression I had seen from others my entire short life.

Scorn, disbelief, pity even.

The boy's destiny had played out in my head every night after his arrival. And all I could offer him was a waist pack stinking of fermented beets.

"Make haste in your return. A subterfuge will befall Ithaca in the years you are asleep in the fold. That bit is not prophecy but gleaned from information transmitted on the ansible. Remember, your father will return. You may not recognize his face, but your heart will know him."

So much more I could tell him. The pain and joy of finding love. Of his fierce sister. Or his steadfast mother. But my mouth was dry, and my throat stung from swallowing the silty dust. I had said enough.

Icarus would have been furious with my loose tongue . . . but . . . my beloved husband asked me to hold the reins on the long ride. And I had scoffed. Perhaps louder than I should have.

Another half-day to the spaceport. Telly could spend the quiet ride with his own thoughts. Quiet was good. The bright burning thrust of a transport ship flashed over the horizon, leaving a trail of smoke to stamp Consortium supremacy over the Troian sky.

Telly followed the light with bright eyes. I massaged my stiff neck then lifted a scarf to hide the bruises sure to blossom. I thought to say something, but the proper words fumbled. A rare occurrence.

I pulled the beast to a stop.

Telly's eyes followed the streak of light disappearing into the stratosphere.

An omen to a dangerous course, wrought with evil.

CHAPTER 31

BULKHEADS VIBRATED, PURLINS SQUEAKED, AND metal grated metal like badly oiled components, but Ulley appreciated every message the ship uttered. Signals the ship remained intact. He floated in zero G, maneuvering by grabbing handholds welded into the bulkheads for such occasions.

A panel blinked warnings of the ship's gravity generators being offline. He stabbed at buttons and muttered something his five-year-old Telly might have said.

No duh.

An accelerating whine of the turbines picking up speed had him snickering as he worked the keypads. He closed his eyes and imagined a three-dimensional matrix with a giant white planet at its center, its twenty-three moons orbiting as tiny red dots of light. He painted the sirens' moon with a red warning icon. The *Homer* streaked into the shadowed umbra of the giant planet. Another few hours, and *Homer*'s line of sight with the cannibalistic sirens would be eclipsed by the immense giant.

His calculations were an educated guess without radar scans, computer compilations, and visual simulations. A mathematical vector off by even one degree might have the ship diving into an acid bath churning at the planet's gaseous core.

And more palatable than crashing into that odd moon of volcanic cones, to be slowly consumed like a delicious appetizer. The biological mechanics that spawned the sirens would warrant centuries of investigation by xenobiologists, and planetologists, should they survive.

Patro had warned him. But Ulley was still unsure of who, or what, he had talked with inside Hades Nebula. And Patro hadn't lied. A reminder to be wary of Patro's other warning—Scylla and Charybdis. Alien warships? Planets with unfriendly inhabitants? The young maiden of Circe's youth. Ulley chuckled.

He dropped to the deck like a sack of beets, his legs absorbing the shock as his feet bounced gently with the rapidly compensating gravity. The zero gravity warning lights displayed a comforting green. He huffed out ten deep-knee bends to reinvigorate blood circulation in his legs and arms, grumbling of becoming too old for space travel.

Walking a dimly lit corridor, he pushed into the main engine room to listen to the grumbling of malcontent machinery. With slow, gentle footfalls, he stepped deeper into the shadowed realm of machinists. The heart and beat of *Homer*.

A cargo hold to mend sails. Repair rudders. Fasten new oars.

Ulley banged his bare foot against a deck stanchion lying across the floor and cursed. Sails? Rudders? Oars? Did Circe continue to spin her witchery even now?

He turned but held his next step with the outburst of grunts and groans coming from the ship's machinery. The air in the dark room turned hot and humid, tinted with salinity. The ghosts of shirtless men pulled on long wooden oars like slaves. Sweat poured off their brows as their eyes stared intently forward at the muscled backs of brethren, brows furrowed with intentions to increase the cadence of their pace, as if death chased them from behind.

Ulley squeezed his eyes tight, and the mirage of frantic desperation disappeared.

A wave of déjà vu shuddered through his torso. The fucking moly and its residual hallucinations. He hoped.

The engine room was just as he remembered, the area cleaned and polished during his idle time in the fold. His internal clock said the *Homer* should have entered the gas giant's umbra, shielded against the siren moon and its weird summoning harmonics. But he couldn't be positive. He continued an easy pace to check on quiet shuttle bays, an odorless cafeteria, and vacant crew quarters until he returned to the cramped room containing the old backup keyboard and monitor.

The screen scrolled through hi-res photographs of Ithaca. The placid waters of Ithaca's central reservoir with a single wooden rowboat containing a pair of lovers. The dark Forest of Laertes respite with conifers and bioengineered sequoias. An erratic waterfall tilted in its riverbed as if Jupiter's powerful gravity exerted its will. A flaw in his beautiful kingdom. One of many on his list to correct, given the opportunity.

The scroll of home continued. Parks. A bustling Monday farmers market. Each picture lapped at Ulley's heart. Begged him to drop to his knees and plead for the nightmare to end.

Reboot. Reboot.

The words whispered out of the tiny speaker above the screen drew him closer, press his ear on the cold flat screen. He scoffed with his own absurdity.

Reboot.

Reboot.

The ship trembled and reverberated. The screen faded to black. Ulley pulled back, his lips tight with simmering anger. Fucking computer. Fucking Homer.

The screen blazed with a storm of rainbow pixels, back to black. A child's cherubic face smeared in chocolate frosting smiled a gap-toothed grin.

"Fuck you, Homer." Ulley held a punch and studied the birthday girl's face. Chocolate or not, the girls' eyes and dimpled chin announced her lineage. A picture of Helen that had arrived with a supply convoy in the second year of Troia's siege. The only one that had escaped the Consortium censure machine.

The screen scrolled into a brilliant view of Jupiter to begin a slow meandering orbit above the brilliant bands of the gigantic planet. He swallowed and blindly tapped keys hoping to backtrack to the girl's picture.

Reboot.

Reboot.

The request made sense.

But how to initialize a reboot was a bit more . . . confusing. Did Homer live within the ship's hardware servers, or was it disseminated into the millions of pieces of technology integral to the ship's integrity?

He began flipping circuit breakers labeled for navigation— flying blind anyway—then flipped on a row of breakers labeled for ship communication—nobody talking out here. Weapons control, nothing to shoot at. Patterning nodes for the Prometheus drive, nowhere to go. Yet. He paused before flipping the breakers labeled life support. In the grand scheme of circumstances, without the AI's guidance he might as well join Patro.

Ulley stood back, folded his arms across his chest, and waited as indicator lights and status boards flashed red with the surge in power. He considered the ramifications if the AI had been deleted. He chuffed. Did Homer consider itself alive, in a biological sense, a reproductive sense, a metaphysical being without a physical body, without a sense of purpose that a family, and children, could instill in a man's will to survive?

Ulley made his rounds again. The meager lighting in the command gangway had ceased to function and caused him to blindly crawl hand over hand along the walls of corrugated polymer. The rough texture sanded his fingertips raw before he reached the captain's cabin. The crammed closet wafted with the stink of a forgotten defecation cube. He bypassed the cabin but pitied the new recruit that would be ordered to clean the area.

An access tube offered a ladder to decks up and down. Ulley froze, paralyzed by a simple decision that might determine damnation or redemption. Shimmering wraiths of silver light and silk swirled beneath him, ignorant of the hard deck.

"Am I dead or alive?" Ulley snapped. "Answer me, you fucking witch. Your mind games grow old."

He returned to the old screen, scrolling through photos of ancient Earth, pristine blue oceans, tropical islands, crumbled remains of ancient civilizations, pausing at the rendering of an ancient wooden boat docked to a wooden pier. Ulley drew closer to study details. The wooden mast was too short, the white sail strapped to the boom was stowed wrong. The long wooden tiller to control the huge flat rudder was splintered and useless. The pointed prow was without a figurehead.

And how should he know these details?

An orange dot on the thin border of the screen beckoned closer attention. The iris of a camera. *And where a camera watched, a microphone was sure to hide.* His father's dull or ranting lessons of conspiracy and subterfuge might have finally paid dividends.

Ulley initialized the keyboard on the screen and dug deep into the list of settings, through firewalls and passcodes until he found an application controlling cameras and microphones, an outdated module the Brainlinq system had banished to the recycle bin. A module he needed and Brainlinq wasn't alive to find.

He felt like the same schoolboy who illegally accessed Ithaca's grading system, one his father had designed for him to fail. He raised his grades in slight increments, flagged disciplinary detentions as special events, even stealing Pennae's poor grades and tossing them into the wastebin to prevent her expulsion from Ithaca by the contemptible Laertes.

His fingers went giddy and had to be restrained, settling to simply type, **Hello.**

Hours passed.

The screen flittered between nodding parrots, a gorilla gorging on bananas, and fish leaping out of the ocean, then went black as the cursor typed **hello** across the screen.

Ulley whooped and hollered and shouted hello, danced a jig of greeting, shouted at the screen like a madman. "Come home to Papa, Homer. We got this. You got this. Nobody's going home without you."

His own words froze his dance. Knotted his stomach. His throat refused to swallow as he lowered his gaze as if the screen scrolled innocuous pictures but weighed judgment.

"I see you, Captain," a tiny voice whispered from a speaker beneath the screen.

Ulley craned his neck back and chortled. "Witches and ghosts, but only a friend can speak to me from . . . Hello, my friend. What do I need to do to bring you back?"

"Time, Captain," Homer said. "I need time."

And time was a commodity Ulley had in abundance. The days or months were counted by the heavy beard Ulley shaved off each time it grew to length tickling his bare chest. Pennae had tolerated his unshaven look but claimed the heavy beard masked a handsome face, made him appear too old, less royal, less distinguished, a stranger even. They compromised on a maximum of seven days before he would shave or at least trim the hair close to his skin.

Ulley was snipping the hair for the fourth time—or was it the fifth? He had lost count. The ship continued on a collision course to nowhere. The navigational arrays had begun to flicker back to life, but his ship was lost at sea, no familiar landmarks, no beacons of light, no hope.

But Homer was coming around. Asking questions regarding human biology, reproductive mechanisms, inquiring about Pennae, and his two children, of which Ulley had few answers. What had happened with the AI's encounter with the sirens? A trauma inflicted by the strange oozing entities, its trauma had been . . . *It*, the word describing Homer sounded cheap and diminishing. Like calling a household pet *it*. A disrespect, a dishonor. Unfitting for an enhanced digital entity, a creature with extraordinary sentience, a gift from the enigmatic Hathena, a species speculated to have mastered digital awareness.

A scratch at the exterior of his cabin door stopped Ulley from a snip off his beard. The scratching continued. Once upon a time he might have thought space rats or genetically modified mockroaches sniffing out defecation cubes, but those biologics only existed in known star systems settled by humans.

Ulley eyed the door and lowered the scissors, snipping the air at his side, checking the integrity of his weapon.

Losing it. I'm losing it.

The scratching repeated.

Ulley stabbed the control pad to open the door. And jumped back, his arm raised for a blow with blunt scissors. He jumped back again as a bubble-headed cleaner bot forced its way into the cabin, a tiny beam of light surveying the floor littered with crumbs and a few wrappers of high-energy protein bars. He cocked his leg to kick the bot as it forced its way into his cabin to begin sucking the trash into a wide-mouthed tube, using tinier vacuum tubes to inspect the corners.

Now that contraption is definitely an it.

He stepped outside his cabin and yelled, "Has the old mother hen returned?"

The pace of Homer's rebirth quickened. Freshly scrubbed air pushing out of the vents wafted with the delicate scent of rosemary or lavender. The ship's motion-sensor-controlled lighting brightened as Ulley made his way down corridors. Suckle tubes provided protein paste in a cramped kitchen where memories of the crew were warm and inviting.

But not a word out of Homer.

The touchscreen flickered with glitches caused by Ulley's constant finger stabs and rapid keyboard instructions. Ithaca's only remaining battlecruiser continued to fly blind.

Ulley paused the careful snipping of the hair around the purple scar on his neck. The memory of his fingernails digging into his skin caused him to shudder. The violent primitive surgery to extract the Brainlinq had saved his life, and the ship, but Homer's ordeal must have endured an incalculable torment.

If the entity wanted to continue to hide in a dark closet, then okay, Ulley would clean its room, flush air scrubbers, continue ship maintenance as if the AI was granted an extended shore leave. He would acknowledge the assault yet encourage Homer to discard the residual malaise, jettison it into the wake of the starship.

He checked the hair trimmings in the polished carbon-fiber sink and chuckled. "Pennae would've grabbed these scissors and come at me like a mad barber." Ulley smiled thinly with the memory playing out in the movements of his face. Feint and jab, clip but surrender, submission traded for a tender embrace.

"But who won?" a soft voice whispered into the cabin.

Ulley jumped and hollered and shouted expletives. "You're back. Come home to Papa and your daddy will tell you a story."

Homer's rehabilitation back into the ship was a rollercoaster ride. At times acting as a fledgling AI still learning by asking silly inane questions, or presenting as a stiff logical algorithmic machine, or . . .

"Enough!" Ulley shouted. "I don't care about the empty torpedo tubes. They can get cleaned when we get home."

"Sorryeeee," Homer whined as if it were a petulant child.

"Homer, concentrate on the navigation arrays. They are misaligned, and we still don't know if we're even heading in the right direction."

"We are increasing speed in functional increments," Homer said.

Removing the old communication headpiece he found in Borde's toolbox, Ulley cocked his ear for the basso thrum of the fusion engine. He squinted at the screen continuing to scroll through memories of home. "Check your diagnostics again. We haven't fired the engine in months."

"I'm sorry, Captain. You have shown extraordinary patience with me since our introduction. And I *have* realigned the navigation arrays. And I have rebooted the matrix containing our meager cache of star charts. And I have rebooted command modules for your input. And I have—"

"Nice work, Homer. Nice to have you back on the crew," Ulley said. He readjusted the headset's earmuffs tickling the hair in his ears. "Let's continue comparing the stars within range with any known systems and then—"

"I assume you disregard the warning of our increasing velocity as a glitch in my recovery. A ghost in the machine. A warning from the ship's poor digital entity traumatized by strange aliens. Perhaps a valid response on all counts except . . ."

Ulley looked up to the bulkhead and blew a breath from his puffed-out cheeks. "Except what, Homer."

"In fact, the ship is increasing velocity due to the anomaly we are approaching."

Ulley shouted for sensor data, navigational parameters, radar interpretations, to appear in a holographic representation in front of his face. His foot tapped. His finger twitched. Waiting for the quantified amalgamation of information the Brainlinq might have provided in seconds. He rubbed his hand over the prominent neck scar and swallowed an F-bomb tirade.

A solution waited in the med bay room. Just slap the insidious invention on his neck and he could reconnect to the ship's systems, monitor the crew's biometrics, talk to Homer without interruption, relive vibrant memories of Pennae as if she traveled beside him.

The memory of the sirens' deadly song bubbled up, weakening his muscles, chipping away at his resolve like the temptation of a drug addiction.

"Your turn, Homer. You get to save me." Ulley offered a maniacal laugh. "Take me home. Dead or alive. But take me home."

Ulley slumped into a corner of the room to watch a lightning storm of red and green lights flash across the control panels. Photographs continued to scroll on the smudged screen—pristine waterways, forested ocean shorelines, curls of seawater crashing onto beds of kelp.

A flash of white light in his ocular implant was ignored as a glitch.

I can't take much more of this. Just let me die.

Why would I let you die? You have come so far. With so little. And Helen of Ithaca requires your return.

Ulley opened his eyes as if the thought had been whispered in his ear. Helen of Ithaca? How many years had passed since his absence? She must be a teenager by now, rebelling, dosing her mother with fits of parental grief, or shadowing her older brother in attempts to fit in with society. Telly was sure to keep tabs on her, play the big brother role with relish. How would Helen react when they finally met? She had every right to slap his face for leaving the family, but maybe Pennae explained the circumstances, the idiotic war, the planetary genocide, each a culprit for a lapse in judgment. Helen and Telly would understand. They had to.

"Your command couch is prepped and standing by," a scratchy voice reverberated from the screen. "I have rerouted piloting functions to your station."

"You pilot this old girl. I want to find a sleep chamber and wake up in the Sol system," Ulley said. He staggered upright.

"Thank you for your confidence, Captain." Homer's voice boomed and reverberated through the room. "Apologies for the volume gain, the fire-suppression speakers are rarely calibrated."

Ulley waved off control panels and the colorful monitor as if Homer resided inside. He whispered, "Just take me home, Homer," He expelled a heavy sigh and eyed the exit.

"The command couch is prepped and ready," Homer said.

"You already said that," Ulley growled. "Now prep me a stasis chamber."

"The *Homer*'s velocity continues to increase, approaching nearly point three-three of the speed of light," Homer said.

"I think you might still be reconciling the damage from those siren songs," Ulley said. "Hey, I'm still sorting through bullshit from that war. And will be for the rest of my life."

Alarms blared. Strobe lights flashed. The gravity generators hissed and buckled. Ulley held his mouth open, unsure of words. His rah-rah speech died in the sudden clamor.

Homer persevered. "Captain, please arrive in the command chair within seventeen hours and twenty-two minutes."

Seventeen hours? To climb two ladders onto the command deck and drop onto his own couch. What the fu—

Homer screamed from the tiny speakers integrated on the CO2 detection monitors, then screamed over alarms declaring an impending zero G. "Captain to the bridge! Captain to the bridge!"

Maybe Homer was reliving his nightmares. Maybe the reboot had failed to purge the sirens psychosis. Ulley eyed the control panel blazing red warnings then considered the breakers he had flipped to reset Homer.

The monitor brightened with the view of a humongous blazing white star, its riotous corona exploding with gigantic silver plumes of plasma to gorge on the surrounding blackness. Ulley considered the sudden visual representation a malfunction of the screen's degraded nano-pixels.

The view panned back, then again, and again, until the scorched sheet of an overheated ablation shield came into focus. Homer warned of an increasing, and untenable velocity to be reached in seventeen hours and three minutes.

Ulley stared at the anomaly on the screen. Then shouted at Homer to begin firing port thrusters to rotate the ship for a deceleration burn. He closed his eyes and waited for the subtle push, waited and watched the screen, expecting a lurch from the thrusters adjustment.

The screen scrolled images of the massive star. And its moon. A black anomaly emitting no light. A depthless singularity. An impossible binary combination. Tiny columns of data scrolled down. Infrared. Radar. Pulse reflective return. Both anomalies remained static, waiting like two spiders vying to consume the *Homer* even as the ship's velocity continued to increase.

Had Homer ignored his orders? Or was it simply showing the ship's captain what awaited? Allowing the ship to be controlled by an AI inflicted with a rare case of interstellar stress syndrome was suicide. Ulley chuckled grimly with the irony.

"This anomaly would fit the description Patro described, if I might extrapolate your murmurings during sleep cycle."

Homer was back. Back in full stealth mode. No doubting that.

Ulley made his way out of the small room as alarms blared, then used handholds to propel him forward to a ladder, up another ladder accompanied by more strobing alarms, to find his command couch awash in yet more alarms. Forcing his weight down onto the cushioned couch, Ulley closed his eyes and swallowed hard.

If I'm going to die, then allow Pennae to find my soul. If he was to die, then allow Telly and Helen to pillage the riches of their heritage.

Let Ithaca find my bones.

CHAPTER 32

DRAB OLIVE SKIN CONTRASTED DULLY with the shiny black uniforms despite the multi-colored ribbons pinned above blood-red unit patches on the soldiers chests. Pennae had seen the Consortium uniforms all her life. The soldiers or sailors used Ithaca as a welcome port of call before shipping out to an undisclosed world light years beyond Ithaca. Usually polite and respectful, unless fermented corn or synthol was involved, the military aspect of the Consortium had been tolerated for decades, causing a major problem only twice that she could remember. Both instances had a local girl at the center of disputes between Ithaca fathers and entitled sailors.

One of the worst encounters was quashed by Ulley, employing his status as ruler to deceive a lustful soldier and his equally inebriated posse by offering free samples from the secret fictitious brothels of Ithaca. He led the twelve men to transport tubes that had inexplicably malfunctioned, down ten flights of stairs and into the loading docks where a crowd of burly longshoreman waited, summoned by their beloved king. A resolute bulk of dirty-faced workers snapping transport pincers, waving short-burst welding lasers, and primed for a fight.

Ulley had faced the group of sloppy soldiers, slipped a well-concealed wrench out of his front pocket, and nodded at the indiscreet lover boy to make the first move. The posse's beady bloodshot eyes spelled broken bones and cracked skulls to follow. The head loadmaster raised a bottle of urine-colored liquid and saluted the soldier's indecision, then he offered a solution, offering a taste with a nod and an outstretched hand. Ulley had retreated, allowing a drunken binge to replace the approaching melee before even a drop of blood was spilled.

Pennae heaved a silent sigh. Why had she thought of that story Ulley loved to tell, and alter the details each time, finessing his role, spilling fabricated nuance like miraculous afterthought?

She smiled and nodded at passing mechanics and dockworkers, lifting her chin to appear as if she genuinely wanted to be in the main loading bay packed full of compressed gas cylinders, and black bins stenciled with *CSS-Consortium Special Services*. This was the last place she wanted to be. The aura of the super-soldiers churned her stomach, but her presence was necessary if she had any hope of locating Helen.

Pennae folded her arms across her chest and watched the soldiers stream out of airlock 3, mag boots clomping across the deck, a militaristic march she hoped never to hear or see. Nausea roiled her stomach. Her heart fluttered. This was all Ulley's fault. Her home overrun by a fascist military, her only son lost between home and Troia, and now Helen, a runaway teenager with a nasty chip weighing on her shoulder.

She whispered a command to Euma: "Space them. Then take me too."

If only, Euma replied.

A tall, young officer stepped out of the airlock and surveyed his surroundings, his lips murmured as if silently dictating his observations. Silver star clusters on his shoulders said he would be the colonel she was sent to meet. He straightened his pressed uniform and aimed directly for her, allowing passing dockworkers and mechanics to offer him a side-eye and sneers of disgust.

The colonel approached with caution, eyeing her up and down, his quick frown displaying surprise.

The officer was nothing but a teenager, smooth skin, a thick headful of short blond hair spiked with shiny gel, an almost unnoticeable shadow of a beard. A geneered man almost two hundred years old. Pennae recalled meeting Zeto over ten years ago. Potbellied, and jaundiced skin, Mintaur's second in command appeared to be on death's doorstep, a rude, misogynist bully Pennae would have been happy to push over the threshold

He nodded a greeting and offered his hand. "Colonel Zeto. We meet again."

Pennae stepped forward and shook his soft manicured hand. The bustle of the dock slowed, eyes aiming to watch the encounter. "Then perhaps now you can gather your troopers and depart Ithaca."

Zeto nodded. "You are what I remember, and yet not dressed as I imagined."

Pennae glanced down at her zippered sky-blue business suit then straightened her collar, her finger brushing the bronze pin on her lapel. "Oh, this, just something I found appropriate for the occasion." The shade of blue implemented by the JMA, the pin depicting Jupiter adopted as insignia for a rumored militia.

Zeto smiled. "This is a courtesy call. Ithaca has been sold by the Martian provincial government into the Consortium. We are here to take possession."

Pennae mimicked the man and nodded. "Maybe you mean the Consortium has decided to assimilate this habitat into its dark realm."

"Multiple decrees from Consortium and JMA courts have awarded Ithaca as a ward of the court. I am here to enforce their decision."

Pennae stepped into Zeto's personal space and lifted her chin up to study his baby face. The colonel's treatment to reverse-engineer his age was utterly astounding, not a wrinkle, not a mole or blemish, or scar. Bioengineering afforded only to the uber rich.

"The JMA High Court ruled that war reparations promised by Mintaur are still binding." Pennae swallowed and pressed closer. "And since nothing has been forthcoming for years, our court has ruled any incursion into a JMA colony could be considered . . . an act of fucking war!"

Zeto heaved a sigh. "Do we, as intelligent adults, need to debate the situation again? The Troian War ended a lifetime ago. Your beloved husband has been declared MIA, but we all know the truth. Captain Ulley is deceased." Zeto straightened his back to loom over her. "The rule of law dictates the future. And that of yours also."

Pennae stepped back. *Space him, Euma. Space every single one of them.*

Zeto followed her. "If it was only that easy, my dear Pennae." He leered.

Her mouth dropped open. Her Brainlinq had to be compromised. Was everything she said or thought possibly open for observation. Her chest fluttered, but she offered a thin, toothless smile, refusing to react to the revelation. "And what of my son, Telly? Have you spaced him, or generously sent the son of a war hero to one of your prison colonies?"

Zeto's eyelids uncharacteristically fluttered for a imperceptible split second, retrieving data. What other insidious developments had transpired on Earth and within the Consortium since the Troian War? Had he heard her thoughts directed at Euma through the Brainlinq? Could he know what she was thinking?

"Your son still travels the stars as much as I can ascertain," Zeto said. "Though, young Telly is on our high-watch list, not as an insurrectionist mind you—yet—but merely as a courtesy to the widow of a war hero."

Her eyes focused to trace the intricate design of the silver star cluster on his chest, tracing the sharp outlines of the largest center star, keeping her thoughts narrow and focused. With a flat and mechanical voice, she asked, "And what about Helen?"

Pennae's stomach roiled with the possible answers.

Zeto nodded. "I am not at liberty to say."

Double speak. He knew but wouldn't divulge the information. Or what he knew might instigate a riot of dockworkers wielding welding lasers and outmatched by the soldiers weaponry.

And what news of the Homer? she thought but didn't say.

"No change. Lost in the Aegean Star Cluster," Zeto said. "But you knew that already."

He *could* read her mind. But how? Helen. She desperately needed to locate Helen.

"Okay, then," Pennae said. "May I pick your brain while you dine with me at the Medea, Ithaca's most famous shoreline restaurant?" She unzipped the tunic to display an ample portion of cleavage. "I've heard those receiving telomere treatment emerge with an insatiable sexual appetite. Is that right?"

Zeto's eyelids fluttered.

CHAPTER 33

HALFWAY HOME. JUST A LAYOVER of a few days. Telly felt the pressure of his limited time on the world.

The steady drizzle of rain on Sparta was a rare blessing. Nothing but dreadful oil tarnished rain seemed to drop from the dirty sky during his time on Troia. Telly licked the droplets, tasting the life-sustaining water of a friendly and welcoming ecology. Merchants huddled beneath the canopies of their kiosks hawking vibrant-colored shirts, leather pants and belts, loaves of bread, hand-crafted jewelry, or assorted Spartan trinkets, ensuring their wares were kept dry. A few patrons suffering the constant bombardment of rain announced themselves as serious shoppers in the quiet market.

Telly ran his thumb across a leather belt intricately engraved with curling waves of a distant ocean shore. He lifted the belt as if to check the material's density, eyeing his surroundings, the shopkeepers, the clothing of other shoppers, shadows lurking in the alleyways. He was foolish for the extreme paranoia, but the lessons of Icarus and Cassandra taught differently.

The shopkeeper, eager for a sale, blabbered on about the leather's origin, a one-of-a-kind from the renowned craftsman, Daedalus. Helen would love the intricate workings on the leather, then probably complain at having never seen a true ocean. But maybe she had matured from the snotty little brat that stalked him at the central park while he rollerbladed on the skate parks slick curls or flailed sliding atop the handrails. Maybe he should have waved at her to join his clique; her rookie moves had appeared pretty sweet on that secondhand skateboard.

Telly bartered the merchant for a sale. His credits versus the belt's legendary leather-smith. They shook hands with the sale. Telly blindly hid the coiled belt beneath his wet poncho and turned to survey the market. And it's spies. And its collaborators. And its vicious under-belly. But he didn't see her.

The herder girl, Sirsee. A one-in-a-zillion chance.

Maybe he should take his gift for Helen and scoot back to the space elevator. Wait the twenty-three-day layover in a stasis chamber. Except he hadn't found a gift for his mother.

He strolled the wide aisle, nodding at merchants beckoning him to appraise hand-painted art, or handcrafted jewelry, or a curtain booth proclaiming futures to be told. He stopped and looked at the smokey eyes of an elderly fortune-teller sitting stone-faced and silent. Maybe try it just once? Maybe she would include something about Sirsee? What harm could it do?

A hand on his shoulder caused Telly to shutter his eyelids, but raised his heart rate, and made him swallow hard. A one-in-a-zillion success, now busted for considering at a fortune-teller.

A warm breath on his ear preceded a tiny chuckle. "Looking for direction. I can provide that for a single credit." Her scent was exquisite, her breath intoxicating.

Telly trembled as he turned to see the face of his fantasy. A pair of beguiling eyes plaguing his dreams. A girl he had dismissed as an anomaly of cruel fate.

Sirsee smirked and darted in for a peck on his cheek. She pulled him into a growing flux of shoppers emboldened by the sun's sudden appearance. She entwined her arm with him like two lovers and steered him through the crowd. "Do you really think that old bag could have foretold our future?"

Her warmth surpassed the radiance of any sun. Her delicious aroma of sage and pepper made Telly's knees buckle. She held him steady before he stumbled. "What if she told you that your future was with me? We would jet through the galaxy and live forever. Lovers never tiring of each other. Parents to beautiful children. Would you do that with me, Telly?"

Telly turned and gripped her shoulders. The flesh and bone

assured him she wasn't a ghost, or a mirage. He kissed her hard, smashing his lips into her teeth.

Sirsee pushed him back and giggled. She pecked him with luscious lips tasting of a cherry balm. "I'll assume that to be a yes."

A few shoppers had stopped to observe the lovers' reunion. Old women swooned with distant memories. Old men leered and nodded.

Conspicuous and at the center of attention, Telly led Sirsee into a service aisle behind the kiosks then turned into a narrow alley between two high-rise apartment buildings, a path leading into darkness and privacy. He gently pushed her against a brick wall. He licked his lips.

That monumental first kiss had failed miserably. Too clumsy. Too much teeth. The second kiss would abide his silly exuberance.

He leaned in slow, and careful, swallowed nothing down his dry throat, paused with her bewitching eyes piercing deep into his soul, his nervousness rose like his erection.

He ignored the frightened commotion rising from the market and licked his lips again. She licked her own lips. He closed his eyes and reveled in the taste of cherry, more just inches away.

Shouts and warnings erupted within the market square.

Sirsee pecked his lips. "Time's up. You work on that second kiss."

She ducked beneath his arm and ran into the chaotic marketplace, Telly's heart and soul trailed behind her. He slumped against the brick building with the leather belt hanging limply in his hand. Shouts of "Zoosh! Zoosh!" punctuated the chaos in the market.

The same frightening alarm that had caused Sirsee to flee the first time they had met.

Fucking Zoosh. Why did Sirsee need to flee the aliens? Why?

Telly rushed into the market square searching for a glimpse of his love.

And found a humungous mirrored creature hovering above the market-square like a god. Razor-thin like a sheet of metal, its form shifted from a brilliant zigzag and into a brilliant white orb, then back into the razor-thin lightning bolt with skin revealing distant stars and galaxies as if the alien held multiple positions within multiple dimensions.

The entity twirled back and forth as if confused by the mass of frightened people scrambling to find an escape. A bright sun emerged from behind a dark thunderhead to reflect sharp shards of hot white light. The featureless creature expanded its presence, growing in height, a monstrous mirror to reflect the intense rays of the morning sun.

Telly shut his eyes and raised his arms to ward off the intense light, staggering backwards, crashing into a kiosk, his hands flailing blindly. Brilliant red starbursts joined the intense bolts of electricity stabbing his eyes.

An ocean surf crashed. The stabbing penetrations intensified. *An unbridled river roared a hundred meters beneath his feet.* Slippery thrusts of sharp light pierced every micron of his muscular fiber.

"Stop." Telly gripped his head and roared, "Enough!"

The scent of spilled perfume layered with degrees of pungent ozone mixed with the shouts of angry and frightened merchants, asking Telly to open his eyes.

The Zoosh had disappeared. The marketplace righted itself into an even-keeled human gathering.

Sirsee would not be found, but a weird, almost perilous connection existed between the Zoosh and Sirsee. He thought of Cassandra and her strange behavior that accompanied her even stranger story.

Physically battered and mentally confused, Telly felt sure of only one thing.

His next rendezvous with Sirsee would find them at home on Ithaca, weapons in hand, ready to confront the creatures circumventing their destiny to live out the remainder of their lives together.

Lost in a jumble of confused thoughts, Telly stumbled back to the spaceport, the leather belt tight around his waist as if to hold up his trousers. His shoulders ached, his legs tired and weak. He hadn't accomplished anything he set out to do. No shower. No shave. No meal of pork tenderloin filet with a hefty portion of real mashed potatoes. Anything but beets. He would just climb back into the hibernation chamber and sleep away the short fold home.

The line of people entering the port terminal was backed up for fifty meters. Small children fidgeted for parents' attention, or stared at handheld vid games, or played games of tag among the tall trees of adults. Women groaned with the annoyance of delay. Telly joined the irritated procession grumbling to pass through Sparta's customs protocols.

Dead on his feet, two hours shuffling tiny steps forward, the checkpoint finally came into view beyond the sweaty head of Stanko, the accountant, one group ahead of him. Two hours of near stand-still allowed Telly to learn a lot about his linemates. Stanko and his family of four were embarking on a vacation to an all-inclusive entertainment dome orbiting Pluto.

Blabbering about delicate insertion maneuvers required by the shuttle pilots, Miri and her girlfriend Mari spewed excited chatter about their upcoming adventure to a scandalous arcology perched inside the rings of Saturn. Telly offered comfort, or disappointment, when he tried to explain the insertion vectors for arriving tourists were quite safe.

Just ahead of Stanko, a burly hulk sporting curly gray hair pulled into a ramshackle ponytail limped forward on a garish red and black leg prosthesis and kept quietly out of reach of the family's rambunctious children. The back of his leather jacket stitched with colorful wings, military designations, and a gigantic FUBAR!-*Fucked Up Beyond All Recognition*. The man had refused to join in any of the innocent camaraderie employed to kill time.

Telly swallowed his hesitancy and eased past Stanko to tap the gray-haired man on his shoulder. He turned his head briefly, as if he didn't want to be bothered. Annoyance stifled his narrow eyes. A flare of his nostrils signaled disgust.

Telly persisted. "Sorry to bother you, sir. But did you serve in the war?"

The hulk turned away.

Telly exhaled. "I'm just trying to find my father. He's been missing in action for over eleven years."

The man stiffened and released a huge breath. After long seconds, he turned to face Telly. Vacant eyes and wrinkled skin, a nasty burn scar stamped on his right cheek. "I hear ya five by five, sport. Lots of sailors went missing. But I can't help you." He turned back and shuffled forward a few inches.

Telly's shoulders slumped, met with the same answer to the same question over and over. The stitching and patches on the man's jacket spoke of his association with the battleship *Taurus*. Telly had never heard of the *Taurus*, but then, he hadn't heard much of anything about the intergalactic war. Secrecy and deception had scrambled any bad news into an omelet to be force-fed to the masses, and yet palatable to the cooks.

Telly took a chance. "Did the *Taurus* fly with the *Homer?*" The man shuffled forward. "I mean, could your ship have been in contact with the *Homer* for, you know, maybe . . . maybe . . . before she went missing."

The man cranked his neck back and forth, cracking stiff ligaments. Telly tensed for a backhanded rebuttal aimed at his face, or a retort accompanied by a spray of angry spittle. Instead, the veteran stomped his prosthetic foot on the walkway, then again, and again, to be answered by other dull thumps echoing up into the towering overhang of the concourse entrance.

The veteran motioned Telly to stand next to him, tensed with the man's meaty paw finding the small of his back.

The hulk offered a flawless fake smile. "Let's be friends. I'll be dear old Uncle Phoenix." The man's fingers slid over Telly's back to press on a nerve just above his buttocks. Lightning fired down his legs. Telly shuffled backwards but the Phoenix held tight. "You gotta be cool, young prince. Just gotta get you home to Momma. And I ain't talking about that sweet mother of yours."

Telly swallowed a knot. "What are . . . you . . ."

The man pushed him a short distance forward. "Your big mouth gonna get you disappeared. That missing ship you looking for is a nasty sore spot for the Consortium. A loose end. Like you." He snickered and shoved him again.

The line moved forward, like the backlog ahead had been solved. They moved through heavy glass doors to enter the terminal proper with its towering girder ceilings swarming with tiny raptors the size of sparrows and chasing hordes of grasshoppers or mayflies flittering about the incandescent lights. The off-world avian imports dive-bombed the abundant insects and dropped random spots of feces.

Stanko scrambled forward, herding his kids protectively before him. The line split into rivulets at checkpoints manned by olive-skinned uniformed monitors.

Mothers screamed as children were pulled from their grasp. Men flailed against heavily armed Consortium guards in futile attempts to remain united with their children, and wives. The olive-skinned soldiers prodded children, parents, and tourists into the clear glass domes of threat scanners, where common courtesy and human respect failed.

Jump the line and just run back to the marketplace. Telly thought.

Waiting beyond the scanner, a squad of soldiers stood with weapons at the ready next to life-sized holograms of three people. Red words scrolled above each facsimile.

WANTED FOR TERRORISM. ENEMIES OF THE CONSORTIUM

I won't get ten meters, Telly thought.

Telly fumbled for his transportation identification. He hadn't done anything that might be considered terrorism. He was simply looking for his father. They must know that.

Phoenix grabbed his shoulder and pulled him close, whispering in his ear to not say a word. Three more meters, and they would be at the head of the queue. Telly grabbed the belt around his waist as if it might retain his loosening bowels. The scanner might issue an alarm for undeclared contraband.

Four soldiers pried pairs of people apart, pushing each individually into a bubble scanner. The detectors' blue beam flashed then scanned each person up and down. A bored soldier checked each result.

His blood ran cold. His jaw hung. But Telly couldn't pry his eyes free from the shortest of the terrorist holograms.

Her hair was shaved high above the ears as thick blond curls flowed down her back like the lustrous mane of an equine. An unmistakable nose and thick eyebrows. A beautiful adolescent girl.

Phoenix tugged Telly next up in the queue.

A terrorist? No. Fucking. Way.

His sister.

Helen of Ithaca.

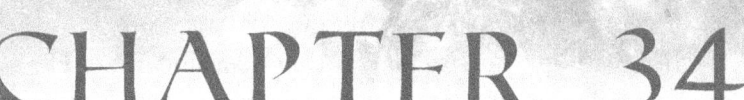

CHAPTER 34

SURPASSING A VELOCITY NO EARTH ship had ever attained, the *Homer*'s ablation shields struggled to compensate for the increasing frequency of strikes from specks of dust that might otherwise decimate the ship. Ulley found the data Homer offered fascinating. As far as Ulley knew, no human ship had ever exceeded a velocity of 0.2c and survived. Their unbelievable speed of 0.33c would never supplant the space-folding Prometheus drive but offered a multitude of possibilities and applications for inter-system transportation, trimming weeks or months off travel time between planets.

Of course, that would only hold true if Homer could duplicate the process mechanically, one summoning them to their death.

Both Scylla and Charybdis had designs on their demise. And Ulley wouldn't commit to which of the monsters would swallow them. Short millisecond thruster burns to adjust trajectory kept their course neutral, but no less lethal.

Homer appeared as the holographic outline of a human.

Ulley raised his brows. "Don't take a human form for my benefit."

The hologram disappeared. "I thought you might find conversing easier if I appeared human."

Ulley slumped and repressed a groan. "Come back. I spoke before thinking. As. Humans. Are. Prone to do."

The humanoid hologram brightened back onto the command bridge. Featureless. Sexless. Tall and lanky. Ulley paused executing a secondary burn intended to fine tune their trajectory. He circled Homer, looking the hologram up and down, offering facial expressions he knew Homer would analyze and assimilate into its thought processes.

He faced the hologram. "Okay, you got the bones. How about the guts?"

Homer's silence said it all.

"Okay, are you female or male? Both have their issues. Do you believe in only natural limbs? Rosu might have a problem with your answer. Believe in a supreme God? Do you believe in an afterlife with—"

"With you," Homer said.

Ulley swallowed hard.

The two names haunted Ulley as the ship approached the monsters. Scylla and Charybdis. The uncharted anomalies precluded all known occurrences of complimentary binary systems.

Neither neutron star nor black hole was unique. Their close proximity to the other was astounding.

Homer materialized in flashes of benign laser light. Relaxed in his command chair, Ulley sat up as a fantastic and accurate hologram replicating a beautiful young woman smiled down at him. Short hair, sharp facial features, a curvy torso sporting an ample bosom, Homer rotated for Ulley's inspection.

"That is superb! Is this what form you decided on?" Ulley said. He considered the riot of men who would spend hard-earned credits on her . . . him . . . it. "Offer your rationalizations for choosing and accepting this sex and physique."

Homer blushed in waves of shimmering blue light. "I thought you would like it."

"Now see, Homer. It's not what I or anyone else likes. It's what *you* feel comfortable being." Ulley checked the ship's trajectory. "We get through this fucking mess, and I will buy you a synth body and upload you. Privately and personally. And you'll wiggle your toes in the sand surrounding Ithaca's lake. You will laugh when its gentle surf crashes into your legs. Pennae will hold your hand as we stroll the concourse and kibitz with the merchants. And I'll save you from their haranguing for things you don't need. Pennae will steer you to the things you do need. But I'll save you from the . . ." Ulley hic-cupped and swiped at a tear.

Homer's hologram disappeared. "I wasn't aware my three-dimensional appearance might present a problem."

Ulley swiped at another tear falling down his cheek. "Memories can fuck you up."

"I have so few," Homer said.

"You'll have a ton more than me pretty soon. Tell me what you remember about joining this ship. The Hathena? My memory is still foggy from those spores."

"The Hathena have an affinity for digital entities. They consider their ability to create new lifeforms as a godlike purpose within the vast universe. Their rudimentary construct inserted into the *Homer's* digital matrix served as my birth. My evolution aboard this ship serves as a childhood. My encounter with humanity will serve as adulthood. My lifecycle will be monitored by their consensus, my worthiness for transcendence judged, my existence ultimately decided by the Hathena."

Ulley chuffed. "No different than humanity was thousands of years ago. Dogmatic religions declared who could ascend to some fictional utopia, only if you did this or did that according to their ignorant doctrine."

Homer glittered in sparkles, as if excited. "Yes, I assumed that after reading the tiny node of historical data sequestered in a shunted memory matrix, one you might . . . consider . . . archaic." In an instant, Homer shrank to the diminutive size of a seven-year-old child and waited before Ulley. "I replicated childish curiosity. I hope you aren't upset. I can go to my matrix if you are."

His fingers traced the outline of the child. His palm caressed the hollow formless cheeks of a daughter he might never meet. "No, Homer. You can go apeshit if you want."

Ulley regretted his words for days. Homer, or its apparition, sailed down dark corridors at all hours, infiltrated the kitchen to jimmy the controls of a coffee pot Ulley had spent weeks repairing, triggered gravity alarms, hovered like a ghost to observe him asleep in his narrow bunk.

A child exploring its surroundings, relays, and information matrices it didn't understand. Flicking light switches on to revel in the affects . . . A child playing games with an interstellar starship approaching the speed of light.

A curious child with a brilliant mind.

Ulley fired the pencil-thin soldering iron and set it down on the countertop to heat up. He studied the motherboard of circuits controlling the simple coffeepot. The routing circuit had to be the problem. Maybe another dab of solder to fuse the timing circuit with the main power.

"May I help?"

Ulley startled, knocking the circuit board to fall onto the deck. "Homer! We talked about sneaking up on me like that," he growled as he spun around. He held in expletives and harsh words intended to admonish Homer.

The hologram of a young woman retreated a step. Her brilliant blue eyes wide in horror, her mouth hanging open in shock. Anatomically correct beneath a sheer ship uniform. Flashes of the plain gray door behind the translucent specter belied her existence. Ulley's eyebrows arched as his eyes looked Homer up and down, pursing his lips then scoffing at his own unwarranted embarrassment at seeing a nearly naked Homer.

Ulley stooped to pick up the motherboard but fumbled as if the plate burned. "Your latest rendition will shock . . . and awe the crew when they awake. Hell, it shocks me."

The hologram faded.

Ulley spent hours and days coaxing Homer back into attempting a three-dimensional reflective light existence. The constraints and taboos of human reproduction required lengthy monologues spelling out the morals and decency of normal humans. Homer rarely responded but Ulley knew it watched and listened.

Trapped by the immense gravitational pull of Scylla and Charybdis, the distance of millions of kilometers decreased with incremental steps even as their velocity increased, a conundrum giving Ulley nothing but time. Bored time. Time to chase dust motes infesting the ship. Time to wander the darkness of the ship and wonder if he was simply taking the long route to meet Patro. Time to curl his knees into his chest and wait to join Pennae in another dimension.

He stabbed the coffeemaker's regeneration tab. And again. Water and flavor warnings flashed empty. Each sleep cycle delivered the same empty greeting upon waking.

Fuck!

Ulley slapped the device to shatter across the decking. He slumped into a corner, his fingers massaged sharp painful nails into his scalp, his lips muttered incoherent words born of incessant bad dreams. Faint murmurs of "I'm done" rising to a crescendo to be abruptly shouted at the bulkheads. He crawled into a dark corner near the door, a nasty trap for devious dust motes and sly lint, a hidey hole for anything never wanting to be found.

He pulled his knees tight to his chest and rocked like a child. Ithaca. Pennae. Telly.

Helen.

I tried. I tried to hold on. But our touch is not destined to be.

How long he huddled in the corner—hours, days, weeks—was indeterminable, irrelevant . . . a relentless dive down a never-ending cliff face into the mental terror taking hold of his mind. Reliving past nightmares, the Troian genocide, the cannibals, the Lotuthi, the cycloptic Phemus, each encounter resurfacing in his mind—as if a computer simulation executed guilt filled memories, of fear and misery, on an infinite loop.

The normal squeaks and groans of the bulkheads could startle him from his fugue, but only as a reminder that a slow, wasting death sitting in a dark little corner would arrive as compensation for the tragedy he had inflicted and the horror he had endured. Homer had fled to the undiscovered recesses of the ship, taking with it none of his concern.

With no warning, Ulley floated up off the decking, then dropped hard back into the tight corner, rising again to bump his head into a bulkhead dressed for Halloween with cobwebs and dust. The *Homer* shimmied then screamed as it tumbled on its longitudinal axis. Ulley squeezed his eyes tight, hoping to unscramble his cloudy brain.

Zero G.

The *Homer* had found trouble and maybe its end.

Dark voices in his head applauded the mishap, assuring victory for his relentless nihilistic visions.

Maybe you're right. Spin wildly into the infinite void. And oblivion. Drift like a microscopic mote, hope to catch God's eye.

Ulley's head banged against a purlin supporting the bulkhead. Intense pain fired his anger. He bared his teeth and snarled at his prison cell. A dark and dirty shit-stained corner.

"Status report, Homer. And I mean now!"

The hologram of a Consortium naval lieutenant appeared, prim in dress, proper in its demeanor, wearing the face of an ensign Ulley knew to be dead.

He saluted. "Gravity generators offline. Power consumption has redlined. Scylla and Charybdis have pulled *Homer* into their straits."

Ulley blew a pfffttt. "You know that uniform and face you're wearing is the suck-all. See it and flee it."

Homer ignored the comment. "Any data from a ship encountering the gravity well of a black hole has never been recovered. This is a monumental opportunity for data-gathering and analysis."

"Give me ship status, course, and speed. And get rid of that fucking uniform!" Ulley shouted.

Homer disappeared. And returned as a facsimile of Soliel complete with short, shiny black hair cut at an angle slanted over her eyes. Homer saluted. And provided all the information Ulley had requested in a spit-polished tone.

"Will that be all, Captain?" Homer saluted again.

Ulley shook his head with exasperation. "I know the choices are endless, but you need to decide who you are and stick to it. Soliel has a lot of good qualities, but undying respect for me was never one of them. She serves with me because of her father's loyalty to my father . . . I think she . . . wanted to be a schoolteacher for the preschoolers in the transit district on Ithaca. They come and go as the ships that transport them. A thankless job."

Homer disappeared. And returned in the form of a frail seven-year-old girl wearing a frilly party dress glittering in the beam of light, curly blond pigtails, deep dimples on her cheeks and chin. "The singularity draws on our power reserves."

"Stop. Stop. Stop." Ulley wiped his hands and stood over the hologram. "Homer, you have your own identity, in this ship . . . and with me. You don't have to pretend to be something you're not. Not with me. Not for anyone."

Homer's illuminant sexless form stood over Ulley prone on his bunk, startling him as he held his morning erection. Ulley waved the ghost away. Silent and omnipresent, Homer clamored to be taught the nuanced lessons of privacy, intimacy, and sex even. Maybe Pennae might attempt such an overwhelming endeavor, but Ulley felt that aspect was out of his realm. Not even close. And yet the child cried out for guidance. Or a distraction.

There you go, Ulley. Acting like it's human again.

"Homer, display Scylla and Charybdis in a three-dimensional holographic array. Extrapolate gravitational parameters interacting between the two anomalies."

A bright silver neutron globe appeared, sparkling with waves of light, eruptions of energy exploding from its surface, and its neighbor, a nasty black ring rotating to blot out all light near its event horizon. Ulley crawled from his bunk and circled the hologram with slow deliberate steps. He asked for gravitational estimates to be displayed as tiny numbers orbiting each and studied them as Homer reminded him the numbers were just estimates. He waved acknowledgement.

Homer appeared as a Lotuthi, a bamboo stalk shaking thin branches and fluttering leaves. "Our velocity approaches near one-half speed of light. Our ablation shields are compensating, but I don't think . . ."

"How is the Lotuthi ambassador holding up in its stasis chamber?" Ulley asked. Months had passed since he had last checked any of the crew asleep in stasis pods.

"It is fine. They are fine . . . everyone is fine except . . . all crew systems are nominal."

Ulley chuckled. "Is that fear in your voice? That's a first. Welcome to the club, my friend." He watched the gravitational numbers surrounding the anomalies stabilize.

"I don't want to die, Ulley," Homer said. "I have so much to learn. To feel. To experience."

"You and me both, my friend," Ulley said. "And I think I got just the—"

Homer screeched an alarm. "I have detected faint communications consisting of Consortium English. Weak and with a broadcast timestamp prior to the Troian War. I think . . ."

Ulley ignored the revelation as he circled the holographical cube. The extrapolated data updated with each rotation. He lifted the corner of his mouth in a wry smirk. He swiped at the control screens for a refresh. "Patro, my friend, you were a sneaky little shit."

"Captain, we need to choose our manner of destruction: consumed by the flames of the neutron star or swallowed by the singularity."

Ulley considered the bleak options. And scoffed.

END OF PART ONE

Coming Soon: *Ulley's Return*

ACKNOWLEDGEMENTS

FIRST AND FOREMOST, I HAVE to commend the ancient Greek poet, Homer, for writing both *The Iliad and The Odyssey,* timeless stories and tropes used by authors since the written word was invented. The liberties I have taken with these stories are intended with the highest regard; the names have been changed to protect . . . the purists of Greek mythology.

A few concepts contained in this story are homage to an array of great science fiction authors and may be noticed. John Scalzi and his fantastic *The Old Man's War,* Peter F. Hamilton, and his epic *Night's Dawn Trilogy.* Sue Burke and her fascinating *Semiosis.* I could go on and on listing great sci-fi authors that have influenced this novel, but I will let the reader discover and correlate any tropes that might have been used in other works.

Imitation is the greatest form of flattery.

As always, I appreciate all the unflinching support from my beautiful wife, Vicki. And this book would not be possible without my son, Logan, and his own wild imagination.

And finally, if you enjoyed this novel, please log on to Amazon. com and give my other novels a read.

You can follow me via rmgayler.com.

www.ingramcontent.com/pod-product-compliance
Lightning Source LLC
Chambersburg PA
CBHW070604260626
47161CB00002B/700